"A big, brilliant novel: sensual, wise, compelling—and utterly magnificent."
—LILY KING, AUTHOR OF *EUPHORIA*

"Deeply satisfying." —*SAN FRANCISCO CHRONICLE*

"Tessa Hadley recruits admirers with each book."
—HILARY MANTEL,
AUTHOR OF *WOLF HALL* AND *BRING UP THE BODIES*

"Hadley is so insightful, such a lovely writer, that she pulls you right
into the tangle of wires that connect and trip up the stressed siblings."
—*PEOPLE*, BOOK OF THE WEEK

"Few writers give me such consistent pleasure."
—ZADIE SMITH, AUTHOR OF *NW*

"Exhilarating. . . . I finished *The Past* sadly—why did it
have to end?—with a sense that I had understood something
profound about both Hadley's characters and my own life."
—*BOSTON GLOBE*

"*The Past* glitters." —NPR

ens and expands your own. She is a true master, and *The Past* is a big, brilliant novel: sensual, wise, compelling—and utterly magnificent."
—Lily King, author of *Euphoria*

"Recalls Elizabeth Bowen's *The House in Paris* in its dovetailing story lines, but the author's genius for the thorny comforts of family—'they sulked for five minutes and couldn't forgive each other, until they forgot about it and went back to their gossip'—are entirely her own."
—Megan O'Grady, *Vogue*

"We come to understand that the past—for them and for us—is merely yesterday's present: ordinary, at times beautiful, and tragic too, a complicated ghost hovering at the edges of our lives. And it is that revelation that elevates the novel, deepening our own understanding of what shapes us."
—Tayari Jones, *O Magazine*

"Hadley brings a keen intelligence and emotional acuity to domestic fiction. . . . *The Past* glitters."
—Heller McAlpin, NPR

"Brilliant. . . . I finished *The Past* sadly—why did it have to end?—with a sense that I had understood something profound about both Hadley's characters, and my own life."
—Margot Livesey, *Boston Globe*

"[An] exquisitely written family drama."
—Liz Loerke, *US Weekly*

"The kind of observant, bittersweet book whose pleasures defy plot summaries."
—Yvonne Zipp, *Christian Science Monitor*

"A lushly written novel about four siblings revisiting their family's country home, *The Past* reads like the lovechild of a nature essay and domestic drama, with all the joys of both."
—Claire Fallon, *Huffington Post*

"Beautiful."
—*Travel + Leisure*

"Masterful. . . . Hadley is the patron saint of ordinary lives; her trademark empathy and sharp insight are out in force here."
—*Kirkus Reviews* (starred review)

"A fresh take on a familiar story of fractious family reunions where old resentments resurface, new alliances form, and long-buried secrets are uncovered. A great read whether at the cottage or just dreaming of one."
—Barbara Love, *Library Journal* (starred review)

THE PAST

ALSO BY TESSA HADLEY

THE PAST

A Novel

Tessa Hadley

HARPER PERENNIAL

NEW YORK • LONDON • TORONTO • SYDNEY • NEW DELHI • AUCKLAND

HARPER ● PERENNIAL

A hardcover edition of this book was published in 2016 by HarperCollins Publishers.

P.S.™ is a registered trademark of HarperCollins Publishers.

HarperCollins books may be purchased for educational, business, or sales promotional use. For information, please e-mail the Special Markets Department at SPsales@harpercollins.com.

Originally published, in a slightly different form, in Great Britain in 2015 by Jonathan Cape.

FIRST HARPER PERENNIAL EDITION PUBLISHED 2016.

Library of Congress Cataloging-in-Publication Data has been applied for.

ISBN 978-0-06-227042-9 (pbk.)

16 17 18 19 20   OFF/RRD   10 9 8 7 6 5 4 3 2 1

TO JACK

PART ONE

The Present

ONE

———

ALICE WAS THE first to arrive, but she discovered as she stood at the front door that she had forgotten her key. The noise of their taxi receding, like an insect burrowing between the hills, was the only sound at first in the still afternoon, until their ears got used to other sounds: the jostling of water in the stream that ran at the bottom of the garden, a tickle of tiny movements in the hedgerows and grasses. At least it was an afternoon of balmy warmth, its sunlight diffused because the air was dense with seed floss, transparent-winged midges, pollen; light flickered on the grass, and under the silver birch leaf-shadows shifted, blotting their penny-shapes upon one another. Searching through her bag Alice put on a show of amusement and scatty self-deprecation. She was famously hopeless with keys. She had come with a young man who was her ex-boyfriend's son and on the train she had been preoccupied with the question of what stage of life she was at, whether people seeing them would think Kasim was her lover, or her child – though he wasn't either. Now he walked away from her around the house without saying anything, and she thought that this mishap with the keys had shrivelled her in his opinion, he was bored already. They were in the country, in the middle of nowhere, with no way back; the house was set behind a cluster of houses on a no through road where there was no café or pub or even shop where they could pass the time.

Behind her smiles she raged at Kasim for a moment. She wished now that she hadn't brought him. It had been a careless suggestion in a moment of feeling bountiful, having this place to offer; she hadn't really expected him to take her up on it and had been flattered when he did. But if she had been alone the keys wouldn't have mattered. It would have been a kind of bliss, even, to be shut out from the responsibility of opening up the house and making it ready for the others. She could have dropped onto the grass in the sunshine. She could have let go her eternal vigilance and fallen deep down here, in this place, Kington, of all places, into sleep, the real thing, the sleep that she was always seeking for and could never quite get. Alice was forty-six, dark, soft, concentrated yet indefinite – she could look like a different person in different photographs. Her complex personality was diffuse, always flying away in different directions, like her fine hair, which a man had once described as prune-coloured; it was soft and brown like the inside of prunes, and she wore it curling loose on her shoulders.

THE HOUSE WAS A WHITE cube two storeys high, wrapped round on all four sides by garden, with French windows and a veranda at the back and a lawn sloping to a stream; the walls inside were mottled with brown damp, there was no central heating and the roof leaked.

On the mossy roof slates, thick as pavings, you could see the chisel marks where the quarrymen had dressed them two hundred years ago. Alice and Kasim stood peering through the French windows: the interior seemed to be a vision of another world, its stillness pregnant with meaning, like a room seen in a mirror. The rooms were still furnished with her grandparents' furniture; wallpaper glimmered silvery behind the spindly chairs, upright black-lacquered piano and bureau. Paintings were pits of darkness suspended from the picture rail. Alice had told her therapist that she dreamed about this house all the time. Every other house she'd lived in seemed, beside this one, only a stage set for a performance.

Kasim didn't care about not getting inside; vaguely he was embarrassed because Alice had made a fool of herself. He wasn't sure how long he would stay anyway, and had only come to get away from his mother, who was anxious because he wasn't studying – at the end of his first year at university he was bored. He imagined he could smell the room's musty old age through the glass; the carpet was bleached and threadbare where the sun patched it. When he found a cheerfully shabby grey Renault parked on the cobbles beside the outhouses he called to Alice. Alice didn't drive and couldn't tell one car from another, but looking inside she knew it must belong to Harriet, her older sister. There was a box with maps in it on the back seat, and next to it on a folded newspaper a pair of shoes neatly side by side, with one striped sock tucked into the top of each. — I know exactly what she's done, she said. — Arrived here and left the car and gone straight off for a walk before the rest of us got here. She's that sort of person. She loves nature and communes with it, in a principled way. She thinks I'm frivolous.

The little display of ordered privacy made Harriet seem vulnerable to Alice; it touched and irritated her.

5

— Perhaps your sister forgot her key too.

— Harriet's never forgotten anything in her life.

Because they couldn't get inside the house, Alice felt obliged to go on showing things to Kasim. She took him into the churchyard through a keyhole gap in a stone wall in the back garden. Her grandfather had been the minister here. The house and the church stood together on the rim of a bowl of air scooped deep between the surrounding hills, and buzzards floated on thermals in the air below them. The ancient stubby tower of the church, blind without windows, seemed sunk in the red earth; the nave was disproportionately all window by contrast, and the clear old quavering glass made its stone walls appear weightless – you saw straight through to the green of trees on the far side. In the churchyard the earth was upheaved as turbulently as a sea by all the burials in it, and overgrown at one end with tall hogweed and rusty dock. Her grandparents' grave, red granite, still looked shiny-new after a quarter of a century. Her grandfather had been very high church, Alice said: incense and the Authorised Version and real hell, or at least some complicated clever kind of hell.

— He was a very educated man, and a poet. A famous poet.

Kasim was studying economics, he didn't care about poetry – though he didn't care much about economics either. Loose-jointed, he ambled after Alice round the churchyard, hands in pockets, only half-interested, head cocked to listen to her. Alice always talked a lot. Kasim was very tall and much too thin, with brown skin and a big nose lean as a blade; his smudged-black eyes drooped eloquently at the corners, the lower lids purplish, fine-skinned; his blue-black hair was thick as a pelt. He was completely English and unmistakeably something else too – his paternal grandfather, a Punjabi judge, had been married briefly to an English novelist. Now Alice was worrying that he would find the country tedious; somehow this hadn't occurred to her when she'd invited him in London. What she loved best in Kington was doing nothing – reading or sleeping. It was obvious now they'd arrived that this wouldn't be enough for Kasim, and she sagged under her responsibility to entertain him. Because he was young and she was forty-six, she was afraid of failing to interest him; she would be crushed if he didn't like it here. Alice was painfully stalled by beginning to lose her looks. She had always believed that it was her personality and intelligence which gave her what power she had. Her looks she had taken for granted.

FRAN – ALICE'S OTHER SISTER, the youngest of the four siblings – arrived next with her children, Ivy and Arthur, nine and six. They'd had an awful journey, the traffic had been hell and Ivy had been carsick. She'd had to sit with a plastic bowl on her knees, and her face – thin, prim mouth and sharp points of nose and chin, high forehead – was drained theatrically white behind her freckles. Trailing into the back garden from the car, through the stone archway overgrown with an aged white rambler rose, the children looked like remnants from an old-fashioned play: Ivy was dressed in a long Victorian skirt of khaki silk with ruffles, and a pink-sequinned top. She was usually running some imaginary other world in her head. Her stories weren't dramas with plots and happenings, they were all ambience – and she loved Kington because here her inner life seemed to touch the outer world at every point. She advanced across the grass into her dream: the old house dozed in the sunshine, and its French windows under their little canopy of dun lead, burdened with clematis montana, might have opened onto any scene of royalty or poetry or tragic forbearance.

Arthur was wearing everyday shorts and a tee shirt but he

was frail and exquisite, with translucent skin and blue veins at his temples; he looked more like a part in one of Ivy's stories than she ever did. Although Fran was resolutely not sentimental, she couldn't bear to cut Arthur's silky pale-gold hair, which had grown down below his shoulders. Fran herself was stocky and definite, freckled, tawny hair chopped off in a neat bob, her green top stretched tight across her breasts and stomach.

— Thank goodness you've come, cried Alice, arriving in the keyhole gap from the churchyard. — I've forgotten my keys!

— I was terribly sick, Ivy announced. — I had to have a bowl.

— You should have heard the fuss. You'd have thought it was terminal. Doesn't Harriet have keys? Her car's here.

— The car was here when we arrived. She must have gone off for a walk.

— Oh well, at least there's you – I could do with a hand unpacking all this shopping. You're looking nice. How slim you are! I'm jealous.

She admired Alice's white dress patterned with blue flowers, her tan, painted toenails, clever sandals. — I wish I had the time to spare for all of that.

Alice said she felt terrible that Fran had had to do the shopping. But she couldn't have brought it on the train, and they somehow couldn't have asked Roland to shop, could they, as they hadn't met his new wife yet? And Harriet would have been too abstemious. Fran reassured her that she hadn't been abstemious at all; Harriet would be horrified when they divvied the costs up later. Kneeling on the tufty rough grass, Alice hugged the children: Ivy holding herself stiffly, convalescent, and Arthur leaning into the kiss, liking the perfumed soft warmth of women. The grass had been cut for their coming by the neighbour who kept up the garden for them, and the grass cuttings strewn all around them were turning to dead straw, smelling sweetly rotten. Fran remembered there were spare keys in one of the outhouses anyway.

— Oh well, it didn't matter. We've been in the churchyard together, visiting graves.

— Who's we?

She was so sure she'd mentioned bringing Kasim. — Dani's son. You'll really like him. I left him meditating on a tomb or something.

— But Alice! You're the one who said only family.

— He's almost family! You met him – don't you remember? – when he was a beautiful little boy, just about yesterday. Now he's a beautiful young man – isn't it frightening?

— You didn't mention it, Fran said.

— And where's Jeff?

Standing over her sister on the lawn, laden with plastic carriers, Fran paused for a dramatic effect that was very like her daughter. She was forceful where Alice was diffuse; her eyes had distinctive shallow lids which made her look as if all her awareness was out on the surface, with nothing hidden. — Guess what. At the last minute, Jeff couldn't make it.

— Fran, you're kidding? I thought he'd really promised this time.

— He really did promise. But he's crap.

Jeff pretended he'd forgotten all about the holiday, Fran said, though it had been arranged for months. He'd booked in gigs for the whole time they were supposed to be away, without telling her; he said might be able to clear some time to come down for a few days. She had told him not to bother. Alice exclaimed and commiserated, though warily, because sometimes when she'd criticised Jeff, Fran had taken offence and begun defending him. And Alice liked him anyway, she was sorry he hadn't come. This really was the last straw, Fran insisted, keeping her voice low to spare the children. It was all over between her and Jeff, she'd had enough. Alice had heard that before as well.

Fran unlocked the front door and the sisters stood hesitating on the brink of the interior for a moment, preparing themselves, recognising what they had forgotten while they were away from it – the under-earth smell of imprisoned air, something plaintive in the thin light of the hall with its grey and white tiled floor and thin old rugs faded to red-mud colour. There was always a moment of adjustment as the shabby, needy actuality of the place settled over their too-hopeful idea of it. Fran began unpacking the shopping in the kitchen, which was the least nice room of the house, unchanged since the nineteen seventies when their grandmother in a fit of modernisation had put in wood veneer wall cabinets and a sink unit and linoleum and an electric stove – at least she had preserved the old dresser built along one wall. Pans and basins left in certain cupboards grew black mould and were sticky with cobwebs, and there were always mouse droppings. Because the kitchen was between the dining room at the front of the house, and the long sitting room which ran all the way across the south-facing back, it was dark, with a neon strip light, and its side window looked out onto a scullery and outhouses.

Their brother Roland's previous wife, Valerie – she had been his second – had seemed to spend all her time in Kington describing her plans for improving it, although she was always reassuring them how much she loved the place. They should make a new kitchen which opened into the garden, she said; put in central heating and more bathrooms. Everyone agreed with her but nothing was changed. There was no money to change anything anyway.

IVY SETTLED BESIDE KASIM WHERE he lay flat among the plumy grasses in the churchyard with his eyes closed. She stretched out her legs alongside his, arranging her long skirt carefully so that only her patent leather shoes poked out, two upright black exclamations, from under its hem. Propped on one elbow, leaning earnestly over him, she ran through her usual repertoire of topics – school, Arthur, the Victorians, food she hated – testing to see what might amuse him. Without opening his eyes Kasim felt for cigarettes in his trouser pockets and then for a lighter. She followed the ritual application of the flame and the first deep-drawn inhalation with respectful interest.

— Watch out, she said. — It would be quite easy to set fire to this dry grass.

He opened one eye to look at her then closed it again.

— My mum doesn't like smoking. She says it gives you cancer.

— Wherever did she get that idea?

Kasim's offhandedness didn't put Ivy off – in fact he was beginning to impress her. She supposed he was her aunt Alice's new boyfriend, and might be the best so far. Most of the adult behaviour children saw, it occurred to her, was carefully infantilised for their benefit – like smoking, which she knew her daddy did, but never where they could see it. Idling, Kasim took out his phone to check his emails.

— You won't get a signal here, she said importantly. — There's only one place, and even then it depends what network you're on. You have to cross into that field with the cows in and then walk up to the gate at the top and sit on it. It's the only way.

Kasim swore – incredulously rather than because he really cared. Perhaps you weren't supposed to swear in front of children, but Ivy was unblinking as if she heard *fuck* every day of her life. He quite liked the idea of dropping off the edge of communication into nowhere, where his friends couldn't find him, nor his father or mother – who were divorced – nor the girl he was half-heartedly half-involved with. The buzzing, rustling summer afternoon, too hot for birdsong, swelled louder and more invitingly in his ears now that he knew it couldn't be cut across by any mediated connect-edness. He was going to ground, he decided, and enjoyed feeling the hard flank of the ground, not at all accommodating, moulded underneath him where he lay. On the other hand, it was irritating that there were children here. Children didn't amuse him. It seemed only yesterday that he was a child himself, he could remember it only too well.

ALICE WENT ROUND THE HOUSE to air it, singing and opening doors and windows. She was all right now she was inside. Leaning out of an upstairs bedroom she called and waved to Kasim coming through from the churchyard; he was trying to shake off Ivy who followed close behind. He waved back without unplugging his cigarette. Turning away from him into the room again, Alice was subject to a leap of promise that had no relation to Kasim or to anyone, certainly not to Dani: light moving on pink wallpaper, the dark bulk of a wardrobe in the corner of her vision, the children's voices from outside, the room's musty air and its secrets, a creak of floorboards – these aroused a memory so piercing and yet so indefinite that it might have only been a memory of a dream. There was summer in the dream, and a man, and some wordless, weightless signal of affinity passing between him and her, with everything to play for. This flare of intimation buoyed Alice up and agitated her, more like anticipation than recollection. Love seemed again luxuriant and possible – as if something lay in wait. She went along the landing breathless, and aware of her heart beating.

Upstairs the house was always full of light, changing dramatically according to the weather. Its design was very simple: a single flight of wide, shallow stairs rose to a long landing with a white-painted balustrade; at each end of the landing, at the centre of the front and back elevations of the house, there rose the tall arched windows that were its distinctive beauty from inside and out. In the front bedroom that was always hers, Alice knelt at the bookshelf – guiltily aware all the time of Fran at work downstairs. The house was full of children's books – not only from her own and her siblings' childhood, but from their dead mother's too. Bookplates, with Alice's name written in the shakily flowing cursive she'd been taught at school, were pasted inside the cover of all hers, with dates. As if in a form of divination she opened one at random – E. Nesbit's *The Wouldbegoods* – and read a page or two. *And then we saw a thing that was well worth coming all that way for; the stream suddenly disappeared under a dark stone archway, and however much you stood in the water and stuck your head down between your knees you could not see any light at the other end.* The very weight of the book in her hands, and the thick good paper of the pages as she turned them, and the illustrations with the boys in their knickerbockers and the girls in pinafores, seemed to bring back other times – the time when she had first read this, and behind that the time when such children might have existed.

Fran was chopping onions in the kitchen sink when Alice came in looking for scissors, wanting to cut flowers in the garden.

— When you decided to invite Kasim, Fran said, — where exactly were you planning for him to sleep?

Alice was blithe. — Don't worry, there's plenty of room. She banged through the drawers in vain, looked hopelessly around her. — Don't we have scissors?

Fran lifted them from their place hanging on a row of wall-hooks, and handed them over. — I mean, I presume that he's not in with you.

— For god's sake! Kasim's something like my stepson, almost.

— Only asking. I never know with you.

— I'm an ancient old woman, as far as he's concerned. The children adore him, by the way. Everywhere he goes, they go in procession after him. Kasim has his hands in his pockets and now Arthur's copying him. He looks so sweet.

— Is there room then? Fran persisted, bent over her peeling. — Molly has to have a room of her own, obviously. She's not a child any longer.

Alice was forced to start counting up bedrooms and beds on her fingers. — Oh dear. I'd forgotten Molly.

— Roland and whatever her name is, the new wife. You, Kasim, Harriet. Molly. That's five bedrooms. There are only six. It means I have to sleep in with the children, in the bunk-bed room.

— Oh Fran, that's awful. You need a break more than any of us. You need your privacy. No. I'll sleep with them instead, it's all my fault. I don't mind, really.

— Don't be silly, Fran said flatly, punishingly. — You know that isn't ever going to happen.

Penitent, Alice got out their grandmother's vases from the scullery and filled them with water on the kitchen table. — Right in my way, Fran grumbled when she was out of earshot. Alice brought in roses and montbretia and purple linaria from the garden, where only the toughest plants survived their long absences. Then she put flowers out all round the house – a posy for every dressing table, white roses and ferns for the new wife. She arranged the supermarket fruit in bowls. Fran had brought new tea towels in bright colours. Rooms filled with the smells of cooking. In between their visits it was as if the empty house lapsed into a kind of torpor, and was frigid and reluctant at first when they had to rouse it back to life.

HARRIET CAME THROUGH THE CHURCHYARD and paused at the keyhole gap to brace herself for the end of her solitude. Her afternoon filled her to the brim: she had taken the route to the waterfall, which at this time of year wasn't much more than a swell of liquid in a sodden long fall of emerald moss. Goldcrests had shrilled in the tops of a plantation of firs, a slow-worm had basked across her path, grey tree trunks surged and the sunlight was filtered through fans of leaves that stirred in movements of air imperceptible on the ground. A cottage whose abandonment they had observed since they were children – with a dim memory of a last inhabitant, an old woman – had sunk further back into the earth at its vantage point at the path's turn, perched high above the steep end of a valley. Long ago she and her brother and sisters had broken a rusty padlock and explored inside the cottage, even climbing upstairs; it would be dangerous to do that now. The place was cut off from all services, there was no mains water, let alone electricity, no one could have lived there any longer. Though sometimes Harriet had thought that she could. She didn't need very much.

She saw that the others had arrived. The French windows were open onto the terrace and a young man was established there on one of the deckchairs, fetched from an outhouse. Ivy, emerging from the sitting room, was bringing him a glass of what looked like gin and tonic, held aloft carefully in two hands; Arthur, following, carried a bowl. Harriet was more shy than anyone knew, and quailed at the necessity of re-entering this peopled world. At first she thought the man must be a new boyfriend of Alice's, though she hadn't heard of there being one. Closer up, she recognised him.

— I know who you are, Harriet said, holding out her hand, startling Kasim because he was finishing reading, attentively contemptuous, the *Metro* he'd picked up on the tube in London. — You must be Dani's son. We met at Alice's birthday a few years ago. You were only a boy then. I'm Alice's sister.

— I've grown up.

— Stupid thing for me to say. Of course you have.

Kasim stood up, he tried to make Harriet take his seat, and then his gin and tonic, and the salted cashews, which were what Arthur had brought.

— This one's yours, said Ivy sternly. — She can have one of her own.

As soon as Kasim saw Harriet he did remember meeting her, because she looked like a more tragic Alice – though her cord trousers and old tee shirt showed that she didn't care about clothes as Alice did. Her face was more haggard than Alice's, though less expressive, like a mask of calm, and her short hair stuck up in a stiff crest and was pure white.

Harriet said she wasn't ready for gin yet, she had better change out of her walking boots first, and then unpack. Arthur asked if he could come.

— He loves women changing their clothes, Ivy explained.

— I'm only changing my boots, Harriet apologised.

Fran, washing salad in the kitchen sink, saw Harriet and Arthur bringing Harriet's luggage – not much of it – to the side door opening into the scullery, which opened in turn into the kitchen. Arthur was solemn with the importance of being slung across with his aunt's binoculars. He couldn't help, with that hair, having a page-boy look: Fran had seen this when she gave him the cashew nuts, and she felt with a pang that she must cut it, but not yet. At least her oldest sister talked to the children as if they were sensible adults – Alice did exaggerate sometimes.

— So you've been for a walk already? she said, kissing Harriet.

— I didn't want to be the first inside, Harriet confessed. — For some superstitious reason.

— I wish I had your energy. No wonder you're so thin.

Harriet sat in the scullery to unlace her boots, while Fran explained about Jeff not coming, and how unfair it was. — We don't know what time Roland's lot are getting here, but I'm making supper anyway and we've started on the gin. We thought we'd better be fortified against the new wife.

— I met Kasim in the garden.

— Dani's son. He's supposed to be very brilliant. But then all Alice's friends are supposed to be brilliant, aren't they?

— He seemed very nice.

Fran dropped her voice. — Alice never thinks about the practicalities. Because she's brought him, I'll have to be in the bunk-bed room with the children.

Harriet bent her hot face over her bootlaces, skewered with guilt because she knew she ought to offer to sleep with the children instead, to give Fran a break, and yet she couldn't do it. Her aloneness last thing at night was precious to her: at home she lived mostly apart from her partner, Christopher, because they both preferred it. Then Alice came into the kitchen, hands bundled full with knives and forks – she was laying the table in the dining room. — Hettie, you're here! Did you have a good walk? So wise, to get straight out into the lovely day. You haven't brought much luggage, to last three weeks. Aren't you austere! It's so like you, to be sensible about clothes. After all, no one's going to see us, are they? Except each other, and we don't care, we're family. And Kasim and Pilar.

— That's her name, Fran said. — I knew it was something architectural.

— I'm only here for a week, Harriet said. — I couldn't take more time off.

Fran whirred the salad spinner, to cover up the blow of Alice's disappointment. Alice's whole demeanour altered exaggeratedly. She dropped the cutlery noisily on the kitchen table. Harriet had promised, she cried. Hadn't they all agreed, to save up their holidays and have three full weeks together, because this might be the last time?

— I didn't promise, Harriet said. — I warned you. I said that it would be difficult, to take time off work for so long.

— I wanted you to be here. It's supposed to be a special occasion. I wanted us all to be here together like the old days.

— She's here now, Fran said. — Let's not quarrel on the very first night.

Upstairs, Harriet found the little posy on her chest of drawers; it seemed to communicate Alice's reproach as she unpacked. Her bedroom was above the kitchen and she could hear her sister's voice rising in continuing indignation downstairs, though she couldn't hear her actual words; when she stomped deliberately heavily on the floorboards, Alice shut up. A chiming of glasses and scraping of chairs came pointedly from the dining room. It wasn't fair of Alice to blame her for spoiling things. No one had protested that she shouldn't have turned up with Kasim, if she wanted this to be a family occasion.

Arthur sat on the bed swinging his legs, watching absorbedly as Harriet put her clothes away. — Are those your best pyjamas? he asked with earnest interest, and she had to admit she only had two pairs and they were both the same – one green check and one red. She regretted not having anything more thrilling to show him than the neat pile of clean tee shirts and the spare underwear and spare pair of trousers, a jumper in case it got cold. Putting away her hay-fever pills and her hairbrush, she slipped her diary under the tee shirts in the drawer. Tonight, when she was alone, she would write in the diary about the quarrel with Alice, and would try to put down both points of view with scrupulous fairness. Then Alice climbed the stairs with a peacemaking gin, and Harriet accepted it, although she didn't like gin much.

— You don't mind being in this room? Alice said, turning away quickly from catching sight of herself in the age-spotted swing mirror, though she couldn't help her hand going up to adjust her hair.

— I don't mind. Why should I?

— Because you have to come through my room, and that's a nuisance for you. You can't go through Roland's room because of Pilar.

— I don't mind.

Arthur asked whether Harriet would like to take his picture and when she said she'd love to he put on an assured, equivocal smile for her camera. Then Alice, also camera-natural, sat beside him on the bed, arm around him, for another picture. Arthur offered to take one of the sisters together, but they wouldn't hear of it. They both had a horror, not ever acknowledged, of how closely alike they looked, and yet unalike. In family groups they made sure they were always one at either end. Harriet's hair turning white had made the resemblance more startling.

THEY WENT AHEAD WITH SUPPER although they hadn't heard from Roland: pasta in a tomato sauce with olives and capers, sourdough bread, salad dressed with olive oil and sea salt. Alice had made the table lovely with more flowers and the tarnished heavy silver cutlery which had been their grandparents' wedding present. She'd found a damp-spotted lace tablecloth that smelled of its cupboard. The sash windows on the side of the house were thrown up and the slanting late sunshine rebounded from the mirror above the sideboard; they ate in its dazzle and the whole scene had something commemorative about it. None of them had dining rooms in the rest of their lives or ever used tablecloths, let alone lace ones.

— Just to think, said Fran, — that this might be the last time we come here.

Alice said she hated thinking about it and Fran shouldn't jump the gun, that was what they had to discuss when they were all assembled. The children, searching from face to face to gauge the collective mood, were poignantly good mannered under its influence: Ivy's peaky face was lifted up towards nothing because she was suspended between this real room and another imaginary one. The telephone rang on its stand in the hall while they ate and when Harriet came back from answering it she looked disappointed.

— It was Roland. They're not coming until tomorrow.

— I knew it as soon as the phone rang, Alice said.

— He always manages to do this, Fran exclaimed. — Every time!

— Oh, it's his little power play. He doesn't know he's doing it.

For a moment they were flattened; expectation of the others' coming had buoyed them all up. Their brother and his wife and daughter – Molly was his daughter by his first wife – had seemed all the more glamorous in their absence, and the evening had been climbing towards the high point of their arrival. — Pretty feeble excuse, Harriet said. — If he really has a meeting tomorrow, he surely could have let us know earlier?

— But actually I'm glad, said Alice, recovering, sitting forwards with her elbows on the table, holding up her wineglass to the others so that her bangles fell chinking down her arm. She had put on a vintage bolero with transparent sleeves over her summer dress. — Isn't this special, just the six of us? I feel quite reprieved, that we don't have to meet Roland's new wife tonight. We'll be fresh tomorrow, we'll be ready for her. But just for tonight – we're perfect without them, aren't we?

— I don't care if they never come, said Kasim cheerfully.

— Roland should think about us when he gets married so often, Fran said. — All over again, we have to learn to live with a new wife. We'd got used to Valerie.

— Sort of used to her.

— I wasn't ever used to her, Ivy said. — Her voice was screechy and her head went like a chicken's when she walked.

— Like this, said Arthur, imitating it.

Alice said wasn't it such a relief, now that Valerie was a thing of the past, to be able to come out with the truth at last?

— Don't encourage them, Fran said. — They're bad enough.

After dinner Alice hunted in the sideboard for candles: electric light was too brutal, it would spoil the magic. And when the washing up was done and the beds were made up and the children were quiet upstairs, the adults sat around the table again, with the windows open because the night was so warm. Poetic moths, significant in a thin soup of lesser insects, blundered about the candle flames. Harriet had put on a cardigan and tied a silk scarf round her neck, a concession to sociability; scarves were Alice's thing, but encouragingly she touched her sister's and exclaimed at how pretty it was. Pulling off her apron, Fran dug out chocolates and a bottle of Armagnac from among the supermarket boxes. Alice stole one of Kasim's cigarettes so she could blow smoke at the insects, then stole another one.

Kasim was quite drunk, warming himself expansively in the tender attention of the three women concentrated on him, each of them old enough to be his mother. They drew out his responsiveness as girls of his own age didn't yet know how: girls thought he was cold and clever. He sprawled back in his chair and stretched his long legs under the table, aware of exerting and stretching his intelligence, and of the sisters' alertness to him – unguarded, because they had outgrown any narrow self-possession. The girls he knew were always performing something, or if they let go of their guard then there seemed nothing behind it. His cleverness in relation to these older women operated like a sexual power in itself – even if the power reached out to no particular end. He tipped the Armagnac luxuriantly round in his glass and slopped it onto his shirt, dropping ash from his cigarette onto the carpet.

He addressed himself to Fran, who was a maths teacher in a comprehensive school, and might have liked him least if he hadn't worked on her. She seemed more definite and perhaps more limited than her sisters. Kasim had once had a crush on his maths teacher, and Fran's freckled plump hands roused a pleasurable memory of equations written out neatly on a whiteboard. Showing off, he talked about optimisation theory and the chain rule in calculus – the amount x of some good demanded depends on price p, which depends on the weather, measured by the parameter w, and so on. Actually maths was dull, moving in its inexorable circles. But he enjoyed frightening them with his solutions to the banking crisis: we ought to have let the banks fail, he explained severely, and let the insurance companies who bought the collateralised debt obligations fail, and let the people who borrowed too much to buy their homes, lose their homes. We need less regulation not more – global finance operates as a set of interlocking cartels and a free market is our only hope of breaking them up.

Alice was horrified, but also proudly vindicated by Kasim's display of himself. Of course he knew what the sisters' opinions were even before they voiced them – their dusty old hopeful leftism, their old-fashioned aspiration for the state to be the instrument of social justice.

— The trouble with capitalism, Alice said, — is that it's always predicated on growth. But we can't go on just making more and more things, and using up more of the earth's resources. We have to cut carbon emissions, to begin with.

— Are you serious? Is there anybody who seriously still thinks there's time for that? Do you imagine that Chinese heavy industry can run on sunshine?

— We have to live differently. We have to learn to do without things.

— Tell that to the Chinese.

Fran said she didn't want to think about global warming, it was too depressing.

— D'you know, Kas, Alice said, — Harriet was a real revolutionary when she was younger! The real thing! You'd be amazed. She was arrested over and over. She went to prison for her beliefs.

— You make it sound as if she was planting bombs or something, Fran said.

— Were you planting bombs? he asked. — More fun than economics.

He was used to his father's friends' nostalgic bragging about their radical pasts.

— Of course I wasn't planting bombs. Harriet looked down uneasily into her coffee, chiming her spoon against her cup. — I wasn't really a revolutionary. Don't take any notice of Alice, she doesn't mean half of what she says. She just talks to be entertaining.

— You used to go on all the protests! You lay down in the road in front of cruise missiles! You filmed police tactics in the miners' strike! You hated being middle class, from our sort of family. And do you know was she does now? She works advising asylum seekers. It's such hopeless work. She's so good. She listens all day to stories of rape and torture.

Tetchily Harriet interrupted her. — Don't try to make a drama out of it, Alice. You turn it into something that it isn't.

— I'm so selfish, Alice persisted. — I only live for myself.

Kasim said it was the only way, live for yourself and make plenty of money.

— At least I've never made any money. I'm not that bad.

— I wish I was that bad, said Fran. — I wish I had money.

Lying awake upstairs, Ivy could hear their voices and laughter: she identified in a frisson of loneliness with a solitary owl calling over the fields outside. Turning her invisible hands this way and that in front of her face in the dark, it was impossible to believe that she ended at the limits of her skin and couldn't surpass it. At last, curling on her side with her knees up, she descended the ceremonial staircase of her sleep, shedding a heavy cloak on the steps behind her, unpinning the dark rivers of her hair, which fell in her dream all the way down her back to the floor.

TWO

KASIM ATE BREAKFAST the next morning in a deckchair in the garden outside the French windows, scowling, retreating inside himself, without even a newspaper or his iPad to hide behind. He had shed the previous evening, choosing to remember nothing about it. The second gloriously fine day in a row already struck him as monotonous – what were you supposed to *do* with fine weather? Ivy and Arthur, who'd been up for hours, watched from a respectful distance where they sat cross-legged on the lawn; when he turned his back on them deliberately, they moved to a new vantage point. Alice and Fran – revealed to him, disturbing, softer, older, in their dressing gowns and without make-up – supplied him solicitously with coffee and orange juice and toast.

He contemplated escape, imagined himself on a train back to London, and asked if anyone was driving into town. But then he saw in Alice's face how she would be crushed if he left; because of his father, Kasim felt exposed whenever Alice showed her vulnerability. Anyway, London wasn't what he wanted, he was already on the run from there. On second thoughts, he said, he would rather stay put. He pretended he had work to do, though actually he hadn't brought any books. Reprieved, with a rich smile, Alice put her cool hand on his forehead as if he was sick.

— You take it easy, she said. — Enjoy yourself.

He tried not to show how much he wanted her to take her hand away. After breakfast he made a little pilgrimage, up through the field with the cows in it to the gate at the top, to check his phone. Ivy and Arthur followed faithfully after him.

— Now, wait here, he said sternly, stopping some little way before the gate, gesturing out an invisible line along the ground. — No coming any closer. This is private, right?

Impressed, they kept back religiously behind his line, standing poised on the very brink of the forbidden, shuffling their feet to be as close as they could get, both making pantomime efforts not to topple forwards, Ivy tugging Arthur fiercely back into his place. Kasim climbed to the top of the gate as Ivy instructed. He didn't know why he bothered. Among his messages there was one from his mother, which he didn't read, and one from the girl; he decided before opening this that if she used any form of text-abbreviation, which he despised, then he wouldn't respond.

— Where r u Kas? she wrote.

With a sigh he switched the phone off and discovered that from this elevation he could see the sea in the distance, looking more like a flat wash of silver light than like water; and beyond the silver wash, a blue line of hills. He had had no idea that they had arrived so close to this other edge of the country – how small it was! He said to himself sometimes that he was more at home in the Punjab, although he hadn't been there since he was fifteen, when his grandfather died.

ROLAND AND HIS SERAGLIO – as Alice called them, though not to his face – arrived at Kington at lunchtime. He drove an old Jaguar XJ6 with all the original beige leather upholstery. His new wife Pilar, Argentinian and a lawyer, was beside him in the passenger seat; she had passed the journey reading through papers, replacing one file every so often in her briefcase and pulling out another. Sixteen-year-old Molly had been stretched along the back seat, either asleep or playing with her iPhone, and every so often she had asked how far it was now, just as she had done when she was six.

They pulled up on the cobbles beside the outhouses. All the noise and forward thrust of travel faded and receded, the engine clicked secretively as it cooled, and when he stood up out of the car Roland experienced the scene for a moment as archetypally English, as if he saw it through Pilar's foreign eyes: the simple white house with its arched window, the surging pillar-like trunks of the great beech trees with their canopies of sombre bronze-green, the dancing silver birch, the old church sunk in its graveyard, the white doves in the stone dovecote belonging to a barn conversion opposite. But it might all seem poky and parochial to Pilar, who had spent her childhood summers on a ranch on the Argentinian pampas, where her uncle raised cattle and bred polo ponies. Her uncle, whom she loved much better than her own father, had been up to his neck in junta politics.

Molly and Pilar yawned and stretched, Pilar fished for her shoes. She had slipped out of her high heels in the car and tucked her feet underneath her on the seat while she was reading, as she always did; her feet were long-boned and slender like her hands. Roland began unpacking their luggage.

— It's a nice example of a small English rectory, he explained to her. — Built about 1820.

She was smiling, willing to like whatever he liked. — It's very pretty.

— I'm fond of it because our mother grew up here. Molly's been coming here all through her childhood. But of course the upkeep's expensive, it needs a lot of work.

— You can't ever sell Kington, Dad, Molly said flatly. — You're not allowed to. It always has to be here to come back to.

— We'll have to see.

Roland had worried that Pilar and Molly wouldn't get on. His own relationship with his only child was unproblematic and doting, but he had thought Pilar might be exasperated by Molly's silences and awkwardness. They seemed to be all right, though; since they first met a few days ago – Molly lived mostly with her mother, his first wife – Pilar had taken her to have her hair cut and her eyebrows threaded, and had bought her new clothes. Molly had been gratefully absorbed in these initiations. Probably Molly's mother wouldn't approve – she was stern on the subject of the commodification of beauty. It was interesting to Roland that a woman's appearance, so seemingly effortless, might in fact entail all this earnest expertise and hard work. Pilar's elegance was accomplished out of sight, a daily miracle. She had never asked for his approval.

Alice and Fran and the children spilled out noisily from the side door of the house; they crowded around Pilar and kissed her and then kissed Molly. — At last! At last you're all here. Welcome! Don't unpack now, leave it, come and eat. We've put out lunch on a table on the terrace. Isn't the weather wonderful? There are going to be three weeks like this, I know there are. Harriet's out bird-watching of course. And Jeff isn't coming! He's done his usual thing, booking himself in to play, claiming he'd forgotten all about the holiday. Are you all right in those shoes, Pilar? Divine shoes! Take care on the cobbles though.

Alice linked her arm into her brother's, walking round into the garden. — I can't believe you in a white suit, Roly. Do you remember, when you were twenty you despised me and Fran because we cared about clothes?

— I've never despised anyone.

— You did, you did! You despised us. Now look at you! It's such a good look. Like one of those academics on television, wandering around a ruined monastery or something. Crumpled and sexy and wise.

Roland was short and compact and calm with blinking brown eyes, the lids very curved; his grizzled, tightly curled hair was cut close to his well-shaped head and his mouth was unexpectedly soft, loose-lipped. His smiles when they came transformed him. He didn't mind his sister teasing him but he didn't respond in kind, he never had: he hadn't been very playful even when he was a child and supposed to play. He had always preferred knowing and explaining things.

Pulling Pilar along, Ivy and Arthur pressed her to admire the lunch table, where they had decorated each place with leaves and sprigs of unripe blackberries. — It's very nice, she said of everything, not quite satisfying them. A bowl on the table was piled high with fruit, another was full of baby tomatoes and sliced cucumber; butter and cheese were laid out on leaves and a loaf was put ready with its knife, yet they sensed that Pilar was not overwhelmed. They let go her hands. She said she didn't want to sit down to lunch yet, she was cramped from sitting for so long in the car.

— There's no hurry, said Alice. — Stretch your legs. Breathe the air.

Ivy groaned, she was starving, she couldn't wait or she would die of hunger. Ignoring her, Fran opened a bottle of something fizzy to toast the new arrivals.

— You should see this place in the spring, Pilar, said Alice regretfully, — when the flowers are so perfect.

— Everything here is left just as our grandparents had it, Roland said, gesturing into the shadowy drawing room. — Our grandpees, as we called them. He was afraid Pilar was seeing the faded beige brocade on the sofa and chairs and the damp stains on the wallpaper, which had peeled away from the wall in one corner. There weren't even many real antiques in the house, most of the furniture was wartime utility, which had come with the house when their grandparents moved in.

She was sympathetic. — These old houses are so expensive to maintain.

— We don't maintain it, Alice cheerfully said. She sat on the terrace steps with her bright face uplifted, hands clasped around her knee, keen to charm her new sister-in-law. — We love it just how it is. Do you know, Roly, that I forgot my keys? When we arrived I could only peer into it from the outside, through the windows. Then it seemed an enchanted place: as if we'd only seen it in a mirror and wouldn't ever be able to get inside it. Now I keep feeling as if I passed through the mirror and I'm living in there, on the other side.

— Our grandfather was minister here for forty years, Roland said. — And he was a poet too: a good one I think. Alice will tell you whether he's any good. Alice is the poet in the family now.

— I'm not a real poet, Alice apologised. — Not like Grandfather. Do you like poetry?

Pilar said she didn't have time to read any and Alice sympathised. — There's never any time, is there? What happens to it?

Molly already had her guitar out of its case. She bent over it, hair falling to hide her face as she bent down to the strings – she might have been showing off except that her playing was so hesitant, made with such minimal movements of her fingers that it barely stirred the air: a little repeated pattern of notes close together, in a minor key. Her fingers hardly seemed to press the frets. Arthur stood watching, compelled by the tiny music.

— I can't believe we're drinking again, said Alice. — We only seemed to stop five minutes ago. I ought to be more hungover than I am. Kasim's in a bad way this morning. He was here at breakfast but he retreated to his room again and hasn't been seen since. He said he was working but we think he's just gone back to bed.

Then she had to explain all over again who Kasim was. Roland tensed visibly, warily. Brought up in a household of women, he found them easier, more stimulating, and resented the idea of an unknown adult male on his territory, let alone Dani's son, who was still in bed in the afternoon. Dani had been a disaster for Alice, Roland thought.

COMING OUT OF HIS BEDROOM, still sleepy, rubbing his eyes bad-temperedly, Kasim met Molly just as she arrived at the top of the stairs with her rucksack. Alice and Fran had mentioned Molly, but he'd presumed she would just be another little girl, a nuisance. Both of them visibly quaked at catching this unexpected sight of each other; not with attraction immediately but with shock at this encounter with one of their own kind – young – in this place where they had both been resigned to being singular, and even relieved by it. The encounter added interest to the whole situation, most definitely, but also pressure. They passed in silence, Kasim on his way to the bathroom and Molly to her bedroom. He carried away her image – delicate little cat's impertinent muzzle, little springy high breasts – imprinted on his mind's eye and digested it afterwards while taking a piss, not too noisily, in case she was listening. Running the cold tap, splashing water on his face, he stared into the mirror above the sink and saw himself differently because she'd seen him; he knew that now, alone in her room, she was digesting his image too.

ON HER WAY HOME FROM birdwatching Harriet crossed a tussocky field, a narrow wedge shape between two stretches of woodland, rising steeply to where it was closed in by more woods at the top. After the woods with their equivocal shade, the strong sunlight was startling when the path opened onto this gap; a red kite ambled in the sky above, small birds scuffled in the undergrowth, too hot to sing, and a pigeon broke out from the trees with a wooden clatter of wing beats. A stream ran down the field, bisecting it, conversing urgently with itself, its cleft bitten disproportionately deep into the stony ground and marked against the field's rough grass by the tangle of brambles that grew luxuriantly all along it, profuse as fur, still showing a few late white flowers limp like damp tissue, and heavy with berries too sour and green to pick yet, humming with flies.

Harriet followed the sound of the stream's boiling and deep chuckle up the field to a place where it tumbled over a stone and fell to foam in a dark pool below, all out of the sunlight, hidden under its thick fringe of growth. Crouching, she reached out her hand to break the water's fall; it bore away from the stone lip in a perfect glassy curve, vividly cold. She wanted to taste it but thought that wasn't sensible – who knew what pesticides they used on these fields? On her solitary walks she was ambushed occasionally by this fear of accidents: what if she fell, and no one knew where she was? So she touched her wet hand to her forehead instead, and the water dried against her skin as she walked towards home, through the woods down to the road and past the restored mill which sold handmade paper to London artists, then onto the disused road which climbed again, along the side of the hill to Kington at the top.

Roland's Jaguar, when she got there, was pulled up between her car and Fran's, and luggage was left on the cobbles – so much good-looking luggage, expensive suitcases and briefcases and laptops, and a lovely straw basket, lined with cotton print, a billowing scarf tied round the leather handles. Harriet stood hesitating – she could hear excited voices, mostly Alice's, coming from the back garden. Entering into that high-pitched sociability would be like breaking through a skin, all eyes would turn on her and see how she was hot and dishevelled from her walk. Harriet dreaded the effort that would have to be made, getting to know Roland's new wife: a stranger was a fearful and impregnable unknown country. Even this luggage intimidated her, with its aura of life lived according to a high, intolerant code that she would never master.

She lingered in the pregnant quiet of the empty yard, until Arthur came wading out from the scullery in cobwebby walking boots, huge on him, that must have once belonged to her grandfather. He didn't seem surprised to find her skulking there.

– You should come round, he said. – They're all here now.

– I suppose I should.

Kindly, Arthur led her by the hand. They went together through the stone archway; the French windows in the drawing room were open onto the terrace and the lawn. A table was set out on the terrace for lunch. They never seemed to stop eating, Harriet thought – although Alice didn't really eat much, she just picked at it, watching her weight. Roland at the head of the table was talking, his fork laden with avocado and tomato and then forgotten: his delivery was always deliberate, full of measured pauses as if he considered every remark, holding it in inverted commas before letting it out in shapely sentences. His sisters half-worshipped his cleverness. *Who'd have thought it?* they said to one another. Being his sisters, they also found it slightly ridiculous, even Harriet did. They could remember him in short trousers, when his glasses were mended with sticking plaster.

Roland's academic position was as a philosopher, but he had also published a couple of popularising books, which didn't popularise too far, on philosophy and film, and now he wrote and reviewed for the national papers. The surprising white suit must be the new wife's influence, Harriet thought, and made him appear worldly and gilded. He was saying that British film had always been limited by its lack of pastoral. — Unlike Italian films, say, or Iranian, we can only do the pastoral as pastiche. We only know how to be nostalgic about landscape, we don't know how to imagine ourselves inside it.

Pilar said that the countryside didn't make her in the least nostalgic. — I love cities. I love London. All the people, all the conveniences.

Her accent was not heavy but pervasive, exotic, tawny.

— She grew up on a ranch, Roland told them. — Twelve thousand acres.

— I'm hopeless at numbers, Alice said. — Is that enormous or tiny?

Pilar was dressed in white too, the shape of her dress seemed stamped against the shadows under the overhanging clematis. Her slim long legs were crossed, a white shoe dangled from the toe of one long foot, her long brown hair was caught up smoothly behind in a clip. When Arthur led Harriet forwards to the table, they were startled as if they'd hardly registered that she was missing – there wasn't a place set for her. Roland over-compensated, kissing her although they didn't usually kiss, then escorting her almost ceremonially to meet Pilar. Harriet put out her hand at arm's length to forestall more embraces, Pilar unwound from her chair and stood up to shake it. She was very handsome, and taller than anyone in their family; in fact, she seemed to be made of a different material to them, less fussy and more polished, simplified to a few strong statements – the dark strokes of her eyebrows, straight long nose, heavy jaw. Harriet was suffused for a moment in the pungent perfume the other woman was wearing, and could smell it on her fingers for hours afterwards.

They were all affected by Pilar's new presence among them – it had the effect of making their talk at the table seem false, as if they were performing their family life for her scrutiny. Alice and Fran were noisy, showing off; Fran exaggerated the drama of Jeff's selfishness, his dereliction. Ivy spilled her drink, Arthur picked out all the cheese from his sandwich, then left the crusts; Kasim when he appeared wouldn't sit down for lunch – he said he wasn't hungry and then carved himself huge hunks of bread, ate them sitting on the grass at the bottom of the garden. Pilar didn't contribute much to the conversation, her remarks were rapid and forceful like her concentrated, liquid glances, as if she closed discussion instead of opening it up. But this might just be cultural difference, the sisters generously thought. Perhaps it was difficult to be tentative in Spanish. When they asked about the situation in Argentina, Pilar said she loathed politics. — Over there everything's political. That's why I couldn't wait to get away.

— She won't let me meet her family, Roland said.

— You will meet them, Pilar promised him. — You will. Just give me time.

— At fourteen she had to fight off her cousin with a riding whip.

— He was just a little over-excited.

The newly-weds were at that stage where every exchange between them had a private reference, tender but cloying to observers. Alice's quick glance found Fran's, across the table. — The trouble is you'll love them, Pilar said. — They'll love you. They'll butcher an animal for a barbecue for you, take you out riding, sleep under the stars, all that. But you don't know the place, you can't really know it. It's so crazy.

— Philosophers love crazy places, Alice said. — More work for them. Roland's got this Latin American thing anyway, it all appeals to him because he's so buttoned-up in his own life, he's such a puritan. That's why he writes about it.

But clearly Pilar didn't want to talk about Roland's character with his sisters. She was only really forthcoming when she was outlining how, since she'd been made a partner in her law firm, she had led a very effective reorganisation, including getting rid of a couple of staff. — I don't mind working hard, she said, — but I can't bear inefficiency. When Harriet asked what area of law she worked in and Pilar said commercial contracts, there was an awkward silence which was not disapproval – what did they know about it, to disapprove of? – they simply could not think of anything to say, could not bring themselves to say, *that must be interesting*. Roland went on cutting cheese steadfastly and cheerfully, as if he refused to help them out. Commercial contracts, he seemed to imply, were as good a topic for discussion as any other.

KASIM SAID HE WAS GOING for a walk. Cobwebby from too much sleep, he wasn't ready yet to take on Alice's brother, and he didn't want this girl to think he was hanging around because of her. He and Molly had not yet spoken. Ivy sprang into supplicant position at her mother's elbow, holding up her hands together in prayer. — Can we go with him? Please, please, Mummy? We can show him the way to the waterfall. He can look after us.

Fran pretended to make a fuss – they were forbidden to climb trees, Arthur mustn't go near the edge of any steep slopes – but of course, Kasim thought, she must be relieved to be rid of them for a couple of hours. Then he had to be laden with the whole apparatus the children might need: bottles of water, wet wipes, biscuits, apples, Elastoplasts, Savlon. They had to pee, they had to change their shoes. Eventually they set out along the road in the opposite direction to the way the taxi had brought him and Alice the day before; he strode with a scowl, hoping the children wouldn't be able to keep up. They were indefatigable though, running up and down like puppies, yapping and chattering. Ivy in a spangled waistcoat, with a scarf knotted under her chin, was disconcerting, a miniature old crone.

The road became more or less impassable for cars not far beyond the little cluster of houses; grass growing through its tar-macked surface was breaking it up and branches had fallen, blocking it, from ancient oaks growing out of the banks on either side. Ivy led the way across a stile then up a steep field to a tree at the top; they followed the left-hand hedge through several more fields before descending through another gate into woods. Yellow way-markers were painted on posts and trees. They couldn't get lost, everything in this countryside was tamed and known, nothing was dangerous.

They had it all to themselves – only a farmer on a tractor,

toiling up and down, his noise no louder than a persistent buzzing insect, did something in a field far off on the opposite hill-flank. Ploughed? But didn't they plough in the spring? In the woods, as if he'd arrived far enough away from the world in which he was on his dignity, Kasim unbent and began to play with the children: he picked up pine cones where the path ran through a plantation of conifers, pelting Ivy with them. She was dumbfounded at first but soon they were pelting him back and having screaming fun – feet thudding as they ran, breath stopping in their chests with delicious fear, some ancient pent-up violence released in the rage of throwing. Ivy called Arthur a spoilsport when he cried because Kasim hit him too hard. Then for a while Kasim carried Arthur on his shoulders.

They arrived at the ruined cottage at the head of a valley, where the path turned tightly round above a steep drop through trees to the stream below, the cottage hanging precipitously on to the edge. After the wood-shadows this clearing seemed a bright simplification; water gurgled in a rocky cleft below them and the treetops stirred. The windows of the cottage were all on its other side, for the view; a wooden porch on their side was collapsing away from the front door. The roof was made of the same slabs as Kington House, thickly mossed, and from one end of the cottage bulged a semicircular bread oven, built of grey stones slotted mysteriously into their curve. A grassy bank opposite the front door was improbably pretty with wild flowers.

— Is this the waterfall? Kasim said, setting Arthur down.

— Oh, not for *miles*.

Kasim dropped down onto the bank and then lay back among the flowers, closing his eyes. — Who cares about the waterfall anyway? This'll do.

Ivy was crestfallen. When she had been leading them so well!

And the promise of the waterfall – with its clear pool at the bottom, where she had once dramatically cut her foot – had been her trump card. Kasim's sleep, or feigned sleep, withdrew his presence as abruptly as if a cloud had crossed the sun – though none did, the sky was cloudless.

— May we explore in the cottage, then? she asked.

Kasim grunted agreement without even looking at it.

THE RUSTY PADLOCK HELD, BUT pointlessly, because the hasp was entirely loose from the door frame; the door stood slightly ajar, and when they tugged at it opened wide enough to let them squeeze through. Inside, the children were aware at once that the cottage smelled awful – not innocently of leaf-rot and minerals like outside, but of something held furtively close, ripening in secret. There was only one room downstairs, which must have been the kitchen and living room combined; once-cream-painted cupboards were built-in on either side of the chimney breast, and a tiled 1930s hearth, its grate stuffed high with dead leaves and feathers fallen down the chimney, still showed traces of red polish. The room was empty except that, theatrically, a cheap wooden kitchen chair lay on its side on the floorboards, as if to make them think that someone had just left in a hurry – although it was obvious that the house had been abandoned for a long time. All its surfaces had lost their shine and were sinking back into the same dun earth-colour, beginning not to look man-made.

Ivy accepted at first that the house had no staircase: its inhabitants must have gone to bed miraculously, through the upper windows. Then Arthur found stairs behind a little door; he felt for her hand as she led the way up. The smell was worse in the two tiny bedrooms. The wallpaper in the first room might have been pink, once; baskets of fruit were looped along diagonal festoons of roses. This room too was empty, apart from a decomposing heap of magazines in one corner away from the window. Their paper had lost its shine and some of them were left open as if a reader had been interrupted, leafing through them. In angry haste, Ivy scanned and repudiated page after page of bloated flaunting bosoms and fat nipples, upside-down perspectives from peeled, parted, meaty thighs. The drooping texture of the pages was disgusting; some of them were glued together with damp, returning to pulp.

— Come on, said Arthur, not interested, tugging at her hand.

The door to the last room was closed and it was half-dark in there because rags of left-behind curtain were drawn across the window. A few fat flies knocked around sluggishly, buzzing against the glass. As the children's eyes adjusted they made out some large dark mess on the floor, something shrivelled and staining which was the centre of the bad smell. Arthur recognised it first.

— It's Mitzi, he said.

Mitzi was Kington's loping, lolloping red setter, belonging to the Pattens who owned the barn conversion opposite the church. The children hadn't missed her because she wasn't always in the village when they were; like theirs, the barn was a holiday home. Ivy saw that Arthur was right: crisp curls of Mitzi's russet hair were stuck to the blackened leathery thing in places, and it had approximately Mitzi's outline. Spikes of white bone stood up in a row out of the collapsed flat bag of the rest.

— Don't be stupid, she said derisively. — How can it be Mitzi? Do you think anyone would just leave her here?

— But it is Mitzi, look!

You could definitely make out one of those velvety, floppy ears, more intact than the rest of her. Arthur went closer and half-crouched with his hands on his knees, examining forensically, wrinkling up his nose for the smell. — Why is she like this?

Ivy began loudly singing nonsense words and laughing. — La, la. I don't know what you're talking about, she sang. — It isn't Mitzi. Arthur is a silly twat. La, la, la.

Arthur's being there with her made her hot, in the presence of that thing: if she'd been alone she could have stared more greedily, without any need for concealment. Partly she was distracting him as an older sister should, saving him from certainty. Mitzi and the rude pictures swam together in her embarrassment: not knowing she was doing it, she began to think that those women were dead.

— Let's go out, she said. — It's only an old stinky mess.

— Yes, it's stinky.

Arthur had been calm in the presence of the horror, but once or twice he looked back sharply nonetheless as they came down the poky stairs; they hurried, and burst out in a muddle through the door at the bottom.

— Don't dare say anything to Kasim. Because he'd be furious.

He nodded obediently, trusting her.

As they squeezed out through their gap into the day again – and Ivy restored the padlock carefully to its locked-seeming position – Kasim lifted his head, blinking, from among the flowers where he really had fallen asleep. To Ivy and Arthur, their usual roles as adults and children seemed reversed for a disconcerting moment, because they had seen what he hadn't: he belonged outside to the innocent sunshine. It occurred to Kasim, too late, that perhaps he shouldn't have let them go inside without checking first that the cottage was safe. But here they were again, unscathed, so it didn't matter. He yawned and announced he was starving. Ivy unpacked their picnic, laying out biscuits, apples, crisps.

— We have to make Arthur eat an apple, she insisted firmly.

— So what's it like in the cottage?

She was nonchalant. — Empty.

Arthur watched everything his sister did; the liquid blue eyes seemed huge in his small, fine face and he looked as if he was courageously suffering. Ivy had to remind herself that he always looked like this, even when he was only thinking about his dinner, or money – he was surprisingly mercenary for his age. As usual, he took a biscuit from the packet when Ivy did, bit into it when she did, took a mouthful of water from their bottle after her, except that as usual he hadn't emptied his mouth properly first – she protested at the bits swimming in the water when he'd finished. Chattering with exaggerated gaiety, Ivy felt the burden of her responsibility for what they'd seen. Everything was changed by it, she thought. They couldn't ever not have seen it, now. It stayed like a blot in the corner of her vision and darkness leaked from it. She could forget it all right when she was looking forwards, but if she turned too quickly, or forgot to be cautious, then it jolted her all over again with its dirty news, its inadmissible truth.

WHILE ROLAND AND PILAR WENT to look around the village, Alice lay reading on the window seat upstairs. She'd picked up this book about a doll's house from the shelf in her room quite casually and fondly, remembering how she had liked it in her childhood, not at all expecting to be ambushed with overwhelming emotion. Every so often she looked up from the page and stared around her as if she hardly knew where she was – but she was at Kington, which was the beloved scene of her past anyway. So her glance through the panes of the old glass in the arched window, to the yellowing rough grass in the garden and the alders which grew along the stream, didn't restore any equilibrium. It wasn't only the recollection attached to the words she was reading – a memory of other readings – which moved her. The story itself, in its own words, tapped into deep reservoirs of feeling. The writer's touch was very sure and true, unsentimental – one of the doll's-house dolls died, burned up in a fire. The book seemed to open up for Alice a wholesome and simplifying way of seeing things which she had long ago lost or forgotten, and hadn't hoped to find again.

Vaguely she was aware of Molly playing something melancholy on her guitar in her room – the same little sad, tentative thing over and over, always breaking down at the same place. Eventually the music faltered altogether. Molly was standing beside Alice's window seat, staring down at her anxiously.

— Aunt Alice, are you all right?

Alice smiled up at her through her tears. — I'm reading something I used to read when I was a girl. This story makes me so happy. It's brought back so many things.

— Oh dear, Molly said helplessly. — I'm sorry.

— Don't be sorry, I don't mind.

Molly was embarrassed by her aunt's excess of emotion. Guiltily, she mentioned to Harriet later that Alice had been reading old books and getting upset. Harriet only said that Alice got upset very easily. How like Alice, Harriet scolded in her thoughts, to make a parade out of her private feelings for everyone's consumption, bewildering the children.

IVY MADE A SCENE WHEN they got home, saying she wouldn't eat the risotto Alice was making; when Fran said that if she didn't she'd go to bed without eating anything, she lay racked with sobbing for a while on the grass in the garden.

— She has to learn to eat what's put in front of her, Fran said.

But Alice couldn't bear it and said she could have cheese on toast instead. Then Ivy and Arthur played before supper in the stream which ran across the bottom of the garden, building the dam they always built, or tried to build. From the kitchen came the rattle of china and cutlery, pan lids chiming, Alice banging the wooden spoon on the side of the pan after stirring. The sun was low and the stream was mostly in shadow. Bare-legged and barefoot inside clammy wellingtons, they fell into a concerted rhythm, satisfied by the push of the water up against their boots as they splashed through it, Arthur following Ivy's orders. They were drawn on by a vision of a spreading, still lagoon, while the stream, hastening over its stony bottom, forced its way through all the gaps they left. Urgent, responsible, Ivy rapped out her instructions. Once, memorably, in a different summer and when the children were sitting on the bank, cows – gigantic at close quarters – had come swishing along this stream, making a tremendous racket in the water, stirring up the mud from the stream bed, playing truant from their ordinary lives in the fields.

— It was Mitzi, Arthur paused to say, a stone in each hand.

Ivy was contemptuous. — Are you still thinking about that old thing?

— But it was.

— I don't care. Who cares?

She shrugged her skinny shoulders, fending off some intimation through a great effort of will. The real evening was brimming and steady around her like a counter-argument to horror, its midges swarming and multiplying in the last nooks of yellow sunshine.

AFTER SUPPER, WHEN FRAN HAD put the children to bed and Molly and Harriet were finishing the washing up, Alice visited the bathroom upstairs and then slipped secretly into her brother's room. She carried the tooth mug full of water, pretending she wanted to top up their flowers. Roland and Pilar and Kasim were sitting outside on the terrace with their coffee and brandy; their voices floated from below through the open windows. Kasim was opening up to them at last – perhaps too much. It sounded as if he was boasting about how he found his university lecturers boring, how stupid most of them were.

Alice found her flowers put aside indifferently on a windowsill, out of the way of all the toiletries and bottles and kit crowded on their dressing table: not only Pilar's expensive make-up and scent but cologne and moisturiser for Roland too. Alice saved the surprise of these for Fran later – after a short and crabbed conversation with Jeff, on the phone in the hall so that everyone could hear her side of things, Fran was watching some detective thing on the grim little television in the study. Who would ever have thought their brother would use moisturiser, or Acqua Di Parma? Alice felt tugged between fond respect for him and a puff of laughter. At dinner there had been a little fuss when he dropped something on the white trousers; crouching beside him, Pilar had mopped at it so seriously and efficiently.

She peered around the bedroom in the dusk, helped by the light from the landing behind. Cases stood open and half-ransacked on the floor: Pilar's dresses and a blouse – in simplified bold shapes and colours, black and white and red – were ghostly presences on their hangers, hooked over the carved rim of their grandmother's huge old wardrobe. Fingering a red chiffon blouse, admiring it, Alice caught sight of herself in the foxed oval mirror in the wardrobe door and was taken aback by something dated and fusty in her own appearance. She had put on that vintage bolero again. Was she letting something slip, had she failed in her vigilance, keeping up her style? Or sometimes too much vigilance was disastrous, as you grew older. A floorboard creaked and Ivy called out subduedly. Alice hurried out through Harriet's room then into her own. — Go to sleep, she said from across the landing.

— I can't!

Alice put her head round the door of the children's bedroom. Ivy was mournful, eyes glittering in the half-dark. She lay flat on her back in bed like a little girl in a folktale, her sharp nose pointing up, her two plaits angled neatly on the pillow.

— Yes you can. Shut your eyes and think of nice things.

— What nice things?

Alice cast around for ideas. — Ice cream? Kittens? A pair of magic shoes to carry you away on an adventure?

She began to tell Ivy the story of the doll's-house dolls, but Ivy only sighed, rolling over, turning her back on Alice. Her eyes were still staring open and she was portentous with her despair, beyond the reach of childish consolations.

HARRIET STEPPED INTO HER ROOM later, closed the door behind her, and stood in the dark in the relief of her own space at last, feeling the evening's sociability drain out of her. Almost at once she was aware that the door in the other wall, which led into her brother's room, had been left open – although she had been careful to close it earlier. The light wasn't on in there either, but she could hear Roland and Pilar moving around; they had come upstairs to finish their unpacking. Embarrassed because they hadn't noticed the door, Harriet slipped out of her shoes and went stealthily across the room to close it. The full moon had risen and was shining in at all the windows on the back of the house; blue light spilled through the open door into her room. Her brother and his wife must be bathed in moonlight.

She put out her hand to close the door – it was only open a few inches. Then through the gap her attention was caught by a movement she couldn't at first interpret – moonlight itself seemed to be coiling and uncoiling inside the looming shape of her grand-mother's heavy wardrobe; Pilar's dresses, hanging like pale body-shapes, swayed in time to it. Whatever Harriet was watching, she realised, she was seeing reflected in the wardrobe's mirror: some knot of light and dark busied upon itself, intent as nothing ever was intent, urgent. It seemed more like work than play. She had watched for too long, too deeply drawn in, before acknowledging that she knew what she was seeing, or half-seeing: the newly-weds were making love. By then it was too late. Putting her forehead against the wood of the doorframe, she touched her own breast with her hand, outside her shirt, unable to leave off looking.

Then a cloud covered the moon and blotted out the light, and she stepped back from the door. She was too horrified to close it now – anyway, they might hear her, and know that she'd heard them. The purposeful low noises of their love-making racked Harriet; in the aftermath (settling sounds, the appreciative hum of fulfilment, a low laugh) she was hollowed out, humiliated. Standing drawn upright, alone in the quiet room, imagining her-self like one of those emaciated worm-eaten medieval carvings, she was assaulted by outrageous longings. Where had these been locked away inside her? With Christopher and with others, she saw now, she had only ever had the husk of the real thing, the dry rehearsal. Creeping out through Alice's room, she shut herself in the bathroom; and then when she returned she came noisily into her bedroom, put on the light, crossed directly to the other door, and closed it firmly. She took out her diary from under the tee shirts in her drawer, and sat with it on the side of her bed as she usually did; she put down the date, then hesitated with her biro poised above the page. After a moment she began to write.

In the field above Bardon Huish I found what I'd never seen before: a waterfall hidden in a cleft in the ground, grown thickly over with brambles. The berries still very green and hard. The little fall of water jetting off its miniature cliff curved purely and perfectly as glass, yet not still but in perpetual motion. I interrupted it with my hand, feeling its force, indifferent to me. Touched myself with the water as if it was a blessing, although of course I knew it might be poisonous.

THREE

KASIM DAWDLED IN the garden the next morning, waiting for Molly to come downstairs. He was setting fire with his lighter to bits of the dried cut grass which lay around, just to annoy Ivy, who hovered on guard nearby, tormented with the responsibility, rushing to stamp out all his little conflagrations, half-delighted and half-exasperated. He knew that Molly was up because he'd listened outside her door hours ago and heard her moving about in her room – they still hadn't spoken one word to each other. Planning to intercept her, he'd lounged for a while on the window seat on the landing with its padded striped cushion, pretending to read the book he'd picked up from the shelf in Alice's room, until the hot sun through the glass made him too stuffy. Arthur had come puffing up the stairs, frowningly intent on some baby purpose: not noticing Kasim, he had knocked on Molly's door and been admitted, swallowed up inside. Then had come a faint noise of the guitar being strummed, first by Molly, who was scarcely competent, and then by Arthur, who was not competent at all. Kasim gave up and took the book downstairs.

What was she doing up there, for fuck's sake?

— Getting ready, Ivy explained.

— Getting ready for what?

When Molly finally appeared, stepping out through the French windows carrying a bowl of muesli and with Arthur devotedly in train, she showed no signs of elaborate preparation. She could have pulled her jeans and cropped tee shirt on in two minutes, she wore no jewellery apart from a plain silver bangle, he could scarcely see that she wore make-up; her ears weren't even pierced. There was something naked in fact in her pretty, neat face – high forehead, slanting long eyes, wide mouth; no wonder she kept the glossy wing of her hair falling forward, to hide it. Her hair had glints of rusty red in it, so did her lashes, and she was dusted across the nose with a few rust-coloured freckles, not too many. She sat on the step, flat belly folding into a neat crease, eating her muesli self-consciously and slowly while Ivy interrogated her. Smiling with her mouth full, Molly only nodded or shook her head in response. Did she like her school? No. What was her favourite lesson? Shrug. Did she have a boyfriend? No: blushing. What did she want to do when she grew up? Shrug. Did she like butter? Yes – a buttercup held under her chin reflected yellow.

Kasim knew Molly knew that he was watching, that she was performing for his benefit and the children were a convenient sideshow as he and she took each other's measure. Molly's self-possession was mysterious as a still inland lake; he hadn't decided yet if she was very deep or very shallow. Now, when she took out her iPhone from her jeans pocket, it was his moment; he saw Ivy open her mouth to explain and sternly he forestalled her, frowning. — What network are you on? There's no signal.

— Oh! Ivy was furious. — I wanted to tell her!

— I'm used to it, Molly said. — I've been coming here for years. Just thought I'd try.

— But it's possible: I'll show you. We have to walk up to that top gate in the field. If you sit on it you might get something.

— I feel cut off without my phone, she confided. — You know?

He was lofty. — I'm not bothering to check mine. Who cares?

Ivy almost protested – he had checked! – then closed up her small mouth upon his fib. The four of them set out up the field in a procession. Kasim reminded the children that they had to stay this side of his line and surprisingly they obeyed, planting their feet as if his new law was a fact of life. Then he leaned on the gate and pretended to be gazing out at the view basking in sunlight, blue-dusky woods and motionless ranks of golden crops, distant birds suspended in the air's pale blue, scrutinising the earth beneath. Molly meanwhile, her bare brown midriff on a level with his eyes, was all absorbed in her phone, giving squeals of satisfaction when she got her signal, growling with real irritation if she lost it again. He stole glances up at her expression, which as she read and texted was the most animated he'd seen it; when she'd finished with her texts she checked Facebook, fingers adept at scrolling, smiling and reacting secretively in collusion with an invisible company of like minds elsewhere.

— Let's take a walk, he said decisively. — Molly, would you like to come for a walk?

The children would accompany them, he calculated: at least on this first excursion. They were his pretext and his cover. Thrilled, Ivy suggested they could go to the Buddhist retreat. — There are people wandering around meditating, and they won't speak to you even if you ask them things.

— No, let's go to the waterfall again. This time I want to actually see the waterfall.

Ivy turned on him, if he'd noticed it, a face that was clouded with complications and reluctance. She accepted stoically, however, that because she was only a child she couldn't determine where they went, could only adapt to what the others chose. Anyway, she half-desired to return to the scene in the cottage, even as she half-dreaded it.

— Will we go in that cottage again? Arthur asked her privately on their way down the field.

— What for? We've seen inside. It's only boring.

IN THE DINING ROOM FRAN replenished everyone's cups with fresh coffee. They were using the good china from the sideboard, the cups weightless and fine, transparent. If you held them up to the light when they were empty you could see set in the base a picture of a woman's head, strands of her loose hair blowing behind her – their grandmother had shown them this miracle when they were children. Alice, still in her dressing gown, was talking too much, leaning animatedly forward across the table among the ends of crust and pots of jam stuck with spoons, showing her cleavage, holding forth in one of her diatribes against modern life. She said everyone was losing the sense that everyday things could be substantial and beautiful. In the old days a peasant carved a bowl and a spoon out of a piece of wood, then used them to eat the food he'd grown in his own garden. — Now everything is banal, objects have no meaning, they're interchangeable.

— I wonder if that's what the peasant thinks, her brother said.

— He's better off carving bowls than working in a factory.

— Well, you'd better ask him.

Roland felt impatient with how Alice simplified – she wanted shortcuts, but the truth about these things could only be understood through a lifetime's intellectual endeavour. It wasn't possible for him to lay out in casual conversation all the complex hinterland to his conviction, his own formulations interwoven with the thoughts of others. — I'm wary of your evaluative judgements, he said. — This is *good* and that's *bad*. The peasant might be better off in the factory and have more leisure time and disposable income. You have to factor that in.

— But is it always stupid, to see the value in other ways of life, and realise what's wrong with our own?

— You have to ask how you know what you think you know, about value.

— It's a bit late for peasants carving bowls, Alice, Fran said. — I don't think you're going to get that particular genie back into its bottle.

— Not just peasants. It's the way that people lived more slowly, and kept the same things all their lives, and took care of them. Our whole relationship to the things we owned was different. I hate how we throw everything away now.

Alice was more of an actress in her private life, Roland thought, than she ever was in the years when she had tried to be one on the stage. She had so *wanted* to be an actress, always – yet in any role apart from her own, to everyone's surprise, her performances had been tentative and lacking in conviction. Roland knew his sister so well. When her words tumbled over one another in this self-dramatising way, he knew she wasn't faking or pretending, it was her real effort to communicate the truth. Pilar asked whether, if she didn't like modernity, she didn't want anaesthetics when she had an operation.

— Of course I'm glad we have those modern things – medicines and sewage and hot showers and low infant mortality. Of course I am. With the treatments they have these days for cancer, our mother could still be alive, probably. But isn't some of it false improvement, false betterment? We're making the world too ugly. We've forgotten how to live.

— You'd be surprised, said Roland, — how long people have been saying that.

— You are an incurable romantic, Alice. Harriet sounded so bitter that everyone looked at her.

— Perhaps I am. Isn't the world ugly, though? And getting uglier.

— You don't know the peasantry, Pilar said briskly. — It's easy to idealise them, but their way of life is very backward. If you saw them, you might change your mind.

Alice was silenced for a moment, unpicking conscientiously her shocked reaction to that word *backward*. After all, what did she know about the Argentinian peasantry, or peasantry anywhere? Roland's sisters looked cautiously at him – he might be scorched, feeling how thoroughly his new wife didn't fit inside their well-worn family forms. Also, they wondered how well this idea of backwardness would go down at his university. Stolidly Roland resisted their interest, keeping his own counsel as he always had, even when it hadn't interested them so much. He knew Pilar didn't enjoy these kind of discussions where there was no practical outcome, no decision to make. She believed social occasions ought to be lubricated with an agreed civility, limited and shallow.

Pilar began clearing the breakfast things onto a tray, refusing help when Harriet offered it. She was wearing a white shirt, and jeans that fitted her curved slim haunches precisely. When they began living together, Roland had been surprised that she put on clean clothes every day – and they were always spotless, never crumpled. At the end of each week, he discovered, she sent everything she'd worn to the dry cleaners or the laundry. This had seemed profligate to him at first, but lately he'd begun to do the same. And Pilar haggled rather brutally if there was the least grease spot or crease when their clothes were delivered back. The people at the cleaners seemed to admire her for it.

— We're going to drive into town, he said to Alice now, — to pick up the papers and find somewhere to check emails. If we do decide to keep the house on, you know, we ought to get broadband. It just makes life easier.

— But that's just what's precious here, Alice protested. — That we're not in connection with everything outside. It's a sanctuary.

KASIM HAD ACQUIRED A MAP from the study. He led them to the waterfall a different way, through a tunnel where a railway line had once passed overhead, then across a stretch of high scrubland with wooden fire towers set at vantage points. They wouldn't pass the ruined cottage until they were on their way home. In the woods they threw pine cones again: Molly screeched unself-consciously when she was hit, racing flat-footed along the path, throwing cones back hard at Kasim – she and Arthur seemed to be in league together against the other two. Collaborating with Kasim, Ivy was happy. Her movements seemed perfectly attuned to his, running among the trees, collecting ammunition and then waiting in ambush.

The waterfall when they eventually arrived was a disappointment. In Ivy's anticipation it had tumbled in a crystal stream, foaming into the pool below; in reality it was a swelling silver rope in a long curtain of vividly green moss. There was no authoritative thunder of falling water, only a subdued trickling. Because she'd talked it up as the climax of their walk, she felt humiliated. Kasim and Molly hardly looked at it. Molly flopped down in the grass and closed her eyes as if she was sunbathing, Kasim sat nearby and began reading a book which he took out of the back pocket of his shorts. In truth they were both – briefly – disappointed too: they had longed, without knowing it, for the éclat of something spectacular and greater than themselves, to overwhelm them. The abrupt cutting off of their attention was a surprise to the children, who were used to being bathed in adult awareness, at least for as long as adults were present. If her mother had been there, Ivy might have made a scene – this exposure, when something fell flat which she had longed for and promoted, was famously one of her tipping points. But she couldn't risk disaster's crescendo with no one to anchor it against. She brought out the story of cutting her foot on a piece of glass in the pool under the waterfall; reduced to words it seemed truncated and paltry and no one listened.

Molly and Kasim appeared to have forgotten each other entirely; then Ivy noticed that while Kasim frowned seriously into the pages of his book he was at the same time tickling Molly's bare midriff with a long piece of grass. He did it so casually that at first Molly didn't know it was him and brushed the grass seed head away carelessly without opening her eyes. When the tickling persisted – as if the grass had a will of its own, nothing to do with Kasim – a smile of knowing came on Molly's face and, still without opening her eyes, she snatched at the seed head and held onto it, crushing it. Kasim's face showed nothing.

Excluded, Ivy was suddenly shy and wanted to do something

childish: she went to paddle in the pool with Arthur. Water babbled in there secretively. A freckled yellow light, refracted in the tea-coloured depths, gilded a scatter of pebbles on the sandy bottom; insects sculled the surface, dodging into the darkness under the ferns. The water was vivid against Ivy's legs as socks of cold. They were wearing their jelly shoes – it didn't matter if you got them wet, and you were safe from glass. Arthur was sternly preoccupied in some game with the thermos cup, pouring water out of the pool into a cleft in the rock. Ivy pressed her palms against the soaking moss of the waterfall – until she thought there might be slugs, and pulled her hand away smartly. Then she was seized by the sensation of seeing herself from a far distance, from the skinny tops of the fir trees stirring high above the clearing: miniature, alone inside herself, cut off at the knees by water.

KASIM PICKED ANOTHER STEM OF grass and dusted its drooping, plumy head, heavy with seeds, against Molly's cheeks and her closed, protuberant, mauve eyelids. With her hair fallen back from her face, he thought, and from his odd angle, she looked quite different – a sleek water animal basking on a rock.

— What are you doing? she said. — Don't! It tickles.

He had forgotten Molly herself, he was so intent upon his explorations – of her ear now, which stood out childishly from her head, its cartilage golden-pink and transparent. Trailing his grass around the whorls of it, he speculated aloud that the grass stem might be sharp enough to pierce its long lobe, then prodded at it.

Molly squealed in protest and sat up: both of them were shocked, looking one another in the eye again after such intimate contact.

— Why don't you pierce your ears? Kasim asked severely. — Or your nose, or at least something.

She explained that she would love to wear earrings but had a horror of the pain of piercing. In fact she couldn't bear the idea of any pain: she told him this solemnly, with innocent self-importance, as if she were telling him she disliked Marmite or classical music. — I've never even had to have a filling at the dentists, thank goodness.

— Ever been stung by a bee or a wasp?

She shuddered at the idea. — Never. I hate them.

— Broken your arm?

— Nope. I sprained my ankle once, that was bad enough.

— Got a staple in your finger from a staple gun?

— Oh god! She buried her face in her hands. — No! Did you ever do that?

She believes she's charmed, Kasim thought incredulously. She thinks she gets a choice. She thinks it's something special about her, and that she's discriminating against pain out of an especially refined sensitivity – as if other people are made differently and don't mind it.

— Ever had a Chinese burn? he said slyly.

— What's that?

— We used to do them in the playground at junior school. Give me your arm.

— I don't want one.

— Give it to me.

He held her arm above the wrist in his two fists, then twisted them opposite ways, pulling the skin lightly but hard enough to hurt her and make her pull away, only half laughing. She rubbed at the place where he'd left a red mark, easy tears welling like lenses, magnifying her tawny irises.

— What about childbirth? he said. — Don't you want children?

— You can have an anaesthetic, Molly said, — from the waist down. My mother did and she said it was fine.

FRAN AND ALICE LAY SIDE by side on a rug on the prickly grass in the garden, with their skirts pulled up to tan their thighs, though Fran's only ever turned pink. — It's not fair, she grumbled. — Why haven't I got your golden kind of skin? Harriet's got it and she doesn't even need it, she doesn't care. So what do you think of the new Mrs Roland?

— My god, she's a Gorgon! Alice exclaimed with pent-up feeling. — Poor Roly. What's he done? He must know what we'd think. No wonder he married her without telling us.

— But he doesn't seem to mind it. He's basking in it.

— He isn't even a womaniser, though. He doesn't lift a finger: it's the women who do it. They see him looking so clever and so lost, so very much married to the wrong person. They come to his rescue; I'll swear he isn't at all active in the whole thing. I mean, everyone knew he needed rescuing from Valerie, but I'm not sure *he* did, until Pilar explained to him. And now he's totally smitten. Sexually smitten.

— I do appreciate Pilar's very attractive. I'd die to have her figure.

— Isn't she a bit heavy in the jaw? Don't you think? Carnivorous. And she so disapproves of us! She thinks we're the worst kind of time-wasters.

— She thinks we aren't worthy of Roland.

— She thinks we ought to be grovelling at his feet. No wonder he's in love. Fran, I feel we'll never have Roly to ourselves again! None of his other wives have taken him away from us like this. We could accommodate ourselves to the others — or they accommodated to us.

— Don't be silly, Fran said. — It won't last.

— D'you mean the marriage won't last?

— I mean this phase of the marriage: you know, the lovey-dovey phase, when everything the other person does seems especially entrancing and original. Before the next phase, when all the same things seem especially irritating.

— Did you go through a lovey-dovey phase with Jeff?

— I suppose I must have, though the memory's so humiliating I've repressed it. I feel as if I've been seeing through Jeff for ever and ever.

Upstairs Harriet was standing in her brother's bedroom. The sash windows were thrown open high and she could hear her sisters' voices from the garden though she couldn't hear their words; she didn't want to. Dust motes swarmed in the sunlight, and the thick hot silence inside the room seemed strongly printed with its absent inhabitants, who had marked it with their scent of cosmetics and perfume and aftershave. They had made up the bed with a duvet cover and pillowcases patterned in swirls of red and orange; the old-fashioned faded furniture seemed to hold stiffly back from an invasion. Harriet, too, was holding herself back – she was rusty, the joints of her spirit creaked and groaned with disuse. And yet she had crept in here. Possessed by what she had seen last night, she could not free herself from its violence, its excitement. She had not reckoned with this power of sex. In all seriousness she had believed that it didn't count for her, that sex was a thing among other things, that you could put aside.

Putting her face up against the scarlet chiffon blouse whose hanger was slung over the wardrobe's upper rim, not touching it at first with her hands, she stood breathing through its veil. The frail fabric rose and fell against her lips and cheeks, lifted by her breath; she tasted its sun-warmed, laundry smell. How grotesque she must look, with this draped over her face, if anyone ever saw. Outside a male voice chimed in with Fran's and Alice's: Simon Cummins, who kept the garden for them. She heard how they flirted with him and how he teased them, and she heard the drowsing, inward-absorbed cooing of the doves, hidden in the full summer skirts of the beech trees. Lifting down the blouse on its hanger, she carried it off into her own room, where she laid it on the bed. When she had closed both the doors, she pulled off her tee shirt, then unhooked her bra and dropped it on the floor. With hasty, clumsy fingers she pulled Pilar's blouse over her head – it floated against her naked chest, the silk was raw against her breasts.

I am inside what she will wear, Harriet thought.

What would it feel like to be Pilar; to be so beautiful inside your clothes, to wear them with such assurance, and fit with that easy grace inside your own skin? It was as if the other woman belonged to a different, superior species. Then she stared at herself, as punishment, in the little round mirror on its stand on top of the chest of drawers. How lucky that her room was on the shady side of the house and the chest of drawers was in the shadows too, on the wall opposite the window. What she saw was something that ought to be kept hidden. The blouse made her grotesque; it insulted her as vividly as a slap or a derisory remark. Its brilliant red sucked away colour from her skin, and its low neck sagged against her jutting, freckled collarbones. She saw that her old woman's haircut – chopped off short at her ears, sticking up on top – wasn't modest or sensible, as she'd hoped, but a humiliating mistake. Reaching up inside the transparent material she touched her breast again, watching herself in disgust. Its flesh was cold, nosing against her hand like an old dog.

Changed back into her own tee shirt, Harriet sat on the side of her bed to write in her diary. *I saw a hawk lift up out of a field*, she wrote. *Such heavy effort of the shoulders, wing tips dipping; the whole noble drama of its movement. I am nothing.*

WHEN HARRIET WENT DOWNSTAIRS AND stepped into the drawing room, thinking she would have it to herself, she found Alice there, kneeling on the floor beside their grandmother's bureau, poking into its lock with something.

— Whatever are you doing?

Alice was startled, but not abashed. — I'm trying to pick the lock, she said. — Do you know how? Dani can do it, but I haven't got his knack. I just have this feeling there are letters in here which might be interesting. Don't you think? Otherwise why keep it locked? I don't know why I haven't wanted to before.

Harriet was horrified by the rage that overwhelmed her. Hadn't she unlearned this years ago? It had been peace, when she had stopped hating Alice.

— You can't do that. Whatever's in there is private, you shouldn't look at it.

— They're dead, Harriet. Don't be ridiculous. If we don't read their stuff, who will? I want to read their letters because I'm remembering them. I love them. Would it be better to forget them?

— Granny would have hated you digging around in her private life. If you do find letters in there you ought to burn them.

Alice sat back on her heels, staring at her sister. — What's got into you? You're in a mood. And what I said at breakfast wasn't just romantic either, by the way. I know you agree with me, that things are ugly and awful. Why are you making up to Pilar? She won't approve of your work with asylum seekers, you needn't think so. I should think she's pretty unsentimental about them. Aren't they all from 'backward' places?

— You're so judgemental, Alice. We hardly know her. You don't know what she thinks, or what her life has been.

Both of them were remorseful, as soon as they were apart, that they had succumbed to quarrelling – it demeaned them, each preferred to think of herself as brightly generous in the face of the other's provocations. Alice was ashamed of judging her new sister-in-law – Harriet was right, there was something crabbed and narrow in how she resented the intrusion into their family. Pilar was admirable and wholesome, as well as intimidating: when she washed up the breakfast things this morning she had scoured the whole kitchen, left it bright and pleasant. And Harriet thought it was true that Alice had loved the grandpees, she had been good to them when they were old, and it surely didn't matter about the letters, if there even were any. What could their grandparents have written that was not blameless?

Alice resumed poking into the keyhole of the little bureau with an unbent paper clip. She tried to remember Dani's swift authoritative movement when he came to her rescue after she locked her passport in a drawer and lost the key; she imitated it now and something gave way inside the bureau, freeing the sloping lid. With a subdued cry of triumph – not wanting to bring Harriet back – she lowered it, letting out its stale, held breath: the past was for a moment intimately at hand. Ink had dried up in a bottle of Quink, pencils and an eraser and a plastic pencil sharpener and Basildon Bond paper were stowed away in their compartments, bills paid long ago were sorted inside the leather clips which had been someone's Christmas present, chequebook stubs were stuffed into a pigeonhole, the lavender in one of the little voile bags her grandmother sewed had crumbled to a powder with no smell. The arrangements preserved the traces of the hands that had last closed the lid, twenty years ago.

There were a few letters; no doubt there would be more in the bureau's side drawers – Alice thought she could open these too, now that she'd got the knack. The first letters weren't interesting: mostly business correspondence from the last four or five years of the old lady's life, when she was a widow and had managed in the house by herself. A carer had visited – first every few days and then daily, driving out from the town – and Alice had come down to be with her grandmother whenever she could, although that was also the time when she was in the thick of her disasters in the theatre. There were some photographs from the 1980s: Roland's graduation and then his PhD graduation, Fran a skinny kid with spiky, punky hair, eyes painted black as pits. Probably Harriet had sent these. It was Harriet who had managed to keep Fran on the rails – attending school, turning up for exams – in the years after their mother died and their father left. Harriet had ironed Fran's school uniform and made her packed lunch, she had helped with her homework.

Alice stared into the photographs of her younger self as if they were oracles – they came with a new shock because she had forgotten they were ever taken, forgotten even possessing the clothes she was wearing in them. What she remembered of that time was insecurity and self-doubt – and yet the young woman in the photographs looked so assured and knowing: blowing out smoke, laughing with her head thrown back and eyes half closed, or haughtily made-up for some party. All that time when she was drowning in the struggle and chaos of her emotions, it was as if her outward identity had led another wholly competent life in spite of her – a life which seemed enviable and even admirable at this distance. She glanced behind her now into the room whose wallpaper was silvery in the light from the garden. No one was there, the room's stillness was all hers: yet the chaise longue and the upright piano and the glass-fronted bookcase with her grandmother's novels in it – Elizabeth Goudge and Rebecca West and L.P. Hartley – seemed drawn up stiffly against the walls in expectation. Again Alice was subject to that intimation of something unknown in wait for her – not from the past, but in her future. Her imagination seemed strained open and consenting, something must come into it, to fulfil it. In her history it had always been a man who filled up that quickened expectation. She was ready for another man.

One bundle of letters and cards were tied together with ribbon: she realised these were condolences written when her grandfather died, along with obituaries cut out from the newspapers. The cards were decorously floral; on one a pair of black gates opened onto an autumnal avenue. Alice imagined her grandmother looking for the ribbon, fastening the letters ceremoniously together before she set them aside. *My dear Sophy, our thoughts are with you . . . your sad news . . . if it's any comfort . . . privilege to have published . . . praying for you . . .* The melancholy and the stuffy smell of old newspaper began to make her sleepy.

MOLLY STOPPED OUTSIDE THE COTTAGE. — Oh, I remember this old place.

Kasim glanced warningly at the children – they knew it meant they must not tell that they'd been inside it.

— Imagine living here, he said as if he was reproaching somebody. — No electricity. No running water. No hot showers. No internet or mobile phone signal.

Molly puzzled over this. — They must have had electricity, surely. Everyone has electricity.

Kasim waved his arms at the sky innocent of pylons, even telegraph wires. — Do you think that it just comes down out of the air?

She looked vague.

— Where my family comes from, he said, — there are hundreds

of thousands of people who live like this. Millions, actually.

The others were impressed. — Where do your family come from?

— But there must be water, Arthur said. — Else, how could you drink?

Kasim made it sound as if he'd spent more time in Pakistan than he ever had. He told them about the deep wells, or fetching water from streams, or from standpipes miles away; he had only a quite vague idea of these things, because his own relatives in Pakistan were wealthy – except that he had drunk water from a well in a country courtyard once, in a house belonging to his great-uncle. It seemed to him now that it must have been exceptionally pure and cold.

— You might die, Arthur said.

Ivy knew he was muddling up the water thing with what had happened inside the cottage.

— Lots of children do, said Kasim. — They die from drinking bad water.

— But not in this country, Molly added quickly, squeezing Arthur's hand.

— So that's all right then, said Kasim, sardonic.

He turned his back on them, but Molly picked up a lump of moss from beside the path and threw it hard at him as he walked off, hitting him accurately between the shoulder blades, spoiling his poise; for a long instant he was astonished and offended, and then to their relief he yelled as if letting go some pent-up outrage, scooped up the moss again and threw it back just as hard at Molly. This was the signal for the resumption of the pelting game they had played earlier: Molly and Arthur went hurrying in search of things to throw. In the slanting, syrupy afternoon light, because they were dreamy with tiredness and heat, they seemed to be bending and shrieking and thudding along the path in pleasurable slow motion.

Ivy hung back in the clearing; soon the shouts of the others sounded remote among the trees below and she had the sensation again that she'd had at the pool, of seeing herself from treetop height, remote and doll-like. Crossing the clearing and tugging at the cottage door, she imagined she was someone else, another more audacious girl in a children's story. Ivy wasn't brave, she was a coward when it came to sports or party games, the kind where you ran in a team and had to burst a balloon by sitting on it. But she also had a greedy curiosity which was like a hunger; she wanted to get clear, all by herself and without the shame of other people knowing she was doing it, the truth of what could happen. Still, squeezing inside the cottage door, she longed to find it scoured and empty, a clean breeze blowing through its harmless shell.

The brown dull light in the downstairs room, and the frozen urgency of the tipped chair, were just the same; her footsteps broke into the silence she and Arthur had left behind them yesterday. Halfway up the stairs she spun round and almost fell with fright when the door swung shut behind her, but this simplified things, because going back now was as dreadful as going on. The magazines and the dead dog had become one composite idea in her mind, the magazines a necessary preliminary to the rest, and she turned the damp-clumped unglossy pages boldly because Arthur wasn't watching, taking possession this time of what she saw, the bleached-paper flesh in all its configurations, on and on, endlessly different and the same. Who were these women? Because she knew the pictures were for grown-ups, she couldn't get over their gratuitous childishness and rudeness. Yet she couldn't discount them completely; they stirred some tingling possibility in her, as well as fierce distaste.

Then she opened the door which she and Arthur had pulled shut behind them, and crossed the threshold into the second room, pinching her nose tight shut with her fingers, breathing through her mouth – still the smell of rot was in her throat, intimate and filthy. The room wasn't as dark as before, light came and went because a breeze was blowing in the scraps of curtain. She had not noticed yesterday that the window was not quite closed. The fat sluggishness of the flies and their inconsequential spurts of buzzing disgusted her; she thought she couldn't bear it if one buzzed against her. Yet once she was actually inside the room she forgot to be frightened. Everything was quiet apart from the flies, even peaceful. There was no one here except herself, she could do what she liked, she could see uninhibitedly.

Mitzi was both something and nothing at the same time: a mass in one corner was darkened and flattened, with a stain spread round it on the floorboards as if fluids had seeped out of it, then dried. Only the patches of russet red curls clinging onto the mass in places made it Mitzi. An eye socket was a pit in the skull, showing white through its leathery covering. When Ivy crouched to examine the remains more closely, not too close, she saw – at first incredulous, then with dawning certainty – that white living maggots fine as threads were wriggling in the dog's body, in the places where the flesh was still clinging to its bones. Reaching this farthest shore of her discovery, Ivy let out a noise that was only for herself: wounded, like a low groan of protest. She was fascinated, though. She didn't move from watching them until she heard the others shouting her name from the woods.

BEFORE SUPPER, FRAN STOOD FROWNING in the shadowy hall, rucking the mat deliberately with her sandal against the che-

quered tiles then smoothing it out again, winding the coiling telephone wire around her hand, hunching her shoulder to hold the
receiver against her ear. The louche old brown telephone, a relic
from the seventies, was isolated on its wooden stand as if it were
ornamental like an aspidistra or a vase: when Molly used it they
had to show her how to dial a number. There was no chair put out
beside it: the grandpees hadn't wanted to invite the cosy, long conversations which were so expensive. Fran was dialling Jeff's number
over and over and not getting through – resentful, she imagined
him drinking beer and playing snooker and smoking with the rest
of the band, his phone ringing pointlessly in his pocket. Roland
and Pilar in the kitchen were roasting two chickens with grapes
and apples: a Spanish recipe. They were collaborating efficiently:
Pilar had everything exactly timed and Roland, tied into an apron,
was following orders, peeling apples and liquidising grapes. This
was a very different regime to the one with Valerie, who had run
around looking after him as if he were helplessly unworldly. Now,
he addressed the cooking processes with earnest technical interest.

Kasim was bored, because Molly was teaching clock patience
to the children. He went to walk by himself in the churchyard, and
from his tall vantage point didn't see Alice until he almost fell over
her; sitting in the long grass, she was leaning back against the grey
stone of a grave. Startled, he was cross for a moment, as if she'd
lain in wait deliberately under his feet. When he was a boy he'd
been humiliatingly aware of Alice's female presence in his home –
her underwear dropped in the washing basket, her perfume on his
father's bed sheets. Now her low exclamation and smiling upwards
glance seemed too softly placatory, they clung to him.

— Kas, spare a ciggy?

She should buy her own, he thought, instead of pretending
that she didn't smoke. But he found them both cigarettes and

dropped to sit cross-legged in the grass with her, his back to a grave opposite hers. Down among the grasses was a different universe, hotter and pleasantly sour with the smells of fermenting sap; out of sight of the encircling landscape, relationship to the huge sky was everything. He twisted to read the words over his shoulder, half indecipherable where the stone was flaking away: *Fell asleep in Jesus, 1882.*

— Fell asleep, and they buried him? Thank goodness I'm a Muslim.

Alice longed to be strong enough not to ask if he was enjoying himself. She shouldn't let him see her need for his approval. — Do you like Molly? she asked instead.

He considered the lit end of his cigarette. Flatly, obediently, giving nothing away, he said he did like Molly. — But who is Molly? What is she?

Alice sang his words, to the tune of *Who is Sylvia?*

— Are you sure she really is your brother's actual daughter? She's not much like him, is she? He's straightforward, she's an enigma.

— You're teasing. But just because Molly's not the brightest, doesn't mean she isn't something special.

— I'm deadly serious. I think she's profound, perhaps presides over the secret to the universe. And while we're on the subject of unknowns, who is Jill Fellowes?

— Oh. Why?

Kasim pulled out from his back pocket the book he'd been carrying round with him all day, not noticing how she flinched at the bent end boards. — Look. The name's written inside it. It's a book of poetry. Is she your grandmother?

Taking the book from him, Alice pressed it tenderly back into shape. — Have you been reading these poems?

— I only pretended to read them, just to intrigue Molly. I'm an economist, I don't know what poetry's function is.

— It's my mother's name. Her maiden name. Lots of those books on the shelf where you found it are books from her childhood. It's so uncanny that you spoke her name, because I'd come in here to think about her. She died, you know, when I was only thirteen.

He was discomfited. — But these aren't poems for children, he said argumentatively.

— They used to be. Now, what we give children to read is mostly anodyne.

Kasim dropped his head melodramatically in his hands; she saw how his hair sprouted from the crown so vigorously glossy and densely black. — Have I said something awful, bringing up your mother's name like that? Are you grief-stricken now? Was she a saint?

— Don't be silly, of course she wasn't a saint, Alice said. — But she was a shining sort of person. Spirited and clever. Imagine her growing up here, in this wonderful place. It was perfect, that just as I closed my eyes to think about her you came in here with her book. Nothing happens by accident.

— Things do happen by accident.

She shook her head wisely, maddeningly. — I don't believe in coincidence.

Light filtered through the stirring straw of the grass stems, bent under the weight of their heavy seed heads, flickering against Alice's heart-shaped face and sooty, smudged eyes, and her soft skin and hair. There was a memorial plaque, she said, inside the church; very beautiful, her grandfather had chosen the words. Of course the death of their daughter, their only child, had broken her grandparents' hearts completely. It had not broken her grandfather's faith only because it was that kind of faith already, hardened in expectation of the cruellest thing possible. When Kasim asked whether Alice's father was still alive, she said he was, somewhere in the Dordogne, probably. She hadn't seen him for a couple of years and didn't much care. After their mother died of breast cancer, their father had gone to pieces – which was forgivable – and run off to France with another woman, leaving his orphaned children behind – which wasn't. It was all ancient history now. Her father had thought he was escaping ahead of old age, but it had caught up with him eventually. She had talked the whole thing over with her therapist for so many years that they'd wrung the subject dry.

— He's supposed to be an artist, she said. — That was his excuse.

— What kind of artist?

— A painter. Not a very good one. Women in landscapes that are sort of dreamscapes: part Van Gogh, part album cover. He's never sold much. His new wife – not the same one he ran off with – earns all the money. She's an estate agent, selling the old farms to British incomers as the French country people go off to live in the cities. Isn't that funny?

— Is it funny?

— I don't mean about the farms and the depopulation. I mean, if you knew some of the fine things my father says about an artist's life.

ALICE WENT INSIDE TO BRUSH her hair before supper. She remembered, as she always did, that her mother had sat at this same dressing table: first as a girl, and then again later, when the children spent their summers here with her and their father went off painting. Slanting late sunlight glinted on Alice's bottles of scent and make-up and nail varnish, the lustre jug with its posy, gold threads in a scarf, the heap of her jewellery – none of it valuable but each piece striking and interesting, rich with sentimental associations. Wherever Alice settled, she had this gift of applying little touches to make the place distinctive and attractive, as if she were composing a scene for a play. She had moved from one room or flat to another very often in London, transforming each one in turn into a nest full of curiosities and nice things. Looking in the mirror now, she held her brush suspended in the air, staring over her reflection's shoulder to the reflected room behind. Quietly she breathed aloud, *my dear*, although she didn't know who she was speaking to. Her fine hair crackled with static, floating up towards the brush.

Breaking her mood, Harriet was suddenly present, blocking the reflected space in the mirror, intruding on her reverie. Of course it wasn't Harriet's fault that she had to come through Alice's room – but she crept about so quietly! Because Alice was startled she couldn't help being annoyed. Harriet made her feel caught out in vanity. She dropped her hairbrush and twisted round from the mirror.

— Goodness, are you spying?

— I thought I ought to tell you, Harriet said gruffly, — that I've arranged with work to take more holiday. So I will be able to stay here longer after all.

Guilty, Alice was aware of overacting her delight. She jumped up from the dressing-table stool to kiss her sister, feeling how Harriet stood stiffly in her embrace, not knowing how to yield to it.

— Oh Hettie! I'm so pleased! Thank you! she exclaimed. — And I know I don't deserve you doing anything nice for me – I'm a grumpy old stick. I'm sorry.

— I didn't do it for you, Harriet said. — It's good for me to have a break. I'm enjoying myself.

She didn't much look like it, Alice thought. She looked strained and there were purple stains on the fine skin under her eyes, as if she hadn't slept – Alice hoped this wasn't because she'd been put in that awkward, poky bedroom. She had some clever concealer which would work wonders with those under-eyes, but she was wary of offering it, thinking Harriet would only despise her.

Harriet prodded around among the bottles on the dressing table.

— I've never gone in for any of this clobber, she said. — What is it all?

Alice was watching her closely.

— Look, she said. — Sit down on the stool. Let me try something on you, just the least little thing. It's only the teeniest smudge of cream. No one will notice, you'll just look prettier.

Harriet's expression as she hesitated brimmed uncharacteristically full with mixed reluctance and yearning. She gave way and sat submissively with her back to the mirror. Alice rummaged in her make-up bag and then very carefully, tenderly, stroked on the concealer, and after that a very light foundation, eye pencil, eyeshadow, mascara. Their two faces for once drew uninhibitedly close without any antagonism, Harriet's vulnerably proffered, Alice absorbed in what she knew supremely well.

— Oh no, Harriet said with horror when finally she looked at her reflection. — It isn't me. It isn't right. Take it off, Alice.

FOUR

FRAN AND ALICE drove into town with the children – Fran wanted fish from the farmers' market, to make a pie. When they'd finished shopping, at the market and in the Co-op, they bought ice cream from the lemon-yellow-painted Esplanade Café, which had endured from the sisters' childhood even though it looked as provisional as a summer house, in its little park of flower beds and crazy golf. In their childhood the ice cream would have been Wall's, between two wafers – now it was made locally, from sheep's milk. Fran and the children had two scoops and Alice had one, then Ivy dropped hers and wept, and needed a replacement. — She always does, Fran said. Leaning on the sea wall to eat theirs, the sisters looked out across the estuary while Ivy and Arthur played on the beach below, turning out buckets of sand decorously and warily because they were latecomers among the family encampments. The air was filmy with heat, blue with stale frying-fat and candy sweetness. The shouts of children ricocheted against the packed sand and the sea wall and the long rock groynes built down onto the beach against erosion.

This seaside town wasn't quite the true seaside, for all the old-fashioned holiday jollity on display in the shops down at that tail end of the high street: buckets and spades and windbreaks and polythene windmills on sticks. The sand was imported from further down the coast; if the tide was out then anyone wanting to swim had to wade, ankle- or calf-deep, for what seemed like miles into rich estuary silt and a disorienting glinting light, laid in long, flat planes across the eye – so that the shore, on turning round to look back, seemed more than left behind, seemed lost. After a rough night the water, opaque with silt, could be as brown as milk chocolate; oystercatchers and curlews and rarer birds fed on the many species of worm left in the mud when the tide slid off it. You saw easily across to Wales – blue hills and the white ghost of a power station at Aberthaw – so that the watery expanse could only ever feel domestic, a known quantity, though notoriously treacherous.

Fran and Alice's gossip rambled luxuriantly around the family – when it was Molly's turn, Fran remarked that she seemed very young for her age.

— She's a bit blank, isn't she? Alice agreed.

— She seems to get on all right with Pilar.

— But have you noticed that although Roland's supposed to adore Molly so much, he never actually talks to her – I mean, about ideas or books? But then, she's very sweet natured.

— She's sweet with the children, bless her. But can she cook an egg?

— And terribly pretty. Kas is smitten. Roly can't bear anyone looking at her in that sexual way, can he? He smoulders whenever

Kas comes near. Though I don't suppose Kas has laid a hand on her. He's quite an innocent, though he thinks he's so wicked and sophisticated.

— I should think he hasn't laid a hand on her, Fran said primly. — She's still a child.

— She's sixteen. What were you up to at sixteen?

— Well exactly.

Fran always maintained that she wouldn't allow any child of hers to get away with what she once did: Alice protested that this was eating your cake and stopping anyone else eating theirs. — Anyway, when it's Ivy's turn, you'll have no idea what she's getting up to. She won't actually *tell* you.

Fran groaned at the idea of Ivy's turn.

— I'm reading through Mum's old letters, Alice said, — written to the grandpees in her first year at Oxford. All she tells them is about lectures and funny things happening – but who knows what she was actually in the thick of?

— It's not healthy you know, Alice, poking around through all that old stuff. It's too depressing. There's no point in looking backward all the time.

— Why not? I like looking backward. It's amazing to imagine her when she was just a girl, and her life hadn't happened to her yet. The sixties and revolution and flared trousers and everything – all that was still to come. Dad was still to come.

— Don't start ranting about Dad, Fran said, — blaming him for everything.

She was the only one of the four siblings who kept up contact with their father; she had taken the children more than once to visit him in France.

— I stopped ranting about him years ago. Now I hardly think about him. What's really striking is that Mum knew so much.

Apart from just Latin and Greek – an awful lot about history and literature, much more than we do. Perhaps people just knew more in those days. A whole lot more than Molly, that's for sure.

— Oh, Molly doesn't know anything.

Fran's phone rang then and she turned away from her sister to walk along the seafront while she spoke into it, hunched intently, lost to the scene around her, the sauntering families eating chips and candyfloss and the supervising glassy-eyed herring gulls on the wall, beaks spotted with ketchup-red. Alice knew it must be Jeff. Mostly Fran's face was bright with a willed confidence, the blue eyes shallowly recessed, fair eyebrows hardly visible. When she spoke to Jeff her expression contracted to a sharper point.

— Any news? Alice asked when she came back. — Is he coming down?

The light seemed particularly insolent at that moment to Fran, flashing from Alice's sunglasses – she saw that people turned their heads to look, wondering if they knew her striking sister from television somewhere. In London Alice didn't show up against the general background of striking people.

— I don't even want him here, I told you, Fran said. — I'm finished with him. What does he ever give? It's always me, giving everything.

— But you love him, you do. He's the one. Don't fight him all the time.

— I'm not going to take any lessons from you, Alice, on how to manage my love life. You don't seem to have made such a brilliant job of yours. Harriet's right, you're such a romantic.

— I'd rather be romantic than jaded. At least I've *had* a love life. Even if the romance does seem unreal sometimes, in retrospect. All that hard work of falling into love and falling out of it again. None of it leaves any trace, not visibly.

— Well, you should have had children then, shouldn't you? Children are real enough. They're a trace.

— Fran, how can you? It hasn't been a *choice*, not to.

— Hasn't it? When did you have time for children, between all your adventures?

Both sisters managed to be offended. They sulked for five minutes and couldn't forgive each other, until they forgot about it and went back to their gossip, which circled eternally. All the siblings felt sometimes, as the days of their holiday passed, the sheer irritation and perplexity of family coexistence: how it fretted away at the love and attachment which were nonetheless intense and enduring when they were apart. They knew one another so well, all too well, and yet they were all continually surprised by the forgotten difficult twists and turns of one another's personalities, so familiar as soon as they appeared.

WHEN ROLAND TOOK PILAR FOR a drive across the moor, Harriet asked if she could come. He would rather have been alone with Pilar, which made him more punctilious in his kindness to his older sister. Just because he felt Harriet's life was dreary, he mustn't let her glimpse this. She wasn't stupid and had read a lot: she turned out, for instance, to be up to date in recent developments in the Argentinian economy. And of course Roland admired what she did at work. But her life seemed so small to Roland, she had no outlet for her thinking in the wider world. She was supposed to have Christopher to talk to, but he was always off cycling. Roland was profoundly unsporting and couldn't take bony, middle-aged Christopher seriously, flaunting himself in in his skintight Lycra.

In the sunlight the moor's distances were harmless, bland lovely tobacco-brown and mauve: they had to explain to Pilar how austere the place could look in winter or bad weather. They got out of the car to see the view, exploring along the bleached dry brush riddled with paths, where the sheep dropped shiny dark pills and left their wool caught in the coconut-scented gorse. Harriet picked a purple sprig of heather, telling Pilar to keep it because it was lucky. Then they drove on to an ancient river crossing, where flat-topped boulders made stepping stones across the water and cream teas were served in a garden. When he set down the laden tea tray on their table, Roland knew that Pilar was drawing glances from the other tourists in her tight trousers and dark glasses.

Roland had wondered whether Harriet would disapprove of Pilar, because of her class and background: no doubt in the past Harriet had belonged to committees protesting the abuses of the Argentinian military. But Harriet seemed more animated and more tentative these days, less judgemental; she was wearing a scarf knotted around her neck too, and had something shiny on her eyelids. Because of her white hair and the way she held herself so stiffly upright, with her bird-like evasive glances, she probably seemed to Pilar more like an elderly aunt than a sister. Now she was expressing an almost exaggerated interest in life in Argentina, which Pilar was reluctant to talk about.

— England must seem very parochial to you, after the sheer scale of things over there: the politics and history as well as the landscape.

— My life is here, Pilar said sharply. — I've chosen England, I've been here ten years, I'm married to an Englishman. People who've chosen to come here don't always want to be looking back.

Harriet blushed, desolated. — Of course you don't. I didn't mean to say you weren't at home here. It's your home as much as it's ours.

She touched Pilar on her bare shoulder to reassure her, and her veined, freckled hand, its unpainted nails bitten as short as a little girl's, was amphibian against Pilar's even-pored brown skin. Pilar accepted the little gesture of obeisance and lifted the heavy teapot, pouring graciously for Harriet first, forgiving her. — Shall I be mother? she said. Assiduously she had set about acquiring these idiomatic English gestures. Yet it was her difference from the Englishwomen Roland knew which attracted him, just as it interested Harriet. He wondered whether mutual incomprehension might not be the most stimulating arrangement in a marriage.

He was touched that Harriet seemed genuinely to like his wife – though he had made up his mind that it didn't matter if his sisters didn't like her. Pilar didn't have the slippery ambiguity which was Alice's specialty. Latin women, he thought, were encouraged to develop more conventionally than English ones – consequently their personalities had firmer and more resilient outlines and they appeared more certain of what they wanted. Of course, his sisters were odd partly because of the oddity of what had happened to them in their teens, when their mother died and they had all managed on their own in the house. Harriet had been in charge when she was only seventeen.

After tea they strolled along the path beside the river. Pilar kicked off her sandals and waded in from a little pebbled strand, squealing and gasping at the cold, trousers rolled up to her knees, sunglasses pushed up onto her hair. — It's nice, she said. — Come on in! Harriet hesitated on the brink, then joined her. When Pilar staggered in the force of the current, which was strong even though the water hardly came halfway up their calves, she had to grab hold of Harriet's arm and hang onto her, laughing; Harriet stood steadily, braced to support her. In the rushing noise of the river, they were cut off from Roland. — My life in Argentina is full of complications right now, Pilar said swiftly to Harriet. — Things are going on with my family, horrible things. I'm happy to be far away from it all.

— Have you talked to Roland about it?

— It's so ugly. He doesn't need to know. He's got more important things to think about. Please, don't say anything to him.

Harriet was stirred by this unexpected confession. In her work with refugees her sympathetic responsiveness was strained continually to the point of pain, and she was ashamed when she thought how she'd come through her own life more or less unscathed. Her own sufferings she counted as nothing. She reassured Pilar: no, of course she wouldn't say anything. Gruffly, not wanting to seem greedy for more, she added that if ever Pilar wanted to talk, she'd be pleased to listen. Under the surface of this decency, though, she was dazzled by Pilar's choosing her to confide in; a breath of drama rose from the fast-flowing water swirling past them.

Watching from the bank, Roland thought he could imagine what Pilar had been like as a domineering, flirting teenager, with a gang of girlfriends. He took a photograph of the two women embracing in the changeable light reflected up from the river. He wouldn't go in himself, he hated putting his feet in cold water and didn't mind presenting a comical target, the Englishman in his linen summer suit, socks and shoes, flinching and smiling benignly on the bank while they flicked water at him.

KASIM SAT CROSS-LEGGED IN THE garden, smoking and watching Molly in the distance. Ivy and Arthur were nearby, also cross-legged and watching Molly. Silhouetted, slender, far off against the sky, perched on the gate at the top of the field, she was lost to them, intent upon her conversations, rocking forwards around her phone or throwing her head back in laughter, her body twisting in delighted appreciation. She was frustrated occasionally if her signal failed. They could just about hear her voice, but not her words. The thin trail of her laughter was somehow entrancing and soporific, creating a rapt silence around the three of them who were shut out: she was as mysterious as if she was talking to herself, hallucinating. In the garden the afternoon was still and hot. Arthur was sorting out the contents of his money box, which Kasim had showed him how to open, though Ivy had protested that he wasn't supposed to open it.

— It's mine, anyway, said Arthur, frowning over his calculations, tucking his long hair out of the way behind his ears. Apparently he was adept with the plastic pennies in the play-shop at school.

— But he's not supposed to have it yet. It's for later when he needs things.

— I need them now.

Ivy, knowing he was only counting to seven then starting over again, had kicked at her brother with the point of her shoe, whose patent shine was scuffed almost to greyness. She was dressed in an old cream nylon petticoat with a lace hem, full-length on her; Alice had found it in a cupboard and tied one of her scarves around the bodice, flattening the stiff breast-shapes. For a while Ivy had walked around with a gliding motion, gazing far away, imagining being watched; the silky fabric against her bare legs had made her feel ethereal. Now the petticoat was stained green from where she had been rolling on the grass, and her jack-knifed knees were sharp points straining its fabric.

They felt as if Molly condescended, returning to their world, when she made her way at last down the field towards them: her contact with what was beyond had left its traces in her expression, skeins of amusement and connection that did not connect her to them. She hummed to herself, some tune they didn't recognise. Dropping to sit beside them on the grass, in her shorts and red bikini top she was all long limbs, awkwardly graceful; her arms and legs were dusted with fine gold hairs, glinting in the sunlight.

— You're addicted to that phone, Kasim accused her disdainfully.

Cheerfully Molly confessed it.

— Doesn't it worry you that you're being fobbed off with second-hand substitutes for actually living? You might be missing out on something. Like reality.

— You're addicted to horrible cigarettes. At least my addiction won't kill me.

Hollowly he laughed. — That's what you think. Wait until they prove the links between phones and brain cancer.

Molly, set-faced, was learning how to negotiate with his intransigence. — What links? If there were any, they'd have told us by now. Everyone uses phones.

Kasim marvelled at her. — I've never met anyone so trusting before. *They?* Who d'you think *they* are? Your kindly uncle? And as it happens I could give up smoking tomorrow.

— I bet you couldn't.

— Only I can't be bothered.

— Like I said, you're addicted.

Superbly, hardly stirring from where he lounged back on his elbows, Kasim picked up the half-full packet of his cigarettes and lobbed it into the stream. It scarcely splashed, bobbed vaguely in a circle, then washed up against a stone where it suddenly just looked like litter, polluting the scene. Looking up from his money, with a small smile to himself, Arthur admired the largesse of the gesture. Ivy, shrieking, jumped up and wanted to wade in and rescue the precious packet, but Kasim held her back by the stretchy skirt of her petticoat.

— I'd have given that fag a bit more thought, he said regretfully, if I'd known it was the last one I'd ever smoke.

— I don't believe you, Molly said, impressed despite herself. — I'll bet you buy more, next time you're in town.

He scowled at her, all his handsomeness in play. — In my country, he said, — a man's promise is a point of honour. I'd rather die than break my word.

— All right, she said. — That's good then.

— It really does give you cancer, Ivy assured him earnestly. — So this is a good thing.

Then in one fluid movement Kasim sprang to his feet. — And now, Miss Molly, I think you ought to give up your phone, if I've given up smoking. My tit for your tat, so to speak.

Before Molly even understood what he was saying, he had snatched her iPhone up from where she had put it down on the grass. Holding it high, he teased her, dancing backwards when she came after him, protesting, across the garden. The children stood up too, thrilling to the anarchy in the others' excitement; Kasim threw the phone to Arthur, calling his name sharply. Exceptionally, Arthur succeeded in catching it, snatching it with both hands to his chest.

Molly pleaded, running towards him. — Please, darling, give it to me.

— To me, to me! Kasim called, urgently.

Carried away by the game and his own treachery, Arthur threw wildly askew, but Kasim dived and saved the phone, scrambled back upright. — Ivy, Ivy! Catch!

The phone sailed through the air in a perfect easy arc that ought to have ended between Ivy's proffered hands – but, tripping over her petticoat, she fumbled it. The phone went past her and fell with an undramatic small wet noise into the water.

— Fuck, Kasim said.

— You shouldn't *swear,* Ivy shouted at him.

Wailing with real grief, Molly waded into the water in her sandals to snatch out the phone, then stood drying it off desperately on her shorts while the stream parted in tiny wavelets around her ankles.

— It will still work, Arthur said firmly.

— It won't! Molly was despairing. — My friend dropped hers in a pub toilet and it was only in there for one second and it never ever worked again. No, see! It's not working! It won't come on.

When she stepped out on the bank they were all four united around the phone, staring at the black screen, willing it to give them any sign of life.

— I'm going to be in such big trouble for this. It was my birthday present. And it's all your fault. Why did you ever do such a stupid thing?

— Ivy dropped it, Kasim said.

Ivy bawled, rubbing grubby fists in her eyes like a child in a book. Molly's outrage was mature and even stately. — It wasn't Ivy's fault. How can you blame your own stupidity on a child? You should be ashamed of yourself.

— At least I didn't drop it, Arthur said.

Arthur worked his hand into Molly's and she didn't shake him off. She said they ought to go inside and try to dry the phone, though she didn't think it would help. Arthur was still hopeful that it might. They all four trooped inside the house and up to Molly's room, huddled in solemn procession as if one of them had been taken ill. Kasim had not been inside her bedroom before – it was surprisingly untidy. He had imagined that everything in here would be as neat and orderly as Molly was in her physical person, but it looked as if she simply took her clothes off at night and dropped them on the floor and left them, then dropped wet towels from the bathroom on top of them. Plates smeared with egg and mugs half-full with cold tea or coffee were on the windowsill and the floor and the bedside table. On the bed, the duvet was kicked to a mound and the bottom sheet was untucked, twisted into a rope across the naked mattress. Molly didn't seem to feel any need to apologise for the mess as she hunted through it for her hair dryer.

— Do you think this might work? Or is it too hot?

Cautiously they turned the iPhone in the warm air from the dryer – but it refused to come to life. Then Molly sat in despondent silence on the edge of the bed, Kasim beside her, the children crouched at her feet on the floor. Her silence was more awful than if she'd cried. Arthur began to stroke Molly's knee, making soothing noises – then Ivy joined in, stroking the other leg. The glossy wing of Molly's hair, scented with shampoo, hung down very close to Kasim, hiding her face from him – he seemed to feel her trembling behind it. Cautiously he put an arm around her bare shoulders. Then, as if he was simply joining in with the children, he began to stroke her head; under the silky, slippery hair he could feel the small, exact shape of her skull. Molly said she would wait until the next day before she told her father what had happened, in case the phone recovered after all.

— Are you really so afraid of him? Kasim asked. — He seems like a teddy bear. I should have thought he was pretty easy to handle.

— I'm not afraid of him. My dad's really good to me, he never gets mad. But I didn't want to let him down. I promised I'd look after it.

Kasim was pierced with remorse and tried to deflect Molly's attention, exaggerating how awful his own father was. — He does drugs, he's an egomaniac, he goes off his head if he thinks you're taking the piss or wasting his time. He's always taking up with different women, he used to bring women back to the house when I was a kid and I had to put my headphones on, so I couldn't hear them.

— Hear them doing what? asked Ivy.

— Never you mind, Molly said.

She was shocked and sorry for him. — I know my phone doesn't really matter, she said. — It's only a thing.

ROLAND AND PILAR, WHEN THEY got back, sat with the news-papers in the garden – she had hers open at the financial section but wasn't reading it, she was dozing in the slanting late yellow sunlight. Her eyes snapped open when Alice emerged from the drawing room to stand at the top of the terrace steps; the French windows behind her seemed to open onto a pit of darkness, as if she came from excavations in an underworld. Roland and Pilar – sitting at a disadvantage below, low-slung on the lawn in deck-chairs – were irritated immediately, co-opted into her stage show. Fran was topping and tailing gooseberries on the terrace steps with a pair of scissors, Harriet was reading her book on a blanket on the grass. All the young ones were somewhere upstairs. Alice was dazzled in the brightness, blinking away tears which, because of her theatricality in that moment, seemed like false tears. Her voice was ripe with feeling.

— Listen to this, Roland. Look what I've found. These are let-ters you wrote to Mum when she was in hospital.

— I doubt it. I don't remember writing any.

— But you did! They're just beautiful. *Dear Mater.* Do you remember, you used to call her that? It was kind of a joke, against that old public school thing, but you sort of also wanted to be like one of those boys, and you were having after-school lessons in Latin. *Dear Mater, Things go on here much the same, except that without you they're not the same, they're pretty dreary.*

Roland lowered his paper warningly. — Don't read from them, please.

— But why not? Don't be ashamed of having feelings. *I expect you're very sorry for yourself in hospital. I know I would be. So here are some little gems from family life to entertain you. Dad makes us tea but it's quite awful, he doesn't have your woman's touch. Even your baked beans, it turns out, are a manifestation of your culinary genius. He burns the toast and then puts too much butter on. Sometimes when I'm in bed I think I can hear your voice downstairs.*

Her brother and sisters sat blenched in the stark light, rigidly still, as if something passing through the garden harrowed them. — You're really insufferable, Alice, Roland said.

— *Mater, I wish you knew . . .*

Getting to her feet, Pilar crumpled her newspaper violently in her lap, then stepped up onto the terrace, snatching the letters out of Alice's hand almost before she had time to flinch. — You can't take them from me, Alice cried indignantly. — They're my mother's letters.

— I'm afraid they're Roland's, in a court of law.

The two women glared, Pilar hugging the letters to her chest. Against the darkness behind them their attitudes seemed frozen, their faces like masks, the light wiping out all nuance in their expressions. — But this isn't a court of law! Alice exclaimed. — It's a family, perhaps you hadn't noticed.

— I noticed all right. Families are always the worst, the most litigious. I prefer the law.

— Well, we're different. We don't live by a set of rules. Perhaps you find it difficult fitting in.

Roland sat uncomfortably, accepting the letters when Pilar thrust them at him but not looking at them. She fished her shoes out from under the deckchair and put them on, then strode past Alice into the house; helpless, they all attended to her footsteps, hollow on the uncarpeted stairs. — Well, that was well-managed, Roland said. Smiling only to himself, he put away his glasses and folded his newspaper and then the letter, returning this to its envelope without reading it. He wouldn't look at his sisters and only conveyed, by the sagging of his shoulders when he followed his wife inside, his patience and resigned tedium at this eruption of stupidity.

— Oh Alice, said Fran. — For goodness sake!

— How could you? said Harriet.

Alice was wounded. — I don't know why everyone's so angry with me. Wasn't it a lovely letter?

— It's your lack of tact. It was Roland's letter.

She seemed genuinely bewildered. — Was I tactless?

Both windows were wide open in Roland and Pilar's bedroom. The sisters couldn't help overhearing what went on up there: they hardly needed to understand what Pilar was actually saying, in her torrent of outraged exclamation in Spanish. They couldn't spare much surprise, in the heat of the moment, at Roland's turning out to be perfectly fluent in Spanish, responding to her – how come he hadn't showed this off to them before? What galling restraint for the couple to have always spoken in English in front of his family, how annoyingly considerate of them. And comically, his Spanish was so English: so placatory and reasonable. Harriet grabbed her book and the blanket, Fran her colander of gooseberries: they wanted to retreat away from the consequences of what Alice had done. Then Roland – it was his only vehemence – pulled down the sash windows, making them shudder in their frames, muffling the voices abruptly. But still they could hear the drawers rattled in the dressing table, the wardrobe door banged open on its hinges.

— Is she packing? Harriet was horrified. — You'll have to apologise, Alice. Go up and speak to her. Go now.

— But I can't, because I'm not sorry.

Fran bore her gooseberries off into the kitchen to make crumble; Harriet lingered, pained, eavesdropping but uncomprehending, in the garden. Alice fled through the keyhole gap into the churchyard and then even went into the church to hide, where she wouldn't usually go – she was afraid of it, superstitiously, because of the succession of funerals there had been inside it: her mother's, then her grandfather's seven years later, and then her grandmother's. Behind her she closed first the mesh gate, to stop birds flying in, and then the ancient heavy door; the dimness and coolness inside swallowed her. Sounds resounded around its quiet, like stones dropped in a well: she refastened the loud latch, then stepped into her own echo, crossing the nave to huddle against the whitewashed, clammy, powdery, green-stained wall at the end of a pew, where she'd be invisible, she convinced herself, if anyone came after her. She wouldn't – couldn't, ever – look at the brass plaque with her mother's name on it, and the dates of her birth and death, and the line from her grandfather's poem. Her grandmother hadn't been able to forgive him that vanity, choosing the words from his own poem.

Light, with a ripple in it like water, quavered through the clear glass in the windows, tinged green from the trees outside. She tried not to move, so that the church could be as it was when she wasn't in it. Its cold breath – eloquent of worm-eaten wood, hard iron, greasy velvet, hymnbooks sour with damp, damp stone – had waited for her all this time. It was damper now, if anything, because it was only used one week in four. She looked around her almost with curiosity, like a tourist, at the musicians' gallery in the west end, at the ancient stone font, its carvings worn almost to inexpressiveness, where Harriet had been christened, but not the rest of them (*we ran out of steam*, her mother had once half-explained, making Alice think for years that babies were christened in hot water). Her grandmother's altar cloth – cream and yellow and black, in the style of that era when she'd embroidered it, John Piperesque bold childlike forms – was spotted with mould in one corner.

She throbbed with the aftershocks of her argument with Pilar, or with everyone – it was a jagged pain. But almost at once, even as she sank into her corner in the pew, Alice gave up defending herself to herself. Conscience – like something weightless, cobwebby – settled on her out of the air; the old church must be thick with it, after all the centuries of soul-searching. It was always a relief, she found, to accuse yourself and lose all the arguments. With the same blundering as when she offended, she went straight to imagining herself forgiven, because she was so sincerely sorry. How could she have read Roland's words aloud like that – making a public parade of his feelings, when he was so private? Probably no one had read those letters before except their mother and grandmother. She wilted and sighed aloud, watching herself doing it in her mind's implacably accusing eye. What showing off! Pilar had been quite right to snatch the letters from her. With a pang, she felt all her new sister-in-law's decency and righteousness mustered in the scales against her, as impeccable as her clothes – which were never studied or too fussy. In a revulsion against her own taste, Alice decided there was something stale in it, that her choices were flaky and unsound; she was always trying too hard.

IVY AND ARTHUR'S DEN WAS hollowed out inside a musty dense hedge on top of the front garden wall, beside the crumbling stone gatepost whose gate had rotted into nothingness long ago. It was easy climbing up from the garden side, but the drop to the stony lane, silted in caramel-brown dust, was much steeper, and so the den was forbidden: Ivy associated danger with the bitter smell of the privet. Arthur muddled up privet and private, thinking they meant the same thing. It was a good place for spying but there wasn't much to spy on, because nothing came that far along the lane; the tractor and its trailers, laden with hay bales or black plastic bags of silage or a few bleating lambs, turned off down the track to the farm before they got as far as Kington House.

Crouched on the mossy flat coping stone that topped the wall, Ivy set out a cramped game of clock patience: her petticoat was a liability in the den, snagging on privet twigs. Arthur watched absorbedly as she turned the cards over, sighing with relief every time it wasn't a king, irritating her with his optimism; the cards stuck together and she envied Molly's deft sliding movement. Would it count if she got the patience out now and no one saw? Nobody would believe them. Heavy with her failure to catch Molly's phone, she cheated once without Arthur noticing. Getting stuck a second time, she gathered the cards up despondently and shoved them into a pocket of the shorts she had on underneath the petticoat.

From their vantage point on the wall, they could see into the yard of the Pattens' barn conversion across the road. The Pattens weren't in residence: the yard had been blankly vacant in the sunshine ever since Ivy and Arthur arrived in Kington, roses blooming and going over with no one to pick them, days burgeoning and ebbing unseen – except that the children saw them – against the pink of the high brick barn wall with its slits at the top where the doves eased in and out. It had been ordinary once, if the Pattens were there, for Mitzi to be sloping around their yard, sniffing in corners and signalling results with her plumy tail, or flopped loose-jointedly on the cobbles in the heat. Ivy wasn't even mad about dogs. She had felt fastidiously about Mitzi's coat – which looked so silky but was greasy to touch – and her bad breath and slobber. Yet now the idea of Mitzi was potent in Ivy's awareness, like something hidden but present in a landscape; the ruined cottage had simplified in her imagination into a perpetual knot of unease. Away from it, she lost her certainty about what was inside. Weren't they too young, to be the only ones who knew anything so important?

When Arthur was upset the veins at his pale temples always showed more blue. – Why do you think they closed the door? he asked.

She pretended she didn't know what he was talking about. – What door?

– Someone might have just shut Mitzi in there for a moment and then gone away and forgotten that they'd done it and been looking for her everywhere.

Ivy was scathing. – Oh, that's really likely, isn't it? Unless they suddenly had total amnesia.

– Or otherwise, Arthur went on (he must have been puzzling all this out by himself) – she might have gone in there on her own. When she finished looking round she could have just pushed at the door with her nose, if she wanted to open it wider to come out.

He made a funny little shoving movement to demonstrate, with his own nose. — But she pushed it shut by mistake instead.

Ivy thought this was plausible, though she wouldn't say so. It was true that Mitzi used to roam for miles in the woods by herself. Pushing the door shut wouldn't even have seemed like much of a disaster at first: she would have sniffed round again in the room, then barked for a bit, then settled down waiting for someone to turn up. She might have found a comfortable place on a pile of leaves. For some reason this quietly meaningless mishap seemed worse than imagining anybody's cruelty or neglect. Stoically she refused to show Arthur, by any least gesture of sympathetic feeling, that what he'd guessed at might really have happened. Her face felt iron-stiff with her refusal.

ALICE WENT IN SEARCH OF Pilar, to pour out her abasement. Fran in the kitchen was mashing potatoes for her fish pie. — They're still upstairs, she said darkly. — But at least it's gone quiet. I'm making a big pie, on the assumption their departure isn't imminent.

Alice almost forgot, in her eagerness, to knock at Roland's bedroom door – remembering, she pulled her hand back from the doorknob as if it burned her. Their voices were not raised now but lowered and tender – she couldn't tell whether they were speaking in English or Spanish. At any rate, the worst of the row was over. When she did knock, she heard from inside the room a certain muffled bustle and protest which she recognised, and her first instinct was to laugh – how funny to catch out her brother Roland when he'd been making love in the afternoon. Then she reminded herself that her brother wasn't her intimate any longer, his sex life was none of her business.

— It's only me, she said apologetically.

Doing penance, she waited a long time on the landing before, soberly, Roland opened the door. Then he stood blocking her way in, fully dressed but barefoot, and as tousled as was possible with his short haircut. She thought he looked her up and down to see what new difficulty she might be landing him in – like a policeman checking whether she had come armed. — I'm such an idiot, Roly, she pleaded. — Can you forgive me?

This didn't get round him – he frowned, wary of more complications. — I was so out of order with Pilar. Does she know that I'm just jealous? I'm like a great baby, wanting all the attention, making a mess of things. My therapist says I've never got over Fran coming along to displace me.

Roland said he hoped her therapist didn't charge too much, if that was as good as she got – but then stood back, relenting, from the door. Both windows in the room were open wide again, frail shadows from the alder trees stirred in the sunlight on the pink wallpaper, the children's voices floated from the garden. Pilar was sitting at the dressing table in her slip, pinning up the rich swathe of her chestnut hair. The flesh of her raised arms was brown and firm and Alice thought she was replete with sexual pleasure, and pleasure in being loved. She met Pilar's eyes in the mirror and stoutly, keeping faith with her new humility, refused to see any sly triumph in them. — Pilar, I'm so sorry for what I said. I was completely in the wrong, and you were right.

Pilar in her reflection held Alice's gaze but hardly unbent, made no gracious protestation that she was guilty too, or had overreacted. — It's water under the bridge, she only said, as if she was trying out a new phrase she'd learned, to see its effect.

— I'm so oblivious sometimes, Alice hurried on, — to other people's feelings.

— Don't overdo it, Roland said. — That will suffice. You're no more oblivious than the next man.

His sister threw her arms round him, embarrassing him; firmly, smiling, he extricated himself. Roland had been very close to Alice for a few years, in that painful early teenage time – they were both clever at school and had done their homework in a frenzy of competition. Later, although she was younger, she had seemed to leap ahead of him into adulthood, beginning to have boyfriends and sex and to be in love while he lagged shamefully behind, hopeless at everything except in the world of his books and his study. It was in this time lag, when he was so crippled by his social ineptitude, that he had gained his advantage education- ally over his sister, and found his path through to his adult self.

Now she had embarked on this project of reading over their grandparents' correspondence. She said she was going to write a book about their grandfather but he didn't believe she would do it, she didn't have the discipline. When they got home from their excursions she was sometimes asleep in bed in the middle of the afternoon, or she looked up at them from along the piles of old letters, face smudged with dust, as if she hardly knew them or was expecting someone else. Roland worried about how she drifted. Since she gave up trying to act she had had a long succession of jobs: waitressing and in bars, front of house for various theatres, some private tutoring. She managed on very little money. She had had a few poems published but she had never given herself over to writing with the ruthlessness that it required; her poems were too slight, he thought, they tried too hard to please. When he suggested they should talk about their plans for the house, Alice pleaded for more time; there was plenty of time, she said. Very soon, they must sit down and have their important discussion. But they didn't need to decide anything just yet. They were enjoying themselves so much, it would be a such a shame to spoil things. Well, she had very nearly spoiled them.

IN BED THAT NIGHT, THE children invented a new game. The cave under Ivy's duvet was some sort of underground hall or temple, and she and Arthur returned there between forays into a dangerous world. They often came back hurt and used magic pine cones for healing – Arthur was particularly moving with his groans and his fainting, eyelids fluttering half open. If the grown-ups heard them playing from downstairs then they took no notice. Ivy snapped out instructions to Arthur. She only mentioned the Dead Women in passing, in an undertone, as if he must know whom she meant: *they* ordered the children to tie their pyjama tops around their heads, or *they* made them bring sacred water in a tooth mug from the bathroom. The Dead Women weren't their enemies exactly, and yet she spoke about them warily, in a guarded voice. The fields outside were staring with blue moonlight and the moon-shadows seemed more substantial than daytime ones. They heard the male owl calling and the female's more subdued response, like a flurry of talk.

— What's the owl doing? Arthur whispered.

— Killing things, said Ivy matter-of-factly.

KASIM WAS DEEPLY ASLEEP THE next morning when Molly pushed open the door to his bedroom. The intrusion must have sounded an alarm in some deep chamber of himself, summoning him to the surface: he sat up quickly with a yell.

— What are you doing in here? What time is it?

It seemed to him it must be unreasonably early – dawn at least.

Molly's hair was wet and she was wearing a towelling bathrobe; her skin was flushed pink and damp from her bath.

— Nine o'clock. Everyone's getting up. I've got good news. Guess what?

Confusedly aroused and sweaty from his dreams, Kasim felt at a disadvantage: probably his breath stank too. When Molly sat down on the side of his bed he imagined he could feel her wetness leeching into his blankets. Was she naked underneath that robe? She announced with glee that her iPhone had started working again. — The hair dryer must have done the trick, she said. — I never though it would. Isn't that great? I'm so relieved.

He was aghast at her prattling on about her phone – as if he cared. And when she'd gone out again he felt exposed because she'd seen inside his room that was too tidy and too empty: austere as a cell, with only a thin rug on bare floorboards, the walls painted a horrible icy pale blue. This décor seemed to stand for a certain kind of middle-class Englishness he loathed, chilly and superior and withholding, despising material comfort. His clothes were piled too neatly on the chair, his trainers tucked too obediently underneath it, side by side. He had created a kind of mystique for the others when he retreated inside this room to be alone, pretending he was working. But now Molly had seen inside it for herself, she knew he had no books with him, and that the room was only bleak and bare.

FIVE

PILAR COMPLAINED THAT she felt out of condition because she was missing her regular swimming sessions; Harriet said there was a pool in a hotel nearby that they could use, and so the two women drove off together in Harriet's car after breakfast one morning. Harriet had used this place before. It was a gloomy Victorian hotel built of red stone at the top of an inlet on the coast, surrounded by a caravan park; the pool was in a basement excavated underneath the building, lit by artificial light. The girl on reception opened it up for them reluctantly, and had to telephone the manager to find out how much to charge them, as non-residents. Harriet wanted to apologise to her sister-in-law – how dismally claustrophobic this pool must seem to anyone used to swimming outdoors. Then she remembered how Pilar had reproached her for always harking back to Argentina. Perhaps she accepted the silly pool as part of an England she was determined to belong to.

Yellow lamps like half shells were set against its walls all round, casting their light oddly upwards so that the water seemed oily, breaking up into shifting flat forms when they disturbed it. Pilar and Harriet changed into similar plain black swimming costumes. They were both strong swimmers, preferring crawl; really the pool was too short for them, but at least they had it to themselves. Swallowed in the muffling, booming underground acoustic, Harriet felt a kind of equality with the other woman for the first time – in the water her body, sleek and streamlined, didn't let her down. Perhaps after all they could be friends; Harriet glowed still, because Pilar had chosen to confide in her, or half-confide. For a while they swam up and down ignoring one another, absorbed in the release of physical exercise. Then Pilar challenged Harriet to a race – four lengths of the pool. Harriet knew that she was faster: she was never normally competitive but now she went all out to win, and felt a surge of power – she could have easily gone on for twenty lengths, or forty. Heaving herself half out against the side of the pool, chlorinated water streaming in her nose and eyes, she was breathless and laughing with triumph. They raced again as soon as they got their breath back. All Harriet's shyness and awkwardness were suspended while she was slicing through the water, buoyed up by her unexpected happiness.

After their swim they stripped out of their sodden costumes and towelled themselves in separate little cubicles, getting dressed side by side, not speaking, hearing each other moving around and bumping against the flimsy dividers. They went outside to drink hot chocolate in the hotel garden, which was built on terraces above a steep wooded coombe, descending to the estuary; the sun on the water below turned its calm surface to a gleaming zinc sheet, too bright to look at. Pilar combed out her wet hair with her fingers. She seemed preoccupied and serious, and began asking questions – brusquely, staring across Harriet's shoulder – about Harriet's old life, when she was involved in politics and an activist for various causes. Did she ever regret what she'd done in those days?

— Why do you ask? That's a difficult question.

— You don't look like a revolutionary, Pilar said bluntly.

Harriet wouldn't have consented to talk about this painful subject with anybody else, but she saw what an effort it took to ask her; mostly Pilar's conversation was practical and impersonal. Roland had told them how the shadow of Pilar's uncle's politics hung over their family – very likely any secrets had to do with him. Harriet said that she hadn't really been much of a revolutionary, she'd never done anything daring or sensational.

— I suppose I did think I was helping the revolution along, which seems ridiculous now. All that campaigning and leafleting, and the meetings and demonstrations. I earned money by temping, in offices mostly – but it was as if the me that worked all day hardly existed. I used to believe I was sacrificing myself for something. I was sacrificing myself – but it was for the wrong thing. It was worse than nothing. It was beside the real political point. Other people were doing the real, political work, trying to change things for the better. We despised them because they were reformists, they weren't revolutionary enough.

Her story seemed far-fetched, told in the sunshine in the country garden. There was no one else out there with them, it was still early; the blanching, scouring light made the white china cups blaze on the table between them. The plastic cloth was weighed down with stones at the corners against any breezes blowing inland, but at that moment the stillness and heat seemed absolute. Nothing stirred, except the bees and other insects, in the flowerbeds planted with tall spiky yucca and acanthus and

ornamental grasses. Pilar was reading Harriet's face intently. —
I'm interested in people who change their minds, she said. —
Switch from one thing to the other. Did you change your mind
all at once? In one day?

— Of course it wasn't in one day, Harriet said. And she hadn't
switched from one thing to another: she hadn't turned into a fas-
cist or a conservative or anything. She hadn't stopped hating injus-
tice and cruelty and suffering, or believing that it was important
to act against them. But she had withdrawn from all the shapes of
her old life, leaving it behind her like a shell. And then she had felt
that she didn't have any shape of her own, without it. She hadn't
any energy left over for a new involvement in the world. She had
been ill for a while, really quite ill. Christopher had helped her
through that bad time – he was an apostate too.

— Revolution here is like a tea party for children, Pilar said.
— In England you take so much for granted. You have no idea.

— We have no idea. I know that.

— Where I come from, revolutionaries are terrible people. And
the other ones are just as terrible. It's all death and endless conflict,
making trouble for people who just want to live their lives.

— What kind of trouble? For your family in particular. You
mentioned something the other day.

Pilar made an angry dismissing gesture, pushing her cup away.
— I can't begin, she said. — I'm not ready to talk about it. I didn't
mean to bring these stupid complications into Roland's life.

Insanely, Harriet found herself wanting to confess everything.
She wanted to explain to Pilar how once she would have judged
against her just because of her background and her type – but
she didn't know how Pilar would respond, she didn't want her to
recoil. She hated to think now about her old mistaken confidence,
when she had divided up the world into the ones who were nobly

wronged, and those who wronged them. Needless to say she had imagined her own family – her bourgeois family – on the culpable side. They hadn't ever been rich exactly, but they had always had education and an assumption of superiority, they were the inheritors and not the disinherited. She had thought that her whole life ought to be a kind of expiation of this privilege. This all seemed histrionic to her in retrospect.

IVY WAS ALONE IN THE den on the front wall, setting out clock patience again, when – breaking into the peace which had seemed impermeable – the Pattens' car was suddenly all noisy presence in their lane. Its shiny red roof slid sinisterly close below her, then the car turned into the courtyard of the barn conversion opposite, crackling over the small stones and spitting them behind it. Hopeful, Ivy watched Janice Patten climb out from the driver's seat: it seemed wholly possible that, through some fluke or break in Ivy's flawed child understanding, Mitzi might come bounding out of the red car when Janice opened the rear door, and pay her necessary visit to a succession of sniffing places around the yard. Then everything would be all right again. But Claude Patten got out of the car instead, and stood stretching and groaning on the gravel. Janice only took some bags off the back seat. But if their dog was dead, how could they be so ordinary?

The last king – diamonds – appeared too soon; Ivy collected her cards together and climbed down from the wall, then wandered inside the house. Alice was playing something melancholy on the piano in the drawing room, and the music filled her with superstitious dread. She retreated upstairs, not announcing to anyone that the Pattens had arrived. Alone in her bedroom, she climbed under her duvet and began reading a book she had borrowed from the shelves in Alice's room, and had read at Kington before. All the time she was aware of voices coming and going downstairs, and felt herself passed over. When at some point she smelled baking she realised, martyred, that she hadn't had lunch. Finishing the book she put it back and took another one. Reading was consoling, when you knew in advance everything that had to happen.

ROLAND DROVE INTO TOWN WHILE Pilar was out with Harriet, to get the newspapers and check his emails – although Alice said they didn't want newspapers, not at Kington. — Can't we not know the news, just for a while? The world will get along fine without us being aware of what's happening in it.

— No one says you have to read them.

— But if I don't they sit expectantly, the news leaks out of them.

Molly asked to come: she wanted to show Kasim the amusement arcades she had loved when she was a child. On the way into town the young ones sat together in the back seat of the Jaguar; Roland imagined Kasim's hand on Molly's leg, bare under her shorts, against the leather upholstery – although he'd never actually seen them touching and there was no sign of anything more between her and Kasim than a frisson of attraction. Roland had always been delighted by his daughter – her easy compliance, her grace; he loved her easily, with a strong current of feeling. Because it was obvious she wasn't intellectual, he had never put any pressure on her to do well at school; that dreary parental fixation on achievement seemed to him a distraction from the real values of art and thought. Now he was taken aback by how much the idea of her sexual life troubled him. He didn't like Kasim; it was a strain keeping ahead of him in conversation, negotiating with his ignorance, his quick cleverness, his high opinion of himself. He flattered Roland almost negligently, as though he were bound to be pleased by it, and cheerfully pronounced his bleak verdicts on politics, on the economy, on the future of the planet. Roland was glad when, after he parked behind the Co-op, they agreed to go their separate ways.

In the library he was scrupulously polite, charming the librarian, then checked his emails among the spider plants and oversized romances and the tiny chairs in the children's section. A publisher wanted a foreword for a new series of film scripts; someone wanted a keynote for a conference on film iconography; his agent had forwarded him some nice remarks on a piece he'd written for the *Guardian* – it all reconnected Roland with his public self. He couldn't imagine a life without work at its heart; it was a frame redeeming everything flawed and incomplete. What he dreaded was coming to the end of his interest, finding himself bored; in his thirties he had panicked, feeling trapped inside his university department, then made strategic efforts to develop a career reaching beyond it. He tried to imagine how it must be for Alice, having pinned all her aspirations on her personal fulfilment and her relationships. Perhaps everything would be different if she had succeeded as an actress.

When he had finished in the library he bought himself coffee and a sandwich, and sat with his newspaper at a café table on the pavement; catching sight of Molly and Kasim wandering past, he pretended not to notice them. Kasim was biting into a burger wrapped in a greasy napkin, Molly was licking ice cream. Strolling along with the crowd of desultory holidaymakers, they didn't look quite like everyone else. No matter how scruffily and carelessly they were dressed they were marked out by their class and education, and by Kasim's brown skin – these old-fashioned resorts were still remarkably white, it was striking when you were used to the crowds in the big cities. Roland couldn't help himself chafing at the narrowness and dullness of the little town. Sitting out like this on the street in any small town in France or Tunisia or Brazil, he'd have felt alive and stimulated, observing everything excitedly, drinking it in. He couldn't enjoy this place, it was too familiar, it was home.

Molly and Kasim had played ice hockey in the arcades, skimming flat discs on a table, then fished for furry toys with a mechanical arm. They had exchanged the reams of tickets they won for a white china vase in the shape of a crumpled boot, which Kasim said he was going to give as a present to Alice, just to watch how it put her on the spot, having to appear grateful when it was the ugliest thing she'd ever seen. They had passed a tattoo parlour on their way up the street, and now he was trying to coax Molly into having a tattoo.

— Just a teeny, teeny little one. Just a tiny butterfly, say. On your ankle.

— You're joking! You must be joking. I'd rather die.

— I don't know what you're worried about. Come on, I gave up smoking, don't you think I'm suffering? It's only a little needle pricking away at the surface of your skin, just the very surface. It doesn't take that long. A couple of hours, say. Little needles full of ink. That's all. They keep them very clean. Your ankle's a long way from your brain.

— You're doing it deliberately, she exclaimed, only half enjoying it. — You're teasing me! I know you are.

IVY'S MOTHER, LOOKING IN SUSPICIOUSLY from the bedroom door, asked what she was up to. — Why aren't you playing outside in this lovely sunshine?

— Why should I? I hate everyone.

— Don't be silly. The Pattens have arrived, and Janice has come over. Alice has made a cake. Needless to say she's left a fine mess in the kitchen.

— I wanted to make a cake, Ivy said. — It's not fair.

Her mother shut the door and went away.

When Ivy heard Janice Patten's voice downstairs in the drawing room – deep as a man's, but chattier – she left her book open on her pillow and dawdled reluctantly down the staircase, first hanging over the banister to listen, then trying to enter the room invisibly: she would have liked to snake along the floor on her belly then conceal herself under a chair. But Janice was on the lookout. — I spy with my little eye, she said in a sprightly, fake-surprised voice, — I do believe it's Princess Ivy.

Janice had an idea that her neighbours were arty and eccentric, and saved up stories about them: they were part of the local history along with their grandfather, even if they were letting that lovely old house decline into a dreadful state. Ivy had forgotten she was wearing the silky petticoat. It was stained and torn now and she had only put it on again this morning as a kind of penance. Giving up snaking, she plonked herself, pouting, in a chair.

— Someone's in a mood, Fran apologised.

— I wanted to do cooking, Ivy said. — Mum, you promised I could.

— Darling, I wish you'd been helping me, Alice said. — Why didn't you say? My cake's a disaster, it's flat as a pancake. Listen, Janice, if you'd rather have a biscuit . . .

Janice reassured her insincerely.

Alice contemplated her cake. — Actually, it *is* a biscuit.

Fran and Alice were so eagerly hospitable – fussing round Janice, bringing out the old story about the lady with the flowing hair in the teacups (Janice was expert in antiques) – that Ivy could tell they wished Janice hadn't come over. She was tall and bulky with a small head and pink skin and small quick blue eyes glancing everywhere; her surprising shock of yellow silky curls was beginning to grey and her silk shirt was tight over her bosom, its button straining under pressure. — Talking of moods, she said, — Claude's taken to his bed. He claims he's exhausted after the journey even though I drove all the way.

— It is exhausting, Alice sympathised. — I'm a back-seat driver and I know just how he feels. In fact I'm exhausted just thinking about driving. I could climb right in there *with* Claude. Well, not literally *with* Claude, obviously.

Janice said Alice was welcome to him, warning that he snored and kicked like a horse. Cross-legged on the floor, Arthur was painting his fingernails with Molly's clear varnish, dipping the little brush in the bottle with scrupulous concentration. — Doesn't anyone think they ought to stop him? Ivy said wearily. — Isn't he bound to get varnish everywhere? That clear stuff is a waste of time anyway. Nothing looks any different afterwards.

— It strengthens your nails, said Arthur.

— He's making a lovely job of it, Fran said. — Molly won't mind.

Arthur lifted his eyes from where he was dabbing the brush on his nails, reproaching his sister without words, soulfully: only she knew how innocent he wasn't. — Why didn't you bring Mitzi? he asked Janice.

— Yes, where is Mitzi? Alice joined in merrily, handing Ivy a slice of cake on a plate.

Janice had just taken a bite of cake, and had to put her hand in front of her mouth while she chewed, signalling distress in her expression, before she could tell them. Too much was at stake to be borne: Ivy dropped the plate – one of the same set as the teacups. There seemed to be a cartoonish moment of suspension, such was the tension, before it bounced and landed upside down on the rug and didn't break; then when she jumped up she pressed it onto its cake under her shoe, and heard it crack.

— Look what you've done now! Fran accused.

Alice said it didn't matter, there were plenty more plates and as far as the cake was concerned it was for the best. — There aren't more plates, cried Ivy. — These are the only ones!

Janice, swallowing, was distressed. — Didn't you know? she exclaimed. — We lost Mitzi! I thought you knew.

— We didn't know. We don't really talk to anyone. We talked to Simon Cummins. He didn't say anything.

Janice had to mop at her tears with a tissue pulled from her sleeve while she told them the story; Arthur all the while appeared absorbed in wafting his nails to dry them, the way he'd learned from watching Molly.

— It was while we were down here at Easter. She just disappeared one morning and at first I didn't think much of it, she was always off on her little escapades. But this time she didn't come back. We hunted for her everywhere for days. Claude thinks she ran out in front of a car, and it's true that she was awfully silly about cars. But I believe she was kidnapped. The pedigrees are worth an awful lot of money. I tell myself she's living the life of luxury with doting new owners somewhere, sleeping on velvet cushions and eating chicken breast and grilled tomato. Do you remember how she loved grilled tomato? Though I still think she'd be pining for us – and how would they find out, about the tomato? We stayed on for days longer than we meant to, because I was just haunted by the idea that she would turn up and we wouldn't be there. I used to think every night that I could hear her scratching at the door and whining, and in the end Claude refused to go down and look, he said I was going potty. It's only a dog, he said.

— It wasn't only a dog, cried Alice. — It was Mitzi!

— If she'd been knocked down, Fran said, picking up the pieces of the plate, — surely someone would have found her body by now?

— That's what I think. But Claude says people who kill dogs don't want to face the music, they drive off with the body and get rid of it at the other end of the country.

— Claude's got a vivid imagination, hasn't he?

— You do hear the most amazing stories though, Alice said, — about dogs coming back to their owners after years and years.

— Oh I know, Janice said. — It's what I'm counting on.

Ivy was aware then of Arthur gazing at her expectantly, and knew she ought to stop them hoping for what wasn't possible: she opened her mouth to speak. But at that moment Fran started sweeping the cake mess crossly from around Ivy with the dustpan and brush, prodding her feet out of the way with the brush-end as though she didn't care about the dog at all. Looking down at her mother on her knees, bent over the sweeping, Ivy was suddenly protective of her secret: in all its ugliness it belonged to her, and she didn't want the grown-ups taking it over, sorting it out and cleaning it up, not yet – although the words unspoken felt stifling in her mouth. Arthur wouldn't say anything, she was sure, if she didn't. She knew that, by refraining, she shut herself out from decency and safety. While they were all still being sorry about Mitzi she announced outrageously that she needed more cake. — No one round here seems to appreciate I'm actually starving to death.

Janice reproached her: she shouldn't use the word starving when there were children in African countries who really were.

Then Alice said Janice made her feel guilty, because she for one was always using it. When Ivy had eaten her dry cake, which almost choked her, she went upstairs again, stomping on every step, burdened, feeling herself impossible. She tried on lipstick at Alice's dressing table, pressing too hard and breaking off the little tube of red paste. Then she wandered next door and rummaged in Harriet's chest of drawers, found the diary hidden under her clothes. Harriet's writing was very small, covering page after page. There didn't seem to be anything secret in it, just stuff about walks and birds and people. *Sat next to P. tonight at supper. Am I happy? I think I'm happy, but it's close to madness.*

Ivy scribbled over the pages with the broken lipstick. She wrote *fuk* upside down, spelling it deliberately wrongly, and then added Arthur's name in sprawling uncertain baby letters which were nothing like Arthur's actual rather careful writing. Harriet's white pillowcase and sheet were smeared with the vermilion lipstick.

THAT AFTERNOON ALICE WENT OUT for a walk by herself. She wanted to be alone: she had chafed at their conversation with Janice in the drawing room, so limited and stale. When the others came back from swimming it wasn't any better; Pilar and Fran were actually discussing house prices. In company Alice was so often disappointed; she dreamed of an ideal sociability, when her most pressing and important thoughts would flow out easily into words and be understood, and she would be equally attuned to the real thoughts of others. Once, she and Roly used to talk on and on for hours about everything – religion and art and death – understanding each other completely. But these days he was so guarded, and put up all his cleverness and his knowledge like a barrier against her, to keep her out. Since he'd arrived at Kington with Pilar, Alice had never had him to herself for a moment.

This wounded her – and yet this morning she had been seized by remorse and affection for her family, after her bad behaviour the other day. She had baked the cake as a warming, heartening surprise, to bring the whole family together – then the cake hadn't risen and no one had wanted it. Also, Janice Patten had turned up. Alice was sorry about their dog, but Janice's sharp eyes went probing everywhere, and you could see she was storing up things to make stories out of; she seemed to be friends with everyone in the village, though she didn't spend any more time in it than they did. She was always telling them news about people whose names they didn't recognise. On the whole Alice preferred Claude to Janice, even though he was pampered and self-indulgent, with a paunch and a bald head like a tonsure, fringed with greasy grey hair straggling down past his shoulders. Claude was an architect – that was why their barn conversion was so nice, although also a bit fake and sterile in its good taste.

All Alice's irritations fell away as she walked. *My beloved,* she thought, tramping along through the first stretch of the woods, where the undergrowth was sparse in a plantation of conifers. She didn't mean Claude Patten – she laughed out loud at the idea. Sunlight pierced the dense pine canopy high above and fell in shafts through the dusty brown space that made her think of an empty theatre. *My beloved, my dear love, my heart's own.* It wasn't Claude! Since she'd been in Kington, her solitary reverie seemed to fall into these cadences like a love letter – a love letter such as, in fact, she'd never written. In her actual love letters she'd always been rather light and dry and funny – either that or anguished and savage. Anyway, nobody wrote love letters any more, nobody wrote letters. Lovers just checked in with each other every hour of the day on their phones, exchanging banalities. But this yearning inward voice of hers was like a tic, a new habit of her heart, which seemed to stumble with excitement in her breast. Yet there was no one. She was living in this keyed-up expectancy, but with no particular man in mind. Was this the form neurosis was going to take, in her middle age? She would have to discuss it with her therapist. Alice called Eva a therapist but she couldn't afford a real one, Eva was more of a counsellor and often overstepped the mark, advising her rather strongly: their talks were more like intimate chats between friends. Once Eva had even told Alice to *pull her socks up*. On the other hand, she didn't charge her if she was short of money.

When she was through the woods, Alice struck into a steep lane that wound up the hillside – she met no one, and no cars passed her. Nothing came this way. The lane was strewn with branches fallen in the last high wind; huge oaks growing out of the banks were contorted and bulging with age, their grey hides deeply fissured and crusty. In the high hedgerows the delicate flowering plants of early summer had yielded to coarsely thriving nettles and bramble and dock, rank in the heat. She crossed a stile, then climbed a stubble field up to where cylindrical bales of straw were stored in a Dutch barn. At the top of the hill the wide landscape was proffered bleached and basking, purged of its darkness: there were views across the shining estuary all the way to the blue hills of Wales and, behind her, inland to the moors. But Alice didn't seek out that sensation of overview, where a place seemed to be explained and put in context as if it was a map laid out: at any given point on a walk, Roland could always tell you which way was north. She would rather burrow into the place she was and lose herself, unsure of how the intricate folds of the hills all fitted together.

On her way down she lay for a long time on her back on the

earth in the hidden corner of a meadow of tall grass, in the half shade under a stand of sweet chestnuts. She was thinking about a science programme she'd seen on television, and felt as if she could see deep into the meaning of the creative and destructive pulses which made up the dynamic of creation. At this late point, now, if it were still possible, would she like to have a child? Was that missing from her life? Mixed in among her grandmother's letters she'd found a number of slips of tissue paper, wrapped round locks of blonde baby hair pale and light as breath, or tiny teeth. These might have been her mother's – or her siblings', or her own; she hadn't shown them to anyone, and they caused her some convoluted pain of exclusion and loss. But the truth was that whenever in the past she'd come close to the reality of having a child, she hadn't felt any joyful anticipation – only a muddled panic, like darkness closing in. All those little eggs which were inside her when she was born: Alice imagined them like clusters of tiny pearly teeth, and the idea of them washing away one by one was a relief as well as a regret.

Then she thought she saw a skylark soar up out of the field, streaming with song, balancing on its invisible jet of air – but as soon as she sat up on her elbows she doubted her identification. The bird was just a dot in the sky, too far off to be certain. Surely the skylarks had gone long ago from this part of the country? Everything was in decline. What a compromised generation theirs was, she thought. Materially they had so much, and yet they were haunted by this sensation of existing in an aftermath, after the best had passed.

IVY UNRAVELLED AT BEDTIME INTO one of her tantrums. The house seemed swollen for a while with her loud weeping and accusations. — I can't sleep in this dirty old bed. All the springs are sticking up through the mattress: look at these scratches on my legs. It's like a torture chamber! I want a bedroom of my own. You never think about me, do you? You only love Arthur. I want to go home to Daddy! Other children get taken on real holidays, in aeroplanes. I hate it here! I wish I was dead. I'm so bored! There's nothing to do.

— Yeah, it's boring, said Arthur, backing her up reliably.

— It's so boring without any computer.

Alice tried to explain why it was good for them to be away from computers, using their own imaginations. Fran was cajoling and calm until she suddenly lost patience and slapped Ivy hard on the legs and shouted at her, making everything worse, telling her she'd had it up to here, and that Ivy was driving her round the bend with her selfishness and behaviour like a spoiled brat. Alice gave Fran one maddening look with her eyes full of feeling, at once disappointed in her and sympathetic. — The children are both overtired, Fran said defiantly when she arrived downstairs, hot-faced with her own outrage and ashamed. — It's probably a bit of heatstroke too. I forgot to make them put on their hats.

The other adults looked incredulous, aghast at the loud grief turning the stone walls of the house to paper. They didn't say anything, but of course each was thinking that they'd never allow any child of theirs to carry on that way. Fran asked herself furiously what any of them knew about bringing up children? Roland had hardly been tested with Molly, who was a docile pudding of a baby, whereas Ivy was a traitor knotted in her mother's chest, devouring her. Fran blamed Jeff; in fact she wanted to phone Jeff this minute and tell him about it, while her injury was still fresh. She shouldn't have lost her temper, though. While she sat on the scullery step with her shoulders rigid and her back to the house, the others crept around in the kitchen behind her, bringing in dishes from the dining table and washing them, exchanging practicalities in low voices, starting up mild jokes which were soon flattened by new blasts of lamenting. Kasim and Molly were play-acting in a kind of dumbshow; she giggled when he threatened her with a skewer from the cutlery drawer. The present was hollowed out as if a birth or a death were taking place upstairs.

Every so often Ivy would emerge again from her bedroom to stand sobbing full-throatedly at the top of the stairs, or begin making a halting, broken-hearted descent until Fran ordered her back. Once Ivy had begun a fight she couldn't let it go, and was drawn again and again to the scene of her disaster, prodding at it and prolonging it, wanting more. — You see, you hate me, don't you? Everybody thinks I'm horrible, I know they do! Everything's ruined now, it's too late.

Tucked virtuously into his bed, Arthur watched his sister's desperate coming and going with a connoisseur's calm appreciation. Eventually, when she had subsided under her duvet into a kind of hysterical coughing, he judged the moment right for climbing out of his own bed and into hers, to console her and put his arm around her, with just a hint of piety. Quivering, racked, her back turned to him, hugging her knees to her chest, she radiated intensity: the knobs of her vertebrae prodded him through her thin pyjamas, and her plait where he lay on it felt as hard as rope. — I was only putting it on, she whispered fiercely. Placatory, Arthur said he'd known she was, and asked her if she wanted to play the game.

— I'm worried, she said, breath ragged with the remnants of her sobs. — I think the Women are angry. There's only one thing we can do.

— What is it?

They needed to make little cuts, she said, with scissors in the bedroom curtains, for a sacrifice. Arthur went obediently to find the nail scissors in the bathroom. Ivy instructed him in a musing, teacherly, expert voice – though Arthur, struggling with the tough material of the curtains, which slid between the scissor blades and wouldn't cut, knew she was making things up as she went along.

— We have to go back to the cottage too, tomorrow, she said. — We have to get samples from those magazines.

— Why didn't you tell the grown-ups? About you-know-what.

Ivy shrugged and said she hated them, she didn't care what they knew.

PILAR WAS WEARING HER CHIFFON blouse that evening, and began to feel chilly; while Alice made coffee, in the calm that finally succeeded Ivy's tempests, she went up to her bedroom to find something to put round her shoulders. Roland came after her, wanting to change his shoes. They were aware of the children scuffling out of sight, not asleep, conferring in muffled voices – probably vengefully. Roland had thrown the sash windows open to their fullest extent in the morning, because these rooms under the roof soaked up heat during the day; now he hurried to close them against the night insects. In the garden the trees were fretty silhouettes against the last of the sky, filled with liquid light; bats flickered between them and an invisible blackbird richly sang; the air inside the room was velvety-ripe. In a vase on the windowsill dead plumes of purple flowers had drooped and were pasted against the glass, a white rosebud had browned and withered unopened in the cloudy water. Pilar asked him about his emails: anything interesting? She was on her knees, searching for her shawl in the drawers of the dressing table. Roland told her about the keynote talk, and the publisher wanting a foreword for a new series.

He was touched by her tender solicitousness for his eminence; she wasn't actually interested in his ideas. Pilar had no idea what philosophy might be for – he wasn't sure she even knew what films were for. Her own professional life didn't have any core of passion in it, apart from the belief she lent to the entire institutional structure of the law, which was wholehearted. An individual's work, as Pilar saw it, was a means of leverage – you ought to make the most of yourself. She interpreted his academic and public career as merely adversarial, a succession of thwartings and triumphant overcomings. And all the time she was questioning him eagerly – so were these useful connections? Did the projects have status? – she was struggling with the ill-fitting drawers in the cheap wartime dressing table. These always got stuck and then flew out, then had to be jiggled and banged into their place again; Roland's grandmother used to rub them with candlewax. He admired his wife's patience, putting up with everything that was hopeless and dysfunctional in the cranky old house; even the bed springs which, as Ivy complained, stuck out through the mattresses.

His sisters clung on to these flaws, as if in themselves they were their link with the past; but Pilar was used to all the latest conveniences working with streamlined ease. He thought that they were a sentimental family; it might be good for them all if they gave the house up. Wouldn't they be relieved, really? Every room in it was printed ineradicably, for Roland, with the quality of the first summer they had spent here without their mother. He had not known until then – he was fifteen – how much material things could be altered by the light, or the absence of light, in which you looked at them. Their mother's death and what it meant, the new vision of things it brought, had seemed to be soaked into the blankets on the beds and the keys on the piano and the stones in the walls.

Expert from long practice, he manoeuvred the drawer into position and pushed it home. Then he stood behind Pilar while she brushed her hair in front of the oval mirror in the wardrobe, looking not at himself but at her. Her emphatic beauty – it was harsh, even – filled him with a yearning whose point was that it couldn't be satisfied. The enchanting surface, drawing him again and again, was all its own meaning, not signifying anything – her beauty couldn't be subject to his understanding. He slipped his hands against her skin under the loose red blouse. — We can go whenever you want, he said. — We've shown our faces now, and you've met everyone. We could leave Molly here and go off on our own for a few days. I know my sisters can be hard work, Alice was awful the other day. We could go to the Veneto, I could show you the villas.

Pilar seemed taken aback by his suggestion. She leaned sinuously into his touch. — Oh no, let's stay. I like it here. It's the real England, isn't it? I'm growing fond of it.

CEREMONIALLY, OVER COFFEE IN THE dining room, Kasim presented Alice with the china boot. — I bought this for you, he said, mumbling and looking away as if he was full of feeling. — I thought you'd like it, and I wanted to thank you, for inviting me down here. It means a lot to me. So I wanted to get you something special.

Alice, unwrapping the boot, only faltered for the least fraction of a second. Her bright face and performance of charmed surprise were always ready to be touched into life. — Oh, it's a marvellous boot, darling Kas. Look how cleverly it's done, with all the leathery little folds! I shall fill it full of flowers. I love it. Thank you.

She was gracious as if she were an actress practised at receiving tributes. Molly suffered physically from seeing anyone deceived, she couldn't bear pitying their foolish hope. — He knows it's not marvellous, Aunt Alice, she said. — He's just kidding you. We won it in the arcades.

— Now Molly's ruined it, Kas said crossly. — Why did you ruin it?

Fran laughed and said she could remember winning one of those boots herself, when she was a kid. Alice's expression was still open and smiling, only faintly bruised, looking from face to face, willing to be amused at her own gullibility. — And I was so touched, thinking you'd chosen it specially for me, Kas. I suppose I should have been insulted.

It was characteristic that, exposed, she didn't recoil into herself but waded in deeper. She told the others then about her walk and the beauty of the landscape and her happiness, lying in that field in the afternoon. She said it had been transcendent, she'd seemed to feel the pulse of the universe through her own body, and had understood at last all those old myths where the gods took on natural forms to make love to mortal women. Roland was embarrassed for his sister; she ought to keep her ecstasies to herself. Why did she always have to bring everything round to sex? She couldn't help herself falling into this mode of charged flirtation, even when there was no one to flirt with. Didn't it occur to her that as far as Kasim was concerned she was halfway to being an old woman, past her best? It was bad enough that her affair with Kasim's father had dragged on painfully for years. Roland resented having to see his sister through the boy's eyes.

Harriet and Pilar were sitting together on the terrace. At

the dinner table Harriet had studied, fascinated, how easily the red chiffon blouse fell against Pilar's brown arms and neck. In the half-light, her shawl slipping down her arms, the red of the blouse retreated and became transparent, so that Harriet could make out what Pilar was wearing underneath it – not a bra, but a glimmering silken slip which slipped and rode over her breasts as she moved. Her silver earrings glinted, catching the light from inside the room. Darkness thickened around them and Harriet gave way to her longing, watching Pilar's mouth move as she talked: the full supple lips, greasy with crimson, pressing together and opening decisively, her ripe accent taking on sensuous form. Native English, by contrast, seemed a limp, attenuated thing. Pilar was complaining that Molly's mother was obstructive and difficult; apparently Roland thought Molly should move to a private school for her sixth form. As Roland had always been keen on state education, it was more likely this idea came from Pilar: Harriet wasn't in sympathy with it, and she liked Molly's mother. Yet none of this shuffling of opinion and judgement meant a thing. She had drunk a couple of glasses of wine. The kiss in her imagination was brilliant and liquid, scalding; she was falling down inside it like a tunnel.

HARRIET HAD NOTICED THE LIPSTICK mess on her sheets in the afternoon but hadn't said anything, not wanting to get the children into trouble. Then, when she went up to bed at the end of the evening, she found her carefully folded tee shirts all jumbled together in the drawer, and her diary defaced with one page torn. It didn't occur to her to doubt that it was Arthur who had written *Arthur* in it, and those other things. She stood staring at his scribbling. Her brother and Pilar were moving around in the next room, preparing for bed, and all the time her awareness of their movements and low-voiced intimacy was raw. How much could Arthur have understood of what he read? He was only a baby, on the first readers in primary school – and she had believed her meanings were more or less hidden in innocent descriptions, available only to herself. Yet the scrawled words made her feel nonetheless as if she'd been found out – he had dragged up out of her diary entries what was most humiliating and raw. *U are stupid. Fuck. Fuk. Fuk you. Leeve me alone.* She summoned her sane understanding: children were capable of random silly malevolence, she should not take this seriously. But Arthur had seemed to like her. She felt his betrayal, and the truth of the violence of passion – *fuk you, fucking, fuck:* ugly and awful as a twisting knife.

SIX

———

ALICE SAT ON the top gate, one shoulder shrugged up, holding her phone against her ear, talking to friends, one after another. Half absorbed in her talk, she also twisted slowly on the gate, taking in the scene around her which her friends couldn't see. The morning was resplendent, weightless: light lay on the fields like gauze. Below her the slate roof of Kington House flashed, solar panels on other roofs in the village drank up power. A family of buzzards held their distances from one another as they floated on thermals above the scooped out valley – and she felt as if she floated too in the blue air: the woods on the valley's other flank were more densely blue, gathering darkness under their canopy. The landscape's pattern seemed as simplified as a child's jigsaw puzzle, locking together in bold pieces. Two old horses ambled to a fence to watch her, cocking their ears at her voice which must seem a silly shiny thread drawn across the mute surface of their day. A fire in the corner of a field far off was weakly orange in all the brilliance, its rising smoke filmy against the light, distorting it like old glass. She imagined she could hear its crackle, amplified by the distance.

— Hello, guess who? It's me. I know you don't know where I am. I'm in a retreat – no, not literally a retreat, I haven't actually taken the veil or anything. Mind you, I really might one day, you never know. I love being cut off from everything, just going deep, deep inside myself. Though I don't think I could bear the early mornings – I mean, if I was a nun. Anyway, how are you? What are you up to? I was thinking about you. I haven't been phoning anyone but I wanted to talk to you.

Quite often she was cut off mid-sentence – the signal wasn't reliable – and didn't bother to call back but went on to the next friend. She could have used the landline in the house, but there was something about the old brown phone in the hall which rebuked frivolity; it was better to be perched up here, with the world unfolded around her, a vision of easy possibility. At least half of the friends she called were men. Alice was good at catching and keeping friends of both sexes, she was loyal and involved and generous with her time, and other people hardly knew about the opposite impulse in her, to crawl away from them and bury herself, inert: she told them about it readily enough, but with such joking confidence that they weren't bound to take her seriously.

Waking this morning, she had felt so strong and young. She had woken from a rather amazing dream of innocent, pleasurable, uncomplicated sex – with someone indistinct, no one she knew. The dream had taken her by surprise; she believed that it must have a message for her, so she had dug out her phone from where she'd pushed it away out of sight in a drawer under her clothes, and plugged it in to charge. Now she was contacting everyone recklessly, promiscuously. One of them must be the one. She was living in such expectation of something happening: there were several possibilities. She felt herself overflowing with sympathetic imagination, ready to fall again, to submit to a new continent of discovery. *You were adored, Alice, adored,* she heard in the air, teasing her. It could be any one of a number of favourite men of hers: a poet, a real one, who taught at Goldsmiths; or a colleague who worked in front of house with her at the theatre, a few years younger than she was but he might not know that; or the gentle, subtle man who had built her some bookshelves in an alcove recently – she didn't actually phone him, she had no excuse unless she wanted him to do more carpentry work, which she couldn't afford.

— It's marvellous here, she said to an old friend, a youth worker who'd recently split up with his wife. — I'm with my brother and sisters and their families. Eating and drinking, sleeping, walking in the fields. Yesterday I lay down by myself under some trees and I felt as if I could really feel the world turning, you know? I thought about the gods and how they came disguised in natural forms to seduce mortal women. I felt like one of those women. Not like Daphne turning into a tree. Is there one who turns into a sod of earth? That's what I felt like, a constituent part of the earth. This is the most beautiful place in England but don't tell anybody, we don't want everyone to find out about it.

Everyone was friendly and pleased to hear from her; there was flirting. She flirted, she heard herself teasing and lingering, she fell into the familiar motions with a lurching sensation as if some well-oiled, habituated machinery were starting into action. And yet nothing ignited her imagination or penetrated her mood: she liked them all but she only liked them, and saw them in a disenchanted clear light, unmuddied by desire or need. When she climbed down from the gate she was as thoroughly alone as she had been at the beginning of all the conversations. She was perfectly all right – in fact she was safer, intact in her own possession. But it was as if some part of the spectrum of her responsiveness, which she had counted on, had shut down as completely as if it had never been. Was this what was in store for her, in her middle age? There was plenty of warm friendship but there was not the other thing – the deepest immersion, the secret underlying all the rest. But where, then, had her dream come from?

AS ALICE RETURNED INSIDE THE house, submerging in the half-dark of the scullery and blind from the brightness outside, Harriet waylaid her, asking her to look at something, saying she needed her advice. Harriet led the way upstairs, then closed the door of her room furtively behind them and pulled out a plastic carrier from underneath the bed.

— You know about this sort of stuff, she said. — I bought this. But probably it's a disaster. I need you to tell me the truth, Alice. Don't do that thing you do when you're just flattering people.

— You bought yourself a dress! How extraordinary! I haven't seen you in a dress in a thousand years. But wherever did you find to buy anything, round here?

Harriet said anxiously that she'd got it from a shop in the High Street, was that a mistake? She was driving to the sea today with Pilar and wondered whether she should wear it. Alice tried not to show in her face that she would not have even looked in the windows of any of those shops. The clothes displayed in them were a kind of doom, she thought – fusty and elderly, unthinkable. Putting them on you would be surrendering all hope of joy. Harriet had bought something flowery and fussy in pink and blue, chiffon lined with cotton, with a full skirt: like a party dress for a little girl. It could at a stretch have looked sexy as a retro parody on a sixteen-year-old, on Molly.

— It's pretty, Alice said, hesitating. — No, no: it is, it's pretty.

— You don't like it.

— You have to put it on, or I can't see whether it works or not. I wish you had let me come with you.

With a bitter face, resigned, Harriet stripped off her tee shirt and trousers and then was smothered momentarily inside the dress, emerging with an odd effect as if a weathered old wooden doll had been stuffed into a Barbie outfit, crucified inside it. Her brown arms and brown muscled calves seemed androgynous against the pale chiffon. — Your expression is a picture, Alice! Is it that bad?

Alice was so sorry. — I'm such a fusspot. It isn't right. It's too – you know – frou-frou. The cut's all wrong for you, and it's baggy over the bust for starters. Can you take it back?

Harriet began clowning as if they were still children, marching up and down the room in a funny stiff walk, swinging her legs from the hips and simpering, to make Alice laugh. — I'm the mad old woman you avoid sitting next to on the bus, aren't I?

— Stop it, really. You just don't have any experience buying clothes. It takes years: you have to know what you're doing, what you want. You have to spend hours of your life actually planning it, concentrating on nothing else. And of course you have to keep up with what the idiotic fashion is. It makes me ashamed of myself, just telling you these things. You haven't been vain enough, Hettie. Look, I'll lend you something if you want to dress up.

— No, I'm going to wear it! Harriet insisted, teasing, escaping into a corner of the room. — I'm going to let everybody see!

Alice made her take off the dress and brought her better

things to try. — You need to dress to flatter this wonderful figure, she said. — You're so lucky to be so lean, without even having to worry. This shape looks marvellous under clothes.

In a spirit of genuine selflessness – she liked these things herself, and never had enough money to buy what she wanted – Alice gave Harriet a grey cord straight skirt and a cream silk shirt with a pretty scooped collar. She stood behind Harriet when she was wearing these new clothes and did something to her hair, pushing her fingers into it tenderly like a hairdresser, fluffing it up, scrutinising in the mirror. — There, she said. — Grow it a little bit until it's softer round your face. We're getting older, we can't afford to be so hard on ourselves. And you need beads or something: just a single strand, nothing fussy. I'll have a look at what I've got. You see, you should go for this understated thing, that the French women do. It suits you, you look distinguished.

— Distinguished, Alice? What's that a euphemism for?

— Not for anything. It's what you are.

Alice rested her cupped hands a moment longer on her sister's head, feeling the warmth in her skull, the stillness of her unexpected submission. She wanted to tell Harriet about last night's dream of sex and how it had coloured her morning, making her mysteriously happy: but of course she couldn't. You couldn't describe those things aloud in your waking life: that move and then this, the affectionate faceless nameless lover, those suffusing pleasurable sensations. There were no words to fit their innocence. Translated into words they would turn into something cheap, Harriet would be disgusted with her.

IVY AND ARTHUR WERE SUPPOSED to tidy their own beds. They only had to put their pyjamas under their pillows and straighten their duvets yet they groaned and protested, dragging their feet as if the work exhausted them. Then while they cleaned their teeth in the bathroom their mother stood over them, plaiting Ivy's long hair, twisting the stretch bands around the ends of the plaits to fasten them in a habituated deft movement.

— Dad never makes us clean them, Ivy complained. — Not in the mornings as well as at night.

— That's just his irresponsibility. Do you want to have bad teeth like your father's, full of fillings?

— His are quite brown, Arthur said thoughtfully.

— This is really *unfair*. They're waiting for us, they'll go without us!

— Of course they won't. And you have to be sensible while you're out, Ivy. You're in charge of making sure Arthur doesn't go too near the edge of the path, if it's steep. Do everything Molly says.

Spitting into the sink, Ivy cast her mother a look heavy with world-weariness. Fran kissed both children while she was drying their mouths on the towel; they twisted their faces away impatiently, though not in hostility, and when they had set off along the road with Kasim and Molly she was at a loss what to do without them. Alice was reading her old letters, Roland was writing something in his room, Harriet and Pilar had gone off to swim. At the end of each term, when the school holidays were approaching, Fran would be longing to escape from her job and get back to her private life, stale from the long enforced confinement with her pupils, chafing at school's repetitions. After a few weeks of holiday her interest began to point the other way, back to the ordered routines of her classroom. Fran was a popular teacher, although she was strict and unsparing, with a biting wit sometimes at the students' expense; she pushed them hard and got them their results. It was a point of honour with her, that she expected as much from the difficult students as from the docile ones. But every day in Kington was so shapeless; she was daunted, having to invent the ways to fill so many empty hours.

Plugging in the radio in the scullery, she began the slow work of washing and rinsing dirty clothes by hand in the big enamel sink. There was always at least this bottom-line grim satisfaction of grinding one's way through the list of things needing to be done. Their grandmother's monstrous ancient electric spin dryer had to be manhandled from its place against the wall; juddering with stunning violence on the stone floor, it spat gouts of its own rust into the rinse water, which Fran collected in a plastic bowl under the perished hose. Every year they expected the dryer to die, or at least electrocute somebody: improbably it persisted, built with the solidity of a tank. Eventually there was pegging out wet clothes in sunshine on the washing line, which for its moment was bucolic. At home Fran had an automatic washer and a tumble dryer. She had half forgotten the fulfilment of pegging out.

Then she sat in the study, with daytime television on. She had bought postcards in town, not quite awful enough to be funny: she chose the one of Exmoor ponies grazing. *Dear Jeff,* she wrote. *The children are missing you. They think I'm a tyrant and that you're much nicer, which is probably true. Only I'm here and you're not.* With the biro she drew a speech bubble on the front of the card, coming out of the mouth of one of the ponies: *I wish I was in a band.*

WHEN THE FAMILY WERE AT Kington, their habit was to stay bunkered down at home, only driving into town, or a mile or two to the beginning of a favourite walk, or on a well-worn pilgrimage

to a favourite second-hand bookshop inland. They excused themselves, saying they never grew tired of the walks which began at
their front door. This was more than just a recoil of laziness: the
past of the place enfolded them as soon as they arrived, they fell
back inside its patterns and repetitions, absorbed into what had
been done there before. Afterwards, they couldn't distinguish
one holiday at Kington from another. All the walks and picnics
and lazy, long sessions of eating and drinking around the dining
table blurred together – sunny days and rainy and snowy ones.
Which year was it when Molly brought two friends who hardly
spoke, except to complain furiously, when they were alone with
her, about the bathroom and the food? Or when Christopher rode
all the way from the station on his bike, up over the steep range of
hills that lay between? All the Christmases they had spent there
looked the same in the photographs: only the hairstyles changed.
Slowly they aged, wearing the same paper hats. The babies grew
into children, Roland's wives replaced one another – in a long procession, Alice said, exaggerating.

Harriet and Pilar were driving all the way to the other side of
the moor, to find a beach to swim from farther down the coast,
where the estuary became the open sea. The break with tradition
felt momentous to Harriet, even though they were only going
thirty miles – she wasn't sure of the way, and had to have Pilar
check it for her on the map. Something lifted in her mood as she
drove, new perceptions seemed possible. Arthur's scribbles didn't
mean anything. Her mistake over the dress was only funny, it
didn't matter. Usually the moor's austerity was reproachful but
today the scrubby, knobbled, tufted earth was mild in the sunshine and seemed an invitation to play: mauve and tan distances
were airy and light hearted. She had looked all right in the blouse
Alice gave her, Alice really was clever with these things. Harriet

might put it on when they went over to the Pattens for dinner. Perhaps it was not ridiculous, to be distinguished.

Everything she thought of was slicked with ease and possibility, because Pilar was beside her in the passenger seat; each time Harriet had to change gear she stole looks at her. The trip had been Pilar's idea in the first place – and it had been obvious she didn't want Roland to come: swimmers only, she had said. *We want to swim in the real sea.* Now that girlish insistence was in abeyance and she was quiet, sometimes staring out at the landscape as if it didn't detain her thought for long. Her hair was fastened back in a sober low ponytail. Harriet was too shy to ask herself what her sister-in-law might be thinking or intending: the other woman's presence – a gift of luck whose shining surface dazzled her – was for submitting to, not interrogating. Harriet kept even her own meanings hidden away from herself, buried inside the changing sunlit scenery of each moment. Pilar's perfume was blown against her in the rush of air through the car; they had to have the windows open in the heat, as needless to say her old Renault didn't have air conditioning. When they stopped halfway across the moor to have lunch in a pub garden, she didn't mind that Pilar hardly spoke. Usually she suffered, blaming other people's silences on her own tongue-tied insufficiency. But her ease with Pilar today, without talking, seemed like evidence of intimacy.

It was exhilarating to feel much farther south and farther west than usual, more remote from everywhere, when they drove down eventually into the steep little seaside town. Instead of the equivocal distances across the estuary and its muddy tides, the light here opened up and the silver sea ran unqualified to the horizon. Human settlement clung nervously in rising tiers to the valley's steep flanks; the little Victorian seaside villas were distinctive as if they were cut out from paper, the pretty fretwork fascia boards like fantasies of peasant art. The place was down at heel, locked in its time warp, over-supplied with cafés and fish and chip shops, and the crowd on the beach too seemed left over from another era. Harriet thought these were eternal children, filling their plastic buckets with sand and poking into rock pools the falling tide had left behind. They sculled face-down on inflatables, jumped and squealed in the ceaseless undertow of the waves swelling and breaking, spilling up the shingle in long curling afterthoughts of shallow foam, tugging and sucking at the grit. Where the cliffs along from the beach ran straight into the water, sea smashed itself against them in a dazzling spume.

They locked their valuables in the boot of the car so that they could leave just the huddle of their clothes and towels on the sand while they swam. Undressing eagerly, they entered the unstable shallows which dipped and retreated, then returned to flood around them; laughing and exclaiming at the cold, they made their way further out, bobbing upright, still hesitating before plunging, holding up their arms out of the way – until the surface, opaque like dark glass, knotty with its flotsam of skeins of weed, was rising and falling around their waists, touching them intimately like gloved chilly hands. Pilar coiled her hair away, to keep it dry under a pink rubber bathing cap, and her long face was austerely naked, the skin seeming softer and more putty-like, blue-shadowed, in the glinting light. Harriet was first to go in, engulfed at once in the huge shock of the different perspective, the horizon settling down at eye level, thick salt water parting before her cleaving hands, the clamour of splashing alternating in her ears with a private underwater peace. The cold of the water began to be translated into her own warmth, buoying her up. — It's gorgeous, she shouted, with the half-treachery of the first in. Pilar eyed her and hesitated, then with a funny gathering movement, as though she pulled on reins, pursing her mouth, threw herself forward towards the sea.

They powered far out of their depth, then back again, to roll inshore with the collapsing waves, then out once more to where they were far off from the small fry at play in the surf. Their pleasure in it was inhuman, almost; transposed out of the air into water, consciousness was silenced and intensified, they moved and submerged in place of speech. Gulls wheeled against the sun, wailing and slicing the air with wings like blades – or they rose and fell inconsequentially on the water surface like toy birds, wings folded, glassy gaze averted. Harriet let herself drop down, once, underneath the water. She opened her eyes to see, so that she could remember it later: through the brown-green murk of sand and spinning motes suspended, Pilar's amphibiously kicking legs, bent beams of sunlight. This seemed a place she hadn't visited since she was a child, she had forgotten it; when she burst again into the clamorous day she half-expected to come up into another life. Then she saw Pilar waving from further out. They swam until they knew they were too exhausted to be safe; getting out, streaming water, they could hardly lift their knees to walk, or stand upright.

Harriet's whole body shook in long spasms; she had to clamp her teeth shut, close her eyes to steady herself, huddled on the hard sand under one of the worn striped towels from the cupboard at Kington. Pilar was anointing herself patiently with suntan oil, the smell of it nutty and spicy like something their mother had once used. No one in England seemed to buy that oil these days. Then Pilar offered to put it on Harriet too. — Come on, you ought to wear something, with your fair skin.

Harriet dropped the towel and kept her head down, neck bent. Business-like, Pilar began rubbing oil into her shoulders;

Harriet closed her thoughts to the shoulders' whiteness and thin angularity.

— I can talk to you, Harriet, Pilar said as she ran strong fingers over the shoulder blades, outlining them, then caressingly forwards around the neck, pressing and smoothing up under the hairline, behind the ears, around the top of the arms, as if it was the most natural thing in the world. — There are things I can't talk to Roland about. I want everything to be nice for him, I don't want to spoil things between us with this worry. Valerie was always nagging at him, wasn't she? But there is a problem with my aunt. This is partly why I'm not keen on returning home for a visit. She wants me to undergo certain tests, I don't want to.

Intelligent thought lagged behind Harriet's awareness of Pilar's competent massage. Her body was melted into her sensations; deliriously she allowed herself to imagine the oiled hands slipping underneath the clinging wet of her costume, foraging further and further, onto her longing breasts and past them, down to between where her thighs were clamped shuddering together, blue-white with cold. No one had touched her so easily as this, not for such a long time, perhaps not ever, not since she was an adult. Reluctantly she dragged her mind to what her sister-in-law was telling her. — What kind of tests?

Pilar rolled down Harriet's shoulder straps matter-of-factly. DNA tests, she explained, because some people believed that her mother and father were not rightfully her parents. She hadn't liked her parents very much, but that didn't mean she wanted a whole new set of relatives; one family was quite enough, thank you. — You don't know what these people are like. These campaigners, these leftists: obsessed, thinking of the same thing day and night. I can understand it of course. But I don't want to belong to them. Do they think any test can bring back their sons and daughters?

Harriet was puzzling it out. — Do you mean you might have been adopted?

— Everyone knows I'm adopted, me and my brother. It was at the time of the disappearances, but it was from an orphanage, everything above board and official. We have all the paperwork. Anyway what can the tests prove? I don't belong to these people, they're in a different world. My uncle says, what's gone is gone.

Digging with her fingers into the gritty sand of the beach, feeling for fragments of shell, Harriet was pierced with guilt and exquisite pleasure both at once: how could she be so selfishly happy, while Pilar was suffering? She knew something about these stories, that the children of the disappeared had been handed over for adoption, to privileged friends of the regime. But she pushed away out of her own sight the complicated justice of the situation, muffled and opaque: immune in her sheltered life, she had no right to enquire into that. What could she know? Pilar seemed magnificent to her, heroic and stoical, living inside the reality of politics, and with the terrible consequences of violence.

KASIM SAID IT WAS ALL right for the children to go inside the ruined cottage. When Molly was anxious it might not be safe, he reassured her airily. — It's been here for a hundred years, it'll last for another hundred. Anyway, they've been inside before, we all went in, there's nothing to be afraid of.

— I'd better go in with them, Molly said. — Even though it's creepy. It smells bad.

She shivered fastidiously, like a cat sniffing at cold water.

Kasim and Ivy had to join forces to dissuade her; he winked at Ivy expressively. — It's our secret, Ivy darkly said. — You can't come in.

— Sit down here on this bank, Kasim said, steering Molly by the shoulders, coaxing her. — Don't worry about the children, they're just fine. I fell asleep here, one day before you came. It's an enchanted place, it makes you sleep. Look, you can still see the outline of where I lay, there where the grass is crushed. Try it.

— I can't see any outline.

He was pressing her down gently but insistently, seemingly intent on her and yet also hardly aware of her, as if he was fulfilling some programme of his own, laid down in advance. She sat cross-legged at first. — No, lie back, you have to lie back. Just try to keep awake, see if you can. Shut your eyes: I bet you're asleep in half a minute. I should think you're highly suggestible, aren't you?

Obediently Molly lay among the grasses with her hair fallen back, eyes closed, her face exposed to the sun. She was pale, the sun had hardly tanned her but it hadn't burned her either – apart from a cloud of indistinct freckles across her nose and a faint effect of rust-colour at her hairline, almost as if she hadn't washed, although he was quite sure she washed exhaustively and often, he heard her running water for hours, day and night, in the bathroom. The purplish lids of her eyes were obscenely huge when they were shut, and her full lips were parted trustingly – they would be cracked and dry, he saw, if she wasn't always putting on that salve from a tube she carried in her pocket, fussing with it, tending to her appearance because she could never quite forget herself. Her small breasts flattened when she was lying on her back, so that it was mostly the crumpled empty padding of her bra that rose and fell under her tee shirt; her belly button was a raised brown knot in the naked hollow, deep as a pool, between her hip-bones.

Kasim hung over Molly without touching her, studying her,

talking to her soothingly, careful that his shadow didn't fall across her and disturb her. He thought that if he could just see her clearly enough he would be able to understand her and see through her: what was this effect of her exterior, that blocked and prevented him? This beauty of hers was only a subjective effect of the moment, evanescent; he was preoccupied by his knowledge that she would grow old and change. He thought about Alice's flirting and the way the flesh was beginning to soften and clot together under her jaw and on her upper arms; not that his mother's arms, sinewy from the gym, were any better.

— My father hasn't got a clue, he said, rambling just to keep her there, just so that Molly didn't open her eyes and return his gaze. — He's such an old leftie, you know? You'd think by now he might be wondering, well, maybe my generation didn't work things out so well, maybe despite all our efforts we didn't really get the socialist dream project off the ground, it all seems to have pretty much ended in the shit. But no: it's never him, it's never his fault, it's always someone else's. If only they'd listened to me and my mates, he thinks, we wouldn't be in this mess now. It's all just one big lost opportunity. That's what I can't stand, Molly, I really can't stand it. He's so energetic. Whoa! Dad! Time to slow down there. Don't start another fucking co-operative whats-it for black youth, just please don't.

Kasim felt an actual gust of irritation at the idea of his father then, as if Dani's pre-emptive maleness cast its shadow over the afternoon. Molly smiled, with her eyes closed. — Stop going on about it, she said. — Never mind, it doesn't matter. Anyway, I thought you said he lived in Pakistan?

— Wherever did you get that idea? He lives in Ladbroke Grove. That's where I live with him, part of the time, when I'm not at the university or at my mum's. I've got to get out, man.

INSIDE THE COTTAGE A KIND of braggadocio came over Ivy. She needed to make free of the place and so she stamped around downstairs, hallooing and kicking at the mass of dead leaves packed in the grate, sending them skittering across the red cement floor. Among the leaves, against her jelly shoe, she felt something softer and more yielding too, which she ignored – though she didn't kick it again. Dead bird? She might have felt the light snap of feathers, or bird bones: any dreamed-of horror was possible. She was showing off to Arthur, asserting her primacy in the cottage, boasting that she'd been here all alone once, without him.

— When?

— The other day, while you were busy playing.

Already that solitary visit seemed enshrined in myth: she could hardly believe in the audacity of that other Ivy, venturing bravely by herself to her tryst with the things upstairs. Arthur was visibly sceptical, jingling coins in his shorts pocket.

— I did come here, I really did! Anyway, why have you brought your money, stupid? There isn't anything to spend it on in the countryside.

He said he'd thought that they might pass a shop; Ivy was scornful, but it gave her an idea. — It's a good job that you brought it actually. It will do as part of the sacrifice we need to make.

— What sacrifice?

She lowered her voice piously. — I told you. Because of the Dead Women.

Arthur took some persuading before she could get him to part with his pound coin – she had to peel back pale fingers finally, one by one, from where he clenched his treasure in his palm. Once he'd let go of it, however, he submitted gracefully to the ritual Ivy invented: upstairs, in the first room, they tore little washed-out pink pieces of body out of the pages of the magazines, and crumpled some of these, arranging them in a heap around the pound coin on the floor. Other samples, as Ivy called them, she thrust in her pocket. Bustling round, preparing the sacrifice, she sometimes almost forgot to be afraid of where she was, opening the door once into the last room almost casually, as if she was simply checking Mitzi was still there. Mitzi was, of course. She wasn't going anywhere – her remains in fact appeared diminished and contracted into a smaller, blander shape, into something leathery. She was beginning to seem part of the same substance as the room, and her smell was changing: still nasty, but more stale and ancient. Ivy's offhandedness, glancing at her, was proprietorial, like the habituated priestess of a cult. Arthur spent longer taking Mitzi in than Ivy did – she was the old hand.

Using Kasim's lighter – which Ivy had picked up from the desk in the study, because Kas didn't need it any longer – they set fire to the twists of paper; these curled and turned brown at the edges as the flame licked round them, and one of the women looked for a moment as if she was stretching, uncoiling luxuriantly to her full length, before she was consumed in a brief flare of heat and light. When they'd scuffed out the last spark responsibly Arthur wanted to have his coin again, but Ivy told him that would be unlucky, it belonged to the Women now; reluctant, gazing behind him over his shoulder when he left, he let it stay there. Their going downstairs wasn't at all like the first time, when nightmare jostled at their heels. Ivy eased the front door open where she had closed it behind them, lifting it on its hinges, Arthur pushing past her into the gap. Both of them saw at the same moment Kasim and Molly on the grassy bank some little way off: framed at eye level in the opening, dazzling and confusing in the suddenly blazing light, oblivious to the children watching.

And at that very moment Molly half-shuffled up on her elbows and reached up her mouth to Kas, who, cupping the curved back of her head in his palm, skewing his shoulders round to come at her from the right angle, reached down his open mouth to kiss her. Their heads moved in deliberate slow rhythm together, like licking at ice cream. This kiss hadn't occurred to the children as a possibility and they were shaken by what was indecently needy and exposed in it, exchanging glances ripe with derision and dismay. As soon as the lovers heard the children coming they sprang apart as if nothing had happened, and the children pretended they hadn't seen anything.

ROLAND AND ALICE DRANK FLAT glasses of leftover fizzy wine, stretched out on the grassy stubble in the garden in the afternoon sun, sharing a bowl of salted nuts instead of lunch. They had the place to themselves, everyone else was out. Roland was voluble from writing all morning in his room on his laptop, working on a review. Alice said that when she was an actress the reviews had almost killed her. The idea of that kind of implacable judgement was awful to her, pinned down in words on a page which couldn't be softened or unwritten. For once, instead of countering Alice – did he notice he was doing it, dissenting with a kind of patient forbearance from everything she put forward? – Roland seemed to attend sympathetically to what she was saying. Where had her self-doubt come from? When they were fifteen or sixteen, you'd have thought that Alice was the confident one, she had been so blithe and poised. No one could have imagined that Roland would come to speak with such assurance, such weight of authority behind him.

— In another era, Roly, you'd have made a wonderful vicar. I mean a really noble one. Founding a monastic order or taking the word to the heathen or something. I can just imagine it. While all of us sat at home knitting warm vests for you, dreadful spinsters, making a cult out of their precious brother and hating him secretly.

— That doesn't sound much fun for anyone.

— Probably more fun for the spinsters. You'd have got yellow fever and been nursed in your last days by a devoted native bearer, but your faith would have sustained you. Do you think our grandfather's faith sustained him? I mean, seriously, when Mum died. Or d'you think he lost it?

On the day of their mother's funeral, Roland remembered, their father had driven off somewhere with Alice in the old Bedford van; they'd arrived back very late when everything was over, and then Alice had thrown up all night from eating too much chocolate. Yet Roland had heard her on two separate occasions, as an adult, talk as if she was present at the funeral – and she seemed to think it had been here in Kington, not in a church in Marylebone. Their dad had claimed he couldn't stand the religious hypocrisy, and Alice had pretended she felt the same, though she had been too young to know what hypocrisy was. Roland had seen through the pair of them, father and daughter: he knew they were only afraid. Alice had been wearing some kind of punky, slippery, inappropriate silver party dress, which showed up her puppy fat and the small beginnings of her breasts; everything that day had been crazy and disordered, even their grandmother couldn't put it right. Roland was pierced with a strong pity for his sister sometimes – although this was out of character, and he wasn't convinced that pity helped anyone. Alice would have been dismayed if she'd known he felt it.

He pushed his fingers through his wiry curls. — I expect our grandfather believed God's providence was inscrutable. That's what the serious Christians think. Which seems reasonable enough. That's just about what I think, only without God.

His skin was faintly freckled with brown and he reminded Alice, with his brown eyes, of a speckled thrush; you could see the current of awareness moving in his face like a current in water. Their closeness for a moment was like the old days, she thought. She scrabbled in the bowl for nuts, got mostly salt. — It is inscrutable, isn't it? I find life pretty terrifying, don't you? And I'm such a coward. I certainly don't know what anything means. I mean, even the ordinary things frighten me, just the sadness of change and growing old and missed opportunities. And then there's the ugly way things are going – with the environment for instance. I know you get annoyed when you think I'm nostalgic for the old days, as if things were always better in the past. Perhaps they really weren't. But aren't you afraid of oceans full of plastic, melting ice caps, factory farms with lakes of pigswill? All the forests of Zambia cut down, and the animals becoming extinct in our lifetimes, and grubbing up the earth for filthy minerals, and everyone forgetting how to make beautiful things. Isn't that all so disgusting and threatening?

— But you've never been to Zambia.

— I read a book about it.

Roland stretched out in the sun, closing his eyes. — Am I afraid? At this moment I seem to feel an animal assurance of wellbeing, against all the promptings of my intellect. Anyway, how did we get so fast to the apocalypse? You bring everything around to the apocalypse, Alice.

— No, be serious. Own up to being afraid.

But Roland wouldn't own up, he smiled with his eyes still shut as if fear were just a phenomenon he was considering among others, interested in working out its implications.

— I really do think Pilar is gorgeous, Alice said. — You know I didn't mean what I said the other day, don't you? I'm sure she can fit in. Though I do find her a little bit intimidating. She's so organised and dynamic, she must think I'm good for nothing. It's nice how well she gets on with Harriet.

Roland clammed up then. He didn't want to talk with her about Pilar.

THEY WERE ALL INVITED ACROSS to the Pattens for dinner, including the children. There was something ceremonious in how they crossed the road in the early evening light, bearing bottles; Ivy concentrated, in charge of a glass dish of Fran's home-made chocolate truffles covered in cling film. Pilar brought white roses, cut from the garden wall. They felt clannish: bound together and identifiable, for once, as a family. Roland had Arthur hoisted on his shoulders as if, male, they ought to combine to overtop the female hordes; Arthur rode his uncle tranquilly, a small smile playing in his expression for no one in particular, steering lightly with his hands in Roland's hair, the boy-prince easy with acclaim.

Wordless, they all seemed to collect themselves in preparation for the hours of chatter to come, scuffing up a cloud of dust around their feet in the road, the women's different perfumes mingling in the disturbed, heavy air. Even Harriet was wearing perfume; even Roland had sprayed on cologne. Harriet carried herself with a self-conscious stiffness which warned off comment; she was wearing the skirt and blouse Alice had given her, and her own little silk scarf knotted at her neck – which Alice would not actually have advised. But Harriet's pretty earrings, bought apparently in some museum she'd once visited, caught the light, and her face was animated, tanned and pink from her trip to the seaside. And Molly moved, after her kiss, with a new languid full-ness which only the children understood; her father, observing her daydreaming, suffered in fact a pang of worry, thinking how childlike and inexperienced she was. Kasim would be late to the supper party because he had chosen this moment to take a bath, though he'd been skulking in his room for hours. Molly hardly missed him: her idea of him was so vivid in his absence, complet-ing her, that she half-dreaded his actual presence, complicating things.

Light from the low sun slanted through the windows of the church behind them, filling the stone interior and making it appear weightless, floating spirit-like among its graves. From inside the church that morning, while some of them were still slothful in bed, they'd heard the quavering of hymns; because it was used in rotation with the vicar's other three churches, they never quite remembered to expect it. None of them ever attended, to kneel on their grandmother's hassocks which were each embroidered with a different local wildflower. If a service was taking place, they only moved around more decorously and guiltily in the old rec-tory, and everyone was made aware of some pattern of significant time passing, marked out behind the succession of their own days, which were not distinguished one from another. The church kept count, while they were distracted.

Now, as they stepped into the Pattens' yard, white doves descended in a kerfuffle of fanned-out feathers, the spread wings backing up before landing with the noise a length of cloth makes when snapped in the air to straighten it. Claude Patten, whatever kind of architect he was (mostly old people's homes and shopping malls) had known better than to encroach upon the barn's ancient dovecote. Janice had researched on the internet which doves to choose, and how to keep them. She was waiting now, pink-skinned from her shower, curls damp, dressed up in a caftan of kingfisher-blue shot silk, full of proud-hostess smiles beside the tall glass doors which stood open to the yard. These let out the rich smells of her cooking: meat slow baked with tomatoes and wine and herbs, home-made bread. Behind her, opaque white globes – suspended on chains from the barn's rafters high above – shone with weak light over the long refectory-style table, laid with blue glass and yellow linen napkins. Alice thought it looked like a showy restaurant. The lamps were still outdone by the big low lemony sun outside – but this was about to sink behind the field of head-high exotic and shabby elephant grass, grown for biofuel, which rose behind the barn to the horizon. Janice hated the elephant grass – *it spoils my view but it isn't that, it's the ecological issue* – and had fallen out with the farmer over it.

She greeted her guests and kissed them and took grateful possession of the roses and the truffles, telling Roland she was afraid of him because he was so clever. Apologetic, Roland lifted Arthur from his shoulders and deposited him carefully. Claude, Janice insisted, summoning him ringingly from wherever he was lurking, must be put in charge of the bottles. Her guests felt that their long moment of silence, crossing the road, was suddenly a tangibly sweet thing between them, as they noisily broke it.

COMING LATE ACROSS THE ROAD – probably too late, he gloomily and indifferently thought, perhaps he shouldn't bother – Kas was almost in the dark. The huge evening sky wheeling overhead was a livid, electric blue, pocked with sparks of stars; it stalled him, so that he stood still in the middle of it, in the middle of the road, as if there was something he'd forgotten. His hair was still wet from his bath, picking up the evening's chill and soaking the collar of his last clean shirt; he had been too proud, or too lazy, to ask where he could do his washing, vaguely he'd been waiting to happen upon a washing machine somewhere. He had seen things drying today, hadn't he, on a line in the garden?

The tall windows in the barn were lit up and wide open and a clamour of voices floated from inside, along with the businesslike chink of cutlery and chiming of glasses. Kasim shuddered, entering the yard, not wanting to belong to that conviviality. He felt he didn't want to be initiated, ever, into any noisy crowd of friends and family, its claim a chummy arm dropped on his shoulders. Now he was alive, now. Apprehension could only be kept keen by being kept apart. Alice was protesting over something in that drawling voice which was always on the verge of either tears or teasing. — I'm afraid of everything, she was saying. — But Roland won't own up to fear, he just won't admit to it.

Disgusted, Kasim imagined them all laughing with their mouths full. But he was bent upon Molly and must go inside: Molly was silent amid the crowd as he was. The memory of their kiss washed over him and he was strained with sexual longing. Then an unexpected fat drop of warm rain struck his cheek, out of the night-blue sky which had seemed cloudless. At first he thought that his wet hair was dripping, then he felt another drop and heard the rain's secretive patter swelling all around, too quietly for them to hear inside, rustling in the Pattens' gravel, sending up little puffs of the parched dust.

PART TWO

The Past

ONE

JILL FELLOWES CAME home to her parents at Kington in 1968, with her three children, in flight from her husband: she believed that she was finished with him for ever. She had never stopped calling herself Jill Fellowes – in her own mind and, mostly, when she met people – although it was useful being married for the benefit of Harriet's school, and at the doctor's. When her mother wrote to her the envelopes were always addressed to Mrs T. R. Crane. Her mother wrote every week, her letters filled with news of the nothing that happened at Kington, salted with her perpetual irony. *The big story around here is that the shop has thrown in the towel and refuses to sell anything apart from sliced bread, they say it's too much trouble, and you know your father won't eat it. I expect this Sunday's sermon will be punishing.* Every week, dutifully, Jill had written back, dry in return. In return telling her mother nothing, nothing.

Late one afternoon in May, Jill's mother, dressed in her old-est slacks and gardening shirt, straightened up from weeding in the front garden of the old white house beside the church, in an empty pause. She was extremely thin – bony, she called it – grace-ful and washed out, with pale grey-blue eyes and iron-grey hair which grew oddly upwards, like a crest. Was she thinking in those moments of her budding roses, and the shepherd's pie for sup-per, like a caricature of a vicar's wife? Just then a noisy arrival broke in upon the sealed, blissful, tedious peace of the place, and her beloved only daughter and her grandchildren unfurled from an unfamiliar panting, juddering car on the road outside, like an apparition, utterly unexpected. The car was a Morris Traveller, with Tudor panelling.

Sophy wasn't really thinking of shepherd's pie. She had slipped, as she often did when she was alone, into the dark pool of herself, beneath conscious awareness: she might have been stand-ing, dreaming of nothing, for five seconds or five minutes. So that when she saw her daughter she really thought in that first instant – uncharacteristically, because she was rational and sceptical, the faith that bound her slender sometimes as a thread – that she was subject to a vision. Of the Stanley Spencer kind: a domesticated miracle. The children were beautiful as angels but also sticky and filthy, Hettie was ghastly pale, Roland's glasses were mended at the bridge with sticking plaster, baby Ali's curls were flattened with sweat, as if she had been roused from sleep against her mother. Whining at being put down on the road, she stumbled after Jill, clinging to her coat so that Jill almost fell over her.

— Keep hold of her, Hettie, will you?

The Morris Traveller wasn't Jill's. She couldn't drive and any-way couldn't possibly have afforded a car. They'd come from London on the train, then the bus, and then finally as they set out to walk the two miles from where the bus put them down, through the winding lanes into Kington – looking like refugees from the dust bowl or something, Jill said – someone passing had taken pity on them and given them a lift. When she had heaved the folding pushchair and a suitcase from behind the back seat, Jill leaned in through the open front passenger window, smiling, and Sophy heard her daughter fulsome and charming as she'd been brought up to be. *So very kind of you . . . saved our lives.* The Morris reversed into the Brodys' farm entrance opposite, and was off by the time Sophy had dropped her trowel and hurried down to the gate.

— My dear ones, my best boy and girls, she said. — What's happened?

— We stink, Jill said flatly. — They'll have to open all their windows to get rid of us. Harriet was sick on the bus, I had nothing to wipe it up with except her own cardigan. The whole journey's been sheer hell. And they weren't actually coming to Kington, they made a detour just for us. No idea who they were, only they seemed to know us. We're badly in need of a bath.

— Oh, but who *was* it?

Sophy worried about an intricate network of obligations and favours. — How nice of them! I'd like to thank them.

— I pretended I knew. Cunningly I said, *So, how are you all?* But their lives were too bland for identification. A daughter called Penny, who rides? Anyway, they were nosy, they wanted to know why Dad hadn't picked us up at the station. I said we'd just come on an impulse. Which we have.

— Darling, you could have phoned the Smiths. How can I feed you all? The loaves and fishes thing doesn't *work* with shepherd's pie, when it's such a tiny one. And you know that the Smiths really don't mind. It's only your father's obstinacy, that he won't have a phone put in. Now the shop's shut. I'll have to go over to Brodys for some eggs.

— We don't eat eggs.

Roland broke the news solemnly.

— Oh *god,* said Jill. — I really began to think we'd never get here, that we'd just have to sleep under a hedge or something. And you're worrying about a little thing like eggs.

— You shouldn't say god, said Hettie. — Grandfather doesn't like it.

— He isn't here. He's visiting the sick.

— Thank god for the sick, said Jill. — We can swear until he gets back.

Sophy put the kettle on for tea. It was astonishing that Jill and her children were suddenly real, and in the house with her. Usually before their visits – or before her own visits to their chaotic, unsuitable flat over a shop in Marylebone High Street – she had time to prepare to be astonished. If only she'd had time at least to change out of these old clothes. She had become more familiar, she realised, with the wistful dream of her daughter than with this actual woman: decisive, her face keen with the extreme leanness of young motherhood, her colouring which made Sophy think of a thrush, the careless switch of her tawny hair swinging from where she pulled it into a ponytail high on her head. Her crumpled shirt dress was so short – she had taken up the hem herself, Sophy could see, sewing in childish big stitches. Pale lipstick had seeped into the cracks in her lips, and she had painted her eyes. When she lowered her gaze, the heavy, strongly convex mauve lids could have belonged to a saint in a vision, but the eyes when they looked up took in everything with too much appetite.

Jill had come wearing her winter coat, because it was easier than carrying it; the coat was too thick for the cloudy, mild spring day, and her cheeks were hectic with the heat. Now she shrugged it off and dropped it on a chair in the hall, strode through the house and out through the French windows, into the garden where she threw herself down, flat on her back on the lawn: the earth's deep chill seeped up through her dress, refreshing her. For a moment it was as if she was still seventeen, and had never left. Then the baby toddled after her and settled crowing with triumph astride her, bouncing until Jill groaned and pushed her off, lifted the little top of her romper suit printed with strawberries and blew noises on her tummy.

Her mother asked Jill carefully, over their cup of tea, where Tom was.

— Oh, he's in Paris. He's revolting.

For once Sophy's irony failed her. — Revolting?

— You know. Isn't that what revolutionaries do: revolt?

— Well, goodness. I hope he isn't getting into trouble.

— That's the whole point of a revolution, Mum, Jill said. — Trouble is what you're hoping for. Anyway, Tom's hoping for it, so he can write about it for his paper.

Evasive, not commenting, Sophy stirred the tea in her cup, chinking the spoon against the porcelain. Her doubts about Tom, transparent to her daughter, mostly went unspoken. — I'll be so interested to hear what he thinks. I don't know what to make of it. Aren't the students going too far? There was a lot of idealism in the beginning. And the French police are brutes, aren't they?

— Not like the nice English policemen.

But Jill didn't want to get into a row about politics with her mother. She was sick of her own tired old opinions and indignation; at this moment, in truth, she couldn't care less about Paris. She could just imagine what was going on over there: everyone denouncing all the wrongs in the world as if no one had ever denounced them before, all those students who'd never done a day's work in their lives, so delighted with their sacrifices on behalf of the 'workers'. Of course when she imagined those things she was really imagining Tom.

She had thought that when she arrived home she would spill over with her sorrows to her mother right away. Through all the difficulties of the long journey with the children, she had had this sensation as if she were holding the burden of these sorrows up out of the way and guarding them with her life: like a messenger in a story carrying something of terrible import, a signal for war or an enemy's severed head. As soon as she was actually in Kington, her urgency diffused. How could she have forgotten this muffling effect of her home, where plain speaking was always deferred until a moment which never came? Instead they worried about eggs – and she found herself joining in, over the eggs, and the sheets and the hot water, as if these would suffice as coded, generalised expressions of affection, and concern. She waited for her mother to ask why she had come so precipitously, without warning. Perhaps Sophy really hadn't read anything between the lines of all the letters Jill had sent, hadn't intuited the failure of her marriage. Jill felt gratified and lonely both at once; loftily so much more experienced than her mother.

Later, when Sophy climbed upstairs with her arms full of the clean sheets she had been airing in front of the Rayburn, she saw through the open door of the bathroom that Jill was naked in the bath with all the children. Startled, she turned her eyes away from all that flesh, from the clambering, slithering, chubby limbs flushed pink in the hot water, and from her daughter's bare breasts, still plump and shapely even though she'd fed three babies. All piled in together, they were splashing water everywhere on the lino. Some people round here would disapprove, Sophy knew, of the promiscuous bathing. She didn't disapprove, but the sight made her afraid for Jill, as if it was a signal from the kind of life Jill had now, which Sophy couldn't imagine: initiated into goodness knows what, in London with Tom. Sophy thought that she had not looked directly for a long time at any adult's nakedness, not her husband's, rarely even her own. Snapping out a sheet, ironed into its perfect squares, over the bed in Jill's room, she was startled by catching sight of an old woman – clothed, thankfully – in the dressing-table mirror: tall, and so thin she seemed made like old bentwood furniture, with all the colour leached out of her, even out of her eyes. The giveaway slippery liver-dark mouth was ugly with doubt, Sophy thought, and the surprising upstanding crest of her hair made her look like an affronted bird: she forgot sometimes to put in the hairgrips to tame it.

When the baby and Roland had been put to bed, and Hettie was reading in the drawing room with her grandmother, Jill paced around the bedrooms in the dusk, in her stocking feet, drying the rope of her hair in a towel. The fresh smell of the fields at evening came in at the windows, tugging at her. It was unexpected to find that leaving a man was not chaste or nun-like; on the contrary, it seemed to have a smouldering sexual content. She looked out from her parents' room at the alders stirring beside the river, heard the water hurrying on with that low-key urgent restlessness which sounded like rain when you woke to it in the night; her reflection surprised her in the mirror of the monumental wardrobe, she looked impatiently away. This reprieve was what she had longed for when she felt trapped and half-crazy, alone with the children in the flat in London, eking out the days with trips to the park, or with visiting friends – the friends had been no solace because she hadn't told them what was happening with Tom, hadn't wanted their opinions or their advice. All her rage and unhappiness and heightened excitement, over the past weeks, had focused in her longing to get home, as if that was a solution. But now she was actually in Kington, she seemed still to be waiting for something else, the next thing.

By the time her father returned the children were all in bed, and Jill had changed into a clean blouse and skirt. — You'll never guess who's here, she heard her mother say in the hall, helping him off with his coat. He strode into the drawing room with an exasperated low hum, resenting the intrusion of visitors, preparing his patience, tightening the belt on the flapping black gown which Tom derided as vanity and pantomime. Grantham Fellowes was small, austerely thin, his skin tanned and burned as dark as old leather. His cheeks and his eye sockets were sculptured pits; above a high naked forehead his thick hair was pure white, and light as down. Tom said Grantham cultivated this look, of a medieval Saint Jerome – or a fake, Pre-Raphaelite, copy of one. Jill was aware of making her own striking picture, sitting with her clean hair loose in the lamplight and a book open on her knee – though in truth she hadn't been reading it, she couldn't concentrate. There was deception in her composure but that was a good thing, she preferred to present him with an impermeable surface, her performance of an accomplished, fulfilled self. She could imagine spilling over in confidences to her mother, but couldn't bear the idea of her father's knowing yet about her failure, and judging it.

— Isn't this lovely? Sophy said.

The surprise put him for a moment at a disadvantage. — Charlie! To what do we owe this unexpected honour?

— Just a whim, Jill said. — Hello, Daddy.

Charlie was his name for her in the days when they went around everywhere together and she had wanted to be a boy; he had started her off on Latin and ancient history while she was still in junior school, taught her elementary botany on their long walks – she had never complained when her legs were tired. She had gone with him into estate cottages without running water or electricity, where old men or women lay sick or dying; once it was a young man whose chest had been crushed by falling straw bales, and whose mother wanted him to pray, though he wouldn't look at the minister. He had turned his head away, gargling and blowing bright terrible bubbles of blood which stained the dirty pillowcase; someone had hurried Jill out before she saw too much, although she already had. Her father had worn himself out campaigning to improve the living conditions of the rural workers, though he never identified with them, and wasn't much loved – his manner was too distant, he didn't know how to put uneducated people at ease. In his poems he wrote about them sometimes as if they were insentient features of the landscape, like old stones or trees. He had a vision of a simple Christian community, toughened by hardship and contact with harsh natural law; he couldn't sympathise when the country people wanted televisions and refrigerators. Now, with the mechanisation of the farms, so many were leaving the countryside to look for work in the cities; his congregation was mostly old women and a few incomers, retirees. Jill knew that he embraced this new turn of his fate as a comic irony, scourge of his pride.

IT WAS ABSOLUTELY DARK IN the bedroom the three children shared, yet in Hettie, lying in bed with her eyes strained open onto nothing, every sense was anxiously alert to the difference from home. Even the dark was different: in Marylebone a street lamp diffused its orange glow into their room so that she could always make out the hump of Roly in his bed – he slept bottom up, with his face in his pillow – and the bars of the baby's cot casting a weak shadow on the wall. There, the headlights of cars passing crossed the ceiling in a deliciously, mysteriously purposeful slow arc; the night was always full of voices from the London street below.

Darkness in Kington was as dense as a hand clapped over her face, and her grandmother's cool sheets smelled disconcertingly of lavender. At home Jill hardly had time to wash their sheets, let alone iron them, and Hettie had grown used to burrowing each night into the crumpled cloth smelling of herself, her dribble and biscuit crumbs and salty hair. Something barked in the woods: a fox, or a wolf? There was so much empty silence in the country that each sound seemed significant in ways Hettie couldn't learn to understand; her dad didn't understand them either. Jill knew the names of all the flowers and could recognise the birds by their songs; when Tom said he didn't care, Hettie was reprieved, and hid away the I-Spy books of the countryside which were the record of her shame, hardly ticked at all. She preferred the wild animals in London zoo, safe behind bars and identified straightforwardly by the labels on their cages, which she was beginning to be able to read.

For a while she lay tormented and sorry for herself, needing to pee, disappointed in her body as she had been on the bus when she knew she would be sick. Eventually, swinging her legs from under the blankets, she slid down the side of the bed until her feet touched the bare boards of the floor, feeling with her toes for the rug: it occurred to her in a clutch of terror that in this darkness reality could be making and unmaking itself dizzily, unforeseen precipices opening ahead of her which were not there when she got into bed. Cautiously, she felt her way around by the wall – Ali stirred in the cot when she knocked against it, and made lip-smacking noises. At least Hettie could discern, once she was out from the bedroom – in a dim light escaping from wherever the grown-ups were talking downstairs – the looming perspectival shapes of so many doors, open and closed, to so many rooms fearfully unused, full with their emptiness. A blue-black sky showed in the uncurtained arched windows at either end of the landing. In the bathroom she peed and rubbed the hard toilet paper between her hands as her mother had showed her, till it was soft enough to use, then pulled the momentous long chain. On the windowsill ends of old soap were dissolving in a jam jar of gloopy water; her grandfather used these to wash his hair, it was one of the funny stories Daddy told about his meanness. Coming out onto the landing again, Hettie was quite blind, after the light in the bathroom.

Jill's voice rang out downstairs, overbearing the murmurings of Granny and Grandfather. – Having the time of his life, she said. – *Vive les étudiants! À bas le C.R.S.*

Hettie had no idea why her mother was speaking in an unknown language, or what her father was doing, but thought her grandfather might make some cutting comment. She was anxiously wary of Grandfather's disapproval on behalf of all her family – Roland because he was fussy over his food, the baby with her clamour and clutching fat fingers, though in fact he was tolerant of these sticky fingers, he liked Ali. Hettie had been drawn fatally, on certain occasions in the past, into the bad behaviour that brought a pained distaste onto her grandfather's face; the more coldly he withdrew his attention, the more insanely she had tried to attract it, dissolving into tantrums and extremes of silliness which she feared he hadn't forgotten. At least there was always Granny, who could be counted on to love you – though consequently Hettie rated her grandmother's approval slightly less.

Tiptoeing in the dark along the landing, she didn't want to climb back into her reproachful lavender-bed. In her mother's room the curtains weren't drawn across and the window was pulled up a few inches, letting in the shock of ripe night air, as cold as water. By touch Hettie identified the familiar loved items unpacked onto the dressing table: hairbrush, face cream, scent bottle. A little lamp with a short chrome neck offered an irresistible upright press-switch in its base; she pressed, and the room sprang into satisfying being, with her mother's library book, Margaret Drabble, and its postcard-marker, and her mother's spare shoes, and the coat in her mother's shape on its hanger. Hettie breathed *L'Air du Temps* on her fingers, and longed to slip for warmth into the insulated space between the pink satin eiderdown and the top blanket; it was so perfect, when she tried it, that she closed her eyes in bliss. Jill woke her later, coming to bed and cross. — In the country when you put on the light at night, she said, — you must make sure the windows are closed first. Look at all the bugs that have come in.

Hettie thought guiltily that she must still be dreaming: the walls of the room were crowded with blundering moth-shadows, looming and receding. — I lost my way. I came in your room by mistake, it's too dark here at night.

Her mother was implacable about returning her to her own bed.
— You're my big girl, Hettie. You have to be sensible.

JILL LEFT THE CHILDREN WITH her mother the next day and caught the bus into town: one ran from the village every morning, returning in the early afternoon. She needed things from the shops – food, zinc ointment for the baby's nappy rash, Tampax. And she had business there too which she didn't mention to her mother: she called in at the estate agents, to make enquiries about properties available to rent locally. It was strange to be back in these streets sodden with familiarity, and it was the first time in weeks – in months even – that she had been anywhere alone. Without the pushchair and the children hanging on to her she was weightlessly afloat. The estate agent she spoke to was someone she had known from primary school; she and he had been set apart together in the little gang of clever ones who would pass the eleven plus. Big-limbed and blushing, he looked displaced now in his poky office, but must have chosen it in preference to a life on the family farm – for the past's sake, Jill felt tenderly towards his freckled pink wrist, clumsy in his clean shirt-cuff. She was aware of putting on a performance as married and sophisticated; she had pinned up her hair in front of the mirror that morning and now she flaunted her wedding ring, crossing her legs conspicuously in their slippery nylon tights under her short skirt. It was important to convince them all that she was sane and worldly, even as she made crazy plans to manage by herself.

— My husband has to travel a lot for work, she said. — If we rented somewhere down here, I could be closer to my parents, my mother could help with the children.

When they shook hands he called her Mrs Crane, and asked if he should send through details of any new properties that came up – but Jill didn't want her parents to know what her plans were, not yet. — Don't bother to post them, she said, smiling, charming him. — I'll call in here whenever I'm in town.

She had time, when she'd finished shopping, for a coffee at The Bungalow on the high street. Tom would despise The Bungalow, where the fake beams were festooned with horse collars and horse brasses, there were plastic flowers in the vases, and the elderly waitresses – wizened, she imagined him calling them – wore black dresses and white organdie aprons with starched frills.

A friend of Sophy's at another table – Women's Institute, tennis – waved to Jill, she waved back. I could live here, all the same, she thought. Because life is just life; I can choose to belong anywhere. Who's to say all our radical friends in London are right, with their condemnations? You live how you can.

Reading through the details the estate agent had given her, she was exultant with self-sufficiency, though she didn't see anything that fitted in the least with her idea – her old schoolmate, not knowing her, had chosen all the modern horrors for her, little boxes new-built on the edge of town, which in any case she couldn't afford. What she dreamed of was somewhere on the edge of social life, where she could be free, not cluttered with falsity. She didn't really know how much she had to spend, except that it was next to nothing – even if Tom sent her half his money, which he would very likely refuse to do. In London she had been getting copy-editing work from a couple of publishers, but she didn't think they'd go on using her if she moved away. Recklessly she ate a buttered teacake, then ordered another one. These past awful weeks, she had gone days forgetting almost to eat; now she was wildly hungry and thirsty.

Sophy's friend – gaunt and powdered and faintly arty, with dangling earrings – stopped on her way out, to ask yearningly after the London theatres. She said she always looked out for Tom's articles, he was so clever. — Sophy didn't mention she was expecting you. Are you staying long? She'll be so happy to have you home. Isn't it term time? Harriet must have started school by now.

Suavely Jill explained something about the children having had feverish colds, needing to recuperate in the country air. Because she was the vicar's daughter, she'd learned to lie from an early age, not caring much if anyone believed her, so long as she firmly deflected further enquiry. When she paid for her teacakes and coffee she found that her mother had slipped a ten-shilling note into her purse – half-infuriating, but useful. Sophy was full of these secret charities, pre-empting you, accomplished with a little shy fuss like a quiver of nerves. Dawdling on her way to the bus stop, Jill saw a card in the wool shop window, advertising for part-time staff, and on an impulse she went inside, not caring who was watching. She didn't recognise the woman who took down her details. The manageress wasn't in today – perhaps Jill could call in again on Monday?

Jill could tell this woman didn't think she was at all the right type for selling wool, with her short skirt and eye make-up and patrician condescending accent – whereas the idea thrilled Jill perversely, to end up here, with her first class in Greats from Oxford. Eagerly she insisted that she could knit, was skilled in knitting: which was perfectly true. She had knitted such lovely things before Hettie was born, including a shawl in 2-ply off-white lambswool, as subtle as a cobweb, in a complicated leaf pattern. She had had a job, while she was pregnant, on reception at a publisher's, and when she wasn't enlisted for tying up parcels of books, had striven away on her needles through long empty hours. The matinee jackets and bootees in the wool shop window – in brash strawberry nylon, and yellow and vermilion – weren't anything like the tasteful old-fashioned things that she had made. She had imagined that motherhood was going to be dreamy and delicately absorbed like her knitting: then all the pretty clothes she'd prepared had turned out to be so wildly beside the point, in the days of shock and violence – as she thought of them – which began with the arrival of the actual baby. The dainty wool vests and cardigans had quickly become matted and tight with washing, and anyway they had given Hettie a rash – and she had outgrown them in a few weeks. Jill had only ever imagined her baby, in advance, as a tiny, wistful, curled-up creature-thing.

THE VICAR WAS AWAY FOR the day at a diocesan meeting and Sophy found Roland in his study, staring into a leather-bound book open across his scabby knees: Herodotus in the original, as it turned out. She stored this up as a funny story to report to Jill; then, in a second impulse of protective tact, decided to keep it to herself. Jill these days seemed to make a joke out of everything, including her children – she believed it was better to jolly them along and not indulge them. Sophy quailed occasionally at her daughter's brittle, brave performance; Jill had mentioned already, as if it was funny, that Roland was slow at learning his letters. – He's a sweetheart, but he isn't Einstein, she had cheerfully said. He was holding Herodotus the right way up, anyhow, and turned the pages with great care, seeming really to be peering closely at the words. His small, intent face was brown and neat as a nut, wrenching his grandmother, and the silky hair curled tight on his skull like a black lamb's. He told her he was reading Grandfather's book.

– How interesting, darling. What is it about?

– All sorts of things, Granny. They can't be said, because I can only read it with my mind.

– Of course, that's very natural, I'm the same way.

– But what is thinking?

Sophy pushed away the idea of those absences of hers, when she sank into deep water: did they count as thought? – I suppose it is a kind of work, she said. – You can feel it in going on in your brain, when you're understanding things. For instance when you're reading words in a book, trying to find out what they mean. This book is in Greek, of course, so Granny can't read it: but your mummy can, and your grandfather.

– And I can.

Roland twitched his nose when he looked up, to keep his glasses in place, with a backwards jerk of his head like a little old man. Sophy blamed this new habit, which distressed her, on the glasses mended lumpily with sticking plaster, which must be a blot in the corner of his vision. At the first opportunity she would take him into Corrigan's, for a real repair. She mentioned it as soon as Jill arrived home off the bus, her basket piled high with shopping – and of course Jill took it as a criticism, although she was in buoyant spirits and forgave her mother easily. – Don't you think I've had them repaired ten times already? He'll only break them again right away. And old Corrigan's creepy, he used to put his hand on my knee. But if you want to, I don't care.

Jill's beauty was startling that afternoon, with her hair pinned up and something scalded and raw in her young face: Sophy had to turn her eyes away from it. She didn't have the refinement of either of her parents, with her straight long nose, lean animal jaw, big lazy mouth, her golden colouring suffused across the cheeks with a rough pink. – I can't believe how everything in town is just the same. I knew everyone. I bumped into Mikey Waller – he's working as an estate agent, did you know? And Ailsa was in The Bungalow. Thank you for the ten shillings. I felt like a schoolgirl on a treat, and ate two teacakes and bought iced buns for everyone.

– Hurrah, hurrah! Hettie shouted, picking up on her mother's mood. She had been tranquil all morning while Jill was away, filling in her colouring book at the kitchen table.

– Ailsa's always in The Bungalow, Sophy said. – No wonder she's jumpy, it's all that coffee she drinks.

– Innocent dear Mummy, Ailsa's drink problem isn't *coffee*.

Sophy frowned across the children's heads and shook her head just perceptibly; alertly Hettie caught it, looking from her grandmother to her mother and back again. – Who is Ailsa? she demanded. – And what *is* her drink problem?

Jill laughed and wouldn't tell her, then when Hettie loudly

persisted she lost her temper, smacking Hettie smartly across the back of the legs. — No iced bun for you!

Hettie's screams awoke the baby early from her nap, and Sophy thought of that flat in Marylebone, where they were all on top of one another. None of this fraught chaos of childcare had seemed to arise when Jill was a child herself. No doubt it was easier with only one – and anyway Jill had been serene from the moment she was born: commanding and forceful, but never naughty. Sophy hadn't realised perhaps how peculiar their family was, with a child who was her parents' easy companion, entering all the concerns of their adult lives: parish war work, the Tennis Club, Latin and Greek and poetry. This childhood seemed even odder in the light of Jill's adult life – she had disavowed her parents' style so wholeheartedly.

Sophy's own experience, she thought, hardly counted as motherhood at all – she had missed out on something more boisterous and transforming. Probably as an adult she had been too childish. Jill was right, she was an innocent – and that was awful. Though she did know about Ailsa. No doubt there were things in Jill's and Tom's life together which made it harder to include children. When Tom played with his children they had great fun, he rolled round on the floor with them, roaring like a bear – but he was quickly bored, and away too often. Poor Jill had to make up the rules for their family life all by herself. And Sophy saw that the children were bruised sometimes by their mother's power, which could be inconsistent and capricious. She thought that Jill adored her son too openly, and was too hard on little Hettie.

JILL TOOK THE CHILDREN INTO the woods to eat their buns: even Hettie, when she'd apologised, was allowed to have one. They spread a rug among the bluebells – which were over, darkened and shrivelled on their stems – and Jill poured out plastic beakers of orange squash. Dwarfed by the woods' tall spaciousness, the children were very calm: the smooth trunks of the birch trees soared up all around them and over their heads the branches broke out in young leaves, tender as scraps of soft cloth caught in the twigs. Out of sight of other adults, Jill let her prickly irony lapse as if it was exhausting. Her children knew this and they loved to be alone with her. Ali stuffed her mouth determinedly with leaf mould and they gave up trying to prevent her: it was only earth after all, as Roland reassured his mother. Colours were clean in the watery light, small birds scuffled in the undergrowth, a wood pigeon took off from time to time, its disruption startling as gunshot. Behind the stillness they felt the surge of spring, pressing everything forwards.

After their picnic Hettie and Roland ran on along the path through the trees, while Jill let the baby stagger at her own pace, in her leading reins, pausing to bend over unsteadily like a stout old gentleman, picking up litter so daintily between two fingertips: a lolly stick, sweet wrapper, cigarette end, all dropped long ago and weathered to the same brown as the woods. Jill had changed out of her heels into a pair of flip-flops she found in the scullery; every so often, to catch up with the others, she slipped out of these and ran barefoot, carrying the flip-flops hooked over a finger, the baby bouncing and hiccoughing with laughter on her hip. She thought she'd take the children to call on the old couple who lived in a lonely cottage perched on a bend in the path, with a well in the garden and a view down through the trees into a secluded valley. They'd called here before, and Mrs Good had given sweets to Hettie – she had given them to Jill too, when she was a child, and Jill had always thanked her politely, then carried them home to bury them guiltily in the vicarage dustbin. She couldn't remember now what she'd been afraid of. Poison perhaps, as if they were sweets in a fairy tale, because of the old lady's name and the equivocal position of the cottage, set apart from the village community.

When they arrived at the cottage and knocked on the door, there seemed to be no one at home. All the windows were on the inaccessible back wall, overhanging the valley below, so they couldn't peer inside; Roland tried the door handle and was taken aback when the door swung open. Stepping halfway across the threshold into the tiny single room on the ground floor, Jill called out in case anyone was lying sick or in trouble upstairs. The silence and stillness inside the cottage was a shock after the perpetual movement outdoors; this air hadn't been stirred for long hours – or days perhaps. Even the light was stale. She felt she'd intruded on something forbidden. The dishes on the painted dresser and rug in front of the hearth communicated the home's emptiness, presided over by the religious pictures on the walls: Jesus was sorrowfully reproachful, or had a lantern and a lost lamb tucked under his arm. The Goods were a remnant of the Bible Christians, who once had a great following among the farm workers.

Jill called out again for Mrs Good, and then when no one responded was relieved to get out of the cottage, pulling the door shut quickly behind her, choosing not to explore upstairs. Roland asked her what she'd seen inside.

— Nothing at all. Just the ordinary inside of a house, when the people are out somewhere.

THERE WAS A MESSAGE WAITING for Jill when they arrived home, sent round from the Smiths who owned Roddings, the biggest and oldest farm in the village, and had a telephone. Tom had called her and left a number he could be contacted on, if she rang him at nine that evening. Mrs Smith had written it out in a fat schoolbook hand, in purple indelible pencil, on notepaper headed with an advertisement for a dairy – a cow kicking up her heels, jumping over a moon.

Jill frowned at it, suspicious. — So is this a Paris number?

The outrage of him: sending his instructions, dictating that she should arrange her life around his convenience. She wouldn't call, anyway. He could sit and wait, expecting the phone to ring, and it wouldn't. Let him have a taste of that.

Peering at the number, Sophy worried. — What do you think?

— It's rather important because of the time difference. I don't think it's Paris, it's not long enough. I think it's London. He wouldn't have thought to take the Smiths' number away with him, he must be back at the flat. I'm surprised he remembered where I wrote it down. By the way, what's happened to the Goods? We went to the cottage and their door was unlocked, but no one was home.

Sophy was vague, her mind was still on Tom. — It shouldn't be unlocked. We ought to see to that. There's a niece who might want things. Didn't I write to you? He died just before Christmas, she went into a Home, poor old thing. Daddy calls on her but she won't see him, she has some rather eccentric religious convictions. I don't know what will happen to the house. No one will live there, without running water.

Jill said that all religious convictions were eccentric, including Daddy's. Her mother was unperturbed. — Well, mine are the most eccentric of all. If you knew the half of the funny things that I have faith in. Just don't start any theological arguments with your father before he's finished supper. He forgets to eat, if he's enjoying himself.

— Oh, you're an old pagan, Jill said. — I know all about that. You're a disgrace to the Church.

She was burning up all the time, with consciousness of Tom's call: it roused her again to that exhilarated anger she'd felt in those last weeks in London, and to those heights of cheerful dissimulation. Whose number was it he had given her? It wasn't his office. Perhaps some other woman's place? He demeaned her and she repudiated out of her exceptional soul the cliché of the old wrong, would not allow sex-jealousy to be the explanation for her leaving. And how dare he presume that she wanted to speak to him?

Yet a few minutes before nine o'clock – the children were all asleep – Jill slipped out of the house in the dark as if under some compulsion, to go to the phone box in the village. Her father was working on his sermon, Sophy was sitting at her bureau, writing to old schoolfriends: Jill didn't want their awareness accompanying her. It was a relief to duck down the stone steps at the front, into the chilly damp under the privet hedge, hearing the voice from the wireless carry on indoors, blithely assured, without her. Moonlight seeped around the edges of a mass of cloud. Sophy had left shillings and sixpences piled up discreetly beside Jill's purse, and she didn't notice how tightly she was gripping them until her fingers ached. Her hate-tryst consumed her, she was bent upon it, aimed in her entirety at the lit-up phone box and its dank sealed-in air, the furtive importance of fumbling in her pocket for the number, the burr in the heavy receiver, the suspenseful moment of waiting, reading over the framed instructions and advertisements in the kiosk without seeing them. Two worlds – here, and elsewhere – were steered into collision.

Tom made a mistake when he answered the phone. She knew him! He would have planned to snatch it up as soon as she rang, and greet her gravely, intimately. But for a moment he'd lost concentration, and forgotten: probably he was reading something he'd picked up while he waited, or scribbling an idea. So he answered the phone in a breezy light voice, without thinking, as he did at the office. — Tom Crane?

She almost laughed.

He changed his voice then hastily, to growly and low, troubled. — Jill, is it you?

— Where are you? she said. — Whose number is this? I don't care: only I need to know.

— Bernie's. I'm staying here. Can't stand being in that flat without you.

— You'll get used to it.

Did she believe him, that he was at Bernie's? His silence tried to be reproachful, but he wasn't very good at silence. — Everything's changed, Jilly. You'd feel differently if you'd seen what I've seen. There's no way things are going to go back to how they were, not after this. Listen, I'll stay with the children at home for a few days and you can go over there, be part of it. I don't mind at all.

— Go over where? she asked coldly. — Oh, you mean Paris. I'd forgotten about Paris. No, I've no desire to go there.

— It's crazy, I'm telling you. The courage of those kids! The police have clubs and gas bombs: they've brought in reservists from Brittany – country boys, reactionary nationalists. Someone said that they're getting rid of bodies in the Seine. And people in the apartments throw down chocolate and *saucisson* for the students, bring them out coffee. The bourgeois drive into the *quartier* from the suburbs on quiet nights, sightseeing, taking photos of themselves on the barricades. Three million joined the march protesting at the police repression. I stood up on a traffic island and I saw a river of them, running all the way down the Boul' Saint-Mich and out of sight. Do you know what they chanted? *Nous sommes tous des juifs allemands* – because of Cohn-Bendit, the authorities threatening to deport him. Isn't that beautiful?

— Three million sounds unlikely. The whole population of Paris is only eight and a half.

Jill knew how he hated her when she was flattening. She was like her father then, with his superior knowledge like a trap snapping shut. — I heard they're cutting down the trees, she said. — The lovely old plane trees of Paris. They won't grow again in a hurry.

Sententiously Tom said that this wasn't a time to be worrying about trees.

— It'll be too late to worry about them afterwards. Anyway, what did you want? You left a message asking me to call.

He changed to the low-toned, coaxing voice he used when he wanted to make love to her. — Just to talk to you, Jilly. I wanted to hear you speak. Listen, I need you. I can't live without you and the children. When are you coming back? You're making a big fuss about a little thing. It was nothing, what happened with Vanda. She drives me nuts, she's stupid, I don't even like her. You're the one, Jilly. You're the only one who understands all this. I miss you so much. I need you.

Jill didn't say anything. She coiled and uncoiled the flex of the phone restlessly around her left hand and held the receiver with her chin against her shoulder, stretching her neck as if her shoulders ached, pressing her back against the heavy door of the phone box until it opened under her weight, letting in the night air. She hardly knew that she watched the barn owl pass, weightless-seeming as a drift of chiffon against the gloom. Luxuriantly she listened to her husband. She didn't want him back. But still, she wanted to hear this, she couldn't help herself. When he fell quiet eventually, listening to her, trying to gauge what meaning there was for him in her silence, she put the receiver back in its metal cradle, cutting him off.

TWO

——

ON SUNDAY MORNING the baby woke up early. Jill was hauled out of her own deep sleep by the creak of the wooden cot as Ali climbed over its side, for the first time. After a pause – for sheer surprise, perhaps, at this brand new freedom, so easily attained – purposeful little steps came padding out onto the landing, then, after a hesitation, along towards Jill's room. Jill was aware of calculating irresponsibly – in exchange for a few seconds more of warmth in bed – that if Ali could climb out of her cot, then she could navigate safely past the top of the stairs. The door of the bedroom was pushed tentatively open and Ali stopped on the threshold, in her sagging night-nappy and the blue pyjamas patterned with yachts that had belonged to Roland. She was staring solemnly, as if she wasn't sure what she might find, in a world no one had prepared for her. Jill couldn't help laughing at the round eyes and fat flushed cheeks: Ali's fair hair was so fine that it hardly counted, she looked bald as an egg. She laughed back at her mother in pure pleasure.

— What do you think you're doing, naughty? Why aren't you in your cot?

Jill slipped out of bed then, to snatch the baby up and kiss her, scolding her in whispers, then listen at the door and quietly close it. As long as Ali hadn't woken up the others, if Jill changed her nappy now and she had her morning bottle of milk – kept ready overnight on the dressing table – there was even a chance of her falling asleep again. Ali was the doziest and easiest of her three babies. With Hettie she had tried too hard to establish a routine, as the books instructed; Roland had frightened her with infantile convulsions.

— It's still night-time, little chicken. You can have your bottle in bed with Mummy if you'll go back to sleep. Shut your eyes now.

Jill held her in the crook of her arm, nestled under the blankets and eiderdown. At first Ali kept her eyes resolutely open as she sucked: brilliant with the joke of the whole occasion, fixed on her mother. When her grin spread irresistibly her mouth slid off the rubber teat of the bottle, milk trickling at its corner. Eventually the heavy eyes fell shut, flicked open, drooped again. Jill put the bottle on the bedside table and tried to go back to sleep herself. The sleeping baby was pressed close along the contours of her own body, burning with her heat, wispy hair blowing in her breath, the stuffy milky smell in her own nose – but in the hollow of her thoughts she was agitated and noisy, full of her argument with Tom as she hadn't been when she went to bed. She saw things with finality in the grey light which developed inexorably around the heavy furniture in the room. From henceforward, she thought, he and she were fated to be enemies, set opposite each other at their different poles of experience. Once, they had been equal in their separate freedoms. They had set out to have children as lightly as if they were playing house, and now her necessarily domestic life bored him, and she was bound to it in her body and imagination. This imbalance was fated, built into their biology.

Jill was afraid for her free self, as if she saw a young woman receding on a road in the far distance. What use was her grown-up knowledge – acquired through such initiations, at such risk – in this world of infants, who had to be kept safe? Tom had said once that anyone could do motherhood: in fact, he added, the less complicated you were, the better mother you would make. This was probably true, but not consoling. The whole silly, flirting, furtive episode with Vanda was enraging just because it was so lightweight and shouldn't have mattered – Tom went ducking and wincing with infuriating flexibility through his obligations, while Jill's humiliation weighed her down. She thought about the Goods' cottage in the woods. Perhaps she could find another kind of freedom, if she lived there. Looking out of those windows day after day, seeing nothing human, only the shifting screens of leaves between her and the sky – what a simplification! Drifting into sleep, she imagined a life alone in those tiny rooms, alone with the children.

SOPHY LOOKED AFTER THE BABY while Jill went to church with the older children. Hettie and Roland felt as if they followed another mother when Jill led the way, in her coat and a hat – a pretty, neat, blue hat, borrowed from Granny, with a feather tucked into its blue ribbon – holding up a big umbrella over all of them against the drizzle. They processed through the keyhole gap between their garden and the churchyard which was their privilege, when all the rest of the congregation had to come in by the church gate. This other mother was more like the ones in books, stricter and yet more poised and equable than her everyday self, more remote. Inside the church Jill always knew confidently what to do, carrying off the mysterious act in such bold style, standing up and sitting down and kneeling even before anyone else did, singing hymns in a strong voice, hardly glancing at the words in the hymn book. They children felt their own disgrace as pagan city-dwellers, fumbling and mumbling their lame way after her. Roland after a while gave up pretending, preferring to stare into the church calmly in silence as if he'd got its measure. He attended to his grandfather's sermon, about Hope, with detached interest. When his mother's fingertips – seeming moved by an awareness quite separate to her own steadied attention to her father – strayed across his warm scalp, among his curls, he shifted away just perceptibly, not wanting the church to catch them out in any absence.

At least Hettie did know the Lord's Prayer. She had learned it at school, and Granny had given them a Ladybird book which was an illustrated version. A dense passage in the middle wound around the trespasses whose very sound – *as we forgive those who trespass against us* – was vexed and bristling, and which were disconcerting morally because you might, Hettie had puzzled out, both inflict them and have them inflicted upon you. She was drawn to those pictures in shamed fascination: a boy put his hand in wet paint where his father was decorating, but it was his sister who had broken the boy's toys, an aeroplane and a crane. Faces were stark with outrage and guilt and hurt. This moral ambiguity was associated, in Hettie's vision, with the building of the church itself, whose stone shape, pierced with glass, soared upwards and yet remained where you could always smell damp earth beneath you. The great Gurney stove, with its iron fins spread like the fanned pages of a book, only ever gave out the faintest indication of heat: her grandparents despaired of it and the parish couldn't afford to buy a new one, so no wonder the hymn books grew mouldy. In the coldest weather they plugged in an electric fire. The altar cloth their grandmother had sewn was the only sumptuous thing in the grave, undecorated place: yellow-haired angels blasted something against cream satin on long trumpets, turning their faces away from the stubby huge nails which they held out as if to prove something. *You see?* These nails looked like the fat wax crayons at school.

The congregation were few and mostly female, not young; distinctive – even if you also knew them as their weekday informal selves – in their padded, sculpted, decisive Sunday clothes, pinned-on hats or tied headscarves. If you were ever seized, to be embraced against a lapel pinned with a scratching brooch, these clothes gave off an odour of something chemical and hostile. Church was a place set apart, Hettie saw, for what in the everyday world had to be muffled and passed over. Death, for instance, was not dissimulated in the memorials on the walls or the floor of the church, any more than on the graves outside: she had been shocked when she first learned to make out what these matter-of-fact dates meant, attached to each name. It was no surprise that their father never came inside here. Hettie thought that he was against death, and all the burden of importance surrounding it. When the congregation gave themselves up to silent prayer, their mother sank her head impressively on her arms on the pew in front, and Roland sat open-eyed, looking around him. Hettie could hear rain buffeting against the church outside, beating on the roof, running down the window-glass, enclosing the still interior in its successive, insistent washes of soft sound.

AT SUNDAY LUNCH TRADITIONALLY, AFTER he'd delivered his sermon, the minster drank a decent wine. He poured for his wife and daughter while Sophy dished up steaming bowls of watery vegetables in the kitchen, passing them through the serving hatch after the roast chicken which was their treat because they had visitors. Jill had begun cutting chicken breast up into morsels for the baby, who was tied into her bib in Jill's old high chair, pounding her spoon cheerfully in her fist.

— Charlie wore the shortest skirt that's been seen in my church, her father said, teasing. — It won't have gone unnoticed.

Jill shrugged. — It's all I brought to wear.

— He doesn't mind, Sophy explained, calling through the hatch. — He likes it. He wishes the church was full of young women in short skirts.

— But don't tell the Bishop, Grantham said.

The atmosphere in the vicarage was exuberant, because the sermon was done for a week and because their daughter was home. Sophy laughed in the kitchen, as if she'd drunk her wine already.

Because Grantham Fellowes had been beautiful when he was young – and despised that, even as he took for granted the power it conferred – he had never lost the habit of commanding a room. A great deal of his spiritual agony had come out of his circular pursuit of his own vanity, which he thought was only intellectual arrogance, not noticing how women yielded to his physical presence, basking in it – and some men too – and how he responded with unthinking entitlement. Only Sophy didn't flutter, among the little group of middle-class women huddled around him in the parish, whom he mostly treated fairly badly, *de haut en bas*. A few of the men hated him. His face now was brown as wood, chiselled with deep trenches, assertively and shamelessly old – he was seventy, and perhaps looked older. Yet still there was something jaunty and haughty in the slanting bones and far-off blue of the small eyes, eloquent with all the punishment he'd inflicted on himself. Jill was susceptible to changes in her father's expression, as if his moods were fastened into her awareness, tugging at her, although she had set her back to him years ago, and sailed in a contrary direction.

When he had carved, they passed around the gravy boat and discussed the sermon. — I knew what it meant, Roland said. — When you hope for something you might get something else instead, which is more useful.

His grandfather was gratified. — From the pulpit I was aware of those sceptical specs, trained on me in critical scrutiny. The boy really was listening! Well done, Childe Roland.

— And I was listening, said Hettie.

— You were a little fidget, her mother said, — twisting your head around to stare at everything.

— I heard it, Hettie said, looking around the table defiantly, trying to be funny, eyes glassy in her flushed, hasty little face. — Grandfather's sermon about a nasty old mouldy-warp.

— An old mouldy-warp, darling? Sophy was bemused and pleased. — I'm sorry I missed that one!

— Take no notice, Jill said. — She's only showing off, talking nonsense. Can't bear anyone else to have the limelight.

— *Forgiver us from evil. For thine is the daily bread.*

— There you are, you see, said Sophy. — She was listening.

— Not very carefully.

The minister had finished the small portion on his plate. Overlooking Hettie's performance, he spooned chopped carrots into the baby's mouth. Even Ali felt his condescension, working the orange mass around in her jaw obediently, dumbstruck. — And what's your opinion, Roland? he asked. — Do we just have to make the best of this useful thing we never hoped for in the first place? Or is that pusillanimous?

Roland was shovelling vegetables with his knife and fork: his mother had warned him that he had to eat them. — Pusillanimity, she added quickly, — is not doing something because you're afraid of it.

Roland considered, twitching his glasses into position. — It would depend on what you got, he said. — The thing you got instead of what you wanted. Whether it really was any use.

His grandfather gave a bark of laughter, approving; his grandmother relieved Roland of his cabbage when no one was looking. Jill knew that her father wanted her praise for his sermon now – and in fact when she had been sitting listening to him, contained inside his voice, in the stark little church washed with wet light that was the core of her childhood and her past, his words had unbound an overwhelming emotion inside her. Putting her head on her arms to pray, she had been afraid for a few moments of falling out of her own control, collapsing to the stone floor or heaving with unseemly sobs – terribly un-Anglican. Grantham had based the sermon on a short Herbert poem, 'Hope'. The limpid, measured words of this poem, and her father's judicious explication of it, had seemed in their moment sufficient to her experience: everything outside them was obliterated. It was peculiar, as she had been so moved, how reluctant she was now for her father to know it.

— What the poet wants, she said to Roland, — is a ring. But God won't send it.

— Why a *ring?* Hettie asked, too loudly, but genuinely bemused. She would like to own a ring herself, but couldn't imagine a man wanting one.

Jill made strong efforts, overcoming her own contrary will. — You were good, Daddy. It was a beautiful sermon.

She'd have been the only one in the church, Grantham pointed out with sour irony, to recognise the Herbert. He always shook praise off like this, as if it was below the mark he aimed at; yet his wife and daughter knew from experience how he hungered for it, and was capable of sulking if it wasn't forthcoming. Tom thought he was all vanity, and wouldn't listen to Jill when she said vanity didn't matter, it existed in a separate part of the self to writing. Anyway, weren't all writers vain?

— Didn't you choose the poem, Sophy suggested enthusiastically, — just because Jill was staying with us?

Grantham disdained this with a little moue of irritation. — I base any number of my sermons on poetry, with no expectation of anybody noticing.

Carefully, Sophy ate a cold mouthful of cabbage. She loved poems but easily forgot them, and she only half-listened to her husband's sermons anyway. This wasn't exactly because she wasn't interested. But part of the oddity of marriage, she thought, was in how unwise it was to attend too intently to the other person. This was the opposite to what she had naively imagined, as a girl. To the unmarried, it seemed that a couple must be intimately, perpetually exposed to each other – but actually, that wasn't bearable. In order for love to survive, you had to close yourself off to a certain extent.

THE CARD HAD GONE FROM the window of the wool shop when Jill was next in town, and when she went inside, the manageress – bustling and bland with thick lipstick, her spectacles inset with little chips of cut glass – hastened up to explain herself. It was obvious that Jill's interest in the job had caused some consternation, and that a pale new girl, with nervous rabbit eyes, had been manoeuvred into place behind the till, to forestall the embarrassment of having to turn Jill down.

— We'll keep you on our books, the manageress reassured her insincerely. — In case anything else comes up.

The idea of spending more than a few minutes in the airless, hot little shop, packed tight with wool-balls, was suddenly a nightmare – how could Jill have imagined it would work? These shops weren't like the shops in London, with a perpetual flow of customers coming and going. She would have died, if she'd been stuck in here with someone like this rabbit-girl for days on end, forced to make conversation, helping old women choose patterns for twinsets and car-coats. Yet she couldn't help feeling a twinge of humiliation, because they hadn't wanted her. — Don't worry, she said with breezy charm, knowing she wouldn't be forgiven for it. — I noticed it because I was looking around for something for a few hours a week. But it's not really the kind of thing I'm used to.

The estate agents would be more suitable, she thought; with her intelligence she would surely be able to pick up the work quickly. She wondered if they needed anyone. As she pushed the door open, a woman looked up from where she was bent over the Gestetner copier, churning out details of properties. Mikey Waller came out of the back office when he heard Jill's voice. — It's all right, Rose, he said. — I'll deal with Mrs Crane.

Jill had the impression that Mikey was pleased she'd called in. He offered her coffee: in one corner of his office he kept an electric kettle, with a jar of Nescafé and mugs on a tray. She imagined suggesting that they went across the road to The Bungalow – but perhaps she should tread carefully, not knowing whether he was married. He set about spooning the Nescafé into two mugs, stirring it to a paste with the dried milk. It still seemed wrong to Jill, finding him confined to this office whose partitions were so flimsily provisional. She could remember when the place was an enchanting chemist's shop: they must have ripped out all the old mirror glass, and the drawers and shelves of polished mahogany. Mikey was too substantial to fit in here, he ought to have gone into some career better suited to his bulky physique and clever, careful hands. The way he concentrated, stirring two spoons of sugar into his cup, reminded her that at school he was always the one the teacher counted on to be sensible, to collect up the litter at the end of sports day or clean the blackboards during playtime. She and he had both been prefects, in the last year of juniors. It must be awful for him having to sell things, show people round depressing houses and talk them into buying. Perhaps he would call in and see her, once she'd found a place to rent. When she enquired about the Goods' cottage, he was incredulous.

— You mean that old place in Cutcombe woods? You couldn't live there. It isn't suitable.

— Why not? The Goods lived there for years. Isn't there still water in the well?

— In the well? He laughed at her. — Nobody gets their water from a well any longer. Not to mention that there's no bathroom or toilet, no electricity – and no access by road.

She hadn't properly thought about the toilet, and had no idea how you dealt with an earth closet, or whatever arrangement the cottage had. Probably Mikey would know how. — People manage without those things.

— Well, maybe you could manage it, he said. — You always were a bit different.

He was taking her seriously, observing her very closely. Mikey wasn't good looking. His sandy hair was limp and his eyelids were freckled, with short fair lashes; he moved his shoulders stiffly, turning his whole torso at once. But Jill thought now that she had always liked his unselfconscious calm, as if he were holding something back. — They probably had an old copper for hot water, he said. — No shortage of firewood. It would certainly be peaceful. I haven't been past it for a while. I suppose I can see you living like that, if you really didn't mind those inconveniences.

For some reason Jill felt ashamed then, as though she'd been showing off. It was the kind of thing her London friends went on about: starting new lives in the countryside, getting closer to nature, doing without modern technologies. Usually she was the one who debunked their fantasies, saying they had no idea what hard labour it was, getting a living out of the earth – and that the countryside wasn't an empty place you could just drop into, like a garden of Eden. Real people lived in it, who mostly took a dim view of outsiders. Now here she was pretending to be a gypsy like any romantic. Mikey promised he would find out who owned the cottage – he thought it was probably tied to one of the big estates, and didn't suppose the Goods had been paying a king's ransom. The place would most likely be left to fall down, if no one wanted it. Jill told him then about trying to get a job in the wool shop. — I wasn't good enough, they wouldn't have me.

— In the wool shop? He was incredulous. — Aren't you a bit overqualified for that?

— There isn't much call for classicists down here. Actually, there isn't much call for them anywhere. And I need the money.

— I forgot you did classics, he said. — You were the clever one.

— You solved all the arithmetic problems at junior school.

He liked remembering that. — Filling up a tank, so many gallons, such a cubic capacity, how long would it take, that sort of thing. Yes, I enjoyed those.

She saw that Mikey was curious, wondering why she needed money if she had a husband who wrote for the newspapers.

Because of her enquiries about the cottage, he must have half an idea that she was up to something, digging her way out of some disaster. Perhaps she could explain herself to him sometime. She would like someone else in the world to know what she was planning and what she felt, and what Tom was – what he really was, once and for all, which nobody saw apart from her. Though that was nonsense of course. People weren't 'really' anything, there wasn't ever any final, definitive version. For a moment she hoped Mikey would say that if she was looking for a job, they needed help with their filing right here in the office. Instead he asked how many children she had. He might have been worrying about the cottage and the earth closet, reminding her of realities and of her responsibilities. Was he reproaching her? You never knew with men, what ideas they got into their heads about how mothers ought to behave.

— Two girls and a boy. The oldest is seven, the baby's eighteen months.

— That sounds like quite a handful.

— Mum's looking after them this afternoon. I can't tell you what a treat this is, just sitting here talking, drinking coffee, not having to worry about anyone behaving badly, or falling over, or needing their nappy changing. What about you? Do you have children?

— Haven't been nabbed yet, he said heartily, rubbing his finger round the rim of his coffee mug as if he was trying to make it ring. — Don't know one end of a baby from the other. I was engaged once, but it didn't work out. Still footloose and fancy-free.

The words sounded as if Mikey had overheard someone else using them: they didn't suit him. It was ridiculous to think of him as footloose, he was too shambling and heavy. They were both embarrassed, and Jill began explaining the kind of properties she was interested in – not the modern houses that were like anonymous little boxes. And not anything in town: she'd rather live out in the country. She might learn to drive, and anyway didn't mind using the buses. — I'd have thought you were the marrying kind, she said while he looked for more property details in a filing cabinet. — The kind women are drawn to.

— Well, they haven't been queuing up lately, he said, searching through papers with a frown. — Here we are. See what you think of these two places. At least these have running water, though they're not exactly all mod cons. I could take you round to have a look, if you were interested. One afternoon later in the week? Or next week?

Jill wondered about Rose in the outer office – she was middle-aged, with a stiff blonde perm, but anything could happen if a man and a woman spent every day together. Then she was afraid that Mikey might be affronted, by her having claimed so high-handedly to know him – or perhaps by her remark about the little boxes. She must sound like a ghastly snob, despising those: most people were grateful to have a roof over their heads, and indoor bathrooms. Beneath his show of being blunt and uncomplicated, she suspected that Mikey was all delicate perception and quick judgement.

SOPHY TOLD JILL, WHO WAS sorting out laundry, that she was going to drop in at Roddings. The children were playing in the garden – Hettie was in charge, making sure no one fell in the river. Eve Smith was doing the church flowers that week, Sophy said, and wanted lilac for her colour scheme. All this was the truth, and before she went she picked an armful of the plumy lilac that grew beside the rectory's front gate. But when she'd handed the lilac over to Eve, and Eve was filling a sink for it in the Roddings back scullery, Sophy also asked if she could use the telephone. Eve had a pink, round, patient face and lank, greying dark hair, forever falling in her eyes; she looked washed out, with all the work of a farm and three grown bullying sons all living at home. She told Sophy to go ahead and help herself, pushing her hair back with a broad mottled arm because her hands were wet. Sophy had brought half a crown with her, to leave discreetly beside the phone as payment, always anxious that it might not be enough, or be too much. You could never forget you were the vicar's wife, with all that brought in the way of wariness in the country women, and a submerged hostility.

The Smiths had their telephone in the farm office, which was off the passage to the yard, a watershed between indoor and outdoor worlds: farm machinery and veterinary equipment were jumbled with boots and socks and waterproofs, an old clock ticked on the mantel above the huge cold fireplace, packets of shotgun cartridges were spilled amongst the paperwork on the desk. Parts of Roddings went back to the fourteenth century, Grantham said; the beams in the low ceiling were twelve inches thick. If John Smith or any of the boys had been at work in the office, Sophy would have abandoned her call: she didn't mind John, but could never have explained to him what she was up to. First she dialled the number for the flat in Marylebone, though she hardly expected anyone to answer, and no one did.

Then, fishing out a scrap of paper from her coat pocket, she tried another number, the one which Tom had left for Jill last week. Sophy had copied it before she gave the note to her daughter – partly out of her usual anxiety over losing things, partly because she was thinking that she might want to contact Tom herself, without letting Jill know. She didn't have much hope of getting hold of him, but it was worth a try. Obviously the two young ones had quarrelled. Sophy dreaded being the kind of mother who insisted on explanations, but she had got it into her head that it was her duty to encourage Tom, and tell him not to be deterred by Jill's intransigence. Her daughter was capable of putting up such a shining, off-putting show of certainty; Jill believed that each time she changed, it was for the last time. She insisted that she hadn't spoken to Tom the other night, though she had taken the handful of coins which Sophy put out for her. Left to himself, Tom might not persevere. He made such a point of being fearless, shocking people with his hair and his jokes and opinions; but Sophy didn't trust him not to give up at the first obstacle. She saw the strain in his eyes sometimes, as if his bravado was hard work.

A woman answered the phone: her voice was breathless as if she'd broken off in the middle of something funny. Sophy asked if she could speak to Mr Crane. There was a hesitation, then the woman proceeded more cautiously, though with something flaunting in her voice, as if her laughter might start up again at any moment. — Who is this speaking, please?

She couldn't possibly say she was his mother-in-law. — It's Sophy.

— Sophy, I'm afraid Mr Crane isn't here.

The woman's voice sounded as if she were putting on a parody of a secretary's clipped professionalism for someone else's benefit, to amuse them. — He's in an important meeting. Terribly important. I don't have any idea when he'll be back. Do you know, Bernie?

Sophy heard a man's voice – it didn't sound like Tom – in the background.

— Bernie doesn't have any idea either. Shall I ask Mr Crane to call you back?

Sophy said she would try again another time. It was strange to put down the phone and look around the unchanged walls of the Roddings office, coloured a deep yellow-brown by the men's tobacco smoke over the years. Her conversation lingered in there, a frivolous rainbow vapour from another world, a younger one. Should she feel anxious, because a woman had answered the phone? Definitely it hadn't been Tom's voice in the background. Probably they were just a couple, friends of his. But disturbing possibilities swam in her imagination, uninvited: just because they were a couple, that didn't preclude other arrangements with her son-in-law, experimental combinations. She found herself wondering, alarmed by her own inventiveness, whether the woman hadn't answered the phone half-naked, propped on her elbows amid rumpled sheets, in the middle of the day. It was extraordinary how much you knew about people, even from such a short exchange. These friends of Tom's weren't straightforward, they weren't serious, they had laughed at her. Sophy felt caught out, as if she belonged to ancient, earnest history.

IN THE MIDDLE OF THE night a noise intruded into Jill's dream and dispersed it. She was sorry, because the dream had been intricate and delicious – tidal, like swimming in shallow warm water through fronds of weed. She assumed at first that she had been woken by one of the children calling. Then the noise came again, thudding against her window-pane, a slushy blow, insolent and insistent: some bird must be bruising itself against the glass, on a crazy mission to get inside. Her first thought was to get up and close the window, which was open six inches or so at the bottom. Jill had been brought up to sleep with her window open, even on the coldest nights.

The front garden was stark with moonlight. There was no wind, and yet the young silver birch seemed to be quivering in agitation; some big animal was rooting round its base. When the animal straightened up she saw that it was a man – it was Tom, in his bulky duffel coat with the hood up. He had been gouging up another handful of earth and stones from around the base of the tree to throw at her window: luckily her parents slept at the back of the house. Furious, she pushed up the window and leaned out, feeling the cold air on her bare shoulders. She was wearing the pink nylon nightdress he had bought for her last birthday – not out of any sentimental attachment, but because it was the only one she'd had clean to bring with her.

— What do you think you're doing? she hissed.

He dropped his handful of earth and came to stand below her, brushing off his hands, turning the pale oval of his face up to her, framed monkishly in its hood. — Come down.

— I don't want you here, go away.

— For god's sake, Jilly, come down and talk to me.

Truly, in that moment she wasn't gratified – even though he'd come all this way just to find her. All her exasperation, which might have been waning, revived at the actual sight of Tom. Of course she couldn't really send him away, though she longed to do it; there was nowhere for him to go from here, in the middle of the night. And she was afraid of his making more noise, waking up her parents, confirming their suspicion that in choosing Tom she had made drastic errors of judgement and taste. She told him to wait, she would come down; then she closed the window and stood in her bedroom at a loss, not knowing what to do with him. This room, where she had slept alone all through her childhood and girlhood, appeared in that moment virginal and sacrosanct – even though she'd spent any number of nights in it with Tom since they'd been married, when they'd come visiting together. But her marriage seemed to her now a flimsy, provisional thing, and the spell of her solitude had grown powerful again. Every nerve was strained in her, against his intrusion.

Pulling her nightdress over her head, she dressed hastily in the clothes she'd taken off the night before, putting on an extra jumper, and then on top of that her coat. Another handful of gravelly soil came thumping against the glass, and she remembered that Tom had no patience: even when his dinner was almost ready he couldn't stop himself sometimes from devouring two or three slices of bread, thickly buttered, spoiling his appetite: his wide eyes would be pleading with her apologetically even while his mouth was still full. Quickly Jill made her way downstairs with her shoes in her hand, then went through the kitchen and let herself out by the side door, unlocking it and closing it quietly behind her, slipping into her shoes and making her way round to the front garden. The sky was a vivid blue, so bright it seemed to stand back from the land in amazement; the swollen moon fumed with light above Brodys' broken old slate roof, which was a sheet of pure silver. She couldn't see Tom at first, then he reappeared loping round the far side of the house. She supposed he'd been looking for a way in at the back. He was a big man, six foot two or three and fourteen stone, but he walked hunching his shoulders like a teenager, with his hands in his pockets, rolling stiffly from the hips.

— Thank Christ, he said. — I'm fucking freezing, Jill. Let me inside.

The duffel coat had its animal smell, like a wet old dog; it must have rained at some point on his journey. Jill snapped at him in an undertone not to swear, not here – seized in a gust of rage she swung her hand at him, slapping him hard across the face, although the hood's hairy fabric deflected the worst of her blow.

She had never hit him before and he was astonished, though comically obedient, keeping his outrage subdued. Really, he might have bellowed. — What's that for?

She could tell he was flooded with self-pity.

— I didn't want you to come here. I didn't ask you.

All this conversation was carried on in a barking whisper, while Jill took Tom by the arm and steered him away from the house, down the garden path. He said plaintively that he'd come because her mother phoned: he'd thought something must have happened to her, or to one of the kids. — I've hitched all the way, it's taken me all night, there was nothing on the roads, it rained. I had to walk the last few miles, from West Huish. And I got lost, I went the wrong way.

— My mother didn't phone, she scoffed. — You've forgotten, we don't even have a telephone!

— Well, she did, she spoke to Carol. Who was at Bernie's, as it happened: I'll explain later what's going down with those two, it's pretty complicated.

Jill thought then that Sophy must have gone through her pockets.

— So that really was Bernie's number?

— Of course it really was Bernie's number, he said indignantly. — All the time I was on the road, I was so anxious, worrying about all of you: now when I've got here you treat me like a pariah. And I'm hungry, I've had nothing to eat since I set out, I've got no money.

Knowing he would be hungry, she had brought out a packet of chocolate mini rolls from the kitchen. Struggling with the foil wrapper in the dark, Tom wolfed down the first roll in a couple of mouthfuls, spitting out bits of foil. — Can't I just come inside? he urged her through chocolate crumbs. — Jilly, we have to talk.

This is getting ridiculous. Just because of one stupid mistake.

— Give me a mini roll. I'm hungry too. You woke me out of my sleep.

— I'm not sure if I can spare you one. I'm famished – and these aren't very filling. But go on then. Look: see how much I love you? What's mine is yours. Disregard that it was yours in the first place.

Jill ate her roll in smaller, thoughtful bites. — If you want to talk to me, we have to walk. I know somewhere we can go. I'm not letting you inside the house; I don't want my parents to know you're here.

He said resignedly that he didn't mind walking. When they opened the front gate, the lane was so pale in the moonlight, between looming dark walls of hedge, that they felt as if they were stepping down into water. They went on whispering, even when they were surely out of earshot of the house. Tom asked over his second mini roll whether she'd told her parents about you-know-what, about Vanda.

— I haven't. I'm too ashamed to tell them.

— Ashamed of me?

— Of myself, that I married anyone capable of anything so dismally ordinary as an affair with his secretary.

— She wasn't my secretary. I don't have a secretary.

— Someone else's secretary then. Talk about second-rate.

Tom gave a low, swooping whistle of mock admiration. — Ten days at home and you really are back to being the vicar's daughter.

She swung round to slap him across the face again and this time he was ready for her, he caught both her wrists easily in his big hands, laughing. — Come on, you have to admit, that did have something of your old man in it. Something of the pulpit.

Jill stopped struggling then and stood very still, with her shoulders slumped inside her thick woollen coat and her head bowed, as if some burden were falling on her out of the dark, some awareness of futility. Tom wasn't stupid, he didn't mistake this for submission to him. He put his arm around her carefully and they began to walk again, more slowly. When they were out of the moonlight they had to slow down anyway, because they couldn't see the road surface. After a while she was leaning into him, letting him take some of her weight, in a way that felt familiar to her and even comforting, though she complained that his coat smelled awful and scratched her face.

— Listen to me, Tom said. — I'm telling you about Paris. A revolution is happening in Paris. The children are tearing down the prison walls. Everything that seemed established and set in stone turns out to be insubstantial as fog.

— Did you write all that in one of your articles?

He said that all the students were asking for was an education – a real one. In the Sorbonne the discussion groups were packed out, day and night. Everyone had their copy of the Little Red Book. Did she know that only eight per cent of the university students in France were working class? The Renault workers came to teach the students about factory work, they told their life stories. It was beautiful. The atmosphere was electric. All the time, everyone was listening to the news on their transistors, even the bourgeois, taking them out in the street so as not to miss anything: not the government channels, but Luxembourg or Europe I. — We had dinner in the *quartier* the other night, and when we came out there was a wall of flame across the street, we had to tie handkerchiefs across our faces for the tear gas. The police are brutes, they beat up the wounded even when they're laid out on stretchers, they beat up the doctors. There's rubbish everywhere, no rubbish collection. And burned-out cars. And you were right about the trees. It's sad about the trees. But they will plant new trees.

They struck off from the lane into the path through the woods; Jill had brought a torch in her coat pocket. What if it was true? she thought. What if this absolute, creative transformation into a new life really were possible, and it was her fault that she couldn't see it, and was stuck inside the old one?

— Journalism's beginning to disgust me, Tom said. — It's just being part of the machine. I'm thinking about taking up my painting again. I've got some ideas. Doing something real for once. Something that's really different, part of how everything's changing.

SHE TOOK HIM TO THE Goods' cottage, and they went inside. It was darker and colder in there than outside in the woods. — We could stop here for a bit, Jill said. — If you really want to talk. — What is this place? Who lives here? Won't they mind? It smells creepy.

— He died and she went off her head. It belongs to no one.

Their voices were flattened in the stale, tiny room; Tom shone the torch around, picking out torn-out coupons stuffed in front of the plates in a dresser, a crocheted antimacassar, Jesus gazing yearningly at them, a wilted magazine – *The People's Friend* – in a wire rack, a dirty crust of sliced bread in a torn plastic bag on the floor. Invisible in the dark aftermath of the torch beam, the room's sparse furniture was more insistently present. Jill had brought matches and she tried to make a fire in the grate – there was kindling in a bucket, she brought in a couple of logs from the pile outside. But the chimney didn't draw well and it smoked. Tom went exploring upstairs and came down with an armful of eiderdowns and blankets. — It's grim up there, he said. — I had a feeling he'd died in that very bed, whoever he was.

The musty damp eiderdowns and the wood smoke made him
wheeze, he had to use the pink rubber ephedrine pump he always
carried with him. They spread the eiderdowns on the floor and
wrapped themselves in the blankets, then ate the last of the mini
rolls; it turned out that Tom had the remains of a quarter bottle of
brandy with him too, although he'd said he had no money. Generously, he let Jill have most of what was left in it. Shuffling out of
the blankets on her hands and knees, she adjusted the logs in the
fire, adding another one – she had a gift for fires and this one had
settled in, it wasn't smoking too badly. While she crouched there
on all fours, taking her weight on her arms with her face to the
flames, Tom tugged out the elastic band from her ponytail so that
her hair fell down loose over her shoulders. Then he slid his hand
against her neck underneath it, making a low noise all the time as
if he were growling in delight, bending his head down to kiss the
back of her ears. At the same time he was sliding his other hand up
between her legs from behind, slithering against the hard nylon
of her tights, pushing up her skirt out of the way, probing around
the waistband of her knickers. Closing her eyes, Jill shifted her
weight so that she was pressing back against his hand. She thought
then that this was really what she had been wanting all along, it
was what she had come for. The wheezing in Tom's chest was as
purposeful as a ship's engine.

— I missed you, Tom said. — I missed you so badly, Jilly.

Jill wouldn't have been able to stop herself going along with
the lovemaking, if Tom hadn't spoken. The spell of this strange
place in the middle of the woods, where neither of them were
themselves, was very powerful – she was half abandoned to it
already. But then she heard such familiar confident satisfaction
in Tom's voice. He was so sure that this would make everything
all right. In one bound she sprang away from him, pulling down

her skirt: she was still on all fours, but now she was facing him. They were head to head, like two fighting dogs. — How can you? How can you just settle back into this, as if nothing had happened?

— I'm not settling back into anything.

— Yes you are! When you say you want to talk, this is what you mean.

— Don't be a prude, he said. — Don't tell me you don't want it too.

— You've got such a coarse mind. I don't just mean sex. I don't mean sex all the time.

— I know you don't, he coaxed her. — Neither do I. But this is still all about Vanda, isn't it? I never thought you'd be so hung up on that old possessiveness. I thought we agreed we didn't own each other.

— You haven't even asked about the children.

— All right, I'm asking about them now.

Jill groaned in exasperation, and said it wasn't just the asking. — It's the way you are, how you can put them out of your mind for days at a time, or weeks even. Just as if you were free. And I can't.

— I said I'd look after them for a bit, if you wanted to go to Paris. Or go anywhere. I don't mind!

— You're not serious about anything. So now it's painting instead of journalism. What will it be next week?

— D'you mean like your old man is serious? The serious miserable fucking poet? And by the way, I don't think sex is coarse. You surely brought me to this weird and wonderful place – I know you – with sex in mind. That isn't coarse. And now you're breaking my balls. Look, I'm serious. Look at me. This is the thing in the world I am most serious about.

Jill looked at him almost tenderly. It wasn't any wonder that other women threw themselves in his way. The firelight played over his long brown face, which was like her idea of a warrior's or a cowboy's: the high, hard, knobbed cheekbones, jutting tense brow. In the grey eyes there was always a suggestion of sleepy satisfaction, something rapt and dreaming. — D'you know what? she said. — I'm going to go back now. I'm going to leave you here.

— You're insane, you can't do that.

— Don't follow me. I don't want you to follow me. I'm going to take the torch, you'd only get lost without it. You'll be all right in here until the morning. There are plenty of logs. In the morning I don't want to see you. I don't want you coming to the house.

STANDING AT HER WINDOW IN the dawn light, Hettie saw the strangest thing. The light often woke her up, here in the country: when her eyes flipped open out of her dreams, the new day waiting in the room was so distinctively, surprisingly present that it was impossible – it was almost impolite – to close her eyes again, as if she hadn't seen it. The children's bedroom overlooked the front garden, as their mother's did. And on this particular day, almost as soon as she took up her post between the silky lilac-coloured curtains – in her nightdress, with her bare feet in the ice-cold which pooled ankle-deep on the floorboards – she saw her daddy walking past in the lane outside. He was wearing his big duffel coat, with the hood down.

In fact she heard him before she saw him; in the stillness of the early morning she had heard the tramp of his boots, coming from the direction of the woods, displacing the little stones on the road, crunching them and sending them skittering. This made her know that he was real. And then when she did see him it was only the top third of him, because the rest was hidden by the garden wall. But she was so sure that it was him. No one else down here had that long hair and that untidy beard and that intent way of walking with his head down and his shoulders hunched up. Yet how could he be coming from the woods, when it was only just light? And strangest of all, he didn't stop at their house and come inside to see them. Of course she was expecting him to turn in at the garden gate and come up the path. She was all ready to fly downstairs and be the one to let him in, and the first one carried round in triumph on his shoulders, announcing to the sleeping house that he'd arrived.

But he went on walking past the gate, and down the lane out of sight, and he never even turned his head to look at the house, though he knew it as well as they did, and must surely have known where he was. He never looked up to see his daughter watching at the window. And then he was gone, though for a while Hettie could hear the noise of his boots in the distance. The whole thing was so improbable that afterwards, as it settled down into her memory, she thought she must have been dreaming, or that she'd confused reality with an illustration in a picture book. Their dad was in London, or somewhere else, Paris: she knew that really. She never mentioned what she'd seen to anyone, because it couldn't really have happened, and her mother got angry if Hettie invented things. When she came to a certain page in their book of nursery rhymes – Mr Foster going to Gloucester in a shower of rain, drawn in a purple pencil and wearing a top hat – Hettie turned over quickly, because it brought back a sharp pain of disappointment.

THREE

THE CHILDREN GOT used to the rectory as the days passed, and began to forget their life in London, as they had done in the holidays before. Hettie settled into not going to school, although from time to time she was aware of the routines of that other existence – which she had been beginning to master – proceeding without her, and had a panicking sense of her deficit. Then she put off this awareness with a quick grimace. They might never go back, perhaps there would never be any more school. The rooms of their Marylebone flat seemed a chaotic muddle in memory – crowded with their landlord's ugly furniture, and with all the apparatus of toys and baby-life, and their mother's distinctive efforts at home-making: splashes of painted vivid colour, exotic textiles draped over sofas or pinned to the walls, art posters and political ones. Jill had found a stuffed heron in a glass case for next to nothing in a junk shop, and a gigantic mirror with dancing, garlanded cupids set into the gilt frame. The sink was always piled with dishes, there were always visitors talking non-stop and drinking tea from chunky ceramic mugs at the kitchen table: alien children were imposed upon them. By contrast, the kingdom of the rectory was theirs alone. There was more space for fantasy in its faded empty rooms – especially in the expectant spare bedrooms upstairs, used for nothing, scarcely furnished except with beds and chests of drawers and skimpy rugs, and smelling thinly of damp.

Who were those beds intended for? The rooms' vacancy, which intimidated Hettie at night, was stimulating by day. A statuesque dressmaker's dummy, like nobody's shape, loomed in one corner. Little crabbed watercolours, relegated to hang amid their expanses of bare wall, took on a momentousness in isolation: the children stared into the smudgy landscapes and feeble portraits as if they were oracles, speaking of the past and the dead. They invented a game of stampeding along the landing, between the arched windows, shouting, as if they were pursuing something or being pursued – Ali could even join in, if they fixed a chair across the top of the stairs to stop her falling down them. There was an additional delicious pleasure in this game if it was raining outside; the sound of the rain, and the sight of it blowing in wet gusts against the bare tall windows, drove them mad, and they dived onto the empty beds, rolling around in them, shrieking. Of course they could only play this if Grandfather were out. Granny didn't mind it: you could even tell, from a gleam in her pale eyes, that it stirred a buried desire in her which she could never act on, to join in and throw herself around. It was just possible to imagine Granny as a lanky, watchful girl-child; impossible somehow to imagine their own mother, ever, as anything but the full-grown finished woman, all curves and certainty. She often talked about her childhood, and there were photographs to prove that time existed – but her children didn't really believe in it.

For hours, when it wasn't raining, or not much, Hettie and Roland waded in wellington boots in the stream in the garden, carrying a bucket, looking for eels or sticklebacks. Or they prowled downstairs indoors, where the day's work proceeded in a way that was more ordered and less fraught than their parents' way. In the mornings Granny appeared to spring from her bed fully dressed, there was no sticky and fractious long interval of dressing gowns and breakfast mess and getting ready, before things could properly begin. In the dining room a cloth was spread on the breakfast table, there were flowers in a vase, and the children dipped bread-and-butter soldiers tranquilly in eggs fetched from Brodys across the road, as if they had been eating eggs all their lives. When she had finished her tea their grandmother held up her cup against the light and showed them a woman's face, hidden in the china. Twice a week a Mrs Cummins – she of the scratchy brooches, known to them from church – came to do the heavy chores, not constrained in the sculpted church-suit, but loose and business-like inside her overall. She manhandled steaming sheets out of the boiler then rinsed them and put them through the mangle, she scrubbed floors on her knees with a contemptuous hissing noise which must have come from her brush, though it seemed to come out of herself.

If their Grandfather was at home, then everything revolved around the invisible work that went on behind the closed door of his study. But even the prohibitions that came with this, the whispering and secrecy – and occasionally, the door torn open, the blast of his cold complaint – had their reassurance and romance. Because he was getting on with what mattered, the women and children could fill their time without responsibility. There was always work to do, women's work – but that was not lofty or exacting like religion or poetry. And then when he did go out, some spring which had held them tightly was released, so that they felt free. Even Jill, at the ironing board or at the sink, could seem to be caught up in the air of mild, sly, jubilation – as if she were another kind of woman, a more ordinary one. When the cat's away, their granny said, the mice can play – though their grandfather couldn't really be called a cat, or any kind of tyrant. Granny would put the kettle on although it wasn't teatime. Peculiarly, this liberation couldn't happen so long as Mrs Cummins was there: she kept them up to the mark in the minister's absence.

In his study even the smells were different to the rest of the house: the smoky brown notes – of pipe tobacco, books, cold cinders in the fireplace, whisky – were half offensive, with their suggestion of something meaty. Hettie and Roland had investigated the cut-glass decanter once, and discovered that the whisky, which looked and smelled promisingly like liquid caramel, tasted poisonous. Could anyone actually drink it for pleasure? It must be one of those forbidding adult initiations, commensurate with the impossible books on the shelves. However Hettie pored over the words in these, spelling them out one at a time, the sentences remained obdurately outside her comprehension. Grandfather told them he was writing poems about somebody in the fifth century who had translated St John's gospel into Greek verse, and also wrote hymns to a pagan god. Roland was maddening, with his calm presumption that he would understand all of this very soon. Hettie couldn't see why the grown-ups found this charming. She reminded him sternly that he couldn't even read yet.

— Grandfather said that doesn't matter, because I'm already thinking about things.

— What things?

— Sorting out what I need to learn, about history and science and stuff, and people speaking different languages.

After lunch their grandmother retired mysteriously to her room, and came down later in a different dress, unless she was gardening. In those late afternoons, their mother sometimes played the piano, and the sound came floating out past Alice, eating through the daisies in her playpen set on the lawn, to where Hettie and Roland were busy in the stream, building a dam across it, Hettie snapping out orders to Roland. The music while it lasted seemed to frame and characterise their life in a way which was poignant and satisfying, as if they could see it from a long way off. The children were always surprised that their mother could play at all; the piano seemed to speak quintessentially of acres of empty time, dedicated to dreamy introspection – which they did not associate with her. Then Jill would break off impatiently, when she made a mistake in the middle of some rippling passage, crashing both her hands down on the piano keys crossly, slamming the lid shut. They were half-aware that their mother was boiling up with trouble, the whole time they were adapting to life in Kington, settling down there. — I can't bear this, she said aloud once rather calmly, with her hands still raised in that impressive way, curving and passionate, poised above the notes.

— WHAT CAN'T YOU BEAR? Sophy said.

She was patting out a soft dough for scones, with floury hands, on the kitchen table. Jill had come in to cook the baby's supper and was crouching, banging through the saucepans in a corner cupboard, looking for a small one.

— Not being able to play through those pieces I used to know. It's so frustrating.

Her mother began pressing a glass into the dough, cutting rounds of scone and setting them out on a baking tray, while Jill sat back thoughtfully on her heels on the linoleum, with the saucepan in her hand. — And that's not all. There's quite a lot I can't bear, just at the moment. My husband, for instance, if you really want to know. That marriage is pretty much over, I should say. I made a mistake with Tom, and it hasn't worked out. So there we are.

She put on a sprightly, debunking voice, as if all this was a subject for a light, bright, clever irony; and Sophy went on pressing down the glass into the dough, close up each time against the last cut-out round, for minimum waste. — I knew something was wrong, she exclaimed, but without looking at her daughter.

— I've decided to come back and live down here, Jill said. — Mikey Waller's helping me look for a place to rent. Perhaps I could find a little job – I thought you wouldn't mind looking after the children, just a couple of mornings a week.

— What kind of little job?

— Anything. I don't care. I thought of asking in the library.

— You're a wicked girl, Sophy said. When she had stamped out as many rounds as she could, she gathered up the leftovers, pressing them together into a new ball, flattening this with deft fingers. — To tempt me so dreadfully. I can't think of anything I'd rather have in the whole world than all of you living down here. I'd be so happy, having you nearby all the time. Or here at the rectory for goodness sake: what are all those spare rooms for? Helping you look after the children. I'd like it more than anything.

— But, Jill said. — You're going to say: *but,* it's not possible. But, I have to be good, or something. We can't all just have what we want in life. You're going to remind me of my duty, that I ought to stay with him. For the sake of the children or whatever.

Those things don't mean anything any more, Mum. They don't count for anything. Women have seen through them. Anyway, you haven't even asked what's wrong.

— So what's wrong?

Jill sighed and put up the cool metal of the saucepan against her face. — He sleeps with other women for a start. That's the easy bit.

Sophy began stamping out new scone-rounds, dipping the glass into the flour bag, grinding it down thoughtfully into the dough. — How many other women?

— Mum, you're funny. What does it matter how many? I don't know. One at least, quite definite, that he's owned up to, recently. I found her underwear, if you want to know the sordid detail, in my bed, when I stripped it to wash the sheets. All crumpled up, sort of fossilised because I don't wash them that often, down over the edge at the end, caught between the layers. He brought her home when I took the children off to Candice Markham's for the weekend. They must have hunted everywhere. She had to go home without her knickers, poor Vanda. She must have thought he'd stolen them, to keep in his pocket or something. Frilly red nylon ones, that couldn't possibly ever have been mine: in the underwear department I'm still very much the vicar's daughter, in my white cotton. Poor Vanda. He doesn't even like her very much.

Jill said she was sure there'd been other women too. — Two at least, that I have suspicions over. He's probably with someone right now. Some dirty little Parisian Maoist he's got off with on the *manif*, the *manifestation*. Or perhaps there's a woman at Bernie's – you may have spoken to her, when you telephoned.

— I think that one's with Bernie.

— Well, who knows? She may sleep around. The point is, Tom doesn't seem to have qualms, as long as he can get away with it.

But the unfaithfulness really isn't the major problem. Maybe he's right that we don't need to own each other. Maybe I could get lovers of my own, we could balance things out.

It was lucky, Jill thought, that she was sitting here on the floor. From her unusual perspective, everything in this kitchen – that was familiar as life itself – looked unexpected: so that these extraordinary words, which didn't belong in here, could flow freely out of her mouth, liberated by the room's new strangeness. She could see from where she was sitting the grubby stained underside of the kitchen table, the side which was not bleached each week by Mrs Cummins, and metal struts that had been screwed in at some point, fastening the top more securely against the legs.

— The real problem is that I don't admire Tom any more. I don't just mean him being unfaithful: though of course that makes me sick and jealous, it's bound to. But I mean intellectually, as a thinker and a writer. I used to believe he was so brilliant. I chose him as my guide to everything, he showed me how to find my way in the world. But now I can see the lazy patterns in his thinking, all the short cuts. He doesn't really know half as much as he pretends he does. He's full of enthusiasms, but doesn't think things through deeply. I can follow a complex argument better than he can, I can see through falsity more quickly, I'm better at connecting things up together. I'm a better writer. What am I supposed to do with that discovery? I don't know how to be with him if I can't look up to him. I'm programmed to believe that the man I choose must be my master. I know that's an absurd expectation, but I can't seem to unpick it from where it's stitched into my psyche.

Jill had never said any of these things aloud before; she hardly even knew if they were true. And her mother didn't care anyway, about cleverness. She wouldn't be on Jill's side over that, she believed that women should keep their scepticism and criticism hidden, not risk exposing themselves – as the men exposed themselves – by pronouncing with any certainty. She would disapprove of the language of intellectual competition which Jill had used, she would have her secret irony at that. But at the same time, she must be at least half-triumphant, hearing all these things about Tom. In recent years Jill's relationship with her mother had often seemed to be a silent tussle, Sophy's unspoken judgement against Tom pushing up against her daughter's defence of him. Now Sophy was painting the tops of the scones with egg and milk beaten together, and she asked what Jill was going to cook for the baby's dinner. Would Alice eat the cauliflower cheese left over from yesterday? Jill stared hopelessly inside her empty pan. — She didn't like it very much, did she? I was imagining some boiled potatoes, with peas and grated cheese on top.

— That sounds like a good solution.

Sophy opened the oven door in the Rayburn with a tea towel, slid the tray of scones inside, rummaged in the vegetable crock for potatoes. — You'd be surprised, she said, — how you can think you've made up your mind about things and got to the bottom of them, and then there's a sort of swerve in the road or you turn a corner, and everything looks different all over again. As if you're driving through a new landscape.

— Really? Does that really happen?

Sophy considered carefully. — To a certain extent.

Jill slumped in her corner, as if a certain extent wasn't enough.

— Incidentally, her mother said, — I don't care as much as you might imagine, about being good. But I really don't think you ought to come home. However much I would love it. I think you ought to stay out there in the world, where things are happening. If I were you, then that's what I would want. I wouldn't want to come back here. There's nothing for you here.

UNDRESSING THAT NIGHT IN HER bedroom, Sophy arranged her dress carefully on its hanger, then hooked this over the carved rim of the wardrobe for airing, and to let the day's creases fall out of the wool crepe. She slipped the straps of her petticoat off her shoulders, then pulled her nightgown over her head, with her arms inside so that she could take off the rest of her clothes underneath it, as she did every night. She preferred, too, not to sit brushing her hair in front of the dressing-table mirror, where she would have to contemplate her own worn face which looked so finished and sad: as if something were completed in her, which was not what she felt. Instead she stood brushing at the window, contemplating the night sky: when she drew the curtains she always left herself this little gap for looking out. She could see her own face here again, reflected in the pane; but she didn't mind her eyes afloat – staring and undomesticated – against the navy-blue dark outside, or the shock of her stiff hair seeming lightened with moonlight, or the pale round of her face like another moon. Their bedroom at the back of the house looked out over the bowl of the valley, so that from her window she had the sensation of swooping down into it, like the owl she often saw passing, hanging from his outstretched wings.

The bed in here was the same one she and her husband had slept in since they first came to this parish and this house during the war, when Jill was a child, four years old. The people here would never accept that Sophy belonged to them, but the landscape and the house had swallowed her tolerantly. Grantham was in the bed already, sitting propped stiff as an effigy against the pillows, holding up his book: they both read in bed at night, often for hours. This wasn't the anodyne reading their middle-class neighbours spoke of, helping you slip over a threshold into sleep, equivalent to swallowing pills, the marker progressing through the book in modest increments. Sophy and Grantham devoured their books: reading was a freedom torn out of the day's regulated fabric. Without ever having spoken of it, each knew that the other approved their habit of having the face of their alarm clock, set for seven, turned away from them, so that they couldn't know how much time passed while they sat up awake and turning pages, couldn't know how rash they were or how much they would pay for it next day. Of course their reading matter was quite different: her novels from the library, his serious books. As was fitting, it was usually Sophy who slipped away first, putting her novel opened face down on the floor – breaking its spine, he complained – and relinquishing her involvement in its otherness with a sigh that was close to sensuous.

Tonight, standing at the window with her back to her husband in bed and her arms up, brushing, she told him that Jill said she was going to leave her husband. — I don't know how far she means it. It may just be a temporary falling out.

She didn't turn round to look at Grantham straight away, knowing how he would dislike her having this advantage over him: getting the news first, and having the power to disconcert him by announcing it. He would be longing to know more, but unable to ask her.

— That's not exactly a surprise, he said. — I knew something was wrong.

Sophy would have to bend first, as she always did, because she didn't care about the little dance of primacy. Yet she felt a perverse impulse to protect Tom against Grantham's condemnation: certainly she would never, ever repeat Jill's story about finding the red knickers in her bed, knowing how that detail would stick to her husband's imagination, burning into it, firing him up with distaste and male challenge. — She says she wants to come back here to live. She's got Mikey Waller looking for somewhere she can rent.

Grantham wanted to know what Sophy's reaction had been, so that he could argue the opposite case. She said she didn't know what there was for Jill, back here. — And then there are the children to think about, their schooling, all the advantages of London.

— They don't need to rent anywhere, he said. — They can come to live with us, there's no question. She would be better off with us. She could pick up her studies where she left them off.

— You know people wouldn't like it.

— I don't care what people like. What is this all about anyway, what's the idiot gone and done now?

— Jill says she sees through him.

— Is that all? It's too easy to see through him.

— He's more persuasive than you will allow.

— He's never persuaded me. I suppose there's another woman? Of course there's another woman. I can't believe he's got away with it for so long. He stinks of women.

Sophy knew he used these violent words to shock her – and actually to jolt himself, because he was upset. He couldn't bear anything to hurt Jill. And she was shocked, although she hoped he didn't notice it; then she wondered about this idea that women – a certain kind of woman – left their scent on men, so that other men could smell it. All kinds of shame seemed to be wrapped up in it: the shame of leaving your civet trace, or the shame of odourlessness, not leaving one. Sitting down on the side of the bed with her back to him, she contemplated the bony mauve of her long bare toes against the carpet. — I think she ought to stick it out, she said. — I expect that this will pass. I dread to think of her bringing up three children alone, without a husband. The children would suffer. People can be very cruel.

— Stick it out? he complained. — You sound like a Girl Guide. Why should she stick it out, if he's no good, not good enough for her? Why shouldn't she be rid of him, if that's what she wants? Isn't that what women do these days?

— Perhaps they do. Off with the old, on with the new.

In bed, while she was finding her place in her book, Sophy felt the familiarity of her husband's lean flank against hers, through the cloth of their nightclothes: they lay close together because the bed hadn't warmed up yet – she had put on her bedsocks as a precaution. The lovemaking part of their marriage wasn't over, but most often these days their contact was merely friendly. After sleeping together for so many years, they hardly had to go through the rigmarole of a rapprochement or a truce before they touched, even if they'd been at odds while they were talking. Their bodies, more prosaic than their souls, were intimate at a level deeper than their argument.

MIKEY WALLER PICKED UP JILL one afternoon in his car, to take her to see a couple of possible rentals. She was taken aback by the car – for some reason she'd imagined him driving something reliably old-fashioned, but he turned up in a bright red sporty Hillman, pleased with it as if he expected to impress her. Sophy came out of the house with the baby on her hip, to say hello to Mikey, shading her eyes with her hand in the watery sunshine. It had been raining all morning but now light was glinting off the puddles on the garden path. Roland and Hettie were collecting snails in a jam jar; Hettie explained that they weren't going to kill them, they were keeping them as pets. She had forgotten her cross self-consciousness for once, looked almost pretty.

Mikey was emollient and affable, joking with the children,

shaking hands and chatting with Sophy. Perhaps there was more of the estate agent in him than Jill had allowed for, when she had thought he might be shy. Flustered, she wanted to show off her children and at the same time regretted that he had to meet them, because when she was talking to him in his office she had felt weightless and carefree, as if she could go back to a bright, hard, selfish time when she had only herself to think about. And she worried uneasily that she might have put on the wrong clothes for looking around properties: she had made up her face and done her hair and sprayed on perfume as if Mikey had invited her for a date. Because the weather was warmer, she had left off her winter coat and was wearing a light anorak; when she climbed into the car passenger seat she pulled at her short skirt and smoothed it down as if she could make it longer. Every time Mikey changed gear – very competently and smoothly, not jabbing the gearstick in the way Tom did – she was aware of her thighs exposed so close beside his hand, as if she had meant to entice him: which perhaps she had, though now this didn't seem such a good idea.

— I expect I seem an ancient old woman to you, she said. — Now that you've seen my great grown children, one of them in school already.

— They look like nice kids, Mikey said. — I never really know what to say when people want me to admire their children. It's a whole world I don't know about.

Jill said he was under no obligation to admire them; she didn't point out that her question hadn't really been about the children. They were driving in one of the winding lanes that led down into the valley, and then up out of it again on the other side; the lane was so narrow that the wet growth in the tall hedgerows brushed against the sides of the car and sappy sharp smells of spring blew in through the open windows. Late primroses were half-hidden at the foot of the mossy banks, purple foxgloves with their pale speckled throats soared up like flares, the hedges were fretted with herb robert and red campion. Dunnocks and yellowhammers broke out on the road ahead of them in little spurts of flight. If they met any vehicle coming the other way, then one driver or the other had to reverse until they reached a passing place: this kind of driving couldn't sink away into a background awareness, Jill and Mikey were involved in it together, Jill craning back over her shoulder to advise him. They talked about her taking driving lessons, if she did move down here.

— I might be leaving my husband, so I need to learn to fend for myself, Jill said, while Mikey was involved in one particularly tricky manoeuvre, getting past a Roddings farm cart. Jill waved at one of the Smith boys driving the tractor, she wasn't sure which. She thought that Mikey was startled by her announcement, crashing the gear change uncharacteristically, then annoyed with himself for bungling.

— I'm sorry to hear that, he said with formal politeness.

— Why should you be sorry? I'm not. I mean I am, of course, for the children and everything. But I'm not sorry to be leaving Tom. He's not really cut out for family life, he's made me quite unhappy.

— Then, why shouldn't you have another chance?

— At happiness? Yes.

She had told him much more than she ought to; just because they had been children together, she mustn't presume that Mikey was interested in her present life. He didn't seem keen to talk about it, anyway, but got on fairly eagerly to the subject of the rentals they were going to visit, explaining things in his practised professional voice, pleasantly reassuring but not selling anything too hard. The first place they looked at was a cottage tucked into a curve in the lane, just before it met the road above: it was ghastly, poky and dark and done up with painted beams and fake bottle-glass window-panes and an inglenook fireplace – and in any case it was far too expensive. The existing tenant showed them round and Jill praised things in her most Oxford voice, eager to get away.

Then Mikey drove fast on to the next one – on the two-lane road which ran along the top of the valley and then left it behind. They hardly met any other cars. Last year's withered leaves hung on in the sombre beech hedges either side of the road, where the the new leaves coming through were a rich bronze-green. In places the hedges had been newly laid: above the woody old masses at the tree roots, thick stems had been gashed across and bent down at right angles, trained to grow parallel to the road. The light flickered behind this tracery, punctuated at intervals by the sturdy grey trunks that had been left to grow straight up. The upland scenery had a sober grandeur, different to the intricacy and intimacy of the valley behind.

The second house they saw was empty and Jill liked it much better: an austere stone box set back from the road, two-up two-down, unfurnished. The empty square rooms, where light shifted on the limewashed walls, seemed hardly differentiated from out-doors – in fact there was ivy growing through one corner under the roof, which Jill didn't mind. She had an excited idea that a life lived up here would be purged of everything unnecessary and distracting: in the evenings when the children were asleep she would be able to write something at last, go back to her Greek translations. She and Mikey stood together at an opened window upstairs, looking out past the woods and Forestry Commission plantations of pine, towards the bare tops of the moor, where the sunlight was falling mildly and sweetly, bringing out the colour of the heather. Jill said she thought she'd be happy in this house.

There seemed some question about exactly what the rent was, but she might be able to afford it.

— It's a long way from anywhere, Mikey warned her. — The weather's not always as nice as this. You could get snowed up in the winter. What would you do to get around until you'd passed your driving test?

— I'm sure there must be a bus, Jill said gaily. — We could get bikes. I could put the baby on the back of mine.

She was staring out at that far-off sunlit patch of colour on top of the moor, and found herself longing to be transported there – as if it were a scene of Elysian pleasures, exempted from heaviness and difficulty. Gravely Mikey was considering her suggestion about the bikes. He said that some of the hills round here were pretty steep, for cycling. — Sorry to be such a wet blanket.

Jill drew her gaze away reluctantly. — You're right. The bikes are an awful idea, we'd probably all be killed. Am I being a terrible nuisance? You've probably got things you ought to be doing in the office.

— Oh, don't worry about me, he said, surprised. — I'm happy. I'd rather be outdoors on a day like this.

— Perhaps this house isn't really practicable. You think I'm not serious about renting, don't you? But I didn't mean to waste your time. I'm at my wits' end, I don't know what else to do.

— That's all right. There are other places to see. Nobody finds their ideal home first time. We'll make a note of this one, I don't think there's been much interest in it, so there's no great hurry. Not everyone's keen on ivy growing through the roof. We could check which buses go past. Or you may turn out to be brilliant at driving, and pass your test first time, you never know.

— But I can't afford the lessons, Jill said. — Or the car.

She turned from the window to face him ruefully, as if across these infinite complications, lifting her hands towards him, palms up in a fatalistic gesture, giving up the lost cause of herself, expressing the comedy of her predicament. Only as she turned towards him he was also turning and opening his hands out, perhaps to console her, and it was as if they combined in an intention that neither had actually intended. Their kiss – just the lightest, delighted hanging on to one another and brushing of lips, at first – was so unexpected that it floated free for a few moments from their real lives, as if it was hardly happening. It was all mixed up, in Jill's sensations, with the tobacco-brown irresponsibility she had imagined on the moor. And because they had had no time to prepare for this kissing, it was surprisingly skilful and suave, not the usual clumsily deliberate thing. It wasn't truly passionate or sexual either, to begin with: tender, like a kiss in a dream. They really were in the middle of nowhere. Afterwards they stepped apart in the strange room with its greenish light, and were quite confused and shy; Mikey apologised.

— Oh, don't be sorry, she said. — I'm not sorry.

She saw how his reddish fair hair was clipped close to the raw skin above his ears and at the nape of his neck, and she thought he was chafing inside his shirt collar and tie and his crumpled suit. It was a long time since Jill had kissed anyone except her husband, and she had forgotten how abrupt the transformation was, how the smiling surface of personalities and faces receded and you were thrust into brash new perspectives, up against the flesh and the inner life of a man, with his heat and his smells, and the nuances of his movements which betrayed how he withheld himself, or gave himself. In Mikey's case, thank goodness, the smells were pleasant: of soap and then something sweetish and lemony, like dried grass. She was still hanging on to him with both hands, grasping his sleeves so that he couldn't pull away from her in his embarrassment. As the married woman, she knew she must take the initiative, if anything more was going to happen between them without drawn-out prevarication. When she kissed him again – pushing harder this time, running the spread fingers of her hand up from his nape through his bristling short hair, cupping the back of his skull and drawing his mouth down more deeply and heavily against hers – she felt how, if she took this lead, then he would follow her. But what now? They couldn't do anything in here, on the bare floor. He didn't even have a proper coat to take off, for her to lie on.

— You know, she said, — we could take a look at the Goods' cottage, the one in Cutcombe wood. In so many ways – I mean, apart from running water and things – that would be more convenient. I know that it's unlocked. We could go there now.

— I did enquire about it. It's not one of the estates we deal with. Strictly speaking.

— But let's take a look, she insisted. — Right now. Not in your professional capacity. Just as a friend.

JILL HARDLY SPOKE, ALL THE way back down into the valley. Only she told him where to park: there was a passing place he could pull into, at the side of the road. She didn't want the excitement which was choking her up and suffusing her to leak away – surely he felt the same, she knew he did. Towards the end of that first dreamlike, innocent kiss, something had changed between them – but if they began talking about ordinary things, then they would lose the way they had torn through the ordinary fabric of the day, to get to what they wanted. The clunk of the car door when Mikey slammed it shut reverberated like a blow inside her, as if her body were hollowed out. She went ahead of him on the path through the woods – this wasn't the same path she had taken with the children, or with Tom, but a steeper one, quicker, weaving down between the trees. They were neither of them wearing suitable shoes, and from time to time they slipped on the leaf mould, grabbing at branches to stop themselves, never quite falling. Every so often Jill looked round at Mikey coming after her and smiled, putting all her encouragement into that smile – nothing could go wrong, they were immune, nothing could touch them. She bent down and took off her heels, then continued in her stocking feet, carrying her shoes in her hand, smiling back at him again, not feeling any pain from the sharp stones and twigs on the path, or the bramble that dragged against her calf, tearing her tights. The cottage door would still be unlocked, they wouldn't meet anyone. She knew all this would work out.

She had supposed that when they pushed open the door, they would find all the mess of Tom's night on the floor in the Goods' cottage. But to her surprise the little room was perfectly tidy; he must have put away all that bedding, although he never so much as straightened the sheets at home. Even the slice of bread in its plastic bag was gone from the floor; only the cold fire in the hearth and the empty brandy bottle were signs that the two of them had ever been in here. Of course she couldn't exclaim over any of this to Mikey. They stood in the doorway, peering into the little room which was a dark cave carved from the brilliance of the afternoon outside. Jill still had her shoes in her hand. She had imagined carrying on with Mikey where she and Tom had left off, on the floor in this room: now that didn't make sense.

— You couldn't live here, Mikey said sternly. — It's horrible.

When they went inside and the door swung shut behind them, they could hardly make each other out until their eyes got used to the dimness: his shirt front was a looming patch of white, unattainable. The house with Mikey in it seemed flimsy as a doll's house – Jill saw its impossibility through his eyes. — Never mind, she said, falsely bright, crossing to the tiny window which was deep-set in the stone wall, looking out into the treetops where the end of the valley fell steeply away below them. — It doesn't matter. It was only an idea.

He opened a cupboard door and found the stairs behind it, disappeared as if he were climbing up inside a well: she heard each step creak with his weight, and then his footsteps as he prowled close above her head. Leaving her shoes at the bottom of the stairs, she went up noiselessly after him. The first bedroom was all but filled up with a double bed, heaped with a tangle of blankets and eiderdowns where Tom must have dropped them; the sloping walls were papered with a pattern of pink baskets overflowing with fruit, and the air was stuffy with the tainted smell of ancient cloth, heated by the sun shining down through the roof. Old clothes and yellowed newspapers and magazines were piled up on the floor all around the bed. There was another, single bed in a second room, with a few rough blankets on it. — In this day and age, Mikey said, — you can't believe people still live like this. You'd be surprised at some of what we see, in the property business.

She told him how Mrs Good who'd lived here used to give her sweets, which she had thrown away. Judging by the mess, he said, that was very sensible.

— When I'm an old woman I want to give everything away, so there's nothing to leave behind.

— You won't be this kind of old woman. You'd never let things get into this state.

— How do you know? I might become one of the crazy ones, frightening children.

He smiled indulgently. — There are decent people and there are people who just don't care. You have to have self-respect.

Jill wondered what Mikey thought about her self-respect – not much, probably, as she'd brought him here. She was losing her confidence that he wanted her; perversely, the more he seemed like a stranger to her, remote and rather stolidly conventional, the more attractive she found him. How had she not seen that his bulky tall physique, cramped in the tiny room, might gain this power over her? She had been a fool, imagining all the power was on her side. Perhaps he was right – there were decent people and she wasn't one of them. — You don't really believe that, do you? she said. — Some people with tidy houses behave awfully and cruelly and aren't decent at all.

Mikey was struggling with the latch on the casement window. He said they could do with some air.

— So you can't imagine me living here?

— It's not a fit place to bring children.

— I could make it nice, she stubbornly said. — Clean it up, clear it out. Put up nice curtains. You'd be amazed what a difference those little details make.

When Mikey finally got the window open the breeze blowing in was a relief, flicking at the newspapers on the floor. He turned back to Jill with a closed and preoccupied look as if he were worried by something else apart from her; for a moment she thought he was going to put her aside regretfully but firmly and head downstairs, saying he had to get back to the office. Instead, without any preamble, he seized her by the shoulders and began kissing her again: not on the mouth this time but on her hair and her neck, pressing her head between the palms of his big hands. Then he was kissing her breasts through the cloth of her blouse, undoing its buttons determinedly one by one, tugging at them if they resisted, so that she had to help in case he pulled them off.

— Do you mind this? he said distractedly.

She reassured him that she didn't mind, and tried to unbutton his shirt in turn and undo his tie, encouraging him to undress; but he wouldn't, and she thought perhaps he didn't want to be naked in such a filthy place. At least she managed to slide the shirt up his chest, so that it bunched under his arms. He undid his trousers and kicked off his shoes, that was all; Jill spread out the slithery pink eiderdown on the bed for them to lie on, then took off her tights and knickers. She could feel that the feathers in the eiderdown underneath her were clumped together with damp. Mikey's body, what she could see of it, was very different to Tom's, so brown and lithe and heedless; Mikey's was thick and white with a flat, broad, sad bottom, and his back was freckled. All the time he was kicking off his shoes, having to yank at the laces, hopping on one foot, then manoeuvring to get on top of her and inside her, he had his eyes closed, or half-closed. And he said strange gasping things, said he loved her and had always loved her — but she was sure this was only the rhythm of his encouragement to himself, giving himself sentimental permission to let go. His extremity helped to bring on some strong sensations of pleasure for Jill, though they didn't get anywhere very far.

— Are you protected? he asked in a shamed voice, muffled against her shoulder, when it was all rather quickly over. — It's a bit late to ask.

— Oh yes. Don't worry about that.

This wasn't actually the truth, but Jill didn't care, it was the last thing on her mind. After Mikey had zipped up his trousers, turning away from her to do it, she saw there was quickly a wet patch darker against the dark material, and thought that Rose would notice in the office, and that the women would notice when he took his suit to the cleaners. She was glad she'd left some mark on him.

ALI HAD FALLEN OFF THE front wall into the road. Now she had a huge blue-green lump on her forehead, and was sitting in all the dignity of her sorrows at the kitchen table, being comforted by her grandmother. Her face was blotched from crying and there was still some low-level snuffling, but actually she was beginning to feel proud of the seriousness of her accident. Sophy was playing pat-a-cake with her and feeding her little bits of buttered toast with jam. Her fall was the other children's fault: Hettie had lifted her up to sit with them in their den in the privet hedge on top of the wall beside the gatepost, but of course she was too little to keep still, and kept leaning over to poke her fingers into the crumbly mortar between the stones, where trailing weeds were rooted and creatures lived. It was a long way down to the road. The others had led her inside with solemn faces, each holding by the wrist onto one of the poor hands with dirty grit stuck in the soft pads of flesh, which were flecked with blood: the blasts of her howling were like trumpets announcing them.

But their grandmother wasn't cross – Hettie and Roland were having buttered toast and jam too, and drinking milky tea copiously sweetened. In the aftermath of the drama the atmosphere in the kitchen was hushed and admonished, almost holy. Hettie got out the painting book Sophy had bought her last time she was in town; you painted with clear water and the colours came out magically in the paper. It was satisfying work, cutting out all the compromise of creative endeavour. Roland sat arranging his plastic letters, pretending he was making words. Then he actually did make one, copying it carefully out of Sophy's cookery book: *plain,* from *plain flour*. Hettie made a big fuss of him. — It's a real word, isn't it, Granny? See now, Roly, you can write! You can really write.

It began to be evening, their mother was late. They had eaten their dinner at midday, so there was no serious meal to cook; Hettie and Roland were sent over to buy eggs from Mrs Brody for their supper, holding hands to cross the road as Granny told them, even though there were almost never any cars. If they'd become positively enthusiastic about eggs, despite the slime, it was partly because they were drawn to what was thrilling and dreadful in this quest to fetch them. The Brodys' farm was dark, not pretty like Roddings where Mrs Smith grew flowers and the windows and doors of the farmhouse were painted a bright jolly green. Even the Brodys' red-brown cows smelled worse than the Smiths' black-and-white ones and seemed more outsize and sinister, stretching their throats and bellowing with eyes rolled back, jostling and clambering onto one another in the muck, in the grim yard of furrowed concrete. Weeds grew through a heap of tyres, and the hens pecked around the wrecks of ancient cars; high in the barn wall above them the evening light shone through the ruined empty dove cote. When Mrs Brody came to the kitchen door she was always nursing a cup of tea against her apron, as if she were keeping it warm – her teeth were brown from all the tea she drank, and sometimes the children didn't understand her because she spoke with a broad accent. She put the money they paid her in a cracked old mug on the window-sill, painted pink and gold, that said *A Present From Ilfracombe*. Their granny always washed the eggs before she used them.

Roland's concentration was entirely taken up, on their way back across the road, by holding on to the precious paper bag, one hand supporting it from underneath. But something made Hettie look around consciously, as if Kington became real to her for the first time – not as a mere background to her thoughts and plans, but having its own authority. The evening was as wide open as a spacious room. There wasn't a cloud in the sky and everything was touched with a warm russet-pink light – the rutted lane, the green growth in the hedges, the clouds of midges so excitedly stirred up. She asked her brother, didn't he just love it here? Even the Brodys' dirty farm seemed part of her happiness. Some bird plummeted past, belly low to the road; then those birds seemed to be all around them, darting and twittering in their high-pitched restlessness which was also soothing. Roland shrugged her enthusiasm off as if it were frivolous, distracting him from his mission. He carried the paper bag scrupulously inside the house.

A car was approaching through the lanes, disrupting the quiet; when it came into sight Hettie recognised the red one from the estate agents. She knew that her mother had been looking around for places they could move into – they might come and live down here in the country, and she would have to start at a new school. Although this prospect was fearful, she felt sure now that it was what she wanted. The car stopped noisily just short of where Hettie waited at the garden gate, and then for a few minutes more her mother didn't get out even though she had seen Hettie and waved to her, but sat on in the passenger seat, talking with the man who was driving. After she had climbed out, she leaned in through the window again, thanking him, telling him she'd be in touch, and then the red car reversed into the Brodys' drive and drove off, its noise subsiding in the evening air. Her mother was standing with the light behind her, and it was shining through her hair which had come down somehow from its French knot while she was out. She was fixing it now, standing in the middle of the road with the hairpins in her mouth, hands up behind her head, twisting round the long tail of her hair and skewering it in place. Because of the brightness, Hettie couldn't see her face properly; she didn't like to rush up to her while she was preoccupied, but began her confession anyway.

— Alice had an accident. She has a bump. It was my fault, I shouldn't have put her up on the wall, only she kept on begging me.

— What kind of a bump?

— On her forehead. But Granny's cheering her up. And Roly's written a real word with his letters: *plain.* He wrote *plain,* all by himself.

— That's a funny word to start off with!

Jill was in her laughing mood, everything was all right. Hettie explained that he copied it from a cookery book. She expected her mother to be businesslike, hurrying indoors to see the others, but instead she lingered outside in the pinkish light, with its promise of summer. — Isn't it lovely here, Het? she said. — Look at the swallows going mad in the field. They're drinking insect soup.

— What's insect soup?

— The air is full of creatures we can hardly see. The birds are feasting on them.

They stood at the field gate, watching in close companionship, and when Jill lifted Hettie high onto the top bar of the gate, she held her tight so that she wouldn't fall.

WHEN SHE'D PUT THE CHILDREN to bed, Jill hesitated in the dusk at the foot of the stairs. There was no lamp switched on yet in her father's study but the fire was lit, its reflection gleaming on the cut glass of the whisky decanter: she was thirsty suddenly for whisky. Perhaps what she'd done that afternoon had opened a door, and she would be buffeted from now on by violent appetites. Stepping inside the room she thought at first she was alone, then realised that her father was kneeling in the half darkness beside the bookcase, not looking round, peering in the firelight to read the gold lettering on the books' spines, as if he didn't want her to know that he knew she was there. Jill picked up the decanter she'd never touched in her life before, to help herself.

— You can pour one for me as well, her father said.

He was stiff, getting up from his knees. Even while he was strong and only middle aged, she'd dreaded any intimation that he might grow old and weak, and thought she wouldn't be able to bear it. — I hear you might be moving home, he said. — Your mother told me.

— It's probably not a good idea, is it?

— We miss you, Charlie. We'd love to have you here.

— Oh well, Daddy, she said, — I miss you. But life goes on. I've got three great big children now.

— You could pick up your work again, if you came down here. Your mother could mind the children, we could try out some translations together. You've got such a good intellect, you know. It hurts me to think that you've thrown it all away.

— I haven't thrown it away. I'm still the same person.

He made an impatient face of fine discrimination, shadows knotting around the deep socketed, disenchanted eyes. — We don't think Tom's such a good idea, you know. Not good enough for you.

— It's too late for that, Jill stubbornly said. — And anyway you don't know him. You don't know what I know. Nobody does.

LATER THAT SAME EVENING, AFTER it was dark, Jill knocked on the side door at Roddings and asked if she could use their phone. She had the money ready to leave for them, and was sure that they always left more than the actual cost of the call – but it was obvious Eve Smith didn't think much of her coming round so late. The Smiths might even have been on their way to bed, though it was only half past nine; there was no sound of any television going in the farmhouse. But Jill didn't care. She knew her apologies sounded insincere and falsely fulsome, in her educated voice, and she was aware for a moment of the person she had been at Oxford, filled up with her cleverness and ambitions for her intellectual life.

Yet this tempestuous life she had instead wasn't anything less. It was surely wrong to think that reading and intelligence had to float somewhere above the thickness of real experience. She was so glad to be in her solid woman's body – used, by men and by her children who'd come into the world through it. Eve switched on the light in the office and retreated to the scullery, not quite out of ear-shot – Jill heard her running water into a tin kettle. The farm office was chilly, bleak in the light from a weak bulb, all its workman-like disorder inert while the farm slept. There was no one in the flat in Marylebone when she rang, so she dialled Bernie's number and some woman answered. — It's Jill Fellowes. I want to speak to Tom.

— He's not here.

— But I expect he is. See if you can find him.

The woman pretended to be bemused, but Jill insisted. Eventually Tom came on the phone, breezy and too ready with his innocence. — Did you hear about de Gaulle?

— I don't want to talk about de Gaulle.

She told him he had to come and pick them up in the morning, to take them home.

— You've changed your mind all of a sudden.

— You'll have to borrow a car from somewhere, she said. — If you want us back, you have to be here by midday. I mean it.

Tom reassured her that it was all he wanted. Nothing else mattered.

PART THREE

The Present

ONE

———

AFTER THE PATTENS' dinner, the rain settled in. Morning after morning they woke in their damp beds to hear it insisting against the windows – not stormily, only steadily, pattering down through the leaves in the big beeches, secretive and pressing. The light and the acoustics in the house were so changed that it seemed a different place, shrunken as if it crouched underneath an assault; landscape diminished to the near-at-hand, airy distances condensed into prosaic grey and crowded close around the windows. The temperature dropped, the clematis dripped on the terrace. A mossy, silvery pattern of wet sunshine bloomed sometimes for a few minutes on a wall on the landing, before it was extinguished again – like a weak message from another existence. *It might brighten up tomorrow*, everyone said. Sometimes the rain was a relief, Alice thought: less was expected of you than in fine weather, you could turn over and go back to sleep. But Harriet and Roland seemed to be up at dawn, Harriet in her sensible checked pyjamas and Roland in his silk ones, putting buckets and plastic bowls underneath the places where there were leaks, their voices reproachful with practicality. Then water pinged, torturously, into the buckets, and Simon Cummins came round to talk to them about repairs. Alice thought that she could give up this house after all, the claims that it made on them.

She was reading gradually through all the children's books on her shelves, losing herself inside them one after another. If Ivy and Arthur joined her in her bed she read to them, and they finished a whole volume of Doctor Dolittle together – not one of the good ones. Kasim drifted into the room and while they watched from the bed he searched through the things on Alice's dressing table and in her handbag without asking or even looking at her, for the cigarettes she didn't have. – No, it's a good thing, he said, when she suggested Fran could drive him into town to buy some. He explained that he'd given up, and was only tempted to start again because he was bored. But when she said they could take him to the station if he wanted, he looked surprised and said that he was all right, he wasn't in any hurry to get home. It might brighten up tomorrow. He liked it here. He didn't mind being bored.

And then he sidled into Molly's room, the children following him, still in their pyjamas, and behind that closed door they seemed to play interminable games of Monopoly – really interminable, one starting up again as the last one finished, Kasim winning every time (*Well, I am supposed to be studying economics*), Molly tranquilly indifferent to losing. Ivy stormed out in a temper, slamming the door behind her because Arthur wouldn't play properly, he wouldn't buy any property, he only wanted to hang on to the money he was given at the beginning. – Don't you understand the idea of it? she shouted. — The idea of it's that you use that money to make more money! Arthur looked from under the blond fringe that hung into his eyes, apologetically but shrewdly, as if he knew better than to trust anything so far-fetched. Between Monopoly games, when Molly was sometimes busy – 'getting ready' – Alice found Kasim slouching on the window seat on the landing, blankly engaged in nothing. She tried to lend him a novel to pass the time, but he said gloomily that he didn't see the point of fiction. — I don't see what it's for. Why would you put out any intellectual effort, understanding something that wasn't actually true?

By the time Alice got up to get dressed, it was often midday, or one o'clock; then in the afternoon she carried more letters upstairs from her grandmother's bureau, or from the drawers of her grand-father's desk in the study, and lay on top of the eiderdown to read through them. She kicked off her shoes and after a while she would slip for warmth into that consoling space between the eiderdown and the top blanket. *Dear Mr Fellowes, I can't tell you how much I was moved and excited by your new collection. It speaks to our moment with a directness and urgency like nothing else I've read this year.*

ROLAND MADE A FIRE IN the sitting room in the afternoons, though the chimney didn't draw very well. Pilar sat hunched over it with her shoes slipped off and her long feet tucked under her, reading through the newspapers, or through the legal papers she had brought with her, making notes. She was determinedly cheer-ful. Fran and Alice agreed in lowered voices in the kitchen that she made everything worse, made them feel the dreariness of the place which they wouldn't have minded if they'd had it to themselves.

— We're used to it being crap, Fran said. — Now I feel like I have
to keep apologising for it.

— Why don't they just go? If they're so obviously bored to
death?

— But it's only Roland who's bored to death: Pilar actually
claims to like it. She must be mad.

— She's needy, Alice said. — She needs something from us. I
don't know what.

Harriet went for long walks despite the weather, and came
back humming to herself, then went upstairs to change her clothes
and confide in her diary. She had to hang out her wet things to dry
– they steamed in front of the fire, depressing Alice. The postman
delivered packages of DVDs for Roland, and he and Pilar cuddled
together under a duvet in the study to watch them – Roland had
bought a new DVD player in town. He bought an oil-filled electric radiator too, which he plugged in wherever they were sitting.
— He thinks he can purchase his way out of boredom, Fran said.
— Well, of course you can purchase your way out of it. But not
down here.

Then Roland had to sit on the gate at the top of the field in the
rain, trying and failing to send off reviews from his phone: on the
way down the hill he even slipped on the grass, getting red mud
on his trousers. Preoccupied when he returned inside the house, he
hurried up to Molly's room and went in without knocking, to ask
for her help – perhaps she could get a better signal on her phone.
She and Kasim were sitting on her bed – upright, it's true, and
fully clothed, but disarrayed, hot-eyed, pulled hastily apart, who
knew which layers untucked or buttons undone? Scalded, banging the door shut again without saying a word, Roland couldn't
forgive either Kasim, or himself for his own idiocy. How had it not
occurred to him to knock? His sisters would have put two and two

together, they would have been deliberately noisy, coming upstairs, they would have knocked, or not even dreamed of going into her room in the first place. Why was he missing those instincts? For the first time in his life he wished he was more ordinary.

— You know what's going on? he said to Alice.

— Well of course I know: isn't it sweet?

— I don't find it sweet. I think I should step in, before things get any worse. What possessed you to bring that boy along in the first place?

— Don't be silly, Roly. What do you mean, worse? Young love: it's a glorious thing. You're just jealous.

— Is it glorious? But I'm so anxious for her.

Alice qualified, more truthfully. — Well, it wasn't exactly glorious for me. But that's only because I was so tortured. Molly's straightforward. I think she knows how to be happy.

Disconcerted, Roland sat down to a long session with Chopin at the old out-of-tune piano whose damper was warped. It didn't soothe him when Pilar marvelled at his performance, because he had no illusions about his playing – in fact it struck him that if she had a cloth ear for music it could be a problem between them. Then when he went upstairs to his own room, he found Ivy and Arthur huddled up against the door to Molly's bedroom, each with a glass tumbler pressed to the door and an ear pressed against the tumbler, listening to whatever was going on inside. Roland roared at them and they fled: even he thought this was amusing as well as alarming. Shortly afterwards, when he was on his way downstairs again, Kasim came out from Molly's room, hands in his pockets, whistling and kicking at the skirting board with exaggerated innocence. Roland thought that the house was intolerably too small and they were all going to go mad if it didn't brighten up soon, piled incestuously like this on top of one another.

— There's something funny going on with those kids, Fran said when he told her about the eavesdropping. — I'll show you what I found in their pockets.

She fetched the little folded scraps of ancient paper from where she'd buried them, perturbed, under her clothes in a drawer upstairs: she was even blushing as she handed them over. After a moment's squinting, Roland and Alice could make out women's body parts, faded to an unhealthy grey-pink. Alice laughed.

— Where on earth could they have got these from? Fran said. — And there's another thing. I'll swear there's money going missing from Arthur's savings. But what's he spending it on? Not just pennies: several pounds I think. They're never out of my sight when we're in town. You don't think that they've been buying porn?

— I know this is the country, Roland said, — but even down here no newsagent in his right mind would hand over dirty magazines to two infants clutching their pocket money.

— Anyway, these magazines are ancient, they smell of old damp.

— Oh, don't *sniff* them Alice, how can you! Maybe they're buying them from some other kid or something.

— Or from Kasim? Roland suggested. — They don't know any other kids down here.

— Roland, that's just an evil thing to say, Alice protested. — You can't mean it seriously, about Kasim.

— All right, I'm not altogether serious. I suppose the children have stumbled on someone's ancient stash, from years ago. No one looks at porn in magazines nowadays. Simon Cummins? He's got a leering look, hasn't he? Or Christopher?

— Christopher? Don't be ridiculous. Whatever made you think of Christopher, of all people? He's only even been here once or twice. And surely he's a feminist or something. He wouldn't look at porn.

— Only an idea. Those Lycra cycling outfits are a kind of sex perversion in themselves. And the feminists are probably the worst.

When Alice suggested she ask the children directly, Fran confessed that, to her own surprise, she'd found she couldn't. — I don't want them to know that I know they've looked at anything like this. But I've no idea what I'm supposed to do. And now they're voyeurs as well! It can't be natural.

— I'm sure it's absolutely natural, Alice said. — Do you want me to ask them?

— Perhaps it's best to just ignore it. Really, though, don't you think Jeff ought to be here?

The sorry little scraps of obscenity on their softened, felty paper contaminated something, Roland thought. Those women with their bloated breasts and shaved pudenda weren't even protected by the sheen of an unreal mannequin beauty; they looked like any housewife he might have met shopping in the streets of the little seaside town, and unsettled him more than he could acknowledge, even to himself. Something overheated and uneasy seemed to have taken possession of their whole household, under siege from the everlasting rain. His own lovemaking with Pilar was more inhibited, as if he was aware of everyone listening in, as if those children might have their glasses pressed against his door. Once or twice he even jumped up out of bed, flinging open the door onto the landing, only to find no one on the other side. Wrung out of him against his will, however, his pleasures seemed particularly acute. In the mornings at breakfast he was ashamed to think who might have been listening.

He tried to persuade Pilar that it was time for them to go,

but she was determined that they see out the whole three weeks.
— It's such a long time since I had a rest, she said. — I feel very
comfortable, here at home with your family.

— But the weather's awful.

— I don't mind the weather.

They drove for a day to look round a great Victorian baronial
pile an hour's drive away, on the other side of the motorway, but
at the last minute Harriet asked if she could come with them. She
said she hadn't seen the place for years, and he didn't know how
to refuse her; then he felt his kindness, which was his fixed habit
with Harriet, strained through a long afternoon. He had wanted
to be alone with his wife, to give her his whole attention, and
to have hers – nothing smothering or soppy, quite the contrary.
Before Pilar met his family, he remembered, their communion had
been simplified and minimal. When he'd told her things, she had
lifted a shapely eyebrow, or curved her lips in a responsive smile:
she only spoke if she had something to say. This had answered
to his deepest need, and he'd never intended for Pilar to be initiated – and so willingly, even eagerly! – into the scruffy, unsound,
makeshift excesses of his own family, which were just what he
wanted to escape from.

Harriet seemed happy enough anyway, all that day: when she
was happy she was surprisingly girlish, chaffing and jokey, bringing up stories from his owlish boyhood until he was annoyed.
He didn't disown the prig he once was, who had worshipped Sir
Mortimer Wheeler and pretended to write plays in Latin, but he
felt tenderly enough about him to keep him more or less private.
He was afraid of seeing the perception dawn in Pilar that he could
be thought ridiculous. Harriet's cheeks as she teased, he noticed,
were surprisingly pink – surely she wasn't wearing something on
her skin? And who'd have imagined that his revolutionary sister

would one day take her pleasures visiting these shrines to the sur-
plus consumption of the aristocracy, exclaiming with Pilar over
a vast billiard table or a cabinet full of lockets with their painted
miniature doll-faces and twists of ancient hair? He was astonished
when they began working out the relationships between the dolls.
Lady Geraldine, she must have been married to the second Earl.

— But don't you want to send them all to the guillotine?

— Don't be such a spoilsport, Harriet said. — I'm having fun.

Roland wasn't in the least revolutionary, but thought nonetheless that the National Trust was opium for the middle classes, and
found he couldn't take much pleasure in it. There were too many
holidaymakers – because it was raining outside, and cold, and
there was nowhere else to pass the time – tramping damply round
the rooms, wondering obediently at the great dining table set out
with damask and silver and Wedgwood, glazed plaster fruit and
dusty plaster fowl and dusty bread rolls, for the delectation of
twenty guests long dead, who'd have despised them. The view
from the back of the house, which should have been down a succession of terraces and parterres to the great gothic threadworks
where the money came from, and beyond that to a dream of hills,
was muffled in grey cloud.

IN THE COLD, WET WEATHER the children's cult intensified:
driven back on themselves indoors, the Dead Women made themselves felt in every shadowy corner blooming with black mould,
and were ever more exacting. Ivy interpreted the signs they left
with confident authority: a pattern of cracks in a broken mirror, a
wet dead mouse left on the terrace, and – unanswerable triumph –
a crude charcoal face found drawn on a wall, once, when she tore
a secret strip of wallpaper away, above the skirting board beside

her bed. She kept Arthur perpetually guessing: was she making all this stuff up, or should he trust her? There was cool calculation in his expression, even while he hurried around after her instructions, digging out Kasim's old dog-ends from the lawn, stealing salt from the crock in the kitchen, peeing into a cup so she could stir up one of her sacrificial potions. He drew the line at touching the mouse, and in the end Alice buried it; their mother had outraged them, telling them to just throw it into the shrubbery. Ivy couldn't, Arthur puzzled, have put the drawing ready under the stuck wallpaper; in fact she had looked for a moment as surprised as he was, finding it there. Everything might be a mere succession of accidents, which his sister wove into her story: he dithered between his belief, and the doubt which was both refreshing and disenchanting.

At least the rain meant they weren't going to the cottage so often, where he had to pay money to appease the Women's powers. They had got nearly all his savings out of him already. According to Ivy, they were building up to some climax of revelation.

— About Mitzi? Arthur asked.

She was fairly contemptuous. — That's old news. It's bigger than that. Something's going to happen.

This expectation became entangled with the time they spent spying on Kasim's and Molly's love affair. The endless kissing and caressing appalled the children but was also enthralling, so that they couldn't bear to miss any developments. Kasim and Molly sat together in the mess of Molly's bed for Monopoly and sometimes forgot – in the long pauses between goes, while Arthur made up his mind – that anyone was watching. They would slip further and further down among the pillows, lost to everything but their own convoluted, mostly mute windings around each other, which seemed so oddly bent upon some purpose, although they had no obvious end in sight. Kasim determinedly clambered half across Molly, Molly responded in adjustments and little noises which were half-protest and half-consent. Ivy would nudge Arthur – lost in contemplation of his troubling property portfolio, which she managed for him – with her foot, and signal with a jerk of her head to see what she saw; then the children stared at each other bemusedly. Their laughter coiled inside them, sensuous in itself, until they had to hide their faces.

Arthur burst out once with his hilarity, hot-cheeked. — Are you two going to get *married* or something? Is he your boy-friend?

— Shut up, small boy, Kasim said, muffled. — Nobody asked you.

Kindly Molly explained that you didn't have to get married just because you kissed someone. Arthur grinned at Ivy. — But you do if you do sex.

Molly sat up abruptly, blushing, pushing Kas away. — You're not supposed to know anything about that!

Ivy was furious with Arthur for drawing the lovers' attention, which meant that they were chucked out from the bedroom for a while – but not for long. It was almost as if the children were part of what was unfolding between the young people: or at least they lent them the necessary cover, so that the grown-ups didn't bother them. Their craze moved on from Monopoly to Scrabble. Alice was sometimes enlisted for advising Arthur and Ivy, although Ivy would agonise between getting a better word and managing by herself; she couldn't believe that she could only see words of three letters, when she could read much harder ones in her books. — Don't tell me, don't tell me! she cried, putting her hands over her ears, scrutinising her tiles fiercely, as if she could glare them into a more sophisticated order. She had finally to turn to her aunt, who was tactful in the extreme. — Look, try this, Alice suggested. — I wonder if this would fit in anywhere?

It turned out that Molly had a gift for Scrabble.

— I've always been good at spelling, she said complacently, putting down *vortex* on the treble word score.

Kasim couldn't bear it. — But you don't even know what half of these words mean! What's a vortex?

— I don't know! It's a thing you get pulled into, like a zone or something.

— And what's a zone?

— Do I have to know? As long as it's a word.

— But I don't understand how you can know it, if you can't use it.

She shrugged. — The word's just sort of *there*, I've heard of it.

Kasim was a bad loser, and even upset the board and stormed out once, when she and Alice wouldn't let him have *Elvis.* — It's a proper name! You know it is! Alice said, laughing at his indignation.

HARRIET WAS SITTING ON THE edge of her bed, writing in her diary, when Pilar knocked subduedly on the door between their rooms. — Do you mind if I come in?

Hastily, guiltily, she closed the book.

— Of course not.

It was the first time Pilar had been inside this room: Harriet saw her look around and take in with a little involuntary shudder how dismally empty it was. Harriet had never known how to do what Alice did, crowding out any space she occupied with her personality, setting out her possessions as if they composed a little tableau, making everything inviting. Even in this wet weather when Alice hardly got dressed, she'd have both lamps switched on in the middle of the day – one beside the bed and one on the dressing table – so that everything was bathed in the glow from under their pink, pleated shades. Harriet hadn't thought to turn anything on, she'd been writing in the dull light from the window and the room was chilly.

— Oh Harriet, I need you, Pilar said, and sat beside her on the bed, seizing her hand, enveloping her in perfume; Harriet stared down at Pilar's wrist, slender in the cuff of her silk blouse, dangling a gold chain. Her English was perfect, and yet there was some nuance in the way that she pronounced *Harriet*, which made it breathily exotic. — I'm so glad we're friends. I have to have someone I can talk to. I don't want to bore Roland.

Trouble showed dramatically in her face: all the strong lines were dragged downwards and there were purple smears of shadow under her eyes and beside her sharpened nostrils. Catching sight of her reflection in the swing mirror, she looked away. — I'm an old witch, she said.

— You? You're not the one who's an old witch. Harriet squeezed her hand, bird-light bones and flesh, impervious stiff bristle of the rings. — You're always beautiful.

— You're so nice to me.

Pilar told her that there was bad news from Argentina: she'd found out when she checked her emails in town that morning. Her brother in Buenos Aires had agreed to have the DNA tests, to help resolve the question over their biological parents. — I don't know, maybe they got to him, put pressure on him, made him feel bad. He's been talking to my aunt. And now I can't tell Roland, it's too late.

— Well of course it's not too late, Harriet stoutly said, though she dreaded the idea of Roland being in on their secret.

— He'll ask why I didn't tell him before, bringing all this trouble. He likes to think I'm so calm and in control.

If Pilar's brother took the tests, it was effectively the same as if she was tested. She said she'd spoken to a lawyer friend in Argentina, who was looking to see whether there was any kind of injunction she could take out to prevent him. — You probably think I'm very selfish, Pilar said, — not to give this satisfaction to people who've lost their children. I must seem like a monster to you.

Harriet tried to imagine this point of view. In another life, she might have thought that Pilar was a monster. Her idea of the women of that guilty class, heir to privileges bought in blood, might have corresponded very much to how Pilar looked at this moment – groomed and impervious and expensive, something hardened in her expression. It was extraordinary that this creature in all her physical perfection sat here beside her on her own poor bed: she looked as displaced as a queen out of a tragedy, or a god in an old painting, descended from another world to ravish mortals. In the presence of the god, the protests of righteousness were puny. Anyway, Harriet's old confidence had collapsed long ago, that the world could be sorted out into the damned and the righteous. In flawed reality, who could blame Pilar for her resistance to being enlisted in some horrible old story? It wasn't her fault, if friends of her friends had once dropped the bodies of dissidents from helicopters into the sea. Who could want to belong to people they didn't know and be claimed by them, even if their wrongs stretched out beyond counting?

— You're not a monster, she said, lifting Pilar's hand to her lips and kissing it. Pilar allowed her to do this, she didn't pull her hand away. There was knowledge in her face, Harriet thought, daring to look into it: a rich gleam of contempt, mingled with amused acceptance of the homage. — If there's anything I can do to help. Really, I would do anything for you.

Pilar wasn't the sort of person Harriet usually got on with: her friends at home were mostly conscientious, wary of judgement, self-deprecating. If Pilar was a queen, it was a drama queen. And Harriet had overheard her say something shocking to Roland once, about Kasim: that she didn't like Asians, didn't trust them – *she ought to know, she had to work with them*. Roland had only mildly demurred, as if her prejudice were amusing, like ignorance in a child. In another life, Harriet might have kept a sceptical distance from Pilar, her lack of irony, partisanship, lack of culture. Had anyone, Alice insufferably said, ever yet seen her with a book? Pilar wanted to belong inside Roland's family because of Roland: she wasn't interested, really, in his sisters' separate selves, and it was obvious that she'd taken against Alice. She had fastened upon Harriet because she needed a confidante, and Harriet was eagerly compliant. Pilar *didn't want to bore Roland*.

When Harriet was twelve or thirteen, she'd had a friend at school whom she'd loved and who had used her, sending her on pointless little errands, finding out where she was vulnerable and prodding there, resorting to her company when there was no one more interesting, dropping occasional kindnesses like crumbs. Harriet had tidied this memory away, believing it belonged safely with childish things; now she remembered her mother's impatience with this friend's exploitation, and her own inability to explain what she knew about it – that the abjection was not a downside, but the essential fabric of her love.

— We two should go swimming again, Pilar said.

— If it brightens up, I'd love that.

Pilar made a face towards the window, shrouded in its grey.

— Will it brighten up? We could go to the little pool in the hotel.

— That awful place. Could you bear to go back there?

— Of course! I liked it!

IN AN INTERVAL OF ONE day which wasn't sunny, but when at least for an hour or two it stopped actually raining, Kasim took the children off into the woods. Molly was doing something to her hair, in her room, and he didn't invite her: he thought she needed reminding that he could enjoy himself without her. Fran made the children put on their wellington boots, so that they could splash through the new lakes of red-brown water blocking the path, and around the troughs of sucking mud, knee-deep where cows had wallowed. Kasim had to negotiate these more cautiously – he'd only brought one pair of trainers, and had spurned Fran's suggestion that he pick a pair of wellingtons to fit him, out of the promiscuous, cobwebby muddle of boots in the scullery. The idea of putting his own foot inside anyone else's dank old castoffs upset him. — Suit yourself, Fran said.

In the woods the light was brooding and subdued. Of course Kas got his feet wet more than once, and muddy, and he cursed, and his pullover was soon soaked and he was freezing, because every bush and drooping bramble shed its load of raindrops if he brushed against it. Streams which had trickled were swollen now and dirty. New undergrowth sprouted livid green, the tan mulch under the pines in a plantation had darkened to ox blood, unripe blackberries were fuzzy with grey mould. Beside a path a bank had sheared away in a smear of red mud; skirting around it they saw into the raw root-gape, like flung arms, of a tree upended, its deep hole whiskery with torn roots. Their senses prickled in the alert quiet; drops merely sifting down through the trees as they passed made them think it was starting to rain again; squirrels startled them, dashing about the tree canopy in crazy fits, sending down showers. Kasim's silence prohibited frivolity; plodding after him, the children knew better than to propose any chasing game. Arthur only stamped his boot once in a puddle to spatter Ivy with liquid mud – Kas quelled her outrage with one look, before it was even uttered. They were regretting coming out, this wasn't much fun. Kasim, with a chill, felt the force of the landscape for the first time, now that it glowered at him.

They were almost surprised, in this altered light, that the cottage still existed: but there it was, greyly enigmatic at the turn of the path as usual, hanging out over the twiggy thin finger-ends of the treetops in the valley below, its windows on that side – the side away from the door – filmed with wet and seeming blind because they knew no one could be looking out through them. As they came past the cottage and emerged into the clearing opposite its front door, a squall of rain blew up, and Kasim suggested taking shelter inside. Couldn't they make a fire in there or something?

— Yes, let's make a fire, Arthur said, inspired.

Anxiously Ivy said that this wasn't a good idea, it might be dangerous. It hadn't occurred to her that Kas might want to come inside, because he never had before: she had planned for one of their sacrifices, Arthur had brought the last of his pound coins. It was awful to have to imagine all over again, with fresh perception, what Kasim would see if he went upstairs – those horrors would become the children's shaming secret, sticking to them. When Kas regretted that he hadn't got his lighter, they were stricken with the recognition that this very lighter lay in full sight on the floor in the magazine room, giving away their familiarity with the Women and with everything else. And – Ivy strained to remember – might they not have left their scissors there on the floor too, along with incriminating fragments of the cut-out pictures? Arthur had developed a knack for cutting out very neatly around the breasts. — Let's not go in, she said.

But Kas put his shoulder to the door and heaved at it, lifting at the same time, until it yielded and opened wider than the children had ever opened it – they stumbled inside together, and he propped it open behind them with a stick. In the changed weather the tiny dim downstairs room was surprisingly dry but seemed somehow even less human, more like a burrow, hardly differentiated from the earth. Perhaps it smelled less of dead dog, but it smelled more of that same mouldy, mineral, rank underground they'd been uneasily aware of earlier, passing the torn-up tree root in the woods. Luxuriantly, obscenely, the cottage was rotting away. If only a clean wind could blow through it! The children looked anxious, as though this desolation were their responsibility.

— How long since anyone lived here? Kasim said shortly.

He poked with his foot at the packed leaves in the grate and then – as if he were looking for something – officiously pulled open and banged shut again the doors of the cupboards built in on either side of it, which the children had never touched. There was nothing inside, except one empty biscuit tin without a lid; the shelves were lined with thick paper, cut in scallops where it overhung the edges. Fatally, they knew he would try the door next which led to the bottom of the stairs – and he did, vanishing behind it. They heard his springy tread on the few steps, taking two at a time, and then crossing the first room. They didn't look at each other, but Arthur shrugged.

Upstairs, Kasim hardly noticed the little mess of scissors and cut out bits of paper on the floor – he knocked the scissors accidentally with his foot into a corner before he saw them, and only then caught sight of the lighter. It didn't occur to him that this was his: it was the cheap kind of disposable you could buy anywhere. He thought simply that someone else had left it, along with some loose change, which he pocketed: presumably whoever had been visiting to enjoy this ancient porn. Trying the lighter, he was surprised that it gave off a strong flame. In one disdainful glance, he spurned the dirty magazines: they mocked and affronted him, the ugly white flesh gloatingly exposed. He hadn't even seen Molly yet without her clothes more or less on, but his knowledge of her body hidden underneath them – intricately folded on itself, taut with secrets – possessed him. He knew that all the kissing and cuddling and hiddenness at some point would not be enough, and must come to feel like failure; desire in him was bitter sometimes, his own equivocation taunted him. Then all at once this lonely place in the woods struck him as an answer to his difficulty and a vision of his fulfilment. He could bring Molly here, undress her finally and make love to her.

Looking out of the window, he could see all the way down the valley. The trees were stirring under successive waves of a light rain, the twigs in their tops springing back as spry as tuning forks. He couldn't possibly have sex with her, proper sex, back at the house, with her father bursting in on them every minute, and the children taking an unhealthy interest, and Alice giving them knowing looks and smiles. Once they were alone in here, they needn't be afraid of anyone. Kasim had made love to several girls already, and none of it been been either a great disaster or a great success, nor had it flowered into any relationship. He wasn't even sure he wanted a relationship, he flinched from intimacy. But he knew that his father's sex life had been going on, pretty much non-stop, from when he was about fifteen, and it made Kas feel that his own was insufficient and paltry. In this place, though, something different might be possible. If he just cleared out the magazines and cleaned up a bit and brought some blankets, there'd be nothing to distract them. He would have Molly to himself, the whole thing could unfold at its own speed. She wasn't like those other girls, she was absorbent and dreamy and would let him be in charge.

Kasim opened the door into the second room and for a short moment was shocked, thinking that something was alive in there – in fact it was only strips of wet curtain, twitching in the squall at the window, which was not quite closed. This tiny dead-end room – it was more like a cupboard, nowhere near the size of his mother's walk-in wardrobe – had advanced much farther into dereliction than the rest of the house. The wall on the window side was stained with rain and black mould, the floor was deep in dead leaves, and there was a nasty mess which looked like a dead animal in one corner, shrivelled leather collapsed onto sinisterly yellow bones, traces of reddish fur. Kas thought it must be a fox, not wanting to examine it too closely, not knowing much about wildlife. He'd have to clear all this lot out before the cottage was ready for Molly. It occurred to him that Ivy and Arthur, who'd been begging almost every day to get into the cottage, must have been upstairs and seen what he'd seen, the magazines and the fox; perhaps they hadn't known what they were looking at. Or more likely it was their guilty little secret, he knew what kids were like. No wonder Ivy hadn't wanted him to come inside.

Downstairs the children waited, hearing him open the second door, close it again; then his tread was noisy once more on the stairs.

— Look what I found, Kas said.

They looked obediently, in dread – but he was only holding up the red lighter. — We could make a fire after all. But I suppose there'll be all kinds of shit stuck in the chimney.

He poked up experimentally with a stick, and a thick tumble of sooty, leafy, feathery mulch fell out gratifyingly at his feet: Arthur put his head in the grate and said he could see the sky. But when they tried, they couldn't really get a fire started, all the wood they picked up outside was too wet.

— We'll bring firelighters next time we come, Kas said enthusiastically. — I'm going to clean this place up. We'll bring a shovel and a broom. We could disinfect it, fetch water from the stream. It could be cosy, don't you think? Burn some incense, get a little fire going.

They'd never seen this boyish Kasim before, excited by his project. Catching on, Ivy suggested that after they'd made it all nice, they could bring Molly to the cottage and surprise her. Kasim was unforthcoming. His plans to bring Molly here, needless to say, did not include the children.

THE FOUR SIBLINGS AND PILAR went out one evening, to eat at a pub in the next village. The Pattens – who had friends staying, down from London – had asked them over to dinner again, and they needed some excuse not to accept. Alice feared that Janice wanted to exhibit them as local colour. Anyway, Roland reminded them, it was time they had their meeting, to decide what to do about the house. Wasn't that what they were down here for? Before they'd even set out, Alice said desolately that they had better let the old place go. — I suppose it's all over, isn't it?

— Wait, Alice, Fran said with real annoyance. — We have to have a discussion first, don't leap to conclusions. We have to think about it logically, what would be best for all of us.

— But it's obvious what you all want.

It should have been a melancholy occasion, but they couldn't quite remember to be sad amongst all the complications of getting in around the table in its little nook, ordering food and drinks – strong drinks, Fran and Alice insisted, to brace them for decision-making. Harriet, squeezed in beside Pilar, surprised them all by asking for a glass of port, and then another one; under its influence they felt her vigilance relax, she told them funny stories about her colleagues at work. Looking from Alice to Harriet, Pilar announced that they were very much alike. — Aren't we? Alice cheerfully agreed for once. — We're like our awful father, I'm afraid.

Harriet said that Alice was the pretty one, Alice said it wasn't true, she was just the fake, with her dyed hair – and in fact Harriet was glowing that evening, dressed again in the nice things Alice had given her. The hollows of her eye sockets and cheeks, which could look haggard, only seemed sculptural and striking; her face was broad and calm like a nun's, her expression open. In the warm artificial light all of them looked ten years younger. It made a pleasant change to be snug in the crooked low-beamed pub, with its wood-burning stove, after the cold and damp of Kington: hungrily they attacked battered scampi and breaded plaice. Roland was troubled from time to time by the idea of Kasim and Molly alone in the house together – but they weren't really alone, the children were allowed to stay up until the grown-ups came back, Kasim couldn't get up to much while those two had him under scrutiny.

It was only Pilar in the end, funnily enough, who sided with Alice in her reluctance to let the house go. Pilar pronounced decisively – almost superstitiously – that there were too many family memories enshrined in the place for them ever to part with it; they were relieved she'd saved them from having to pronounce it for themselves. Then Harriet said simply that she didn't need two homes. The place was going to start falling down round their ears, they all agreed, and they none of them could easily find the money to spend on repairing its fabric. But hadn't they had so many happy holidays down here, for free – or almost free? Roland said its charms had rather palled on him, Fran said she'd rather go abroad for a change. Mightn't one of them want to move down here to live, some day? They looked warily at one another, no one owned up. What emerged to dominate, as the argument went backwards and forwards, was the clinching, immediate problem of the roof. It all came back to the roof, which had needed attention even in their grandparents' day. No one knew what it would cost to put on a new one: ten thousand pounds, fifteen, twenty? More? And who could find time to be on the spot, supervising repair work on that scale? They couldn't ask Simon. Alice couldn't bear the idea, anyway, of replacing those ancient mossy slates with modern ones, even if they were letting water in. — I'd rather even leave the house behind, I think, than change those slates.

— Well there we are then, Fran said. — We're all agreed, it's time to go, we can't bear the idea of the new slates, or actually changing anything. I'm sure Jeff and I can do with the money. There can't be any harm in just getting a valuation, at least. We'll contact Wallers, they're the best people. How much d'you think we'd get for it, Roland?

He hadn't a clue, no one knew. Three hundred thousand? Or more, or less, because of the condition it was in? — We could hold out, suggested Harriet, — and say we'll only sell to local families.

— We could, Roland considered doubtfully.

Fran hated that idea. — And then sell to some local builder who sells it on as a second home for twice the price! Of course we'd do better ourselves if we borrowed the money to do it up, then sold it.

Nobody wanted to be bothered with that.

— I know you're right, Alice said. — It's time to sell. I do agree with you all, really. I never know what's good for me. It may release me into a new phase of life, not clinging to the past. I'll become a new person, even. You won't recognise me! Happy at last!

— Alice, don't be silly, Fran said. — You're happy now, you know you are. Anyway, we can always come back here to visit. There are plenty of places to stay, some lovely B&Bs in the area.

Alice looked horrified. — I never would. I can't ever come back, not anywhere near here, once we've sold the house. That will be the end of it, for me.

TWO

———

THE CHILDREN LOATHED housework if their mother ever asked them to do any, but they threw themselves with enthusiasm into Kasim's new project of cleaning out the cottage. They escaped from home in any intervals when it wasn't raining, or wasn't raining much, smuggling out a plastic bucket and a dustpan and a brush and cloths and bottles of cleaning stuff, returning them later without anyone noticing. If the grown-ups asked where they were off to, so preoccupied and important, they said evasively that they were playing a new game in the woods. Ivy wore her long silk skirt because it conferred extra dignity upon their mission, though it dragged in the mud. Fran wondered where the bucket was, but it didn't occur to her that the children had it; when she found filthy wet cloths dropped in a corner in the scullery, she thought crossly that Alice must have been cleaning her room in one of her fits of energy. Alice had mostly stayed in bed since they'd made their decision to sell.

Fran had felt sorry for her, and taken her cups of tea – then she made that little face of disappointment, if you didn't bring it in the pretty cup she liked.

Molly was half in on the cottage secret, but Kas made her promise not to tell. He liked having something to hold back from her. — It's a surprise for you! he said. — Wait until tomorrow. I'll take you to see it tomorrow evening, I promise.

— But why can't I come now?

He was smiling down into her face, holding her shoulders, his face close to hers, so that she couldn't help reflecting back his smile. Between their two faces, each feasting on the looks of the other, even when they weren't kissing there was a tingling aware-ness of the sensations of kissing. — It's not ready for you yet, he assured her. — We've got to get rid of all the spiders.

He knew he mustn't mention the dead fox, or he'd never get her inside.

She shuddered. — Spiders! I hate spiders.

This gallantly tender Kasim was very different to the grim-faced businesslike one, with a dirty smudge on his cheek, who made a fire in the clearing outside the cottage, helping it along with firelighters and a dash of lighter fuel, while the watching children stood serious and impressed. The three of them hardly spoke all the time they were working – sweeping and scrubbing and carrying out armfuls of dead leaves – except in curt practi-calities. Arthur hunted around in vain for his pound coins. The fire spat and crackled, threatened to go out, and then regained force: sparks whirled up into the wet grey day, making the chil-dren step back smartly. Kasim propped open the cottage door and ran up and down the poky staircase again and again until his tee shirt was wet with sweat, bringing out the piles of magazines on a shovel he'd found in one of the outhouses at Kington, as if he didn't deign to touch them with his hands. No comment in relation to this mystery of the Women ever passed between the three, while they fed the fire with their naked images and watched them burn, blackening sulkily to nothing, the paper turning to a heavy ash that kept its shape as pages. Only Ivy told Arthur in bed that night that the Women's power was broken now: they'd taken his money, and were satisfied. At some point she threw away the little trove of sacred things and signs they'd collected, as if they were all suddenly just trash.

When the magazines were disposed of, Kasim went upstairs again with the shovel. The children looked at each other.

— Does he know that it's Mitzi? Arthur asked.

Ivy was scornful. — He doesn't even know Mitzi ever existed.

— Tell him, then.

— You tell him.

— No, you.

They were both silent when, more cautiously, and with his head twisted fastidiously away, Kasim came out with what must be the dog's remains held out at arms' length on his shovel. These were scrambled now out of their meaningful shape, to a mere nasty heap of contaminating mess. This didn't burn well, until – ordering the children sternly to stand behind him – Kasim threw on more lighter fuel, and more of the dry kindling he'd lugged in his rucksack from the house; then a great flame shot up and everything blazed, and afterwards settled to smouldering and fuming with a greasy black smoke which hung around for hours afterwards, making Ivy feel sick although she didn't say so. It took three trips upstairs before Kasim had scraped the whole thing up. He set to work next on the floor in that last room, with a stiff broom and buckets of water taken from the stream, tearing down the rags of curtain and burning those too, along with all the dead leaves shored up under the window, scrubbing with bleach at the walls blackened with damp and the persisting dark stains on the floor. The children couldn't look at what was left, when the fire burned down – bones, which Kasim kicked away into the undergrowth.

Fran couldn't believe how filthy the children were when they got home; they left a scummy grey watermark on the sides of the bath. When she drove into town the next morning to talk to the estate agents, Kasim and the children asked to go with her, and then mysteriously shopped. — It's for our game, Ivy explained. Kas chose a bottle of wine – rosé, which he thought Molly would like. In a place called The Four-Leaved Clover, ducking under a whole orchestra of wind chimes pinned to the low ceiling, he purchased cones and sticks of incense and scented candles – fairly incredulous at the prices – and an aromatic oil called ylang-ylang which the girl recommended. Telling the children to wait outside, he also went into the chemist's for condoms. Then they went back to the cottage together for the last time, arranging the candles on the shelves and windowsills, sprinkling the whole bottle of oil around. When the candles and the incense were lit, their perfumes mingled exotically with the rooms' pungent damp and smell of bleach. Kasim had stuffed his rucksack with blankets taken from the airing cupboard at Kington, and now he folded these into a corner; he'd also borrowed two glasses and a corkscrew, and put these with the wine and a couple of packets of crisps.

As an experiment, he lit a fire in the grate downstairs. This changed the house completely, as if they awoke something alive in it; he and Arthur crouched side by side on the hearth to watch protectively over the tentative flame with its noisy crackle, Arthur's fists clenched on his dirty bare knees, his long hair pushed behind his ears, the fire's light on his face. Excitedly Ivy entered into the spirit of the transformation, arranging pink flowers in a cup without a handle which she'd found in the tall grass outside the door. She wound trailers of wet greenery along the mantelpiece and above the door to the stairs, around the old nails which were stuck randomly here and there in the walls.

— Are you going to bring Molly here? she asked. — Isn't the wine for her?

— I am going to bring her, Kasim said, looking round from the fire with earnest importance. — And you two aren't going to come with us. Molly and I have something serious to sort out, which we can't discuss in the house. We need to be alone. D'you understand that? If you try to follow us, I'll kill you.

They nodded solemnly.

— Are you going to marry her? Ivy said.

— Don't be ridiculous.

THE HOTEL WITH THE SWIMMING pool was smothered in a sea mist; Harriet and Pilar couldn't even see the sea. It was impossible to believe they had basked so recently in the hot sun in this garden – those plants still dimly visible through the mist were bowed and dripping, upturned chair legs protested on the tables. While they waited in the hotel car park for the engine to die, Pilar showed Harriet two photographs, taken from a manila envelope in her handbag. She explained that these were the two married students who had disappeared in the nineteen seventies, along with their baby son and unborn child. Now, Pilar said, the parents of these students were hounding her and her brother, fixated on the belief that they were the children of these lost children. It wasn't good news about the injunction; her brother might go ahead with the testing, though he seemed to be hesitating at the last moment.

He wouldn't speak to Pilar on the phone, she had only spoken with his wife.

The photos were in black and white, printed on computer paper; they weren't very clear, areas of the black ink had fused together. The young man was wearing glasses, rather expressionless and affronted, as if his picture had been taken for passport ID. The young woman's was more informal: she was smiling up at the photographer, confident of her attraction – she might have been caught in the middle of lively conversation. Her long hair, parted in the middle, fell around her shoulders, solid in the printout like a dark cape. All Harriet could think, staring into their faces, was how thoroughly dead they were. The secret of their deaths had become the central fact about them, blotting out everything else, devouring all the decades which were stolen from them, when they couldn't change out of themselves. Their present had faded gradually out of fashion.

— What do you feel? she warily asked, putting her hand on her friend's.

— Nothing, Pilar said impatiently, shaking her off, busy with something in her bag, her lipstick. — What am I supposed to feel? I'm sorry for them, as anyone would be sorry. But they don't mean anything to me. Do you hate me for that?

She redid her lipstick with scrupulous care – even though they were about to swim – using the mirror on the visor over the passenger seat, pressing her lips together on a tissue, opening her eyes rather wide at the sight of herself. Harriet didn't take the trouble to say she could never hate her. — Do you think they are your parents? She does looks like you.

— You can't tell, Harriet. And anyway it doesn't mean anything. A sperm and an egg. My parents – god forgive them! – are the two fine clowns who brought me up, made a rare mess of it.

Harriet tried to focus on the moral dimensions of Pilar's story. But it was as if some charged low storm cloud – like the darkened, blinded day beyond the steamy windows of the car – blocked her clear perception whichever way she looked. She couldn't straighten up to see past this blockage clearly, through the next minutes and hours into any future. Now that they'd decided to sell the house, she was surprised how much this change seemed like the end of a world, and a crisis in which anything might happen. The end of their holiday was drawing near, the weeks of this summer were ringed already, in retrospect, in a lurid glare of nostalgia for something unrepeatable. Harriet might not see her brother's wife again for months, she didn't know if she could bear that. And because the time left in proximity to Pilar was so short, it was gathering density: as if the hours remaining were backing up against a closed, an untried door. Harriet did not let herself think of what might lie behind the door. She wanted something more from her new friend, that was all – something that sometimes Pilar seemed to be holding out to entice her, like one of the bright jewels in her rings: promising and tantalising. Yet Harriet couldn't be oblivious to a hard limit of calculation in Pilar's look. Hope and doubt pulsed back and forth in her, in their alternating current.

THAT AFTERNOON, KASIM AND MOLLY quarrelled. He had been feeling particularly fond of her, making her laugh, cherishing his secret of the cottage's transformation. Ivy and Arthur were sworn not to say anything. It seemed to him that he'd made extraordinary concessions, in all his preparations, to everything in Molly that was susceptible and sweet and female. Fran put out lunch for the children on the kitchen table and Kasim and Molly joined in, then when she smelled coffee Alice came down too, in her dressing gown. Kasim read out depressing headlines from the *Guardian* which Fran had brought from town. Alice pleaded with him to stop and he found worse and worse ones until she put her hand over her ears. *Gaddafi loyalists held over bomb blasts. UK self-sufficiency in food falling. Violence during Eid celebrations in Syria.*

— It's not funny, Molly said suddenly, frowning down furiously at the bread she was buttering, as if some pent-up condemnation burst out of its bounds. — You can't just use people's sufferings to make a joke.

Kasim was taken aback. — It's better than pretending they're not happening.

— Is it really better?

Molly insisted with a bitterness that hadn't been any part of Kasim's plan; he was wounded and offended. — She doesn't even read the newspaper, he said, appealing around the table. — She doesn't even know where Libya is.

— I'm such a coward, Alice said, conciliatory, smiling from one to the other. — I definitely want to pretend.

— *I* know where Libya is, Ivy cautiously contributed, although she didn't.

— I don't want to know where it is, Molly cried. — I don't have to.

She was looking intently down at her plate and the nakedness of her dropped purple eyelids was reproachful, chastening; cutting slices of cheese, she layered them on her bread, then added sliced tomatoes, coleslaw. When she looked up, her eyes flared with indignation. — Just knowing things without doing anything doesn't help anybody. What's the point of having an opinion about everything? I think it's better not to know. It's more *kind*, just to feel sorry for people.

Kasim thought that was hilarious. — You mean just feel sorry for people generally, without even knowing whether they're actually suffering from anything?

— I know what Molly's trying to get at, Alice put in.

— At least I believe in people, Molly said, — which is more than he does.

— I *believe* in people all right. I mean, I think they're real, they actually exist.

— But you've got such a gloomy outlook. Everything's always going to turn out for the worst. In real life there are lots of good people: nurses and social workers and postmen and councillors and everything. There are people who change things and make them better. Don't you have any hope?

— Hope! That's a fucking message on a birthday card.

— Do you mind? Fran protested. — There are babies here.

Ivy and Arthur said indignantly that *they* weren't babies, Molly ran up to her room leaving her sandwich, and Kasim sat on in high dudgeon at the table, eating through his own sandwich and then hers too, to show his indifference. Fran remarked that he seemed to have eaten his way through a fair amount of food over the holiday, though she hadn't noticed he'd contributed anything – but he hardly seemed to hear her. Then the children had to run between Kas and Molly with important faces all afternoon, peacemaking, carrying messages back and forwards between where Molly sat in tears amid the rich chaos of her room, and Kasim, with an intransigent bleak face, in the empty tidiness of his. Estranged from her, he felt exposed, as though some shelter had been ripped away where he'd been leaning into it.

Postmen? he wondered, with a savage irony only for his own benefit. Did she seriously include *postmen* in her kindly fucking team of do-gooders? Straight out of her first reader in infants – or

Postman Pat, more likely. Morally and intellectually, she's still an infant.

HARRIET AND PILAR HAD THE pool all to themselves again: its strange space seemed to have awaited them, sealed underground, without windows, soundless and motionless, intact through all the days since they last left it, unchanging whatever changed in the weather outside. The effect of the yellow lights, upward cast, was to make them feel as if they slid into some other element than water, something molten or oily, turning choppy as they broke it up. Because any sound in the pool was amplified and distorted, and then swallowed, they felt a prohibition against speaking, as distinctly as if someone had turned to them with a finger across sealed lips. Swimming up and down, again and again, in a smooth continuous motion, they turned almost without a splash, and didn't race: instead of trying to beat Pilar, Harriet adjusted her pace to stay with her exactly, as if she swam in the other woman's wake. She let herself be absorbed in their communion, she told herself it was sufficient happiness, in the time that was left to them, that they moved like this in concert without touching, cleaving through the chlorinated water, up and down the thwarting short length of the pool.

Pilar was the first to have had enough. Streaming water as she climbed the steps, giving out a little grunt of exhaustion or gratification, she pulled off her rubber cap, letting down the dark mass of her hair.

That's it, then, Harriet thought resignedly. It's over.

Then standing at the poolside with her back to Harriet, Pilar casually pulled off her wet swimming costume too, tugging it by the shoulder straps down past her waist, stepping out of it, stooping swiftly to pick up the diminished sodden scrap – though any stranger, a guest at the hotel, might have come through the door at any moment. This peeling away of the last minimal layer of Pilar's covering, and the revelation of her nakedness, the sight of her swinging breasts when she half-turned, was overwhelming for Harriet in the confined space. Pilar's waist was strikingly narrow, the curve into her buttocks was as exaggerated as if she was corseted; the sight of her naked full bottom was frankly intimate, friendly, teasing. Wringing out her costume as she went, she disappeared, flat-footed, round the corner to the showers and changing cubicles. Left behind and treading water, Harriet was sure that this gesture could not mean nothing. It was too flaunting, not to have some message in it for her – one of those messages she had no doubt failed to heed, in the waste of her youth. Now this time, before it was too late, she mustn't fail. Mustn't even think; not thinking was the key.

Pilar was facing her, when she followed, under the shower without having pulled the curtain across, working the shampoo into a lather in her hair, her head bent forward under the onslaught of water and steam. Probably she couldn't see Harriet. Her nakedness was more terrifying from the front: even half-veiled by the water which was slanting off her breasts, streaming in the pubic hair shaved to a black line. She was like a goddess under a waterfall, thought Harriet – the sight made her more afraid. But she mustn't miss life, just because she was afraid. So she stepped into the shower and put her arms round Pilar, whose flesh was yielding, slippery, hot from the hot water. There was a little scuffle, a scream, Pilar exclaimed loudly in Spanish. The whole scene was over in a matter of a few seconds.

Then Harriet was outside the shower again, stumbling, dripping with wet. She might have seen the impression of white finger marks on her upper arms where Pilar had seized her and shoved her, or might have imagined them. The pink plastic curtain had been snapped across and behind it the hot shower still streamed, soapy water swirling around Pilar's long feet – visible below the curtain, toenails painted cherry-red – and into the drain. She was rinsing the shampoo out of her hair.

— I'm so sorry, Harriet said, raising her voice above the water's noise. — I'm so sorry. Forgive me. I misunderstood.

But Pilar was not English, so there was no exchange of apologies, mumbled embarrassment, grudging concession. Her outrage was the goddess's, implacable. In one scouring lightning flash, Harriet saw everything: all her hopes were a mistake and a sad delusion, her transgression was grotesque. Pilar had flirted with her no doubt, tantalising her, bestowing her favour in kind looks and touches. But between their types – the blessed, beautiful type and the other one – there ought to exist an impassable threshold. It had not occurred to Pilar that Harriet could succumb to the gross error of trying to cross over it.

Harriet fled in her shame to the poor privacy of her changing cubicle, pulling her own pink curtain across behind her. She thought for a long moment that she would freeze there where she stood, shuddering in the cold wet costume clinging to her – it would be a relief if she turned into something wooden and need not move ever again. But then she remembered that she had to drive Pilar home. She must dry herself, pull on her clothes over stiff limbs, start up the car, and sit beside Pilar – who had been, an hour ago, her friend and confidante but now would not speak to her, not ever again, and would never even in the least degree acknowledge that she had herself played some small role in Harriet's error. It seemed impossible that Harriet could do these things, and yet she knew she must, and that she would. The twenty-minute drive would be her punishment.

And while she was dressing Pilar came from the shower and put on her own clothes. Harriet flinched from the uninhibited indignation on the other side of the thin partition – as unmistakeable as if Pilar had banged on the walls and stamped on the floor. Would Pilar tell Roland what had happened? It seemed likely she would: she might tell everyone. Harriet couldn't live, she thought, with her brother and sisters knowing what a mistake she'd made, how she was humiliated. Pilar's closeness in the next cubicle squeezed her until she couldn't breathe and couldn't move. Crouching with her face buried in the darkness on her knees, she could only finish dressing when Pilar had gone – without any forgiving word – presumably to wait for her in the hotel reception.

EVERYONE KNEW THAT SOMETHING HAD happened. When the two women arrived back it was as if some tail end of a storm came licking into the house with them, through the scullery door which they left open behind them – until it banged shut in the wind. Their not speaking thrust loudly into everyone's awareness, as their everyday voices wouldn't have. Pilar went upstairs at once, the scrape of her heels significant on every uncarpeted step and resounding against the bare walls, around the empty rooms: the abrupt intolerant clatter condemned them all, the place and its shabbiness, their pointless way of life inside it. Roland had been talking to Alice in the study, they were falling back into their old friendly way of rambling around whatever subject Alice started up – but he was stopped mid-sentence by some message for him in his wife's noisy ascent; then he hated the way Alice significantly didn't look at him, too alert to the sound of trouble. While he followed Pilar upstairs, Alice went to find Harriet, who was standing quite still, holding the kettle under the scullery tap, which she hadn't turned on.

— We've had coffee, Alice said. — Why didn't you have some at the hotel?

Harriet put down the empty kettle, as if she'd forgotten why she'd picked it up. Her hair was so wet it was plastered to her head, her face was luminous with misery, pale eyes staring so that they seemed almost lidless, like some sea-animal's.

— What the matter? Alice said. — You ought to dry your hair.

Her sister hauled her voice with weary effort out of the depths of herself. — Nothing at all's the matter.

— I don't believe you. Have you two fallen out or something?

— You can believe what you like. Anyway I'm going out.

— Out where? It's pouring with rain. You've only just come in.

— I feel like getting out. It was a mistake, the whole holiday has been a mistake, three weeks is much too long, Alice. I should have trusted my own judgement in the first place.

Harriet said she was going to get her waterproof; Alice heard her hurrying up into her own room, closing the door. There was bustle upstairs, more doors opening and closing, brisk footsteps in the back bedroom, pragmatic voices – Roland's and Pilar's, Molly's. At the end of ten minutes, Roland came down to tell Alice and Fran that he and Pilar and Molly had decided to leave, as the weather was so disappointing. They were going to set off soon, in time to stop for a meal somewhere on the way home. Pilar wasn't feeling all that well, she was overtired and also something had cropped up at work, she needed to get back. And Molly had said she wanted to go with them. Alice exclaimed that they couldn't just leave like that. If there was something wrong, couldn't they sort it out? They ought to all have one last meal together, at least. Fran said she'd shopped for nine, how would they eat it all? Alice wanted to ask Roland what had happened, but when she put her arms around him felt how he held himself fractionally apart from her, as if he could only be in sympathetic communion with one woman at a time.

Then he went upstairs again to pack and meanwhile Harriet slipped out through the kitchen, in her waterproof with the hood drawn up over her head. — Don't be silly, Alice called after her. — You'll catch cold if you go out in the rain with that wet hair. Don't you want to say goodbye to Roland? Did you know they're leaving?

They heard the scullery door open, and then close again.

— Do you think they quarrelled over politics? Fran wondered.

— Something worse, Alice said.

— Harriet's driving? She crawls along, it's just as dangerous as going too fast.

— Or perhaps she spilled something on the white trousers.

The sisters dawdled in the kitchen, drying cups and knives, not knowing how to fill in the uneasy time while they waited for the others to have left. Roland toiled purposefully up and down the stairs, piling up bags and cases in the hall – all that impressive luggage! – and the house seemed tensely suspended between two eras. The children were playing clock patience on the hall floor, right in the way, just where Roland needed to come past; Ivy, dealing out, was grimly sceptical of them ever triumphing. Then when Roland started taking things out to the car, wiping his feet on the mat, propping the scullery door open, an uneasy wind blew everywhere downstairs. There seemed to be nowhere comfortable to sit, and no one wanted tea. — It's awful being left behind, Alice said. — It's always more glamorous to be the ones going.

Upstairs, Molly opened the door to Kasim's room, sidled in and closed it soundlessly behind her. Then she waited with her back to the wall, her hand on the doorknob as if for an easy getaway. Kasim was sitting on the side of his bed with his elbows on his knees, scowling down at his phone, playing a game of Angry Birds. She told him that her dad was leaving, and that she'd said she'd go with him.

— No problem, he said, not looking up. — Have a good trip. Been nice knowing you.

— It's something to do with Pilar's work, she has to get back.

— Fair enough.

— I mean, I needn't go, I could stay here with my aunts for a few more days, they could give me a lift to the station when they leave.

— Up to you.

— But what do you think?

— Makes no difference to me.

They waited. She tightened her hand on the doorknob and began slowly to turn it, making Kasim look up at her at last: she was wearing shorts and a white tee shirt, her long legs and feet were bare, and she was standing balanced on one leg, with the other one tucked up, foot flat to the wall, behind her. She was like a white bird beside a lake, he thought. Her face was faintly swollen from crying.

— Though it's a shame you never got to see the cottage, he said. — I mean, the way I've sorted it all out. I did it specially for you. You'd have liked it.

— That *is* a shame, she agreed, heartfelt, hesitating. — Well, I could stay.

— I could show you tonight.

— All right then.

— If you stayed.

— I will. I'll go and tell them now.

AT LAST THEY WERE GONE. Up until the moment of their departure, their leaving had seemed dreadful – they were tearing an irreparable gap, which must be the beginning of the end. The old house must be finished with now, the others felt, and they might as well leave too. Farewells were shallow and perfunctory, as if they suddenly couldn't wait not to see one another any longer. Pilar smiled and squeezed Alice's hand, but her eyes were truthful and her insincerity was even somehow righteous. With a hand on the roof of the Jaguar she hesitated, about to fold herself sinuously into the passenger seat, and Alice wondered whether it had occurred to her to leave some message for absent Harriet – if it did, then the next moment she thought better of it. Roland held out his cheek for his sisters to kiss as if he were elsewhere already. He sent his love to Harriet – so Pilar hadn't told him about their quarrel yet, whatever it was, or at least hadn't insisted that he take sides. He was pained because Molly had chosen to stay – her aunts had promised to keep an eye on her, but he didn't trust them. Embracing his daughter, he was punctiliously affectionate, but Alice saw how he withheld his approval, and in Molly's face saw the shadow of her fear of disappointing him.

And yet Molly had nonetheless stayed! Keeping Molly made the stayers-on triumphant. And as the Jaguar slid between the old gateposts always gaping their welcome promiscuously, those left behind – Fran and Alice and the children, Kas and Molly: Harriet hadn't yet returned from her walk – were suddenly jubilant, relieved, saved, shutting the front door behind the departed ones, putting on the kettle. After all, the present moment closed around them, and they needn't think of the future yet: they needn't think of leaving, or any endings. The four young ones went to play more Scrabble; Fran made tea, while Alice built a fire in the sitting room. Outside the French windows the afternoon changed and glowed with a mild light, the rain eased, a blackbird singing in a birch tree made it shiver and shed silver drops. Fran carried four tea mugs upstairs, all milked and sugared in different proportions, then brought Alice her pretty cup. — This is cosy, she said whole-heartedly, pulling her feet up under her in an armchair opposite Alice's armchair. — Now at last we can say what we think.

Kneeling at the hearth, Alice coaxed her fire with expertise, nudging a log into place with a stick of kindling, putting her hair behind her ears with the back of a smutty hand. — D'you mean, about Pilar?

— And everything.

— She isn't our type. But then perhaps our type is awful. Or at least, isn't good for Roland.

— We are awful.

— Relentless. Always pouncing on things, analysing them to bits.

— Do you remember how we tortured him when he was studying for his A levels? Leaving bits of our underwear in his sock drawers, writing him fake love letters. No wonder he's con-fused when it comes to women.

— Our type is no good to him. He needs someone who just thinks a remark is a remark, and a fact is a fact, a feeling is a feeling.

— But I mean, come on, Alice. She *stamped* on every step on her way upstairs!

— I was watching his face, and I think the only thing he minded was that I heard it. I don't think he cares much about scenes. It isn't scenes he hates: it's complications, and grey areas. He likes clear-cut situations.

— But whatever was going on between her and Harriet?

— I don't know, Alice said doubtfully.

UPSTAIRS, THE CHILDREN WERE GETTING Molly ready (after she'd won at Scrabble as usual). They wouldn't let Kasim into her bedroom, they told him he wasn't allowed to see her yet, he could see her at supper time. After supper, Kasim was taking her to the cottage: what was she going to wear? She said she would just wear her shorts as usual, but Ivy picked up a dress from where it was thrown over the back of a chair – Harriet had given it to Molly, saying she'd bought it and never worn it, Molly could give it to a charity shop if she didn't like it. Molly hadn't even bothered to try it on, she never wore dresses. Now Ivy fingered the filmy flowered chiffon wistfully, exclaiming that it was beautiful and she must wear it for her wedding. – It's not my wedding, Molly said.

– It is, it is, the children insisted, drunk with all the excitement in the house. – It's a pretend wedding.

So Molly stripped off her shorts and tee shirt and pulled the dress over her head: it was baggy across her bust, sleeveless, with a scoop-neck and fitted waist; the chiffon skirt with its blue cotton underskirt was cut in a full circle and hung limply to just above her knees. She wore it with her trainers and no socks, and looked as poignant as an orphan dressed in an old lady's cast-offs. Then she sat on the edge of her bed while Ivy knelt beside her with an intent face, doing Molly's hair in tiny plaits all over her head, weaving in beads and bits of ribbon and lace. Molly only ever wore one silver bangle but had bags full of accessories she never used: diamante chokers and sequined brooches and hairgrips stuck with pink butterflies, all grubby from being jumbled in with tubes and pots of the make-up that she didn't use much either. They heaped her with jewellery – her own and then everything else they could find. – We're dressing Molly up, they said to Alice. – Can we borrow some of your necklaces?

Alice was enthusiastic and also lent them a lace scarf and clip-on white earrings, round and matte like mint imperials, which she told them had belonged to their great-grandmother, Sophy. –

Oh, *that* dress, she said when she saw Molly. — I knew that Molly would look lovely in it.

Ivy pinned the lace scarf in Molly's hair like a veil, then they painted her face; Arthur was allowed to put green on her eyelids with a brush, concentrating furiously, the tip of his tongue protruding between his lips. Ivy pencilled her eyebrows strongly in black, then put blusher on her cheeks and did her lipstick. — Go like this, she said, bringing her a square of toilet paper from the bathroom, pressing her own lips together to show Molly how to blot them.

Molly laughed when she saw herself in the mirror.

— Goodness, Fran said. — What have you done to the poor girl?

— She *likes* it, Ivy insisted.

Arthur started to tell his mother that it was for Molly's wedding, but Ivy kicked him and frowned at him, shaking her head. Kasim said she looked like a nightmare and would have to take it all off, but Molly who thought it was funny was suddenly stubborn and said she wouldn't. Remembering their argument at lunchtime, he decided after all that it didn't matter, though he regretted the white bird she had been. So she ate supper with them in all her finery, her painted face unreal as a mask, not saying much or eating much. The others chattered around her almost as if the real Molly was absent; but they were also disconcerted and touched by the presence of this eerie, hieratic figure amongst them. She was like a doll or a gaudy image of a saint, brought down out of her niche for her feast day, conferring her importance on their meal.

STILL HARRIET HADN'T RETURNED. AFTER supper Alice stood with a tea towel in her hand at the front door, looking out for her, then walked up with the tea towel through the church-yard, expecting to meet her taking the short cut home. Fran was washing up and Alice ought to be helping; Harriet would only be cross with her for worrying. If they did meet, she would give Alice her shrivelling look: why did she have to make such a fuss out of everything? But Alice was susceptible to this panic of wait-ing for nothing in particular; expectation beat against the eve-ning's serenity. The sky overhead was glassy now, as if it had been washed clean; in the west a mass of cloud on the horizon, navy blue and edged in rosy light, was like a whole city in the distance whose existence they'd somehow overlooked, or forgotten. Noth-ing in this bland external world resounded with Alice's anxiety; while she stood watching at the church front gate, Kas and Molly passed, walking hand in hand on the road. Molly had pulled a jumper over her dress because the temperature was dropping; her hair was still in plaits, though she seemed to have scrubbed her face clean and looked more like herself. They said they were going for a stroll; distractedly, Alice told them not to stay out too long, it would be getting dark soon.

Fran didn't know why Alice was worried: Harriet was well known for walking off her moods. — You know her: she'll have a torch with her and a packet of Kendal Mint Cake and a compass. Anyway, how could she get lost anywhere round here?

— But she didn't take the torch, Alice said, — it's on its hook in the scullery. And what if she's fallen somewhere, and can't move?

She wandered upstairs and, when she'd used the bathroom, went into her brother's room, which was not restored to self-sufficiency by the absence of its visitors, but seemed changed by their passage, as if they had stripped away a surface and left it bereft. Empty coat hangers, hooked over the rim of the wardrobe, jangled to her footsteps; the duvet and pillows denuded of their covers were a white mound on the mattress, tinged pink by the low sun; a forgotten sock lay in her sightline just under the edge of the bed. In the wastepaper basket were cotton wool balls dirty with make-up, an empty water bottle, yesterday's newspaper; she looked for those letters Roland had written to their mother, but he must have taken them with him. The flowers she had put out more than a fortnight ago were mummified on the windowsill, in a remaining half-inch of evil-smelling thick green water. Alice was about to pick up the vase to take it downstairs when instead, on an impulse, she opened the door in the corner which led out of this room into Harriet's.

Her fear returned as soon as she crossed this threshold: something in her sister's room – or just nothing, precisely the minimal trace that Harriet left – seemed at last to speak to her own dread. The room was too thoroughly empty, as if Harriet might never return to it. With an effort, scolding herself for her melodrama, Alice repressed a picture that rose before her mind's eye, of a body laid out under a sheet on the narrow bed, their family gathered in grief around it. This was nonsense, of course – at the worst, Harriet might have broken an ankle, or perhaps a leg. Then, with a sister's unerring instinct for finding what she was not supposed to see, Alice went straight to the drawer where Harriet's diary was kept, felt for it confidently under the clean underwear. She told herself she mustn't look inside it, but then immediately afterwards that she must. And the book fell open naturally onto the pages where Arthur had scrawled lipstick obscenities, and his name.

But it wasn't Arthur, Alice understood at once. It must have been Ivy, in one of her tempers, who wrote these things, putting on the fake misspellings too inconsistently: *Leeve me alone, Fuk you, U are an ugly sow.* This was only childish naughtiness. Alice even laughed out loud at it in sheer surprise, imagining Ivy's sour little face as she wrote, twisted with vicious invention. Yet Harriet surely ought to have said something, she ought to have protested; Alice seemed to feel how her sister had taken these stabbing insults inside herself, to let them work in her. Sinking down to sit on the side of the bed, turning on the bedside light to see better, she began reading the words written behind them, in biro, in Harriet's distinctive small hand with its Greek *e*: the letters were all made separately, never joined in a cursive flow. *Is this happiness? My feelings seem crazy, a sickness, when I think of how P. has suffered in the real world. But tonight after she'd used the bath, rescued her long hairs where they blocked the plughole, kept them and touched them.*

Alice guessed, she turned the pages in haste, leaping quickly ahead, following the story through. *Hope and doubt, I don't know what to think. P. touched my hand, haven't washed it all day. I'm like an idiotic child because I don't know how these things are done. I hate Roland, because he has her in there.* Ivy's dirty words, defacing the page, must have felt like Harriet's own judgement on herself. And in fact when Alice turned to find the last written entry, she saw that the neatly printed lettering broke off in violent strokes of Harriet's own pen down the page, digging into the paper, tearing at it. *Stupid, stupid, you stupid . . . How could I? What have I done? It's all over.*

THE SKY SEEMED MORE FULL of light, as it drained from the earth. On her way down the disused road, Alice could still just about see, if she looked up, though not her own feet, not in the tunnel of darkness under the trees, knotty thick-leaved branches black against jewel blue, like a wild wood in a children's book. A white house floated on the road below her; this was the mill where they made paper for artists. Emerging from the tunnel,

she saw bats like clots of darkness breaking away from the gathered darkness in the trees and under the eaves of the house; these
felt like the forms of her own anxiety clotting in her, breaking up
inside her thoughts. She had only come out – grabbing a pullover
and someone's clammy waterproof in the scullery, stripping off
her strappy sandals and plunging her bare feet into damp anonymous wellingtons – because it was intolerable waiting at home. —
But you don't even know which way she went! Fran said.

Beyond the paper mill the road climbed up again, and at the
top Alice crossed a stile, onto a path over a field. This was the way
they most often came to walk when they were children. She was
wading now in a cold, white evening mist, risen out of the damp
field, that swirled around her knees as dense as milk; she had
brought the torch but she didn't want to put it on, not yet – who
knew how much life the batteries had in them? Anyway, she could
still see, it was not quite dark, a few swallows were swooping and
twittering in the broad space of the field in the last light, dipping
into the mist and darting out of it.

Alice began to call her sister's name. *Har-riet! Het-tie!* The
sound of her voice singing out was comforting and strange, as
if it wasn't her own but came from somewhere outside, echoing
against the curve of the field sloping sharply up. But ahead was
the dark entrance to the wood, like a hole burrowed in the barrier of the wood's darkness. When she had to pass through that,
she thought, she wouldn't be able to do it, she'd never have the
courage. Her search was pointless anyway, and her bare feet were
rubbing painfully in the wellingtons. Harriet could have gone anywhere in the hills and valleys round about, she might be miles
away: Alice would never find her. Her imagination failed, she felt
a disenchanted flatness. There was only fear, and her own insufficiency in the empty dark: she was almost certainly only heading

into nothing. In the daytime, in all weathers, she had always liked this gate into the wood with its promise of what lay beyond – she had thought of the birch wood's shadowed interior, and the grace of its trees in summer and winter, like a lovely room. When she arrived at the gate now, and leaned on it, she called again into nothingness, and her voice seemed an intrusion into the wood's withdrawn self. The invisible trees loomed vividly present to her other senses, unfriendly and portentous. At its edge the birch wood had been planted with a few pines, felled recently and now stacked beside the path, their resin pungent in the wet air, the fresh sawdust showing up in pale patches.

And then she had opened the gate and gone through, was immersed in the darkness of the wood and couldn't bring herself to call out again. When she switched on the torch it was as though what surrounded her leaped back, but not reassuringly, gathering intensity rather at the edges of the narrow light-tunnel of her vision. If she swung the light beam around, then the crooked slender trunks, ghost-pale, seemed drawn up in ranks, spelling something significant. What violence was it she feared, though she wasn't ever afraid in a city street? When with a crashing rumpus some animal – a deer? – broke unseen out of the dark ahead, bounding away, Alice was wrenched with shock. She told herself that she'd go through this first stretch of woodland, and no further; when she reached the wedge-shaped field – beyond which there were more woods – if Harriet wasn't there, she would turn back.

Climbing out of the wood, across another stile, she was surprised that there was so much light left in the sky. Milky mist was pooled here at the field's bottom below her; above her she could still make out distinctly the tall rocky banks and mounds of bramble, stunted thorn trees. Weren't those cows, standing at the top of the field across the stream, looking down attentively towards her? Some white shape, anyway, against the gloom. It was a relief to be out in the open. The deep cleft of a stream, overgrown with more brambles, bisected this field in a meandering line; unseen, it babbled in its hollows like a muffled clapper in a bell. Again Alice called out, sing-song. *Het-tie! Har-riet!* She stared up at the distant white shape, which seemed to be lying now along the ground, then started towards it, stumbling on the tussocky rough grass, torch beam jerking inconsequentially.

— Hettie! Is it you? Are you there?

If it was a cow, it might scramble to its feet and charge at her, knock her down. Everything in the night was alive with threat. And Alice couldn't understand, if the shape was Harriet – too slender, and too tapered, after all, for a cow – why she didn't move, and why she showed up in that distinctive way, an inert pale smudge against the gathering darkness of the field. If it was Harriet, she seemed to be turned away, concentrating intently over something private. Alice's ears were filled with her own gasping for breath as she hurried up the slope, boots slipping in the wet. She fell and cracked her knee sickeningly against a rock, struggled up again. Water boiled somewhere nearby in a cold rage, the stream must be falling over a lip of stone. Peering ahead, poking the torch beam, Alice saw then in one scrambled recognition that her sister lay naked on the grass, fork-limbed, face down, bottom up. The violence of the night had been made real, the worst had happened – even though Alice in her horror refused its truth with all her force, protesting aloud against it. It couldn't be so, but it was. The protest, even as she made it, seemed directed at no one present who could hear it. *No! No, no, no!*

Then Harriet lifted her head, twisting her neck to look up over one shoulder, squinting into the torch beam. — Oh Alice, why did you come? she said. — I wanted to die.

Alice was overwhelmed. She couldn't bear Harriet to know she'd believed she was dead, and directed the torch at her accusingly, dazzling her. — But what are you doing here? Where are your clothes?

— I threw them in the water, so that I couldn't change my mind.

— Change your mind about what?

— I don't know. I just wanted to die. I'd had enough.

— You're kidding. You're not serious. Whoever, in the whole history of idiocy, tried to kill themselves by catching cold in the middle of summer?

— I don't know. It turns out I don't even know how to die.

Shining the torch around, Alice found Harriet's woollen jumper, caught in a bramble bush and not quite fallen in the stream. One cuff was soaked where it had dangled down. — Put this on. At once.

— But I haven't got my underwear.

— Have you gone mad? Oh yes, I forgot, obviously you have gone mad. It doesn't matter about your underwear, you idiot. I'll give you my jumper too, to put on top. We have to stop you getting hypothermia – not that I seriously think you *could* get hypothermia at this time of year. I'll give you my skirt as well.

While they talked, Alice was dressing her sister as best she could, pulling the jumper over Harriet's lolling head, rolling up the wet cuff, then taking off her waterproof and her own jumper, putting these on Harriet too. Harriet was compliant but she didn't help, she let Alice put her clothes on for her as if she were a child; her arms were heavy, quite separate things from any will of hers, Alice had to lift them and force them into the sleeves. Harriet said that she was numb. The night was cold, but not unbearably; at first Harriet wasn't even shaking, and then when she began she couldn't stop.

— You see, we have to put everything on you, Alice said. — I'm all right, I'm warm, it really isn't that bad, you've just got yourself into a state. Although I hope we don't meet anyone when we get to the village, me in my knickers. What were you thinking of? What were you thinking?

— You've no idea what's happened to me, what an awful thing I've done.

— Yes I do, Alice said. — I do have some idea. You made some kind of pass at Pilar and she turned you down. Don't worry, she hasn't told anyone, she won't. No one knows. I just guessed. This stuff happens to everyone. It's happened to me a million times over. I mean, mostly with men, it's true, and not with women. But actually, it did happen with a woman once.

Miserably Harriet turned her face away, closing her eyes.

— I know that just because it happens to everyone, that doesn't make it any better. But didn't you *think* about the rest of us, Hettie, and how we love you? Look at me, open your eyes! Isn't it amazing that I found you? I *knew* you'd be here, in this field at the end of the first wood, I knew. I came out because it was unbearable, waiting at home and worrying. And Fran said it was such a bad idea, because we hadn't a clue which way you'd gone, and she was perfectly sensible of course, I was the daft one as usual. But I just had this instinct! Something guided me, although it was all so dark and so awful. You know I've always believed in all that stuff. And now I've found you, thank goodness! And I've saved you! Isn't that amazing!

— But I didn't want to be saved.

— Yes you did. You did really. You just don't know it yet.

KASIM MADE MOLLY WAIT OUTSIDE the cottage for a few minutes while he hurried about inside, lighting the candles and the fire which he'd laid ready, spreading out the blankets on the floor in front of the fire. It didn't smell too bad. Molly was afraid of the dark, she pressed up against the far side of the door, moaning through the crack in her distress. — Can't I come in yet? *Please*, Kas! Let me in. It's horrible out here.

Then he was suddenly nervous when he did let her in, in case she made fun of what he'd done in the cottage, which he was so proud of. He watched her face uneasily; he couldn't get used to how different she looked with her hair sticking out all over her head in those weird plaits – exposed and mocking at the same time, like a clown. She was a stranger whom he hardly knew. When she smiled around her, liking everything, he remembered that women bestowed those bright smiles to encourage men's efforts and be kind to them, whatever they really thought. So he didn't trust her, and felt slightly vengeful.

— Oh, it's lovely, Kas. You've made it lovely. I'm so glad I stayed.

He got busy with opening the wine – it turned out to have a screw top, no need for the corkscrew – and emptying a packet of crisps into a bowl. They sat down on the blankets in front of the fire, which was burning well – he'd been drying the wood in preparation for a few days. Everything at least was going as he had planned. Still, Molly's idea of what happened next might not be quite the same as his. She might just think that they were going to spend the evening kissing and touching each other and getting worked up as usual, and then blow out the candles and go home. Strategically, according to his plan, Kas ought to be topping up her wine every time she tasted it. But when he tried, Molly put her hand across the top of the glass, saying she didn't want to get too drunk. Then she kissed him and her mouth was full of wine, which flooded into his mouth, shocking him. Had she done that deliberately?

So he kneeled up to kiss her back, more forcefully, bearing down on her from above, pushing his fingers up between the knotty plaits on the back of her head, lifting her face towards his, so that she was craning upwards. After a minute or so she twisted away, complaining she'd get a crick in her neck. — So, she asked him, beaming as if she had some secret. — Are you getting used to seeing me in a dress?

Kas couldn't believe that she was still worrying about what to wear. — It's a ridiculous dress, he said. — It looks awful.

Molly leaned forward to whisper, her breath tickling his ear. — All right then.

— All right what?

— If you don't like it, I'd better take it off.

Before he'd even understood, she stripped the dress in one easy movement over her head. Underneath it, she had nothing on. Her body was known to his hands, or half-known, but he was seeing it for the first time, as if she was newborn in the firelight licking over her: the little tipped-up breasts with blunt pink nipples, the long hollow of her stomach with slightly protruberant navel, the shadowy fluff at the crux of her, where she knelt with her thighs pressed together. She smiled at him shyly; she still had her mint imperial earrings on. — So, what do you think? Do you like me?

Kasim hardly knew where to begin.

— Don't be too anxious about this, he said. — I'll be very gentle. I've had quite a bit of experience.

— I've had some too, Molly said. — So I'm not anxious.

THREE

———

FRAN AND ALICE took turns all night to sit up with Harriet. Alice had told Fran everything. First they made Harriet drink hot tea with sugar and brandy in it, then they put her in her own bed to sleep, dressed in her pyjamas with a tee shirt underneath. They filled hot water bottles in relays – wrapping them in towels, careful not to put them too near her skin – and piled two duvets on her. Her flesh had felt so cold and unresponsive when they helped her take off her outdoor clothes – she'd lolled against them, not speaking, with her eyes half rolled up into her head. Fran phoned Jeff, to ask him to check on the internet whether they were doing the right things, or whether they ought to call a doctor. The brandy, it turned out, might have been a mistake. But she did seem warmer now, when they slipped a hand to check between the layers of her bedding. She had turned on her side to sleep, with her knees pulled up, and sometimes she snored. They didn't know how long she'd been exposed out in the field. Probably she'd only taken off her clothes when it began to get dark.

Alice also had to have hot tea, and sit with a blanket round her, and the electric heater turned on in the room; she wanted the brandy even if Jeff said it would make her worse. The horrors of her adventure – dressed only in her knickers and the wellingtons and a shirt, fortunately a long shirt, getting Harriet back through the wood and across the field – were already hardening into legend as she narrated them. Harriet had managed to walk, leaning heavily on her, stumbling and slithering. At least she hadn't thrown her boots into the stream along with her clothes – apparently she'd thought at the last moment that they might be useful to somebody. Fran said that Alice was a hero. They told the children, who weren't in bed yet when Alice and Harriet arrived home, that Harriet had had a fall, and couldn't move till Alice found her – which was what they'd told Jeff, and agreed to tell everyone.

— It's just such amazing luck that you persisted, Fran said again. — I feel so guilty! What if you'd listened to me?

— It wasn't luck. I knew. Something was guiding me, or someone. Don't you think it was our mother?

— Oh no, Alice, no. Don't say that, that's awful. What nonsense. You don't really believe it.

Fran was strictly rational, she put it all down to Alice's psychological insight. Harriet opened her eyes out of her sleep every so often, as if making sure they were still sitting there. — Say something, Harriet, Fran urged her. — We need to know you're compos mentis.

— I am compos mentis, she mumbled, closing her eyes again.

The bedside lamp shed a rosy light; Alice had thrown a red silk scarf over its shade. Outside a wind began to blow, unexpected after the afternoon's stillness, buffeting the house and rattling the windows. When Alice woke from dozing, in the armchair they'd carried in from Roland's room, again her sister's eyes were open, staring at her – but as soon as Alice spoke she closed them and pretended to be asleep. There was something almost voluptuous, Alice thought, in how Harriet was submitting to their attentions, allowing them to dress and undress her, spoon tea into her mouth, talk about her over her head. Ordinarily, in her austere life, there was no one to indulge her or make a fuss of her – certainly Christopher didn't. She held herself stiffly apart from anyone's pity. But now she claimed their care as unselfconsciously as a child, not even trying to thank them or to apologise for making trouble. It stirred Alice but also made her fearful, to see how far her sister was straying from her old self, undoing the vexed knots which had held her tight. She knew from her own experience what a great labour it was, binding up again all the mess of self, which in your extremity you had unbound.

When Fran had put the children to bed, she came back into Harriet's room and didn't sit down, kept going to look out into the darkness, through the window – which didn't look out onto anything much, only the scullery and the outhouses and back door. A light outside this door illuminated the wind tearing into the beech trees, raking through the leaves and stripping them, twisting them so that they flashed pale-side out. Fran didn't want to worry Alice, but there was no sign of Molly or Kasim: she had turned on the outside light in the hope of guiding them home if they were lost. Where on earth had they disappeared to? — What's the matter with everyone today? she protested.

So that second anxiety kept them up all night, began to consume them as the hours passed, and they took it in turns to catch half an hour's sleep. It seemed better somehow to keep a vigil through the young ones' absence than sleep through it. Should they phone Roland? But what was the point of worrying him, when there was nothing they could do until the morning? Should they phone the police? Alice said she was sure Kas and Molly were all right somewhere, she had a feeling. — And even if they were out all night, they could keep each other warm. Like the babes in the wood.

Fran groaned. — Are you allowed to be fanciful for ever now, just because you've found one missing person? It's horrible out there.

— Probably they got lost and then they walked until they found a pub somewhere, had a few drinks and booked a room to stay over.

— Though you'd think they could have called us in that case.

— I'll bet they haven't got the number.

— And if it turns out, Fran added, — that they have spent the night together in a room in a pub, let's not tell Roland.

IN THE MORNING FRAN WENT in early to the children's room, to interrogate them in case they knew anything. Because the day was brilliant, scoured clean by the night's storm, as she was about to pull the curtains open she noticed the light shining – like sequins or a burnished silver thread – through a number of tiny crosswise slits in the cloth, as if it had been deliberately nicked. Rousing the children, she demanded to know what had happened, but they met her with bemused blank faces. Confused and hot from their sleep, still in thrall to their dreams, it genuinely hardly seemed to Ivy or Arthur as if they were the same selves who knew all about the curtain-slits. But this first refusal set them fatefully on the primrose path of denial. Glumly they shook their heads when Fran asked them next if they knew anything about where Kas and Molly had gone. At the kitchen table, tousled and stuffy in their pyjamas, they bent their heads far down in silence over their bowls of rice krispies and golden nuggets, scooping in milk like model children who only wanted to be left in peace to play.

Harriet this morning had drunk tea and eaten toast with appetite, then turned over abandonedly into her sleep again. When Alice came downstairs to get more tea, all the doors were open onto the resplendent day – which intruded inside the house, casting light-rhomboids and dancing light motes on the walls and floors, exposing dingy corners. Only a litter of twigs and leaves in the garden, and spatters of rose petals on the soaked earth, gave any clue to the night's tantrums. Now that the day seemed so promising, Alice was more afraid. She walked to the front gate and looked up and down the road; puddles flashed in the sun, but she was undeceived. — We'll give them another hour, she said sourly in the kitchen, thinking the worst, — and then we'll call the police.

Arthur's and Ivy's startled glances – they hadn't known that they were in *that* deep – snagged and then disengaged, in instinctual self-preservation. An hour seemed an impossibly elastic interval, none of them knew what to do with it; all of them looked up hopefully every time there was any change in the light or sound from outside, and then were sick of themselves hoping. In her armchair in Harriet's room, Alice turned the face of the alarm clock away so that she didn't have to watch the time pass. Fran, because she hadn't slept, was bursting with a scratchy energy. She cast her look around the kitchen and lit upon Arthur's long pale gold locks, falling forward around his face like tent flaps as he focused on spreading his toast, holding his knife clumsily too far down the handle, bent on getting a skim of Nutella to the toast's edges. It struck his mother

295

that her son wasn't as innocent as once he had been. In the general mood of ominous expectation, she felt resigned to the truth that everything good had to be spoiled eventually, and announced that she was going to cut his hair.

— Get on the stool, she said. — I'll do it in your pyjamas.

Arthur was startled. He knew that in some complicated way his long hair fastened him to his mother – he'd always trusted that his dad, when the necessary moment came, would be the one to insist it was cut off. But it was Ivy who began to make a fuss, jumping up from the table, managing to spill milk from her cereal bowl and knock over her chair at the same time. — You can't cut his hair! What are you thinking of? You don't know what it means to me. I'll never feel the same about him if his hair's different. This is the Arthur I'm used to!

Fran paused without turning round, in the middle of her gesture of reaching for the scissors in their place on the row of hooks on the wall. — Just don't, Ivy. Don't start. Don't even dream of it.

And something in her voice made Ivy submit for once. Meekly and without another word she fetched the kitchen paper and used reams of it to mop up her spilled milk. Arthur perched on his high stool gave off the tragic aura of a martyred prince, but Fran was remorseless. She wasn't superstitious, but it crossed her mind that she was sacrificing something precious, to propitiate whatever fates there were. Ivy, when she'd finished mopping, watched in fascination. As the long coils dropped one after another onto the green linoleum, around the legs of the kitchen stool, a new Arthur seemed to come into being: without his old baby sweetness, shrewder, more bony and less soft, more unequivocally male. Hidden behind his hair, he'd been able to develop into a new self without their noticing. The hair's under-colour, left behind

– dented with the marks of clipping like a shorn lamb – was pale mouse-brown, without a hint of gold. As Fran cut she didn't say a word. By a strong effort of will she repressed her sorrow.

When she was more than halfway round his head, there were steps outside and they all looked up in expectation, hearts lifting at the idea of a reprieve. But it was only Janice Patten, blocking the light at the door. Fran was suspicious at once that Janice was nosing around because she'd heard something about Harriet; Alice had hoped that no one saw them on the road last night, but in the country somebody was always noticing something. Or they might have discovered Harriet's clothes, thrown into the stream: Alice had been going to rescue those later, if she could find them. Janice was dressed nautically in a blue-striped tee-shirt dress, with a peaked pink cap jammed down on her grey-blonde frizz. She took in the momentousness of the scene.

— Oh no, his lovely hair!

Fran guessed from something complacent in Janice's protest at the shearing that she approved of it. Perhaps people had talked – all those people they didn't even know, down here, whom Janice knew – about how she made a pet of her little boy. Vengefully she tugged at another lock, sawed into it; Arthur only grimaced, swaying stoically on his stool. And Fran looked at the clock: the hour was almost up. She might as well expose all their disasters.

— Yes, I thought it was about time. He can't stay a baby for ever. And we're in such a mess today: sorry Janice, I can't offer you coffee. We've got to go to the police: we've lost Molly. We've lost Kasim too, but he's not our responsibility. They haven't been back all night. They went off yesterday evening – we've no idea where. And Harriet's poorly.

Janice looked around their faces, miming distress; this was almost too much news at once, Fran thought, for her to properly enjoy. — Oh, you poor creatures, what a worry! What's wrong with Harriet? She's never ill, is she? But Kas and Molly – those two have a bit of a thing going on, don't they? Don't panic, they'll turn up!

Ivy was sepulchral. — Isn't that what they said to you about Mitzi?

For a moment Fran couldn't imagine who Mitzi was; with sorrowful dignity Janice reminded her, adding that it was not at all the same kind of case. — He's probably taken Molly off to a hotel somewhere. What does Roland think?

Fran, hard at work with the scissors, shook her head with her mouth pressed shut. She couldn't bring herself to confess that Roland didn't know. — Oh, they left yesterday.

— I saw the car. I noticed Molly wasn't with them.

Arthur was feeling his hair with his hand, to discover whether his mother was finished. Because he felt satisfied, patting at the absence where his pretty locks had been – he'd had to fight over them a few times already at school, just some minor kicks and punches in retaliation when anyone called him a girl – he was inspired to tidy things up all round. — We know where they are, he said, sounding clearer to himself because he wasn't muffled by his hair. — And where Mitzi is too. Or where she was – because Kas took her out when he was cleaning up.

Fran felt she hardly knew this boy with his bleak, naked head and calm authority. — Don't be silly, Arthur. They lost Mitzi months and months ago.

— And we found her, in the cottage in the woods.

— What cottage? Janice was bewildered. — Is Mitzi OK?

It was time to explain, Ivy decided. — Oh no, I'm sorry. Actually she's dead.

— Really dead, Arthur said. — All rotted and horrible. But

Kas shovelled her up and put her on the fire. He was cleaning everything out, so that he could take Molly there.

— Are they just showing off? Janice asked Fran. — Is any of this true?

Fran honestly couldn't say.

— They really love each other, Ivy insisted. — It was a kind of wedding. Don't worry, not a real wedding, only a pretend one. That's why we dressed her up.

ALICE HAD FORGOTTEN ABOUT THE time, she was lost in her thoughts in the armchair when Fran opened the door of the bedroom a crack, beckoning her over to whisper through it. Apparently Kasim and Molly had spent the night in the ruined cottage, the one on the way to the waterfall. So that was why Kas had wanted candles! The children had known about it all along, they were in big trouble.

— Don't be too cross with them, Alice pleaded.

They were all setting out for the cottage, as soon as the children were dressed. — And I've cut Arthur's hair!

— You haven't! I'll bet he looks lovely.

Fran made an unhappy face. — Alice, I don't like it. He looks like a real boy. He isn't blond at all. And Janice is coming with us.

— Why on earth?

— Oh, it's her wretched dog. Everything's going wrong.

— Don't worry. As long as you find Kas and Molly.

Alice went back to sit in her armchair. She heard the children's voices, and Fran insisting that they put on suncream, and then the crunch of little stones under all their feet on the drive as they went off, Janice having fetched her Nordic walking poles from across the road. The faded silky curtains were pulled across the bedroom window, so that the bright sun wouldn't bother Harriet. In the mauve light the dark old utility furniture, made of varnished cheap wood, seemed to float indistinctly.

— This is peaceful, she said when she saw Harriet was awake.

— I've made a dreadful fool of myself, Harriet said. Her face was yellow against the pillowcases, and her white hair stuck up like bristles where she'd slept on it. Involuntarily Alice's hand went up to touch her own hair, and her sister saw it.

— No you haven't, Alice said. — You're never foolish, you're one of the most serious people I know.

— I hate my own seriousness.

— Think of the wonderful work you do. And Pilar doesn't think you're a fool.

— I don't want to talk about her.

— She's just feeling sorry, right now, that you had a good friendship and it turns out it meant something different to each of you.

Harriet turned her head on the pillow to stare at Alice.

— Doesn't it ever wear you out, gushing and being charming all the time? It must take such an effort. I suppose you read my diary? I don't care about you reading it. Actually, I don't even care about making a fool of myself. But I feel very bitterly, Alice. Other people's lives, and the lives I read about in books, seem richer, mine seems so threadbare.

Alice was only jolted in passing by her sister's assault on her, like travelling over a familiar bump on a road. She sat up straighter, determined to talk with her truthfully for once, in this exceptional moment. — Threadbare? Do you think that's because you didn't have children?

— You don't have children, do you? And your life doesn't seem threadbare.

Alice said that it did sometimes, but Harriet snapped at her. — Don't try to cheer me up. You don't always have to make everything all right.

Well, did she feel that she had wasted that time when she was young, and so dedicated to politics? But Harriet said she'd asked herself that question often, and come to believe she'd chosen to be dedicated because of the way she was, politics hadn't made her that way. And it was true that the work she did now was valuable, she wouldn't change it for the world. But it didn't help to solve her own problems.

— What everybody wants is life: all our clients, all the asylum seekers and everyone. You're doing your best, trying to help them to get a roof over their head, security, enough money coming in. And you've got all those things, so in one way you're lucky, almost unimaginably lucky. But still you haven't got life.

— It isn't true, Alice said. — You're just seeing things the wrong way round, because you're sad.

— But what if I'm seeing them the right way round?

— And what about Christopher? You've got Christopher.

— Yes, Harriet said after a moment. — He's a good friend. They contemplated each other frankly.

Alice sighed. — What you mean is that you've missed out on love.

Harriet picked at some imaginary mark on the duvet cover. She was embarrassed by Alice using that word, which rolled so ripely and fluently off her tongue because she'd used it so many times before, ten thousand times.

— Yes, I suppose that what I mean comes somewhere under that heading, she said gruffly. — And now it's too late. Don't say that it isn't, will you, whatever you do. Because it's in me anyway, the thing that makes love not happen. Or rather, the thing that makes it happen isn't in me. Allure. Or sex appeal. Whatever you call it. It's not in my genetic code.

Alice protested, saying that couldn't be how it worked. There must be something you could do to give yourself allure, if you made up your mind to it.

— But maybe there isn't.

— All the great passion there's been in the world can't be based on anything so arbitrary as a genetic code.

Harriet shrugged. — Maybe it is, though. But don't worry about me. I'm not going to try again, anything so silly. That was my Victor Hugo moment. There won't be another one.

The sisters stopped to listen then, hearing footsteps outside: someone was coming to the scullery door. Could the others be back already? When Alice parted the curtains, to her surprise she saw a man in the yard below. It was Jeff: rucksack slung across one shoulder, guitar on the other. He hadn't told anyone he was coming. Banging on the glass she waved to him excitedly. He must have caught the eleven o'clock bus from the station and then walked – it was such a fine day. Now Fran would be happy. And when Jeff stepped back in the yard to look up at Alice, squinting into the sun and grinning at her, she remembered how nice he was: skinny as ever, with his jeans sliding down his narrow hips, tee shirt hanging out, muscular strong arms although he never did any exercise, tan-skinned although he spent his life in bars and clubs. He hadn't taken care of his teeth, they were crooked and stained with nicotine, and the flesh which had been so tender was beginning to be leathery. But still he had his look of a keen youth: liquid black eyes and dead-straight nose, long face with those distinctive flattened cheekbones, which Arthur had too. Running alongside Alice's exasperation with her teasing, satirical, lazy brother-in-law, there was always a frisson of harmless flirtation. They could do with a man in the house, she thought, for these last few days. Roland hadn't counted because he was their brother, and Kasim was too young. Jeff's arrival seemed to rebalance something.

ALICE HAD MEANT TO TELL Harriet her news. And then Jeff had arrived – and anyway, before that, she had worried that if she brought it out in the middle of their conversation, she could seem to be trumping Harriet's own crisis, or trying to put her somehow in the wrong. So she decided to put off telling anyone. Anyway, it wasn't really news, not yet. It might turn out to be nothing: this small lump she had found in her breast in the middle of one night, a week or so ago, after the Pattens' dinner party. The lump was new, she was sure of it; but it might only be benign. She had woken and put her hand straight to the place; it seemed to have called her out of her sleep, as distinctly as a tiny alarm going off. And she had phoned the next day for an appointment with her doctor, as soon as she got back to London. That margin of delay – she supposed she'd have gone right away, if she was sensible – was the only sign she gave herself that she was afraid.

No, of course she was afraid, that went without saying – especially when she woke alone in the night. And she was conscious of the lump at every moment, even sitting here in the garden with Jeff, drinking beer with him happily, waiting for the others to get back. But for the time being the fear stayed in its separate compartment from the rest of her life; and it was not as bad, not yet, as she might have expected. After all, there was every reason to be hopeful. Even if it was cancer, so many cancers were treatable these days. Their mother might not have died, they had sometimes said, if she'd had access to the latest developments in medicine.

Alice surprised herself with her own resilience. No doubt when she was back in London the reality would lunge from its dark tunnel, mowing her down. But that hadn't happened yet. The lump still belonged to her and had some meaning for her. She told herself it was connected to that intimation on her first day at Kington, when the light moving on the wallpaper in her grandparents' bedroom, and the voices from outside, had pierced her with memories of such intensity. She had known then that something lay in wait for her, something was promised. Only she had mistaken what it was.

THEIR PROCESSION THROUGH THE WOODS was sombre. Fran and Janice made stilted conversation about the National Park, on which subject Janice was darkly conspiratorial. Her Nordic walking poles, Fran felt, were the last straw. Christ, it was a signposted woodland walk, you could have done it in high heels! Ivy had a pinched expression because in her fantasy she was on her way to the altar, or alternately to the scaffold – although she was vague about what happened next in either place. Her outfit was inspired by Molly's yesterday: along with her nylon petticoat and pink sequined top she wore a veil made from a lace doily, borrowed from under the telephone in the hall and fixed with hairgrips. Arthur was experimenting with swivelling his new head, which felt weightless on his neck. Approaching nearer to the cottage, they noticed a faint mist hanging between the trees; none of them were interested in it, putting it down in their city ignorance to some peculiarity of the weather. The mist thickened, glittering in the sunbeams, as they reached the stretch of path leading up to the head of the valley and along the side of the cottage; Arthur began to cough behind his hand, and they all tasted dust. With the help of her poles, Janice was slightly ahead of the others, and saw it first.

— Oh, goodness gracious, she exclaimed, stopping short on the path.

The whole of the back of the cottage had sheared off – along with a great slide of rocks and red mud – and fallen into the wooded gully fifty feet below, where a rubble of bricks and mortar smoked tranquilly in silence among the splintered and smashed trees. The silence – or rather, the ordinary restored quiet rustling and burbling and birdsong – was somehow the strangest thing of all, as if the actual moment of disaster itself might have been soundless, abstract, a technicality. The front facade, with about a third of the depth of the cottage still attached to it, was left hanging out over the sheer slope: exposed from behind, each room seemed like a miniature room from a doll's house, with its own wallpaper, and painted dado, and paler outlines on the walls where pictures had once hung. The cream-tiled fireplace, sticking out into nothing, still had cinders in it, and a wine bottle was rolled on its side on the floor. Ivy shrieked once theatrically, then shut up just as abruptly. Very subduedly, Fran began murmuring to herself: *oh my god, my god, my god.* They seemed to stare at what they saw for whole minutes, reactions suspended, as if waiting for some explanation that might be forthcoming from it.

— Can we climb down there? Fran said.

Janice thought there was a long way round by the path, which took you down. — But one of us should go back for the emergency services. They'll send a helicopter. Should I go? I'm not that fit, but I'll do my best to jog. Or should we send one of the children? Can they be trusted?

— Janice, stay with me another moment. I'm not thinking straight.

Fran crouched down on the path in front of her daughter. —
Ivy, I have to know. How certain are you, on your honour, that
Molly and Kasim were in there?

Dumbly Ivy nodded, lace doily quivering.

But Arthur had run ahead, and now he was waving to them
from where the path swung round. — They're here! They're here!
he shouted.

As they hurried out into the clearing, Kas and Molly, fully
dressed, holding hands, were approaching from the path on the
other side. They seemed every bit as astonished as the others
were by the cataclysm that had occurred in the cottage. Its front
facade, facing onto the clearing, was in fact oddly intact, like a
pretence kept up – for decades now – that domesticity was going
on behind it as usual. But the front door swung open onto the blue
air beyond.

— Oh my god, you stupid pair, what have you *done?* Fran
shouted at the two young ones, and then turned on her own children. — And just don't tell me that you two have been climbing in
and out of that awful place over the past couple of weeks? Don't
tell me these irresponsible idiots allowed you to do that, when I
put them in charge?

Then she burst into furious loud tears and couldn't be comforted, because although Arthur put his arms round her, all she
could see every time she looked at him was his sad, shorn, unfamiliar little poll.

MOLLY TOLD THEM THAT SHE had woken in the dawn light.

— It had been so windy in the night, and then I looked out of
the front door and the wind had stopped, it was all still, everything was shadowy and perfect. And I thought that I'd never

actually seen the dawn before. Well, I'd seen it, on car journeys and things, but I'd never actually been in it. So I woke up Kas, and we got dressed and decided to walk to the waterfall. You should see the waterfall, Ivy, it's like a raging torrent compared to when we went there before. And we saw a deer. I didn't know they still had wild deer in the country.

— But dawn was hours and hours ago, Janice said. — It's almost midday.

Studiously, Kas and Molly didn't exchange looks. They'd fallen asleep again, she explained, on the grass beside the waterfall, once the sun came up and it was so lovely and warm.

Because of the drama of what had happened, and their close escape, no one made any effort to pretend that these two hadn't been making love – probably half the night and all morning. Even the children must have guessed something. The little plaits sticking up all over Molly's head were fuzzy from their embraces, and as she spoke, full of her story, words tumbling out in her excitement, her face shone with a dreamy languor. What a lucky escape! Just imagine it! What would have happened if she hadn't woken, and insisted they go out? Kas had grumbled, he hadn't wanted to go anywhere. If he'd had his way, they'd both be in that pile of rubble now.

But you could see she didn't really for one moment seriously believe that this death was possible. The life in her had such force, it felt inviolable.

— We probably wouldn't, Kas said. — I expect there was some kind of warning noise. Anyway, not all of it has gone down. I'll bet we could have managed to scramble out somehow.

— You must have heard *something*, Janice insisted. — Even from the waterfall. It must have made quite a racket when it came down.

Molly frowned vaguely. — Well, I may have, perhaps. A sort of smash. Or a roar, like bottles being tipped out. I just thought it was industrial. A factory or something.

— You didn't mention it, Kas said. — Of course there are a lot of factories round here.

— I didn't want to wake you. You look so sweet when you're asleep.

Janice asked Kasim, at some point on their way back through the woods, whether it was true that they'd found Mitzi in the cottage. Kasim said he had cleaned out the remains of a fox from one of the upstairs rooms: Janice was relieved and Arthur and Ivy looked at each other, deciding wordlessly not to interfere. They felt upon them again the prohibition of the Women. Even in his newly toughened boy-self, Arthur seemed to half believe in them. Probably the cottage had fallen down by accident. But he remembered those dirty rags flickering at a window, and the dead dog in a corner which might have been a fox, and that mystery of the magazines, which had grown upon him while he cut them out: one naked body after another in numbing repetition, as if they must add up to something. Why weren't there men's bodies?

They took the shortcut up through the churchyard; Alice was talking and laughing with someone in the garden. Fran was thinking about school, trying to be the person she was when she was there: smart and flexible and competent, parrying her pupils' remarks with her quick sarcasm, flattening them. But everything got so confused in her own family, and she made such drastic mistakes. It dismayed her that Janice Patten had seen her in tears, and that her children seemed so unhealthily fascinated by Molly's sex life, and that she'd allowed them to stray into such danger in that place. She closed a door in her mind on that vision of smoking rubble, squeezing it tightly shut – but even the squeezing made her feel blank and sick. If only Jeff were here, she thought. Full of self-doubt, she let go the eternal litany of her complaints, and longed for him – the familiar, loved, wiry puzzle of his body and his familiar exasperating self, his character – as if he was the particular and only solution to the problem of her.

HARRIET WAS MUCH BETTER; SHE was very quiet. A card had arrived for her one morning, inside an envelope addressed in a foreign handwriting: she picked it up from the hall floor under the letter box before anyone else saw it, and took it into her bedroom to read, shutting both doors quietly. What was she hoping for? Some word that could unfasten what she'd done? The card was a picture of Malmesbury Abbey, with its ruined windows in the clerestory: perhaps Pilar and Roland had visited there on their way home. On the back Pilar had only written: *The tests were negative.* Harriet was amazed. How could Pilar imagine that she still cared one way or another about those tests? Why would she care, if she couldn't have Pilar? Harriet wouldn't ever have believed, in her life before, that she was capable of such selfish love, cold greed. But there it was.

The estate agent came one afternoon to go over the house and give them a valuation. They had spent all morning cleaning and making everything look nice, and Alice had put out flowers again in all the rooms. She noticed that someone was sitting out in the man's car on the drive; he explained that this was his father, who wasn't much involved with the business any longer, but liked to come with him for the ride sometimes. He'd been forced to give up driving himself, because of problems with his peripheral vision; frustrating for him, his son said, because he was very fit and active otherwise. Alice said his father was welcome to come inside, she'd make him a cup of tea. But apparently he preferred waiting in the car.

Mikey Waller sat there for a while, and then when the sun came out and the rain stopped spitting he got out to stretch his legs, walking down the road to take a quick look inside the church, because his hobby was church architecture. His thatch of sandy-white hair was neatly trimmed and his colour was ruddy as if he might have high blood pressure; he was one of those tall, shambling men who look too raw when they're young and then, without trying for it, accumulate gravity and style later in life. He didn't take long inside the church, not wanting to keep his son waiting. When he turned into the rectory drive again, he saw that a young woman – anyway, she looked young enough to him – had come out of the house with a bowl of washing, children's clothes, which she was pegging on the line. He watched her, though he had to be careful not to seem to stare, because of the problems with his field of vision. He supposed she must be one of Jill Crane's daughters. How many children were there: three? Or four? This one was petite and plump and decisive; she didn't look much like her mother, as far as he could see – the same red-gold hair perhaps. So the family were going to sell the house, after all these years. Mikey regretted this. He felt a special attachment to the old place, and had always liked to think of the Cranes using it. This was because he'd loved their mother once, for a long time. She'd gone away, though, and he'd had to make his life without her.

ACKNOWLEDGEMENTS

My most heartfelt thanks to Dan Franklin and Caroline Dawnay, Jennifer Barth and Joy Harris, who once again all lent their wisdom and their kindness. I have borrowed my structure – The Present, The Past, The Present – shamelessly from Elizabeth Bowen's superb novel *The House in Paris*, and I have borrowed some details of *les événements* in Paris, May 1968, equally shamelessly from Mavis Gallant's fascinating account of them in her *Paris Notebooks*. I'm always grateful to my university, Bath Spa, which supports all kinds of art-endeavour and makes a writing life easier – and for my friends and colleagues and students there who care about good books. I'm grateful to Katherine Ailes and Sophie Scard and Deirdre Molina, for such thoughtful reading. And to Eric for everything.

Insights,
Interviews
& More . . .

Meet Tessa Hadley

I was born in Bristol, England, in 1956.
My father was a schoolteacher (he's also
very musical and still plays the jazz
trumpet); my mother gave up her
dressmaking business (gratefully, she
says) and stayed at home to look after me
and my younger brother. For next to
nothing they bought one of the old
Georgian houses nobody wanted in
those days—five stories tall, with a leaky
roof and an unsafe wrought-iron balcony
on the front, also an assortment of
sitting tenants. I was shy, bookish,
skinny, freckled, hopeless at games. I
promoted myself to adult books in the
local library at quite an early age and
read lots of them without understanding
much of what was going on—it all seeps
in to the sum of one's knowledge
somewhere. I was happy at junior school,
miserable at secondary school which was
all girls and very driven academically. I
wanted to be left alone, and I didn't want
to belong to anybody's tribe. In an act of
courage that surprises me retrospectively
(I was still shy), I left that pushy school
and went to the ordinary state one where
my brother was, and was much happier.
There, to start with, were boys, who were
different and wittier and fascinating.

I studied English at Cambridge (oh
dear, another tribe), which had its good
moments but didn't convince me that
academic ways of reading literature were
close enough to the real experience of
reading (or writing—I was guessing

then). So I wasn't tempted to try to prolong my life in academia: probably I took some of its luxuries of thought and time too much for granted, assuming they'd always be there for me. Then after a brief doomed idealistic ineffective flurry as a schoolteacher I had babies and stayed at home. Even walking up and down at night with a crying baby on my shoulder, I thought: 'this is better than facing the classroom tomorrow'. I liked the sort of semi-solitude you get, bringing up children. I read lots—always imagining there were other people elsewhere who'd read so much more (there were, of course): which is a great spur. And I did write. Shamefacedly, badly, tainted with failure and falsity: with moments of power and joy and long hours of despair, wondering why it mattered so much, and why I couldn't be decently happy without it. I wrote at least three, maybe four (I've forgotten) bad novels in these years. Solitude is good but I think I was too solitary. I needed to rub up against the audience I was writing for; I didn't have any living sense of them.

My husband was a schoolteacher, and then trained teachers (now in his retirement he's unleashed his passion for theatre, and singing, and studying history). We lived in Cardiff, Wales, for almost thirty years—four years ago we moved to London, for an adventure. We have three sons; the eldest is thirty-five now with two sons of his own, the youngest twenty-four. Two are political and love history like their father; the youngest likes poetry and novels and writes songs. I also have three stepsons and six step-grandchildren, and all the lovely young women that come attached to all those boys. It's impossible to write without mawkishness, or efforts of expression equivalent to the hard work of literature itself, how much one feels about these marvels of relationship, these precious surprises of personality and talent and charm.

In my late thirties I went back to university—about time I think, because I was so ready (belatedly) for making myself a life in the outside world. I'm sure my daughters-in-law can't imagine a retreat so complete and dull-seeming as those years of shopping and cooking and cleaning and waiting in the school playground. They're right, probably. Though there's something to be said for all that slow invisible work the mind does when it isn't buoyed along by anything outside. And there are lessons you learn, too, knowing you're weak and unimportant and socially invisible— ▶

these lessons ought to keep you sane and clean and unillusioned. Anyway, I went back to university and began to teach and write and loved the teaching hugely (I still do) and wrote my book about Henry James, then worked my way round gradually to writing a few stories I wasn't ashamed of. When you do finally make your way into the writing personality that is your real one, it's such a relief (however small that personality might be, however partial). It's like wandering round for years and years in a writing wilderness and then letting yourself in at last to your own house with your own key.

I could write short stories before I managed a novel. So I had the idea of writing a novel by writing a series of short stories about the same characters and in chronological order, then putting them end to end. It isn't really cheating. It solves two problems. First, if each 'chapter' is structured as tightly as if it was a free-standing short story, then you won't risk the slack passages the novel is prone to due to sheer length. Second, it helps solve the problem of needing to find an overarching grand theme of discovery or revelation to pull your novel together. The writer is tempted into finding an 'explanation' for a life, some hidden clue or secret which will release its truth. Of course the good novels don't do this. But it's a temptation.

I published a story-novel, *Accidents in the Home*, in 2002, and since then I've written five more novels. And all this time I've also been writing short stories, and I've published two collections of these, *Sunstroke* and *Married Love*. Writing makes me very happy. Or perhaps I could put it more negatively. All those years I couldn't do it, and had no reason to think I would ever be able to do it, writing was a painful, awful absence in my life. I can't quite explain this rationally. I love paintings, but it's never hurt me that I can't paint for toffee. Which bit of myself, and when, elected to *need* to write, in order to be me—and through what mental process? I used to feel (this is disturbing) that life itself wasn't quite real, unless I could write about it in fiction. Now that I am writing, and being read (most important), that mild insanity has dropped out of sight. I have a fear, of course, of its returning, if ever writing failed. ∾

Playing with Time: A Conversation with Tessa Hadley

This interview first appeared in the *Los Angeles Review of Books* on February 6, 2016.

TO SAY TESSA HADLEY is good with words is beyond an understatement, for her vivid imagery explodes somewhere in its travels from the page to the brain. With sublime prose, Hadley does justice to the beauty of the English countryside, the all-important setting of her latest novel, *The Past*, in which four grown siblings get together for a vacation in their grandparents' West Somerset cottage, to decide whether they should sell a house laden with family history, or hold on to it for generations to come.

The story of three sisters, one with two young children, the others childless, a brother, his Argentinian third wife and teenage daughter, and a teenage boy-interloper of no familial relation, jammed together for three sticky summer weeks to reflect on their lives and navigate their relationships sounds difficult to sustain for more than three hundred pages. Yet Hadley makes it work—with each chapter adding a new layer of forward momentum, this novel marks a more fluid narrative than her often episodic structure.

Despite the London-based author's obvious literary prowess, having penned six triumphant novels and two short ▶

story collections in the last thirteen years, Hadley's talent wasn't always obvious to the writer herself. Her path to success was plagued with self-doubt—she published her first novel at the age of 46, not for lack of trying—but she's content to hold on to those decades of struggle, and to remember them through her writing. They brought her here, to her lilting prose, to her status as a *New Yorker* darling, and to a place of real confidence. It seemed only right that in talking about *The Past*, we talked about her past, too.

JANE GAYDUK: *What was the most challenging part of writing* **The Past?**
TESSA HADLEY: Probably making such a small space of time, the three weeks of the summer holiday, last so long. That sounds silly but it's quite a challenge to write, actually. It's easier to move fast and move on to the next thing and get a change of scene— those inject the natural forward momentum into a narrative. And yet, what one rather wants is to dwell. You think, actually I want to give this room to breathe and I want to give this conversation room to really draw out, not just be a few snappy samplings, but really let [the characters] talk. But it's harder. Slow is harder. Of course one of the ways I manage to make my three weeks sustain its tension across the novel was my decision, which happened late on while I was writing, to drop back thirty years in that middle section. That was like putting in a tent peg to hold the whole thing up. It was a huge help.

Since the central conflicts in this novel are inside the characters themselves, what techniques do you use to keep the plot moving?
I like finding the tensions inside people instead of exerting that tension by using a lever from outside. I'm just that kind of writer, I tend not to have a huge machinery outside the characters which presses on them and produces action and consequences; it's just instinctively the way I've always wanted to write. You look inside people and what you see is not coherence but fracture and ambiguity and ambivalence and you press on that. For instance, Harriet, who seems extraordinarily self-controlled, perhaps you might even say repressed, has something missing. There's

something omitted from her life, so obviously it cries out for a painful, devastating eruption of all the things that she's keeping out of the frame. That's the dynamic that generates change and discovery, which is what I think interests most novelists of the kind of novel I'm aspiring to write.

What kind of novels are you aspiring to write?
One of the things I feel passionately about is the urgency of writing novels about our contemporary moment in the West. And perhaps, if you like, in bourgeois culture, middle class, relatively comfortable culture. And the more our awareness is globalized and the more we see that our own experience is only a tiny fragment of the world, instead of wanting to abandon that little island of experience, it sort of makes me cling to it with all the more passion. Because it's everything I know, and it's everything I've read, and everything I've been brought up in. It's very far from a perfect way of life or sensibility, but it's the only one I can be an expert in. And so in the new light of the global awareness that we have now, it's very interesting to look back at ourselves; that new light is quite lurid, it makes us feel differently. And so I want to write contemporary novels, not historical novels— though occasionally I flirt with that idea—and I want them to be about quite ordinary middle-class people who aren't undergoing huge, life-changing adventures, even though I know the world is full of huge, life-changing adventures. But you have to write about what you know in some sense.

You shift the point of view to so many different characters of different ages and generations. Which age group is the most difficult to narrate from? Which is the easiest?
I think maybe the teenagers [Kasim and Molly], although I thoroughly enjoyed narrating Kasim. I didn't really narrate Molly—she's one of my "mutes" if you know what I mean. She's one of the characters that we do only see from the outside, which is a whole different, interesting question. But I think there is a technical difficulty in writing teenagers.

I think there's something wonderfully eternal about kids. Despite the changes that come with people sitting in front of ▶

computers instead of playing on the street, it's amazing how transferable a child's sensibility is from one generation to another. And then, I suppose I'm at home with middle-aged characters in my book because that's sort of where I am.

But the teenagers are so subject to rapid cultural change—the slang they use—that's always scary, are you going to get that wrong? Are you going to get something that was fashionable five years ago and no teenager would be caught dead saying now? So I listen carefully. Luckily I've got rather a big family, I've got an endless supply of young people and I try and catch what they're saying. And sometimes I test things out on them: I say, "Would you say that? Would you use that word?" I think they're the hardest, but if you're writing something and you're in somebody's point of view and it feels really hard, I think the answer is you have to stop.

That happens to me sometimes, there's just a resistant character and I can't do them from the inside and the answer probably is—it's not because that character is dead, it's because I know them from the outside. I watch them but I don't know what's going on in their narrative. Sometimes you just have those characters in the book where you mustn't go inside. I couldn't have done Pilar, the Argentinian wife; the whole way she works in the book is that she is mysterious. The power she exerts on that family is that she's inaccessible to their way of imagining and thinking. She's closed to them, and that's how she's powerful. So I wouldn't have dreamt of doing anything from her point of view.

And you also chose not to narrate from Molly's point of view, the teenage daughter.

It's funny, because I don't know how one would find the words for Molly. In some way—and the middle-aged women complain about this a bit—she doesn't seem to know very much or be interested in very much, and yet she's intensely alive. She's alive in her body in a way, whatever all that mysterious "getting ready" is that she's always doing. But she is [getting ready], she's getting ready to be a woman, of course. And yes, she has all kinds of mysteries in her that we can't fathom. To put her into an internal narrative, her voice would be weak in relation to the power she actually has as a person.

The Somerset setting plays such a vital role in the story. Do you have any personal connection to the British countryside?
Yes, I do. We live in London, though we've only lived in London for four years; before that we were in Cardiff, Wales. But very fortunately we have a cottage we have shared with the rest of my family since the 1980s, since my children were very small. It's in west Somerset, which is exactly the area I've written about. It's written with great love and intimate knowledge—I've just come back from three weeks there. It sort of belonged to my parents, and now they live nearby. Now it sort of belongs to me, and my brother shares it a bit, and the family all uses it.

Do you have a favorite character in this novel?
I think I'm divided between Alice and Harriet, since I can feel bits of myself in both of them, though neither of them are in fact like me. I identify with little, anxious bits of Harriet and I identify with some of Alice. And I am the little girl as well.

I don't know that I do have a favorite character. I like Jill; well, I don't like Jill, but I feel that Jill is the most powerful person in the book, and that her absence in a way brews over everything. She is a force. There's something kind of certain about her, that none of her children quite have, that her mother doesn't quite have either. She's pretty amazing; I enjoyed creating her, a force in the world. ∾

Tessa Hadley:
By the Book

"By the Book" by Tessa Hadley originally appeared in the *New York Times* on December 31, 2015, and is used here by permission.

What books are currently on your night stand?

On top, a copy of Henry James's *Wings of the Dove,* for my Henry James reading group; just the first thirty pages for this week, the marvelous slow opening where Kate Croy waits for her father, walking up and down in his grubby lodgings, hating the fraudulent thing he is. She looks at herself in the mirror, seeing her beauty as her great good luck, her chance for escape. But her father is beautiful too, and he hasn't escaped. "Why should a set of people have been put in motion, on such a scale and with such an air of being equipped for a profitable journey, only to break down without an accident?" The excited sense, as always with James at his best, that words are freedom, anything is possible. And the exact realism of the detail; her father's lie about his illness, the armchair upholstered in a glazed cloth, slippery and sticky at once.

Also, a little book someone gave me, probably in vain, called *Seven Brief Lessons on Physics,* by Carlo Rovelli. James's sentences are more or less transparent to me these days—most of them—but I'm bewildered by the mysteries in here: energy quanta, which are localized at points in space, which move without dividing. I sense their beauty, but they're closed to me, my mind is the wrong shape, and I can't take them in.

Also, a subtle and tender book by Alexander Nemerov, *Silent Dialogues,* about the relations, or nonrelations, between his father, the poet Howard Nemerov, and his aunt, the photographer Diane Arbus. Howard couldn't bear the photographs; he kept the one Diane gave him in a drawer. But Alexander traces deep connections between the two artists.

What's the last good book you read?
A new novel, *Playthings,* by Alex Pheby, which I finished yesterday. It's based on the life of Schreber, one of Freud's patients, and I opened it warily, thinking it might be too clever and self-conscious. Hasn't that material been worked to death? Well, *Playthings* is certainly clever, but I also thought it was marvelously surprising and vivid, something new. Somehow inside the shape of an old story he traces fresh experiences as if for the first time. The detail is so sensuously precise. Impressed as I haven't been by a new novel for a while.

What moves you most in a work of literature?
Is it just too obvious to say, the words? Because those come first, rather than the themes or the stories or the analysis. When you're standing in a bookshop opening up a novel or book of short stories by someone you've never read before, there's a period of rapid testing, where you enter into the sentences. It's in the arrangements of the language that the intelligence and the taste show up. Are those words, in that sequence, clumsy? Banal? Hyped-up, or showing off? And then, if not, if the book's good, you settle into trusting it. If the book's good, each successive sentence adds something you've never known before.

Tell us about your favorite poem.
(There isn't just one favorite poem, of course. There couldn't be.) Pasted inside the trains on the London Tube, amongst the advertising, we have Poems for the Underground. A few months ago they used a bit of Yeats which I didn't recognize (it comes from a longer poem, "Vacillation"). "My fiftieth year had come and gone, / I sat a solitary man, / In a crowded London shop, / An open book and empty cup / on the marble table-top." There's ▶

more; it's about one of those blazes of irrational well-being, occurring in the midst of ordinary life. My fiftieth year had certainly gone, and I was going shopping—the mythic and the everyday seemed to collide, which is what I love in Yeats. I'm loving Louise Glück's latest collection too, *Faithful and Virtuous Night* (gorgeously funny title). There's a short prose poem in there about "A Work of Fiction." Reading a novel is like smoking a cigarette, she says. "How small it was, how brief . . . but inside me now."

And your favorite movie adaptation of a book?

I'm a great fan of Rumer Godden, whose novels were often made into films, because the plots are so rich, so good. Not only *Black Narcissus*—I'm not sure about that film, Powell and Pressburger make me uneasy (Godden hated it). But there's also *The Greengage Summer,* and *The River,* made into an odd and beautiful film by Jean Renoir. Last Christmas my stepson gave me a charming little British film from the '50s, *Innocent Sinners,* directed by Philip Leacock and based on Godden's *An Episode of Sparrows.* It's about children playing in the ruins of the bomb damage in postwar London; perhaps it's as close as British cinema gets to Italian neorealism, though being British, it's much safer, less searing.

Who is your favorite fictional hero or heroine? Your favorite antihero or villain?

I've drawn great comfort from Alice Munro's drifting heroines, messing up their lives, wanting more than they have, drawn fatally to the men who won't give it. In the background of their imagination, inherited from their past, there's a different universe of hard work and discipline and dutiful routine. Her heroines feel the power of those possibilities, but can't seriously consider putting the genie of their freedom back in its bottle. And yet they don't quite trust their freedom either.

No one writes plausibly evil characters quite like Paula Fox. They're usually mothers. The mother in *The Widow's Children* is one of literature's convincing monsters—and we feel her monstrousness from the inside, as well as watching her perform it, tyrannizing everyone around her. What power in her cruelty, in her ruthless play, teasing with her favor and then snatching it back. And how awful it feels to be monstrous. Monstrosity is such a reality in psychology, but perhaps most novelists flinch from writing it head-on, in case it comes out as caricature. The drunk husband in that novel is brilliantly awful too. So difficult to write that drunkenness, petulant and terrifying, lurching among perceptions, awash with panic.

What kind of reader were you as a child? Which childhood books and authors stick with you most?

Did I live to read? That's almost how I remember it now. I didn't possess all that many books—not many children did. But I went with my class to the local library every Friday afternoon and took out my three books, and if I'd finished them before the week was up I turned to an old favorite for rereading. I loved the promise of books that came in whole series, taking up half a library shelf, like *Anne of Green Gables* or *Swallows and Amazons.* I think I was really afraid of each book coming to its end (like Louise Glück's cigarette); behind each particular volume in a series there stretched a reassuring hinterland. When I read E. Nesbit's *The Wouldbegoods,* I had no sense of distance between my own 1960s world and her Edwardian one. Those children seemed to live in the next room, their idiom and their moral code seemed as natural as my own.

What book read for school had the greatest impact on you?

Once I got to secondary school, the books we read seemed to be spoiled for us. Was it something to do with that horrible pedagogical pattern where questions lay in wait on the last page, spoiling everything? I wasn't happy at that school. I vividly remember reading through Frost's "Mending Wall" and seeing the stodgy questions looming up ahead, making my heart heavy. "Why does the man say good fences make good neighbors? What is it that 'doesn't love a wall'?" The questions stopped me being able to read. My strongest instinct was that reading ought to be freedom; it belonged at home, in precious irresponsibility. At that school we read through one masterpiece after another—*Kim,* and *Silas Marner,* and *Cranford,* and *Northanger Abbey.* Now, I'm impressed by what they chose. But at the time, I hated every one, and it was years before I could return to any of those books.

If you had to name one book that made you who you are today, what would it be?

It's quite frightening to think about the books that form us. It's not just Emma Bovary who makes her life decisions—rather ▶

Tessa Hadley: By the Book (*continued*)

seriously unwise ones (or are they?)—based on something that she's read. I suspect that Lawrence's *The Rainbow* had a significant impact on the way I was when I was twenty. It made me pretty casual, for instance, about higher education—I believed that, like Ursula Brangwen, I'd seen through the fake prophets in their false priesthood. Or something of the sort.

What author, living or dead, would you most like to meet, and what would you like to know?

I've never really been desperate to meet the writers I most admire. What is there to say to them that isn't just embarrassing adulation? Superficial social relations can't hope to match the intimacy you have with an author in their words on the page. Having said that, there is a magical power in actual presence. When I was very young and hadn't published anything, I once sat in the back of a radio studio to hear Nadine Gordimer give an interview. Her glance fell on me accidentally in passing, and I haven't forgotten it.

Whom would you want to write your life story?

No one. It isn't really very interesting. Interesting to me, of course—but really a fairly quiet life, ordinary. I don't very often like biographies; they're so sad: so much youthful hope and then the inevitable ending. The rhythms of fiction are more mysterious; they hold out more promise, and consolation. The best biographies read something like fictions (like Penelope Fitzgerald's biography of Charlotte Mew).

What do you plan to read next?

Maybe I'd better read the next (short) chapter of my physics book. It's called *Probability, Time and the Heat of Black Holes*. I know this stuff is stunning. I know it transforms everything. And I know the little simplifying book is a lovely idea. I'm perplexed by my own failure to understand. ∿